Grimm's Fairy Tales

with illustrations by
Walter Crane
and
Arthur Rackham

Grimm's Fairy Tales
Illustrations by Walter Crane and Arthur Rackham
Translation by Margaret Raine Hunt

ISBN 978-1-910880-64-7
Published by The Planet, 2018
© Marie-Michelle Joy, 2018: book design
www.the-planet-books.com

Contents

The Frog-King, or Iron Henry

I N OLD times when wishing still helped one, there lived a king whose daughters were all beautiful, but the youngest was so beautiful that the sun itself, which has seen so much, was astonished whenever it shone in her face. Close by the King's castle lay a great dark forest, and under an old lime-tree in the forest was a well, and when the day was very warm, the King's child went out into the forest and sat down by the side of the cool fountain, and when she was dull, she took a golden ball, and threw it up on high and caught it, and this ball was her favourite plaything.

Now it so happened that on one occasion the princess's golden ball did not fall into the little hand which she was holding up for it, but on to the ground beyond, and rolled straight into the water. The King's daughter followed it with her eyes, but it vanished, and the well was deep, so deep that the bottom could not be seen.

On this she began to cry, and cried louder and louder, and could not be comforted. And as she thus lamented, someone said to her, "What ails thee, King's daughter? Thou weepest so that even a stone would show pity."

She looked round to the side from whence the voice came, and saw a frog stretching forth its thick, ugly head from the water. "Ah! old water-splasher, is it thou?" said she. "I am weeping for my golden ball, which has fallen into the well."

"Be quiet, and do not weep," answered the frog, "I can help thee, but what wilt thou give me if I bring thy plaything up again?"

"Whatever thou wilt have, dear frog," said she—"my clothes, my pearls and jewels, and even the golden crown which I am wearing."

The frog answered, "I do not care for thy clothes, thy pearls and jewels, or thy golden crown, but if thou wilt love me and let me be thy companion and play-fellow, and sit by thee at thy little table, and eat off thy little golden plate, and drink out of thy little cup, and sleep in thy little bed—if thou wilt promise me this I will go down below, and bring thee thy golden ball up again."

"Oh, yes," said she, "I promise thee all thou wishest, if thou wilt but bring me my ball back again."

She, however, thought, "How the silly frog does talk! He lives in the water with the other frogs and croaks, and can be no companion to any human being!"

But the frog, when he had received this promise, put his head into the water and sank down, and in a short time came swimming up again with the ball in his mouth, and threw it on the grass.

The King's daughter was delighted to see her pretty plaything once more, and picked it up, and ran away with it.

"Wait, wait!" said the frog. "Take me with thee. I can't run as thou canst."

But what did it avail him to scream his croak, croak, after her, as loudly as he could? She did not listen to it, but ran home and soon forgot the poor frog, who was forced to go back into his well again.

The next day when she had seated herself at table with the King and all the courtiers, and was eating from her little golden plate, something came creeping splish splash, splish splash, up the marble staircase, and when it had got to the top, it knocked at the door and cried, "Princess, youngest princess, open the door for me."

She ran to see who was outside, but when she opened the door, there sat the frog in front of it. Then she slammed the door to, in great haste, sat down to dinner again, and was quite frightened.

The King saw plainly that her heart was beating violently, and said, "My child, what art thou so afraid of? Is there perchance a giant outside who wants to carry thee away?"

"Ah, no," replied she, "it is no giant, but a disgusting frog."

"What does the frog want with thee?"

"Ah, dear father, yesterday when I was in the forest sitting by the well, playing, my golden ball fell into the water. And because I cried so the frog brought it out again for me, and because he insisted so on it, I promised him he should be my companion, but I never thought he would be able to come out of his water! And now he is outside there, and wants to come in to me."

In the meantime it knocked a second time, and cried,

"Princess! youngest princess!
Open the door for me!
Dost thou not know what thou saidst to me
Yesterday by the cool waters of the fountain?
Princess, youngest princess!
Open the door for me!"

Then said the King, "That which thou hast promised must thou perform. Go and let him in."

She went and opened the door, and the frog hopped in and followed her, step by step, to her chair. There he sat still and cried, "Lift me up beside thee." She delayed, until at last the King commanded her to do it.

9

When the frog was once on the chair, he wanted to be on the table, and when he was on the table, he said, "Now, push thy little golden plate nearer to me that we may eat together." She did this, but it was easy to see that she did not do it willingly.

The frog enjoyed what he ate, but almost every mouthful she took choked her. At length he said, "I have eaten and am satisfied; now I am tired, carry me into thy little room and make thy little silken bed ready, and we will both lie down and go to sleep."

The King's daughter began to cry, for she was afraid of the cold frog which she did not like to touch, and which was now to sleep in her pretty, clean little bed. But the King grew angry and said, "He who helped thee when thou wert in trouble ought not afterwards to be despised by thee."

So she took hold of the frog with two fingers, carried him upstairs, and put him in a corner. But when she was in bed, he crept to her and said, "I am tired, I want to sleep as well as thou, lift me up or I will tell thy father."

Then she was terribly angry, and took him up and threw him with all her might against the wall. "Now, thou wilt be quiet, odious frog!" said she.

But when he fell down, he was no frog but a king's son with beautiful kind eyes. He by her father's will was now her dear companion and husband. Then he told her how he had been bewitched by a wicked witch, and how no one could have delivered him from the well but herself, and that tomorrow they would go together into his kingdom.

Then they went to sleep, and next morning when the sun awoke them, a carriage came driving up with eight white horses, which had white ostrich feathers on their heads, and were harnessed with golden chains, and behind stood the young King's servant, faithful Henry.

Faithful Henry had been so unhappy when his master was changed into a frog that he had caused three iron bands to be laid round his heart, lest it should burst with grief and sadness.

The carriage was to conduct the young King into his kingdom. Faithful Henry helped them both in, and placed himself behind again, and was full of joy because of this deliverance. And when they had driven a part of the way, the King's son heard a cracking behind him as if something had broken. So he turned round and cried, "Henry, the carriage is breaking."

"No, master, it is not the carriage. It is a band from my heart, which was put there in my great pain when you were a frog and imprisoned in the well."

Again and once again while they were on their way something cracked, and each time the King's son thought the carriage was breaking; but it was only the bands which were springing from the heart of faithful Henry because his master was set free and was happy.

Cat and Mouse in Partnership

CERTAIN cat had made the acquaintance of a mouse, and had said so much to her about the great love and friendship she felt for her, that at length the mouse agreed that they should live and keep house together. "But we must make a provision for winter, or else we shall suffer from hunger," said the cat, "and you, little mouse, cannot venture everywhere, or you will be caught in a trap some day."

The good advice was followed, and a pot of fat was bought, but they did not know where to put it. At length, after much consideration, the cat said, "I know no place where it will be better stored up than in the church, for no one dares take anything away from there. We will set it beneath the altar, and not touch it until we are really in need of it."

So the pot was placed in safety, but it was not long before the cat had a great longing for it, and said to the mouse, "I want to tell you

something, little mouse; my cousin has brought a little son into the world, and has asked me to be godmother; he is white with brown spots, and I am to hold him at the christening. Let me go out today, and you look after the house by yourself."

"Yes, yes," answered the mouse, "by all means go, and if you get anything very good, think of me, I should like a drop of sweet red christening wine too."

All this, however, was untrue; the cat had no cousin, and had not been asked to be godmother. She went straight to the church, stole to the pot of fat, began to lick at it, and licked the top of the fat off. Then she took a walk upon the roofs of the town, looked out for opportunities, and then stretched herself in the sun, and licked her lips whenever she thought of the pot of fat, and not until it was evening did she return home.

"Well, here you are again," said the mouse, "no doubt you have had a merry day."

"All went off well," answered the cat.

"What name did they give the child?"

"Top off!" said the cat quite coolly.

"Top off!" cried the mouse, "that is a very odd and uncommon name, is it a usual one in your family?"

"What does it signify," said the cat, "it is not worse than Crumb-stealer, as your god-children are called."

Before long the cat was seized by another fit of longing. She said to the mouse, "You must do me a favour, and once more manage the house for a day alone. I am again asked to be godmother, and, as the child has a white ring round its neck, I cannot refuse."

The good mouse consented, but the cat crept behind the town walls to the church, and devoured half the pot of fat. "Nothing ever seems so good as what one keeps to oneself," said she, and was quite satisfied with her day's work.

When she went home, the mouse inquired, "And what was this child christened?"

"Half-done," answered the cat.

"Half-done! What are you saying? I never heard the name in my life, I'll wager anything it is not in the calendar!"

The cat's mouth soon began to water for some more licking. "All good things go in threes," said she, "I am asked to stand godmother again. The child is quite black, only it has white paws, but with that exception, it has not a single white hair on its whole body; this only happens once every few years, you will let me go, won't you?"

"Top-off! Half-done!" answered the mouse, "they are such odd names, they make me very thoughtful."

"You sit at home," said the cat, "in your dark-grey fur coat and long tail, and are filled with fancies, that's because you do not go out in the daytime."

During the cat's absence the mouse cleaned the house, and put it in order, but the greedy cat entirely emptied the pot of fat. "When everything is eaten up, one has some peace," said she to herself, and well filled and fat she did not return home till night.

The mouse at once asked what name had been given to the third child.

"It will not please you more than the others," said the cat. "He is called All-gone."

"All-gone," cried the mouse, "that is the most suspicious name of all! I have never seen it in print. All-gone; what can that mean?" and she shook her head, curled herself up, and lay down to sleep.

13

From this time forth no one invited the cat to be godmother, but when the winter had come and there was no longer anything to be found outside, the mouse thought of their provision, and said, "Come, cat, we will go to our pot of fat which we have stored up for ourselves—we shall enjoy that."

"Yes," answered the cat, "you will enjoy it as much as you would enjoy sticking that dainty tongue of yours out of the window."

They set out on their way, but when they arrived, the pot of fat certainly was still in its place, but it was empty.

"Alas!" said the mouse, "now I see what has happened, now it comes to light! You, a true friend! You have devoured all when you were standing godmother. First top off, then half done, then——"

"Will you hold your tongue," cried the cat, "one word more, and I will eat you too!"

"All gone" was already on the poor mouse's lips; scarcely had she spoken it before the cat sprang on her, seized her, and swallowed her down. Verily, that is the way of the world.

The Story of the Youth who Went Forth to Learn What Fear Was

 CERTAIN father had two sons, the elder of whom was sharp and sensible, and could do everything, but the younger was stupid and could neither learn nor understand anything, and when people saw him, they said, "There's a fellow who will give his father some trouble!" When anything had to be done, it was always the elder who was forced to do it; but if his father bade him fetch anything when it was late, or in the night-time, and the way led through the churchyard, or any other dismal place, he answered, "Oh, no, father, I'll not go there, it makes me shudder!" for he was afraid. Or when stories were told by the fire at night which made the flesh creep, the listeners often said, "Oh, it makes us shudder!"

The younger sat in a corner and listened with the rest of them, and could not imagine what they could mean. "They are always saying 'it makes me shudder, it makes me shudder!' It does not make me shudder," thought he. "That, too, must be an art of which I understand nothing!"

Now it came to pass that his father said to him one day, "Hearken to me, thou fellow in the corner there, thou art growing tall and strong, and thou too must learn something by which thou canst earn thy living. Look how thy brother works, but thou dost not even earn thy salt."

"Well, father," he replied, "I am quite willing to learn something—indeed, if it could but be managed, I should like to learn how to shudder. I don't understand that at all yet."

The elder brother smiled when he heard that, and thought to himself, "Good God, what a blockhead that brother of mine is! He will never be good for anything as long as he lives! He who wants to be a sickle must bend himself betimes."

The father sighed, and answered him, "Thou shalt soon learn what it is to shudder, but thou wilt not earn thy bread by that."

Soon after this the sexton came to the house on a visit, and the father bewailed his trouble, and told him how his younger son was so backward in every respect that he knew nothing and learnt nothing.

"Just think," said he, "when I asked him how he was going to earn his bread, he actually wanted to learn to shudder."

"If that be all," replied the sexton, "he can learn that with me. Send him to me, and I will soon polish him."

The father was glad to do it, for he thought, "It will train the boy a little."

The sexton therefore took him into his house, and he had to ring the bell. After a day or two, the sexton awoke him at midnight, and bade him arise and go up into the church tower and ring the bell.

"Thou shalt soon learn what shuddering is," thought he, and secretly went there before him; and when the boy was at the top of the tower and turned round, and was just going to take hold of the bell rope, he saw a white figure standing on the stairs opposite to the sounding hole.

"Who is there?" cried he, but the figure made no reply, and did not move or stir. "Give an answer," cried the boy, "or take thyself off, thou hast no business here at night."

The sexton, however, remained standing motionless that the boy might think he was a ghost.

The boy cried a second time, "What dost thou want here?—speak if thou art an honest fellow, or I will throw thee down the steps!"

The sexton thought, "he can't intend to be as bad as his words," uttered no sound and stood as if he were made of stone.

Then the boy called to him for the third time, and as that was also to no purpose, he ran against him and pushed the ghost down the stairs, so that it fell down ten steps and remained lying there in a corner. Thereupon he rang the bell, went home, and without saying a word went to bed, and fell asleep.

The sexton's wife waited a long time for her husband, but he did not come back. At length she became uneasy, and wakened the boy, and asked, "Dost thou not know where my husband is? He climbed up the tower before thou didst."

"No, I don't know," replied the boy, "but someone was standing by the sounding hole on the other side of the steps, and as he would neither give an answer nor go away, I took him for a scoundrel, and threw him downstairs, just go there and you will see if it was he. I should be sorry if it were."

The woman ran away and found her husband, who was lying moaning in the corner, and had broken his leg.

She carried him down, and then with loud screams she hastened to the boy's father. "Your boy," cried she, "has been the cause of a great misfortune! He has thrown my husband down the steps and made him break his leg. Take the good-for-nothing fellow away from our house."

The father was terrified, and ran thither and scolded the boy. "What wicked tricks are these?" said he, "the devil must have put this into thy head."

"Father," he replied, "do listen to me. I am quite innocent. He was standing there by night like one who is intending to do some evil. I did not know who it was, and I entreated him three times either to speak or to go away."

"Ah," said the father, "I have nothing but unhappiness with thee. Go out of my sight. I will see thee no more."

"Yes, father, right willingly, wait only until it is day. Then will I go forth and learn how to shudder, and then I shall, at any rate, understand one art which will support me."

"Learn what thou wilt," spake the father, "it is all the same to me. Here are fifty thalers for thee. Take these and go into the wide world, and tell no one from whence thou comest, and who is thy father, for I have reason to be ashamed of thee."

"Yes, father, it shall be as you will. If you desire nothing more than that, I can easily keep it in mind."

When day dawned, therefore, the boy put his fifty thalers into his pocket, and went forth on the great highway, and continually said to himself, "If I could but shudder! If I could but shudder!"

Then a man approached who heard this conversation which the youth was holding with himself, and when they had walked a little farther to where they could see the gallows, the man said to him, "Look, there is the tree where seven men have married the ropemaker's daughter, and are now learning how to fly. Sit down below it, and wait till night comes, and thou wilt soon learn how to shudder."

"If that is all that is wanted," answered the youth, "it is easily done; but if I learn how to shudder as quickly as that, thou shalt have my fifty thalers. Just come back to me early in the morning."

Then the youth went to the gallows, sat down below it, and waited till evening came. And as he was cold, he lighted himself a fire, but at midnight the wind blew so sharply that in spite of his fire, he could not get warm. And as the wind knocked the hanged men against each other, and they moved backwards and forwards, he thought to himself, "Thou shiverest below by the fire, but how those up above must freeze and suffer!"

And as he felt pity for them, he raised the ladder, and climbed up, unbound one of them after the other, and brought down all seven. Then he stirred the fire, blew it, and set them all round it to warm themselves. But they sat there and did not stir, and the fire caught their clothes. So he said, "Take care, or I will hang you up again."

The dead men, however, did not hear, but were quite silent, and let their rags go on burning. On this he grew angry, and said, "If you will not take care, I cannot help you, I will not be burnt with you," and he hung them up again each in his turn.

Then he sat down by his fire and fell asleep, and next morning the man came to him and wanted to have the fifty thalers, and said, "Well, dost thou know how to shudder?"

"No," answered he, "how was I to get to know? Those fellows up there did not open their mouths, and were so stupid that they let the few old rags which they had on their bodies get burnt."

Then the man saw that he would not carry away the fifty thalers that day, and went away saying, "One of this kind has never come in my way before."

The youth likewise went his way, and once more began to mutter to himself, "Ah, if I could but shudder! Ah, if I could but shudder!"

A waggoner who was striding behind him heard that and asked, "Who art thou?"

"I don't know," answered the youth.

Then the waggoner asked, "From whence comest thou?"

"I know not."

"Who is thy father?"

"That I may not tell thee."

"What is it that thou art always muttering between thy teeth?"

"Ah," replied the youth, "I do so wish I could shudder, but no one can teach me how to do it."

"Give up thy foolish chatter," said the waggoner. "Come, go with me, I will see about a place for thee."

The youth went with the waggoner, and in the evening they arrived at an inn where they wished to pass the night. Then at the entrance of the room the youth again said quite loudly, "If I could but shudder! If I could but shudder!"

The host who heard that, laughed and said, "If that is your desire, there ought to be a good opportunity for you here."

"Ah, be silent," said the hostess, "so many inquisitive persons have already lost their lives, it would be a pity and a shame if such beautiful eyes as these should never see the daylight again."

But the youth said, "However difficult it may be, I will learn it, and for this purpose indeed have I journeyed forth."

He let the host have no rest, until the latter told him, that not far from thence stood a haunted castle where anyone could very easily learn what shuddering was, if he would but watch in it for three nights. The King had promised that he who would venture should have his daughter to wife, and she was the most beautiful maiden the sun shone on. Great treasures likewise lay in the castle, which were guarded by evil spirits, and these treasures would then be freed, and would make a poor man rich enough. Already many men had gone into the castle, but as yet none had come out again.

Then the youth went next morning to the King, and said that if he were allowed he would watch three nights in the enchanted castle. The King looked at him, and as the youth pleased him, he said, "Thou mayest ask for three things to take into the castle with thee, but they must be things without life."

Then he answered, "Then I ask for a fire, a turning lathe, and a cutting-board with the knife." The King had these things carried into the castle for him during the day.

When night was drawing near, the youth went up and made himself a bright fire in one of the rooms, placed the cutting-board and

knife beside it, and seated himself by the turning-lathe. "Ah, if I could
but shudder!" said he, "but I shall not learn it here either."

Towards midnight he was about to poke his fire, and as he was
blowing it, something cried suddenly from one corner, "Au, miau! how
cold we are!"

"You simpletons!" cried he, "what are you crying about? If you are
cold, come and take a seat by the fire and warm yourselves."

And when he had said that, two great black cats came with one tremendous leap and sat down on each side of him, and looked savagely
at him with their fiery eyes. After a short time, when they had warmed
themselves, they said, "Comrade, shall we have a game at cards?"

"Why not?" he replied, "but just show me your paws." Then they
stretched out their claws. "Oh," said he, "what long nails you have!
Wait, I must first cut them a little for you." Thereupon he seized them
by the throats, put them on the cutting-board and screwed their feet
fast. "I have looked at your fingers," said he, "and my fancy for card-
playing has gone," and he struck them dead and threw them out into
the water.

But when he had made away with these two, and was about to sit
down again by his fire, out from every hole and corner came black cats
and black dogs with red-hot chains, and more and more of them came

until he could no longer stir, and they yelled horribly, and got on his fire, pulled it to pieces, and wanted to put it out.

He watched them for a while quietly, but at last when they were going too far, he seized his cutting-knife, and cried, "Away with ye, vermin," and began to cut them down. Part of them ran away, the others he killed, and threw out into the fish-pond.

When he came back, he blew up the embers of his fire again and warmed himself. And as he thus sat, his eyes would keep open no longer, and he felt a desire to sleep. Then he looked round and saw a great bed in the corner.

"That is the very thing for me," said he, and got into it. When he was just going to shut his eyes, however, the bed began to move of its own accord, and went over the whole of the castle. "That's right," said he, "but go faster."

Then the bed rolled on as if six horses were harnessed to it, up and down, over thresholds and steps, but suddenly hop, hop, it turned over upside down, and lay on him like a mountain. But he threw quilts and pillows up in the air, got out and said, "Now anyone who likes, may drive," and lay down by his fire, and slept till it was day.

In the morning the King came, and when he saw him lying there on the ground, he thought the spirits had killed him and he was dead. Then said he, "After all it is a pity—he is a handsome man."

The youth heard it, got up, and said, "It has not come to that yet." Then the King was astonished, but very glad, and asked how he had fared. "Very well indeed," answered the youth; "one night is over, the two others will get over likewise."

Then he went to the innkeeper, who opened his eyes very wide, and said, "I never expected to see thee alive again! Hast thou learnt how to shudder yet?"

"No," said he, "it is all in vain. If someone would but tell me!"

The second night he again went up into the old castle, sat down by the fire, and once more began his old song, "If I could but shudder!"

When midnight came, an uproar and noise of tumbling about was heard; at first it was low, but it grew louder and louder. Then it was quiet for awhile, and at length with a loud scream, half a man came down the chimney and fell before him.

"Hollo!" cried he, "another half belongs to this. This is too little!"

Then the uproar began again, there was a roaring and howling, and the other half fell down likewise.

"Wait," said he, "I will just blow up the fire a little for thee."

When he had done that and looked round again, the two pieces were joined together, and a frightful man was sitting in his place. "That is no part of our bargain," said the youth, "the bench is mine."

The man wanted to push him away; the youth, however, would not allow that, but thrust him off with all his strength, and seated himself again in his own place. Then still more men fell down, one after the other; they brought nine dead men's legs and two skulls, and set them up and played at nine-pins with them.

The youth also wanted to play and said, "Hark you, can I join you?"
"Yes, if thou hast any money."

"Money enough," replied he, "but your balls are not quite round." Then he took the skulls and put them in the lathe and turned them till they were round. "There, now, they will roll better!" said he. "Hurrah! now it goes merrily!"

He played with them and lost some of his money, but when it struck twelve, everything vanished from his sight. He lay down and quietly fell asleep.

Next morning the King came to enquire after him. "How has it fared with thee this time?" asked he.

"I have been playing at nine-pins," he answered, "and have lost a couple of farthings."

"Hast thou not shuddered then?"

"Eh, what?" said he, "I have made merry. If I did but know what it was to shudder!"

The third night he sat down again on his bench and said quite sadly, "If I could but shudder."

When it grew late, six tall men came in and brought a coffin. Then said he, "Ha, ha, that is certainly my little cousin, who died only a few days ago," and he beckoned with his finger, and cried, "Come, little cousin, come."

They placed the coffin on the ground, but he went to it and took the lid off, and a dead man lay therein. He felt his face, but it was cold as ice.

"Stop," said he, "I will warm thee a little," and went to the fire and warmed his hand and laid it on the dead man's face, but he remained cold. Then he took him out, and sat down by the fire and laid him on his breast and rubbed his arms that the blood might circulate again. As this also did no good, he thought to himself, "When two people lie in bed together, they warm each other," and carried him to the bed, covered him over and lay down by him.

After a short time the dead man became warm too, and began to move. Then said the youth, "See, little cousin, have I not warmed thee?"

The dead man, however, got up and cried, "Now will I strangle thee!"

"What!" said he, "is that the way thou thankest me? Thou shalt at once go into thy coffin again," and he took him up, threw him into it, and shut the lid.

Then came the six men and carried him away again. "I cannot manage to shudder," said he. "I shall never learn it here as long as I live."

Then a man entered who was taller than all others, and looked terrible. He was old, however, and had a long white beard. "Thou wretch," cried he, "thou shalt soon learn what it is to shudder, for thou shalt die!"

"Not so fast," replied the youth. "If I am to die, I shall have to have a say in it."

"I will soon seize thee," said the fiend.

22

"Softly, softly, do not talk so big. I am as strong as thou art, and perhaps even stronger."

"We shall see," said the old man. "If thou art stronger, I will let thee go—come, we will try."

Then he led him by dark passages to a smith's forge, took an axe, and with one blow struck an anvil into the ground.

"I can do that better still," said the youth, and went to the other anvil.

The old man placed himself near and wanted to look on, and his white beard hung down. Then the youth seized the axe, split the anvil with one blow, and struck the old man's beard in with it.

"Now I have thee," said the youth. "Now it is thou who wilt have to die!"

Then he seized an iron bar and beat the old man till he moaned and entreated him to stop, and he would give him great riches. The youth drew out the axe and let him go. The old man led him back into the castle, and in a cellar showed him three chests full of gold.

"Of these," said he, "one part is for the poor, the other is for the king, the third is thine."

In the meantime it struck twelve, and the spirit disappeared; the youth, therefore, was left in darkness. "I shall still be able to find my way out," said he, and felt about, found the way into the room, and slept there by his fire.

Next morning the King came and said, "Now thou must have learnt what shuddering is?"

"No," he answered; "what can it be? My dead cousin was here, and a bearded man came and showed me a great deal of money down below, but no one told me what it was to shudder."

"Then," said the King, "thou hast delivered the castle, and shalt marry my daughter."

"That is all very well," said he, "but still I do not know what it is to shudder!"

Then the gold was brought up and the wedding celebrated; but howsoever much the young King loved his wife, and however happy he was, he still said always, "If I could but shudder, if I could but shudder."

And at last she was angry at this. Her waiting-maid said, "I will find a cure for him; he shall soon learn what it is to shudder."

She went out to the stream which flowed through the garden, and had a whole bucketful of gudgeons brought to her. At night when the young King was sleeping, his wife was to draw the clothes off him and empty the bucketful of cold water with the gudgeons in it over him, so that the little fishes would sprawl about him.

When this was done, he woke up and cried, "Oh, what makes me shudder so? what makes me shudder so, dear wife? Ah! now I know what it is to shudder!"

The Wolf
and the Seven Little Kids

HERE was once on a time an old goat who had seven little kids, and loved them with all the love of a mother for her children. One day she wanted to go into the forest and fetch some food. So she called all seven to her and said, "Dear children, I have to go into the forest, be on your guard against the wolf; if he come in, he will devour you all—skin, hair, and all. The wretch often disguises himself, but you will know him at once by his rough voice and his black feet." The kids said, "Dear mother, we will take good care of ourselves; you may go away without any anxiety."

Then the old one bleated, and went on her way with an easy mind.

It was not long before someone knocked at the house-door and cried, "Open the door, dear children; your mother is here, and has brought something back with her for each of you."

But the little kids knew that it was the wolf, by the rough voice. "We will not open the door," cried they, "thou art not our mother. She has a soft, pleasant voice, but thy voice is rough; thou art the wolf!"

Then the wolf went away to a shopkeeper and bought himself a great lump of chalk, ate this and made his voice soft with it. Then he came back, knocked at the door of the house, and cried, "Open the door, dear children, your mother is here and has brought something back with her for each of you."

But the wolf had laid his black paws against the window, and the children saw them and cried, "We will not open the door, our mother has not black feet like thee; thou art the wolf!"

Then the wolf ran to a baker and said, "I have hurt my feet, rub some dough over them for me." And when the baker had rubbed his feet over, he ran to the miller and said, "Strew some white meal over my feet for me."

The miller thought to himself, "The wolf wants to deceive some-one," and refused; but the wolf said, "If thou wilt not do it, I will devour thee." Then the miller was afraid, and made his paws white for him. Truly men are like that.

So now the wretch went for the third time to the house-door, knocked at it and said, "Open the door for me, children, your dear little mother has come home, and has brought every one of you something back from the forest with her."

The little kids cried, "First show us thy paws that we may know if thou art our dear little mother."

Then he put his paws in through the window, and when the kids saw that they were white, they believed that all he said was true, and opened the door. But who should come in but the wolf! They were ter-rified and wanted to hide themselves. One sprang under the table, the second into the bed, the third into the stove, the fourth into the kitch-en, the fifth into the cupboard, the sixth under the washing-bowl, and the seventh into the clock-case.

But the wolf found them all, and used no great ceremony; one af-ter the other he swallowed them down his throat. The youngest in the clock-case was the only one he did not find. When the wolf had satis-fied his appetite, he took himself off, laid himself down under a tree in the green meadow outside, and began to sleep.

Soon afterwards the old goat came home again from the forest. Ah! what a sight she saw there! The house-door stood wide open. The table, chairs, and benches were thrown down, the washing-bowl lay broken to pieces, and the quilts and pillows were pulled off the bed. She sought her children, but they were nowhere to be found. She called them one after another by name, but no one answered.

At last, when she came to the youngest, a soft voice cried, "Dear mother, I am in the clock-case."

She took the kid out, and it told her that the wolf had come and had eaten all the others. Then you may imagine how she wept over her poor children.

At length in her grief she went out, and the youngest kid ran with her. When they came to the meadow, there lay the wolf by the tree and snored so loud that the branches shook. She looked at him on every side and saw that something was moving and struggling in his gorged belly.

"Ah, heavens," said she, "is it possible that my poor children whom he has swallowed down for his supper, can be still alive?"

Then the kid had to run home and fetch scissors, and a needle and thread, and the goat cut open the monster's stomach, and hardly had she made one cut, than one little kid thrust its head out, and when she had cut farther, all six sprang out one after another, and were all still alive, and had suffered no injury whatever, for in his greediness the monster had swallowed them down whole.

What rejoicing there was! Then they embraced their dear mother, and jumped like a tailor at his wedding.

The mother, however, said, "Now go and look for some big stones, and we will fill the wicked beast's stomach with them while he is still asleep."

Then the seven kids dragged the stones thither with all speed, and put as many of them into his stomach as they could get in; and the mother sewed him up again in the greatest haste, so that he was not aware of anything and never once stirred.

When the wolf at length had had his sleep out, he got on his legs, and as the stones in his stomach made him very thirsty, he wanted to go to a well to drink. But when he began to walk and to move about, the stones in his stomach knocked against each other and rattled.

Then cried he,

> "What rumbles and tumbles
> Against my poor bones?
> I thought 't was six kids,
> But it's naught but big stones."

And when he got to the well and stooped over the water and was just about to drink, the heavy stones made him fall in and there was no help, but he had to drown miserably.

The Good Bargain

HERE was once a peasant who had driven his cow to the fair, and sold her for seven thalers. On the way home he had to pass a pond, and already from afar he heard the frogs crying, "Aik, aik, aik, aik." "Well," said he to himself, "they are talking without rhyme or reason, it is seven that I have received, not eight." When he got to the water, he cried to them, "Stupid animals that you are! Don't you know better than that? It is seven thalers and not eight." The frogs, however, stood to their, "aik, aik, aik, aik."

"Come, then, if you won't believe it, I can count it out to you," and he took his money out of his pocket and counted out the seven thalers, always reckoning four and twenty groschen to a thaler.

The frogs, however, would not pay any attention to his reckoning, but still cried, "aik, aik, aik, aik."

"What," cried the peasant, quite angry, "since you are determined to know better than I, count it yourselves," and threw all the money into the water to them. He stood still and wanted to wait until they were done and had brought him his own again, but the frogs maintained their opinion and cried continually, "aik, aik, aik, aik," and besides that, did not throw the money out again. He still waited a long while until evening came on and he was forced to go home. Then he abused the frogs and cried, "You water-splashers, you thick-heads, you goggle-eyes, you have great mouths and can screech till you hurt one's ears, but you cannot count seven thalers! Do you think I'm going to stand here till you get done?"

And with that he went away, but the frogs still cried, "aik, aik, aik, aik," after him till he went home quite angry.

After a while he bought another cow, which he killed, and he made the calculation that if he sold the meat well he might gain as much as the two cows were worth, and have the skin into the bargain. When therefore he got to the town with the meat, a great troop of dogs were gathered together in front of the gate, with a large greyhound at the head of them, which jumped at the meat, snuffed at it, and barked, "Wow, wow, wow."

As there was no stopping him, the peasant said to him, "Yes, yes, I know quite well that thou art saying, 'wow, wow, wow,' because thou

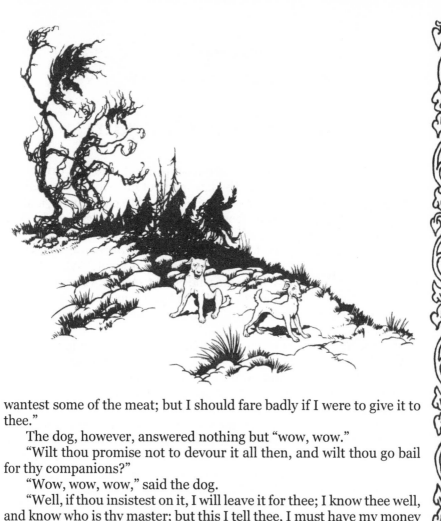

wantest some of the meat; but I should fare badly if I were to give it to
thee."

The dog, however, answered nothing but "wow, wow."

"Wilt thou promise not to devour it all then, and wilt thou go bail
for thy companions?"

"Wow, wow, wow," said the dog.

"Well, if thou insistest on it, I will leave it for thee; I know thee well,
and know who is thy master; but this I tell thee, I must have my money
in three days or else it will go ill with thee; thou must just bring it out
to me."

Thereupon he unloaded the meat and turned back again, the dogs
fell upon it and loudly barked, "wow, wow."

The countryman, who heard them from afar, said to himself, "Hark,
now they all want some, but the big one is responsible to me for it."

When three days had passed, the countryman thought, "Tonight
my money will be in my pocket," and was quite delighted. But no one
would come and pay it. "There is no trusting anyone now," said he;
and at last he lost patience, and went into the town to the butcher and
demanded his money.

The butcher thought it was a joke, but the peasant said, "Jesting
apart, I will have my money! Did not the great dog bring you the whole
of the slaughtered cow three days ago?"

Then the butcher grew angry, snatched a broom-stick and drove
him out.

"Wait a while," said the peasant, "there is still some justice in the world!" and went to the royal palace and begged for an audience.

He was led before the King, who sat there with his daughter, and asked him what injury he had suffered. "Alas!" said he, "the frogs and the dogs have taken from me what is mine, and the butcher has paid me for it with the stick," and he related at full length all that had happened.

Thereupon the King's daughter began to laugh heartily, and the King said to him, "I cannot give you justice in this, but you shall have my daughter to wife for it—in her whole life she has never yet laughed as she has just done at thee, and I have promised her to him who could make her laugh. Thou mayst thank God for thy good fortune!"

"Oh," answered the peasant, "I will not have her, I have a wife already, and she is one too many for me; when I go home, it is just as bad as if I had a wife standing in every corner."

Then the King grew angry, and said, "Thou art a boor."

"Ah, Lord King," replied the peasant, "what can you expect from an ox, but beef?"

"Stop," answered the King, "thou shalt have another reward. Be off now, but come back in three days, and then thou shalt have five hundred counted out in full."

When the peasant went out by the gate, the sentry said, "Thou hast made the King's daughter laugh, so thou wilt certainly receive something good."

"Yes, that is what I think," answered the peasant; "five hundred are to be counted out to me."

"Hark thee," said the soldier, "give me some of it. What canst thou do with all that money?"

"As it is thou," said the peasant, "thou shalt have two hundred; present thyself in three days' time before the King, and let it be paid to thee."

A Jew, who was standing by and had heard the conversation, ran after the peasant, held him by the coat, and said, "Oh, wonder! what a luck-child thou art! I will change it for thee, I will change it for thee into small coins, what dost thou want with the great thalers?"

"Jew," said the countryman, "three hundred canst thou still have; give it to me at once in coin, in three days from this, thou wilt be paid for it by the King."

The Jew was delighted with the profit, and brought the sum in bad groschen, three of which were worth two good ones.

After three days had passed, according to the King's command, the peasant went before the King.

"Pull his coat off," said the latter, "and he shall have his five hundred."

"Ah!" said the peasant, "they no longer belong to me; I presented two hundred of them to the sentinel, and three hundred the Jew has changed for me, so by right nothing at all belongs to me."

In the meantime the soldier and the Jew entered and claimed what they had gained from the peasant, and they received the blows strictly counted out.

The soldier bore it patiently and knew already how it tasted; but the Jew said sorrowfully, "Alas, alas, are these the heavy thalers?"

The King could not help laughing at the peasant, and as all his anger was gone, he said, "As thou hast already lost thy reward before it fell to thy lot, I will give thee something in the place of it. Go into my treasure chamber and get some money for thyself, as much as thou wilt."

The peasant did not need to be told twice, and stuffed into his big pockets whatsoever would go in. Afterwards he went to an inn and counted out his money.

The Jew had crept after him and heard how he muttered to himself, "That rogue of a King has cheated me after all, why could he not have given me the money himself, and then I should have known what I had? How can I tell now if what I have had the luck to put in my pockets is right or not?"

"Good heavens!" said the Jew to himself, "that man is speaking disrespectfully of our lord the King, I will run and inform, and then I shall get a reward, and he will be punished as well."

When the King heard of the peasant's words, he fell into a passion, and commanded the Jew to go and bring the offender to him.

The Jew ran to the peasant, "You are to go at once to the lord King in the very clothes you have on."

"I know what's right better than that," answered the peasant, "I shall have a new coat made first. Dost thou think that a man with so much money in his pocket is to go there in his ragged old coat?"

The Jew, as he saw that the peasant would not stir without another coat, and as he feared that if the King's anger cooled, he himself would lose his reward, and the peasant his punishment, said, "I will out of pure friendship lend thee a coat for the short time. What will people not do for love!"

The peasant was contented with this, put the Jew's coat on, and went off with him.

The King reproached the countryman because of the evil speaking of which the Jew had informed him.

"Ah," said the peasant, "what a Jew says is always false—no true word ever comes out of his mouth! That rascal there is capable of maintaining that I have his coat on."

"What is that?" shrieked the Jew. "Is the coat not mine? Have I not lent it to thee out of pure friendship, in order that thou mightest appear before the lord King?"

When the King heard that, he said, "The Jew has assuredly deceived one or the other of us, either myself or the peasant," and again he ordered something to be counted out to him in hard thalers.

The peasant, however, went home in the good coat, with the good money in his pocket, and said to himself, "This time I have hit it!"

Faithful John

HERE was once on a time an old king who was ill, and thought to himself, "I am lying on what must be my death-bed." Then said he, "Tell Faithful John to come to me." Faithful John was his favourite servant, and was so called, because he had for his whole life long been so true to him. When therefore he came beside the bed, the King said to him, "Most faithful John, I feel my end approaching, and have no anxiety except about my son. He is still of tender age, and cannot always know how to guide himself. If thou dost not promise me to teach him everything that he ought to know, and to be his foster-father, I cannot close my eyes in peace."

Then answered Faithful John, "I will not forsake him, and will serve him with fidelity, even if it should cost me my life."

On this, the old King said, "Now I die in comfort and peace." Then he added, "After my death, thou shalt show him the whole castle: all the chambers, halls, and vaults, and all the treasures which lie therein, but the last chamber in the long gallery, in which is the picture of the princess of the Golden Dwelling, shalt thou not show. If he sees that picture, he will fall violently in love with her, and will drop down in a swoon, and go through great danger for her sake, therefore thou must preserve him from that."

And when Faithful John had once more given his promise to the old King about this, the King said no more, but laid his head on his pillow, and died.

When the old King had been carried to his grave, Faithful John told the young King all that he had promised his father on his death-bed, and said, "This will I assuredly perform, and will be faithful to thee as I have been faithful to him, even if it should cost me my life."

When the mourning was over, Faithful John said to him, "It is now time that thou shouldst see thine inheritance. I will show thee thy father's palace."

Then he took him about everywhere, up and down, and let him see all the riches, and the magnificent apartments, only there was

33

one room which he did not open, that in which hung the dangerous picture. The picture was, however, so placed that when the door was opened you looked straight on it, and it was so admirably painted that it seemed to breathe and live, and there was nothing more charming or more beautiful in the whole world.

The young King, however plainly remarked that Faithful John always walked past this one door, and said, "Why dost thou never open this one for me?"

"There is something within it," he replied, "which would terrify thee."

But the King answered, "I have seen all the palace, and I will know what is in this room also," and he went and tried to break open the door by force.

Then Faithful John held him back and said, "I promised thy father before his death that thou shouldst not see that which is in this chamber, it might bring the greatest misfortune on thee and on me."

"Ah, no," replied the young King, "if I do not go in, it will be my certain destruction. I should have no rest day or night until I had seen it with my own eyes. I shall not leave the place now until thou hast unlocked the door."

Then Faithful John saw that there was no help for it now, and with a heavy heart and many sighs, sought out the key from the great bunch. When he had opened the door, he went in first, and thought by standing before him he could hide the portrait so that the King should not see it in front of him, but what availed that? The King stood on tip-toe and saw it over his shoulder.

And when he saw the portrait of the maiden, which was so magnificent and shone with gold and precious stones, he fell fainting to the ground. Faithful John took him up, carried him to his bed, and sorrowfully thought, "The misfortune has befallen us, Lord God, what will be the end of it?" Then he strengthened him with wine, until he came to himself again. The first words the King said were, "Ah, the beautiful portrait! whose is it?"

"That is the princess of the Golden Dwelling," answered Faithful John.

Then the King continued, "My love for her is so great, that if all the leaves on all the trees were tongues, they could not declare it. I will give my life to win her. Thou art my most Faithful John, thou must help me."

The faithful servant considered within himself for a long time how to set about the matter, for it was difficult even to obtain a sight of the King's daughter. At length he thought of a way, and said to the King, "Everything which she has about her is of gold—tables, chairs, dishes, glasses, bowls, and household furniture. Among thy treasures are five tons of gold; let one of the goldsmiths of the kingdom work these up into all manner of vessels and utensils, into all kinds of birds, wild beasts and strange animals, such as may please her, and we will go there with them and try our luck."

The King ordered all the goldsmiths to be brought to him, and they had to work night and day until at last the most splendid things were prepared. When everything was stowed on board a ship, Faithful John put on the dress of a merchant, and the King was forced to do the same in order to make himself quite unrecognizable. Then they sailed across the sea, and sailed on until they came to the town wherein dwelt the princess of the Golden Dwelling.

Faithful John bade the King stay behind on the ship, and wait for him. "Perhaps I shall bring the princess with me," said he, "therefore see that everything is in order; have the golden vessels set out and the whole ship decorated." Then he gathered together in his apron all kinds of gold things, went on shore and walked straight to the royal palace.

When he entered the courtyard of the palace, a beautiful girl was standing there by the well with two golden buckets in her hand, drawing water with them. And when she was just turning round to carry away the sparkling water, she saw the stranger, and asked who he was.

So he answered, "I am a merchant," and opened his apron, and let her look in.

Then she cried, "Oh, what beautiful gold things!" and put her pails down and looked at the golden wares one after the other. Then said the girl, "The princess must see these, she has such great pleasure in golden things, that she will buy all you have." She took him by the hand and led him upstairs, for she was the waiting-maid.

When the King's daughter saw the wares, she was quite delighted and said, "They are so beautifully worked, that I will buy them all of thee."

But Faithful John said, "I am only the servant of a rich merchant. The things I have here are not to be compared with those my master has in his ship. They are the most beautiful and valuable things that have ever been made in gold."

She wanted to have everything brought to her there, but he said, "There are so many of them that it would take a great many days to do that, and so many rooms would be required to exhibit them, that your house is not big enough."

Then her curiosity and longing were still more excited, until at last she said, "Conduct me to the ship, I will go there myself, and behold the treasures of thy master."

On this Faithful John was quite delighted, and led her to the ship, and when the King saw her, he perceived that her beauty was even greater than the picture had represented it to be, and thought no other than that his heart would burst in twain.

Then she got into the ship, and the King led her within. Faithful John, however, remained behind with the pilot, and ordered the ship to be pushed off, saying, "Set all sail, till it fly like a bird in air."

Within, however, the King showed her the golden vessels, every one of them, also the wild beasts and strange animals. Many hours went by whilst she was seeing everything, and in her delight she did not observe that the ship was sailing away.

35

After she had looked at the last, she thanked the merchant and wanted to go home, but when she came to the side of the ship, she saw that it was on the deep sea far from land, and hurrying onwards with all sail set.

"Ah," cried she in her alarm, "I am betrayed! I am carried away and have fallen into the power of a merchant—I would die rather!"

The King, however, seized her hand, and said, "I am not a merchant. I am a king, and of no meaner origin than thou art, and if I have carried thee away with subtlety, that has come to pass because of my exceeding great love for thee. The first time that I looked on thy portrait, I fell fainting to the ground."

When the princess of the Golden Dwelling heard that, she was comforted, and her heart was inclined unto him, so that she willingly consented to be his wife.

It happened, however, while they were sailing onwards over the deep sea, that Faithful John, who was sitting on the fore part of the vessel, making music, saw three ravens in the air, which came flying towards them. On this he stopped playing and listened to what they were saying to each other, for that he well understood.

One cried, "Oh, there he is carrying home the princess of the Golden Dwelling."

"Yes," replied the second, "but he has not got her yet."

Said the third, "But he has got her, she is sitting beside him in the ship."

Then the first began again, and cried, "What good will that do him? When they reach land, a chestnut horse will leap forward to meet him, and the prince will want to mount it, but if he does that, it will run away with him, and rise up into the air with him, and he will never see his maiden more."

Spake the second, "But is there no escape?"

"Oh, yes, if anyone else gets on it swiftly, and takes out the pistol which must be in its holster, and shoots the horse dead with it, the young King is saved. But who knows that? And whosoever does know it, and tells it to him, will be turned to stone from the toe to the knee."

Then said the second, "I know more than that; even if the horse be killed, the young King will still not keep his bride. When they go into the castle together, a wrought bridal garment will be lying there in a dish, and looking as if it were woven of gold and silver; it is, however, nothing but sulphur and pitch, and if he put it on, it will burn him to the very bone and marrow."

Said the third, "Is there no escape at all?"

"Oh, yes," replied the second, "if anyone with gloves on seizes the garment and throws it into the fire and burns it, the young King will be saved. But what avails that? Whosoever knows it and tells it to him, half his body will become stone from the knee to the heart."

Then said the third, "I know still more; even if the bridal garment be burnt, the young King will still not have his bride. After the wedding, when the dancing begins and the young Queen is dancing, she will suddenly turn pale and fall down as if dead, and if someone does not lift her up and draw three drops of blood from her right breast and spit them out again, she will die. But if anyone who knows that were to declare it, he would become stone from the crown of his head to the sole of his foot."

When the ravens had spoken of this together, they flew onwards, and Faithful John had well understood everything, but from that time forth he became quiet and sad, for if he concealed what he had heard from his master, the latter would be unfortunate, and if he discovered it to him, he himself must sacrifice his life. At length, however, he said to himself, "I will save my master, even if it bring destruction on myself."

When therefore they came to shore, all happened as had been foretold by the ravens, and a magnificent chestnut horse sprang forward.

"Good," said the King, "he shall carry me to my palace," and was about to mount it when Faithful John got before him, jumped quickly on it, drew the pistol out of the holster, and shot the horse.

Then the other attendants of the King, who after all were not very fond of Faithful John, cried, "How shameful to kill the beautiful animal, that was to have carried the King to his palace!"

But the King said, "Hold your peace and leave him alone, he is my most faithful John, who knows what may be the good of that!"

They went into the palace, and in the hall there stood a dish, and therein lay the bridal garment looking no otherwise than as if it were made of gold and silver. The young King went towards it and was about to take hold of it, but Faithful John pushed him away, seized it with gloves on, carried it quickly to the fire and burnt it.

The other attendants again began to murmur, and said, "Behold, now he is even burning the King's bridal garment!"

But the young King said, "Who knows what good he may have done, leave him alone, he is my most faithful John."

And now the wedding was solemnized: the dance began, and the bride also took part in it; then Faithful John was watchful and looked into her face, and suddenly she turned pale and fell to the ground as if she were dead. On this he ran hastily to her, lifted her up and bore her into a chamber—then he laid her down, and knelt and sucked the three drops of blood from her right breast, and spat them out. Immediately she breathed again and recovered herself, but the young King had seen this, and being ignorant why Faithful John had done it, was angry and cried, "Throw him into a dungeon."

Next morning Faithful John was condemned, and led to the gallows, and when he stood on high, and was about to be executed, he said, "Everyone who has to die is permitted before his end to make one last speech; may I too claim the right?"

"Yes," answered the King, "it shall be granted unto thee."

Then said Faithful John, "I am unjustly condemned, and have always been true to thee," and related how he had hearkened to the conversation of the ravens when on the sea, and how he had been obliged to do all these things in order to save his master.

Then cried the King, "Oh, my most Faithful John. Pardon, pardon—bring him down."

But as Faithful John spoke the last word he had fallen down lifeless and become a stone.

Thereupon the King and the Queen suffered great anguish, and the King said, "Ah, how ill I have requited great fidelity!" and ordered the stone figure to be taken up and placed in his bedroom beside his bed. And as often as he looked on it he wept and said, "Ah, if I could bring thee to life again, my most faithful John."

Some time passed and the Queen bore twins, two sons who grew fast and were her delight. Once when the Queen was at church and the two children were sitting playing beside their father, the latter full of grief again looked at the stone figure, sighed and said, "Ah, if I could but bring thee to life again, my most faithful John."

Then the stone began to speak and said, "Thou canst bring me to life again if thou wilt use for that purpose what is dearest to thee."

Then cried the King, "I will give everything I have in the world for thee."

The stone continued, "If thou wilt will cut off the heads of thy two children with thine own hand, and sprinkle me with their blood, I shall be restored to life."

The King was terrified when he heard that he himself must kill his dearest children, but he thought of faithful John's great fidelity, and how he had died for him, drew his sword, and with his own hand cut off the children's heads. And when he had smeared the stone with their blood, life returned to it, and Faithful John stood once more safe and healthy before him.

He said to the King, "Thy truth shall not go unrewarded," and took the heads of the children, put them on again, and rubbed the wounds with their blood, on which they became whole again immediately, and jumped about, and went on playing as if nothing had happened.

Then the King was full of joy, and when he saw the Queen coming, he hid Faithful John and the two children in a great cupboard. When she entered, he said to her, "Hast thou been praying in the church?"

"Yes," answered she, "but I have constantly been thinking of Faithful John and what misfortune has befallen him through us."

Then said he, "Dear wife, we can give him his life again, but it will cost us our two little sons, whom we must sacrifice."

The Queen turned pale, and her heart was full of terror, but she said, "We owe it to him, for his great fidelity."

Then the King was rejoiced that she thought as he had thought, and went and opened the cupboard, and brought forth Faithful John and the children, and said, "God be praised, he is delivered, and we have our little sons again also," and told her how everything had occurred.

Then they dwelt together in much happiness until their death.

The Pack of Ragamuffins

HE cock once said to the hen, "It is now the time when the nuts are ripe, so let us go to the hill together and for once eat our fill before the squirrel takes them all away."

"Yes," replied the hen, "come, we will have some pleasure together."

Then they went away to the hill, and as it was a bright day they stayed till evening.

Now I do not know whether it was that they had eaten till they were too fat, or whether they had become proud, but they would not go home on foot, and the cock had to build a little carriage of nut-shells. When it was ready, the little hen seated herself in it and said to the cock, "Thou canst just harness thyself to it."

"I like that!" said the cock, "I would rather go home on foot than let myself be harnessed to it; no, that is not our bargain. I do not mind being coachman and sitting on the box, but drag it myself I will not."

As they were thus disputing, a duck quacked to them, "You thieving folks, who bade you go to my nut-hill? Wait, you shall suffer for it!" and ran with open beak at the cock.

But the cock also was not idle, and fell boldly on the duck, and at last wounded her so with his spurs that she begged for mercy, and willingly let herself be harnessed to the carriage as a punishment.

The little cock now seated himself on the box and was coachman, and thereupon they went off in a gallop, with "Duck, go as fast as thou canst."

When they had driven a part of the way, they met two foot-passengers, a pin and a needle. They cried, "Stop! stop!" and said that it would soon be as dark as pitch, and then they could not go a step further, and that it was so dirty on the road, and asked if they could not get into the carriage for a while. They had been at the tailor's public-house by the gate, and had stayed too long over the beer. As they were thin people, who did not take up much room, the cock let them both get in, but they had to promise him and his little hen not to step on their feet.

Late in the evening they came to an inn, and as they did not like to go further by night, and as the duck also was not strong on her feet, and fell from one side to the other, they went in. The host at first made many objections, his house was already full, besides he thought they could not be very distinguished persons; but at last, as they made pleasant speeches, and told him that he should have the egg which the little hen had laid on the way, and should likewise keep the duck, which laid one every day, he at length said that they might stay the night. And now they had themselves well served, and feasted and rioted.

Early in the morning, when day was breaking, and everyone was asleep, the cock awoke the hen, brought the egg, pecked it open, and they ate it together, but they threw the shell on the hearth. Then they went to the needle which was still asleep, took it by the head and stuck it into the cushion of the landlord's chair, and put the pin in his towel, and at last without more ado they flew away over the heath.

The duck who liked to sleep in the open air and had stayed in the yard, heard them going away, made herself merry and found a stream, down which she swam, which was a much quicker way of travelling than being harnessed to a carriage.

The host did not get out of bed for two hours after this; he washed himself and wanted to dry himself, then the pin went over his face and made a red streak from one ear to the other. After this he went into the kitchen and wanted to light a pipe, but when he came to the hearth, the egg-shell darted into his eyes.

"This morning everything attacks my head," said he, and angrily sat down on his grandfather's chair, but he quickly started up again and cried, "Woe is me," for the needle had pricked him still worse than the pin, and not in the head.

Now he was thoroughly angry, and suspected the guests who had come so late the night before, and when he went and looked about for them, they were gone. Then he made a vow to take no more ragamuffins into his house, for they consume much, pay for nothing, and play mischievous tricks into the bargain by way of gratitude.

The Twelve Brothers

NCE on a time there were a king and a queen who lived happily together and had twelve children, but they were all boys. Then said the King to his wife, "If the thirteenth child, which thou art about to bring into the world, is a girl, the twelve boys shall die, in order that her possessions may be great, and that the kingdom may fall to her alone." He caused likewise twelve coffins to be made, which were already filled with shavings, and in each lay the little pillow for the dead, and he had them taken into a locked-up room, and then he gave the Queen the key of it, and bade her not to speak of this to anyone.

The mother, however, now sat and lamented all day long, until the youngest son, who was always with her, and whom she had named Benjamin, from the Bible, said to her, "Dear mother, why art thou so sad?"

"Dearest child," she answered, "I may not tell thee."

But he let her have no rest until she went and unlocked the room, and showed him the twelve coffins ready filled with shavings. Then she said, "My dearest Benjamin, thy father has had these coffins made for thee and for thy eleven brothers, for if I bring a little girl into the world, you are all to be killed and buried in them."

And as she wept while she was saying this, the son comforted her and said, "Weep not, dear mother, we will save ourselves, and go hence."

But she said, "Go forth into the forest with thy eleven brothers, and let one sit constantly on the highest tree which can be found, and keep watch, looking towards the tower here in the castle. If I give birth to a little son, I will put up a white flag, and then you may venture to come back, but if I bear a daughter, I will hoist a red flag, and then fly hence as quickly as you are able, and may the good God protect you. And every night I will rise up and pray for you—in winter that you may be able to warm yourself at a fire, and in summer that you may not faint away in the heat."

After she had blessed her sons therefore, they went forth into the forest. They each kept watch in turn, and sat on the highest oak and looked towards the tower.

When eleven days had passed and the turn came to Benjamin, he saw that a flag was being raised. It was, however, not the white, but the blood-red flag which announced that they were all to die.

When the brothers heard that, they were very angry and said, "Are we all to suffer death for the sake of a girl? We swear that we will avenge ourselves—wheresoever we find a girl, her red blood shall flow!"

Thereupon they went deeper into the forest, and in the midst of it, where it was the darkest, they found a little bewitched hut, which was standing empty. Then said they, "Here we will dwell, and thou Benjamin, who art the youngest and weakest, thou shalt stay at home and keep house, we others will go out and get food."

Then they went into the forest and shot hares, wild deer, birds and pigeons, and whatsoever there was to eat; this they took to Benjamin, who had to dress it for them in order that they might appease their hunger. They lived together ten years in the little hut, and the time did not appear long to them.

The little daughter which their mother the Queen had given birth to, was now grown up; she was good of heart, and fair of face, and had a golden star on her forehead. Once, when it was the great washing, she saw twelve men's shirts among the things, and asked her mother, "To whom do these twelve shirts belong, for they are far too small for father?"

Then the Queen answered with a heavy heart, "Dear child, these belong to thy twelve brothers."

Said the maiden, "Where are my twelve brothers, I have never yet heard of them?"

She replied, "God knows where they are, they are wandering about the world."

Then she took the maiden and opened the chamber for her, and showed her the twelve coffins with the shavings, and pillows for the head. "These coffins," said she, "were destined for thy brothers, but they went away secretly before thou wert born," and she related to her how everything had happened.

Then said the maiden, "Dear mother, weep not, I will go and seek my brothers."

So she took the twelve shirts and went forth, and straight into the great forest. She walked the whole day, and in the evening she came to the bewitched hut. Then she entered it and found a young boy, who asked, "From whence comest thou, and whither art thou bound?" and was astonished that she was so beautiful, and wore royal garments, and had a star on her forehead.

And she answered, "I am a king's daughter, and am seeking my twelve brothers, and I will walk as far as the sky is blue until I find them." She likewise showed him the twelve shirts which belonged to them.

Then Benjamin saw that she was his sister, and said, "I am Benjamin, thy youngest brother."

And she began to weep for joy, and Benjamin wept also, and they kissed and embraced each other with the greatest love. But after this he said, "Dear sister, there is still one difficulty. We have agreed that every maiden whom we meet shall die, because we have been obliged to leave our kingdom on account of a girl."

Then said she, "I will willingly die, if by so doing I can deliver my twelve brothers."

"No," answered he, "thou shalt not die, seat thyself beneath this tub until our eleven brothers come, and then I will soon come to an agreement with them."

She did so, and when it was night, the others came from hunting, and their dinner was ready. And as they were sitting at table, and eating, they asked, "What news is there?"

Said Benjamin, "Don't you know anything?"

"No," they answered.

He continued, "You have been in the forest and I have stayed at home, and yet I know more than you do."

"Tell us then," they cried.

He answered, "But promise me that the first maiden who meets us shall not be killed."

"Yes," they all cried, "she shall have mercy, only do tell us."

Then said he, "Our sister is here," and he lifted up the tub, and the King's daughter came forth in her royal garments with the golden star on her forehead, and she was beautiful, delicate, and fair.

Then they were all rejoiced, and fell on her neck, and kissed and loved her with all their hearts.

Now she stayed at home with Benjamin and helped him with the work. The eleven went into the forest and caught game, and deer, and birds, and wood-pigeons that they might have food, and the little sister and Benjamin took care to make it ready for them. She sought for the wood for cooking and herbs for vegetables, and put the pans on the fire so that the dinner was always ready when the eleven came. She likewise kept order in the little house, and put beautifully white clean coverings on the little beds, and the brothers were always contented and lived in great harmony with her.

Once on a time the two at home had prepared a beautiful entertainment, and when they were all together, they sat down and ate and drank and were full of gladness. There was, however, a little garden belonging to the bewitched house wherein stood twelve lily flowers. She wished to give her brothers pleasure, and plucked the twelve flowers, and thought she would present each brother with one while at dinner. But at the self-same moment that she plucked the flowers, the twelve brothers were changed into twelve ravens, and flew away over the forest, and the house and garden vanished likewise.

And now the poor maiden was alone in the wild forest, and when she looked around, an old woman was standing near her who said, "My child, what hast thou done? Why didst thou not leave the twelve white flowers growing? They were thy brothers, who are now for evermore changed into ravens."

The maiden said weeping, "Is there no way of delivering them?"

"No," said the woman, "there is but one in the whole world, and that is so hard that thou wilt not deliver them by it, for thou must be dumb for seven years, and mayst not speak or laugh, and if thou speakest one single word, and only an hour of the seven years is wanting, all is in vain, and thy brothers will be killed by the one word."

Then said the maiden in her heart, "I know with certainty that I shall set my brothers free," and went and sought a high tree and seated herself in it and span, and neither spoke nor laughed.

Now it so happened that a king was hunting in the forest, who had a great greyhound which ran to the tree on which the maiden was sitting, and sprang about it, whining, and barking at her. Then the King came by and saw the beautiful King's daughter with the golden star on her brow, and was so charmed with her beauty that he called to ask her if she would be his wife. She made no answer, but nodded a little with her head. So he climbed up the tree himself, carried her down, placed her on his horse, and bore her home. Then the wedding was solemnized with great magnificence and rejoicing, but the bride neither spoke nor smiled.

When they had lived happily together for a few years, the King's mother, who was a wicked woman, began to slander the young Queen, and said to the King, "This is a common beggar girl whom thou hast brought back with thee. Who knows what impious tricks she practises secretly! Even if she be dumb, and not able to speak, she still might laugh for once; but those who do not laugh have bad consciences."

At first the King would not believe it, but the old woman urged this so long, and accused her of so many evil things, that at last the King let himself be persuaded and sentenced her to death.

And now a great fire was lighted in the courtyard in which she was to be burnt, and the King stood above at the window and looked on with tearful eyes, because he still loved her so much.

And when she was bound fast to the stake, and the fire was licking at her clothes with its red tongue, the last instant of the seven years expired. Then a whirring sound was heard in the air, and twelve ravens came flying towards the place, and sank downwards, and when they touched the earth, they were her twelve brothers, whom she had delivered. They tore the fire asunder, extinguished the flames, set their dear sister free, and kissed and embraced her.

And now as she dared to open her mouth and speak, she told the King why she had been dumb, and had never laughed. The King rejoiced when he heard that she was innocent, and they all lived happily ever after. The wicked step-mother was taken before the judge, and then put to death.

Little Brother and Little Sister

HE little brother took his little sister by the hand and said, "Since our mother died we have had no happiness; our step-mother beats us every day, and if we come near her she kicks us away with her foot. Our meals are the hard crusts of bread that are left over; and the little dog under the table is better off, for she often throws it a nice bit. May Heaven pity us. If our mother only knew! Come, we will go forth together into the wide world."

They walked the whole day over meadows, fields, and stony places; and when it rained, the little sister said, "Heaven and our hearts are weeping together."

In the evening they came to a large forest, and they were so weary with sorrow and hunger and the long walk, that they lay down in a hollow tree and fell asleep.

The next day when they awoke, the sun was already high in the sky, and shone down hot into the tree. Then the brother said, "Sister, I am thirsty; if I knew of a little brook I would go and just take a drink; I think I hear one running." The brother got up and took the little sister by the hand, and they set off to find the brook.

But the wicked step-mother was a witch, and had seen how the two children had gone away, and had crept after them privily, as witches do creep, and had bewitched all the brooks in the forest.

Now when they found a little brook leaping brightly over the stones, the brother was going to drink out of it, but the sister heard how it said as it ran, "Who drinks of me will be a tiger; who drinks of me will be a tiger."

Then the sister cried, "Pray, dear brother, do not drink, or you will become a wild beast, and tear me to pieces."

The brother did not drink, although he was so thirsty, but said, "I will wait for the next spring."

When they came to the next brook, the sister heard this also say, "Who drinks of me will be a wolf; who drinks of me will be a wolf."

Then the sister cried out, "Pray, dear brother, do not drink, or you will become a wolf, and devour me."

The brother did not drink, and said, "I will wait until we come to the next spring, but then I must drink, say what you like; for my thirst is too great."

And when they came to the third brook, the sister heard how it said as it ran, "Who drinks of me will be a roebuck; who drinks of me will be a roebuck."

The sister said, "Oh, I pray you, dear brother, do not drink, or you will become a roebuck, and run away from me."

But the brother had knelt down at once by the brook, and had bent down and drunk some of the water, and as soon as the first drops touched his lips he lay there a young roebuck.

And now the sister wept over her poor bewitched brother, and the little roe wept also, and sat sorrowfully near to her. But at last the girl said, "Be quiet, dear little roe, I will never, never leave you."

Then she untied her golden garter and put it round the roebuck's neck, and she plucked rushes and wove them into a soft cord. With this she tied the little beast and led it on, and she walked deeper and deeper into the forest.

And when they had gone a very long way, they came at last to a little house, and the girl looked in; and as it was empty, she thought, "We can stay here and live."

Then she sought for leaves and moss to make a soft bed for the roe; and every morning she went out and gathered roots and berries and nuts for herself, and brought tender grass for the roe, who ate out of her hand, and was content and played round about her. In the evening, when the sister was tired, and had said her prayer, she laid her head upon the roebuck's back: that was her pillow, and she slept softly on it. And if only the brother had had his human form it would have been a delightful life.

For some time they were alone like this in the wilderness. But it happened that the King of the country held a great hunt in the forest. Then the blasts of the horns, the barking of dogs, and the merry shouts of the huntsmen rang through the trees, and the roebuck heard all, and was only too anxious to be there.

"Oh," said he to his sister, "let me be off to the hunt, I cannot bear it any longer;" and he begged so much that at last she agreed.

"But," said she to him, "come back to me in the evening; I must shut my door for fear of the rough huntsmen, so knock and say, 'My little sister, let me in!' that I may know you; and if you do not say that, I shall not open the door."

Then the young roebuck sprang away; so happy was he and so merry in the open air.

The King and the huntsmen saw the pretty creature, and started after him, but they could not catch him, and when they thought that they surely had him, away he sprang through the bushes and could not be seen.

When it was dark, he ran to the cottage, knocked, and said, "My little sister, let me in."

Then the door was opened for him, and he jumped in, and rested himself the whole night through upon his soft bed.

The next day the hunt went on afresh, and when the roebuck again heard the bugle-horn, and the ho! ho! of the huntsmen, he had no peace, but said, "Sister, let me out, I must be off."

His sister opened the door for him, and said, "But you must be here again in the evening and say your pass-word."

When the King and his huntsmen again saw the young roebuck with the golden collar, they all chased him, but he was too quick and nimble for them. This went on for the whole day, but at last by the evening the huntsmen had surrounded him, and one of them wounded him a little in the foot, so that he limped and ran slowly. Then a hunter crept after him to the cottage and heard how he said, "My little sister, let me in," and saw that the door was opened for him, and was shut again at once. The huntsman took notice of it all, and went to the King and told him what he had seen and heard.

Then the King said, "Tomorrow we will hunt once more."

The little sister, however, was dreadfully frightened when she saw that her fawn was hurt. She washed the blood off him, laid herbs on the wound, and said, "Go to your bed, dear roe, that you may get well again."

But the wound was so slight that the roebuck, next morning, did not feel it any more. And when he again heard the sport outside, he said, "I cannot bear it, I must be there; they shall not find it so easy to catch me."

The sister cried, and said, "This time they will kill you, and here am I alone in the forest and forsaken by all the world. I will not let you out."

"Then you will have me die of grief," answered the roe; "when I hear the bugle-horns, I feel as if I must jump out of my skin."

Then the sister could not do otherwise, but opened the door for him with a heavy heart, and the roebuck, full of health and joy, bounded into the forest.

When the King saw him, he said to his huntsmen, "Now chase him all day long till night-fall, but take care that no one does him any harm."

As soon as the sun had set, the King said to the huntsmen, "Now come and show me the cottage in the wood;" and when he was at the door, he knocked and called out, "Dear little sister, let me in."

Then the door opened, and the King walked in, and there stood a maiden more lovely than any he had ever seen. The maiden was frightened when she saw, not her little roe, but a man come in who wore a golden crown upon his head.

But the King looked kindly at her, stretched out his hand, and said, "Will you go with me to my palace and be my dear wife?"

"Yes, indeed," answered the maiden, "but the little roe must go with me, I cannot leave him."

The King said, "It shall stay with you as long as you live, and shall want nothing."

Just then he came running in, and the sister again tied him with the cord of rushes, took it in her own hand, and went away with the King from the cottage.

The King took the lovely maiden upon his horse and carried her to his palace, where the wedding was held with great pomp. She was now the Queen, and they lived for a long time happily together; the roebuck was tended and cherished, and ran about in the palace-garden.

But the wicked step-mother, because of whom the children had gone out into the world, thought all the time that the sister had been torn to pieces by the wild beasts in the wood, and that the brother had been shot for a roebuck by the huntsmen. Now when she heard that they were so happy and so well off, envy and hatred rose in her heart and left her no peace, and she thought of nothing but how she could bring them again to misfortune.

Her own daughter, who was as ugly as night, and had only one eye, grumbled at her and said, "A Queen! that ought to have been my luck."

"Only be quiet," answered the old woman, and comforted her by saying, "when the time comes, I shall be ready."

As time went on, the Queen had a pretty little boy, and it happened that the King was out hunting; so the old witch took the form of the chamber-maid, went into the room where the Queen lay, and said to her, "Come, the bath is ready; it will do you good, and give you fresh strength; make haste before it gets cold."

The daughter also was close by; so they carried the weakly Queen into the bath-room, and put her into the bath; then they shut the door and ran away. But in the bath-room they had made a fire of such deadly heat that the beautiful young Queen was soon suffocated.

When this was done, the old woman took her daughter, put a night-cap on her head, and laid her in bed in place of the Queen. She gave her too the shape and the look of the Queen, only she could not make good the lost eye. But in order that the King might not see it, she was to lie on the side on which she had no eye.

In the evening when he came home and heard that he had a son, he was heartily glad, and was going to the bed of his dear wife to see how she was. But the old woman quickly called out, "For your life leave the curtains closed; the Queen ought not to see the light yet, and must have rest."

The King went away, and did not find out that a false Queen was lying in the bed.

But at midnight, when all slept, the nurse, who was sitting in the nursery by the cradle, and who was the only person awake, saw the door open and the true Queen walk in. She took the child out of the cradle, laid it on her arm, and suckled it. Then she shook up its pillow, laid the child down again, and covered it with the little quilt. And she did not forget the roebuck, but went into the corner where it lay, and stroked its back. Then she went quite silently out of the door again.

The next morning the nurse asked the guards whether anyone had come into the palace during the night, but they answered, "No, we have seen no one."

52

She came thus many nights and never spoke a word: the nurse always saw her, but she did not dare to tell anyone about it.

When some time had passed in this manner, the Queen began to speak in the night, and said,

> "How fares my child, how fares my roe?
> Twice shall I come, then never more."

The nurse did not answer, but when the Queen had gone again, went to the King and told him all. The King said, "Ah, heavens! what is this? tomorrow night I will watch by the child."

In the evening he went into the nursery, and at midnight the Queen again appeared and said,

> "How fares my child, how fares my roe?
> Once will I come, then never more."

And she nursed the child as she was wont to do before she disappeared. The King dared not speak to her, but on the next night he watched again. Then she said,

> "How fares my child, how fares my roe?
> This time I come, then never more."

Then the King could not restrain himself; he sprang towards her, and said, "You can be none other than my dear wife."

She answered, "Yes, I am your dear wife," and at the same moment she received life again, and by God's grace became fresh, rosy, and full of health.

Then she told the King the evil deed which the wicked witch and her daughter had been guilty of towards her. The King ordered both to be led before the judge, and judgment was delivered against them. The daughter was expelled from the town, and the witch was put to death. And as soon as she was dead, the roebuck changed his shape, and received his human form again, so the sister and brother lived happily together all their lives.

The Three Spinners

 HERE was once a girl who was idle and would not spin, and let her mother say what she would, she could not bring her to it. At last the mother was once so overcome with anger and impatience, that she beat her, on which the girl began to weep loudly.

Now at this very moment the Queen drove by, and when she heard the weeping she stopped her carriage, went into the house and asked the mother why she was beating her daughter so that the cries could be heard out on the road?

Then the woman was ashamed to reveal the laziness of her daughter and said, "I cannot get her to leave off spinning. She insists on spinning for ever and ever, and I am poor, and cannot procure the flax."

Then answered the Queen, "There is nothing that I like better to hear than spinning, and I am never happier than when the wheels are humming. Let me have your daughter with me in the palace. I have flax enough, and there she shall spin as much as she likes."

The mother was heartily satisfied with this, and the Queen took the girl with her.

When they had arrived at the palace, she led her up into three rooms which were filled from the bottom to the top with the finest flax. "Now spin me this flax," said she, "and when thou hast done it, thou shalt have my eldest son for a husband, even if thou art poor. I care not for that, thy indefatigable industry is dowry enough."

The girl was secretly terrified, for she could not have spun the flax, no, not if she had lived till she was three hundred years old, and had sat at it every day from morning till night. When therefore she was alone, she began to weep, and sat thus for three days without moving a finger.

On the third day came the Queen, and when she saw that nothing had been spun yet, she was surprised; but the girl excused herself by saying that she had not been able to begin because of her great distress at leaving her mother's house.

The Queen was satisfied with this, but said when she was going away, "Tomorrow thou must begin to work."

When the girl was alone again, she did not know what to do, and in her distress went to the window. Then she saw three women coming towards her, the first of whom had a broad flat foot, the second had such a great underlip that it hung down over her chin, and the third had a broad thumb.

They remained standing before the window, looked up, and asked the girl what was amiss with her? She complained of her trouble, and then they offered her their help and said, "If thou wilt invite us to the wedding, not be ashamed of us, and wilt call us thine aunts, and likewise wilt place us at thy table, we will spin up the flax for thee, and that in a very short time."

"With all my heart," she replied, "do but come in and begin the work at once."

Then she let in the three strange women, and cleared a place in the first room, where they seated themselves and began their spinning. The one drew the thread and trod the wheel, the other wetted the thread, the third twisted it, and struck the table with her finger, and as often as she struck it, a skein of thread fell to the ground that was spun in the finest manner possible.

The girl concealed the three spinners from the Queen, and showed her whenever she came the great quantity of spun thread, until the latter could not praise her enough. When the first room was empty, she went to the second, and at last to the third, and that too was quickly cleared.

Then the three women took leave and said to the girl, "Do not forget what thou hast promised us—it will make thy fortune."

When the maiden showed the Queen the empty rooms, and the great heap of yarn, she gave orders for the wedding, and the bridegroom rejoiced that he was to have such a clever and industrious wife, and praised her mightily.

"I have three aunts," said the girl, "and as they have been very kind to me, I should not like to forget them in my good fortune; allow me to invite them to the wedding, and let them sit with us at table."

The Queen and the bridegroom said, "Why should we not allow that?"

Therefore when the feast began, the three women entered in strange apparel, and the bride said, "Welcome, dear aunts."

"Ah," said the bridegroom, "how comest thou by these odious friends?" Thereupon he went to the one with the broad flat foot, and said, "How do you come by such a broad foot?"

"By treading," she answered, "by treading."

Then the bridegroom went to the second, and said, "How do you come by your falling lip?"

"By licking," she answered, "by licking."

Then he asked the third, "How do you come by your broad thumb?"

"By twisting the thread," she answered, "by twisting the thread."

On this the King's son was alarmed and said, "Neither now nor ever shall my beautiful bride touch a spinning-wheel."

And thus she got rid of the hateful flax-spinning.

The Seven Ravens

HERE was once a man who had seven sons, and still he had no daughter, however much he wished for one. At length his wife again gave him hope of a child, and when it came into the world, it was a girl. The joy was great, but the child was sickly and small, and had to be privately baptized on account of its weakness.

The father sent one of the boys in haste to the spring to fetch water for the baptism. The other six went with him, and as each of them wanted to be first to fill it, the jug fell into the well. There they stood and did not know what to do, and none of them dared to go home.

As they still did not return, the father grew impatient, and said, "They have certainly forgotten it for some game, the wicked boys!" He became afraid that the girl would have to die without being baptized, and in his anger cried, "I wish the boys were all turned into ravens."

Hardly was the word spoken before he heard a whirring of wings over his head in the air, looked up and saw seven coal-black ravens flying away.

The parents could not recall the curse, and however sad they were at the loss of their seven sons, they still to some extent comforted themselves with their dear little daughter, who soon grew strong and every day became more beautiful.

For a long time she did not know that she had had brothers, for her parents were careful not to mention them before her, but one day she accidentally heard some people saying of herself, "that the girl was certainly beautiful, but that in reality she was to blame for the misfortune which had befallen her seven brothers."

Then she was much troubled, and went to her father and mother and asked if it was true that she had had brothers, and what had become of them? The parents now dared keep the secret no longer, but said that what had befallen her brothers was the will of Heaven, and that her birth had only been the innocent cause.

But the maiden took it to heart daily, and thought she must deliver her brothers. She had no rest or peace until she set out secretly, and went forth into the wide world to trace out her brothers and set them free, let it cost what it might. She took nothing with her but a little ring belonging to her parents as a keepsake, a loaf of bread against hunger, a little pitcher of water against thirst, and a little chair as a provision against weariness.

And now she went continually onwards, far, far, to the very end of the world. Then she came to the sun, but it was too hot and terrible, and devoured little children. Hastily she ran away, and ran to the moon, but it was far too cold, and also awful and malicious, and when it saw the child, it said, "I smell, I smell the flesh of men."

On this she ran swiftly away, and came to the stars, which were kind and good to her, and each of them sat on its own particular little chair. But the morning star arose, and gave her the drumstick of a chicken, and said, "If thou hast not that drumstick thou canst not open the Glass mountain, and in the Glass mountain are thy brothers."

The maiden took the drumstick, wrapped it carefully in a cloth, and went onwards again until she came to the Glass mountain. The door was shut, but she put the drumstick in the door, and succeeded in opening it.

When she had gone inside, a little dwarf came to meet her, who said, "My child, what are you looking for?"

"I am looking for my brothers, the seven ravens," she replied.

The dwarf said, "The lord ravens are not at home, but if you will wait here until they come, step in."

Thereupon the little dwarf carried the ravens' dinner in, on seven little plates, and in seven little glasses, and the little sister ate a morsel from each plate, and from each little glass she took a sip, but in the last little glass she dropped the ring which she had brought away with her.

Suddenly she heard a whirring of wings and a rushing through the air, and then the little dwarf said, "Now the lord ravens are flying home."

Then they came, and wanted to eat and drink, and looked for their little plates

and glasses. Then said one after the other, "Who has eaten something from my plate? Who has drunk out of my little glass? It was a human mouth."

And when the seventh came to the bottom of the glass, the ring rolled against his mouth. Then he looked at it, and saw that it was a ring belonging to his father and mother, and said, "God grant that our sister may be here, and then we shall be free."

When the maiden, who was standing behind the door watching, heard that wish, she came forth, and on this all the ravens were restored to their human form again. And they embraced and kissed each other, and went joyfully home.

Rapunzel

HERE were once a man and a woman who had long in vain wished for a child. At length the woman hoped that God was about to grant her desire. These people had a little window at the back of their house from which a splendid garden could be seen, which was full of the most beautiful flowers and herbs. It was, however, surrounded by a high wall, and no one dared to go into it because it belonged to an enchantress, who had great power and was dreaded by all the world. One day the woman was standing by this window and looking down into the garden, when she saw a bed which was planted with the most beautiful rampion (rapunzel), and it looked so fresh and green that she longed for it, and had the greatest desire to eat some. This desire increased every day, and as she knew that she could not get any of it, she quite pined away, and looked pale and miserable.

Then her husband was alarmed, and asked, "What aileth thee, dear wife?"

"Ah," she replied, "if I can't get some of the rampion, which is in the garden behind our house, to eat, I shall die."

The man, who loved her, thought, "Sooner than let thy wife die, bring her some of the rampion thyself, let it cost thee what it will."

In the twilight of evening, he clambered down over the wall into the garden of the enchantress, hastily clutched a handful of rampion, and took it to his wife. She at once made herself a salad of it, and ate it with much relish.

She, however, liked it so much—so very much, that the next day she longed for it three times as much as before. If he was to have any rest, her husband must once more descend into the garden. In the gloom of evening, therefore, he let himself down again; but when he had clambered down the wall, he was terribly afraid, for he saw the enchantress standing before him.

"How canst thou dare," said she with angry look, "to descend into my garden and steal my rampion like a thief? Thou shalt suffer for it!"

"Ah," answered he, "let mercy take the place of justice, I only made up my mind to do it out of necessity. My wife saw your rampion from the window, and felt such a longing for it that she would have died if she had not got some to eat."

Then the enchantress allowed her anger to be softened, and said to him, "If the case be as thou sayest, I will allow thee to take away with thee as much rampion as thou wilt, only I make one condition, thou must give me the child which thy wife will bring into the world; it shall be well treated, and I will care for it like a mother."

The man in his terror consented to everything, and when the woman was brought to bed, the enchantress appeared at once, gave the child the name of Rapunzel, and took it away with her.

Rapunzel grew into the most beautiful child beneath the sun. When she was twelve years old, the enchantress shut her into a tower, which lay in a forest, and had neither stairs nor door, but quite at the top was a little window.

When the enchantress wanted to go in, she placed herself beneath it, and cried,

> "Rapunzel, Rapunzel,
> Let down thy hair to me."

Rapunzel had magnificent long hair, fine as spun gold, and when she heard the voice of the enchantress, she unfastened her braided tresses, wound them round one of the hooks of the window above, and then the hair fell twenty ells down, and the enchantress climbed up by it.

After a year or two, it came to pass that the King's son rode through the forest and went by the tower. Then he heard a song, which was so charming that he stood still and listened. This was Rapunzel, who in her solitude passed her time in letting her sweet voice resound. The King's son wanted to climb up to her, and looked for the door of the tower, but none was to be found. He rode home, but the singing had so deeply touched his heart, that every day he went out into the forest and listened to it.

Once when he was thus standing behind a tree, he saw that an enchantress came there, and he heard how she cried,

> "Rapunzel, Rapunzel,
> Let down thy hair."

Then Rapunzel let down the braids of her hair, and the enchantress climbed up to her.

"If that is the ladder by which one mounts, I will for once try my fortune," said he, and the next day when it began to grow dark, he went to the tower and cried,

> "Rapunzel, Rapunzel,
> Let down thy hair."

Immediately the hair fell down and the King's son climbed up.

At first Rapunzel was terribly frightened when a man such as her eyes had never yet beheld, came to her; but the King's son began to talk to her quite like a friend, and told her that his heart had been so stirred that it had let him have no rest, and he had been forced to see her.

Then Rapunzel lost her fear, and when he asked her if she would take him for her husband, and she saw that he was young and handsome, she thought, "He will love me more than old Dame Gothel does;" and she said yes, and laid her hand in his. She said, "I will willingly go away with thee, but I do not know how to get down. Bring with thee a skein of silk every time that thou comest, and I will weave a ladder with it, and when that is ready, I will descend, and thou wilt take me on thy horse." They agreed that until that time he should come to her every evening, for the old woman came by day.

The enchantress remarked nothing of this, until once Rapunzel said to her, "Tell me, Dame Gothel, how it happens that you are so much heavier for me to draw up than the young King's son—he is with me in a moment."

"Ah! thou wicked child," cried the enchantress. "What do I hear thee say! I thought I had separated thee from all the world, and yet thou hast deceived me!"

In her anger she clutched Rapunzel's beautiful tresses, wrapped them twice round her left hand, seized a pair of scissors with the right, and snip, snap, they were cut off, and the lovely braids lay on the ground. And she was so pitiless that she took poor Rapunzel into a desert where she had to live in great grief and misery.

On the same day, however, that she cast out Rapunzel, the enchantress in the evening fastened the braids of hair, which she had cut off, to the hook of the window, and when the King's son came and cried,

"Rapunzel, Rapunzel,
Let down thy hair,"

she let the hair down. The King's son ascended, but he did not find his dearest Rapunzel above, but the enchantress, who gazed at him with wicked and venomous looks.

"Aha!" she cried mockingly, "thou wouldst fetch thy dearest, but the beautiful bird sits no longer singing in the nest; the cat has got it, and will scratch out thy eyes as well. Rapunzel is lost to thee; thou wilt never see her more."

The King's son was beside himself with pain, and in his despair he leapt down from the tower. He escaped with his life, but the thorns into which he fell, pierced his eyes. Then he wandered quite blind about the forest, ate nothing but roots and berries, and did nothing but lament and weep over the loss of his dearest wife.

Thus he roamed about in misery for some years, and at length came to the desert where Rapunzel, with the twins to which she had given birth, a boy and a girl, lived in wretchedness. He heard a voice, and it seemed so familiar to him that he went towards it, and when he approached, Rapunzel knew him and fell on his neck and wept. Two of her tears wetted his eyes and they grew clear again, and he could see with them as before. He led her to his kingdom where he was joyfully received, and they lived for a long time afterwards, happy and contented.

The Three Little Men in the Wood

HERE was once a man whose wife died, and a woman whose husband died, and the man had a daughter, and the woman also had a daughter. The girls were acquainted with each other, and went out walking together, and afterwards came to the woman in her house. Then said she to the man's daughter, "Listen, tell thy father that I would like to marry him, and then thou shalt wash thyself in milk every morning, and drink wine, but my own daughter shall wash herself in water and drink water."

The girl went home, and told her father what the woman had said. The man said, "What shall I do? Marriage is a joy and also a torment."

At length as he could come to no decision, he pulled off his boot, and said, "Take this boot, it has a hole in the sole of it. Go with it up to the loft, hang it on the big nail, and then pour water into it. If it hold the water, then I will again take a wife, but if it run through, I will not."

The girl did as she was ordered, but the water drew the hole together, and the boot became full to the top. She informed her father how it had turned out. Then he himself went up, and when he saw that she was right, he went to the widow and wooed her, and the wedding was celebrated.

The next morning, when the two girls got up, there stood before the man's daughter milk for her to wash in and wine for her to drink, but before the woman's daughter stood water to wash herself with and water for drinking. On the second morning, stood water for washing and water for drinking before the man's daughter as well as before the woman's daughter. And on the third morning stood water for washing and water for drinking before the man's daughter, and milk for washing and wine for drinking, before the woman's daughter, and so it continued.

The woman became bitterly unkind to her step-daughter, and day by day did her best to treat her still worse. She was also envious because

67

her step-daughter was beautiful and lovable, and her own daughter ugly and repulsive.

Once, in winter, when everything was frozen as hard as a stone, and hill and vale lay covered with snow, the woman made a frock of paper, called her step-daughter, and said, "Here, put on this dress and go out into the wood, and fetch me a little basketful of strawberries—I have a fancy for some."

"Good heavens!" said the girl, "no strawberries grow in winter! The ground is frozen, and besides the snow has covered everything. And why am I to go in this paper frock? It is so cold outside that one's very breath freezes! The wind will blow through the frock, and the thorns will tear it off my body."

"Wilt thou contradict me again?" said the stepmother. "See that thou goest, and do not show thy face again until thou hast the basketful of strawberries!" Then she gave her a little piece of hard bread, and said, "This will last thee the day," and thought, "Thou wilt die of cold and hunger outside, and wilt never be seen again by me."

Then the maiden was obedient, and put on the paper frock, and went out with the basket. Far and wide there was nothing but snow, and not a green blade to be seen. When she got into the wood, she saw a small house out of which peeped three dwarfs.[1] She wished them good-day, and knocked modestly at the door.

They cried, "Come in," and she entered the room and seated herself on the bench by the stove, where she began to warm herself and eat her breakfast. The elves said, "Give us, too, some of it."

"Willingly," said she, and divided her bit of bread in two, and gave them the half. They asked, "What dost thou here in the forest in the winter time, in thy thin dress?"

"Ah," she answered, "I am to look for a basketful of strawberries, and am not to go home until I can take them with me."

When she had eaten her bread, they gave her a broom and said, "Sweep away the snow at the back door with it." But when she was outside, the three little men said to each other, "What shall we give her as she is so good, and has shared her bread with us?"

Then said the first, "My gift is, that she shall every day grow more beautiful."

The second said, "My gift is, that gold pieces shall fall out of her mouth every time she speaks."

The third said, "My gift is, that a king shall come and take her to wife."

The girl, however, did as the little men had bidden her, swept away the snow behind the little house with the broom, and what did she find but real ripe strawberries, which came up quite dark-red out of the snow! In her joy she hastily gathered her basket full, thanked the little

---

[1] In the original *Haulemännerchen*—i.e., Höhlen-Waldmännlein. They are so called because they live in caves in the forests. They are little dwarfs with large heads, and are supposed to steal unbaptized children.—TR.

men, shook hands with each of them, and ran home to take her step-mother what she had longed for so much.

When she went in and said good-evening, a piece of gold at once fell from her mouth. Thereupon she related what had happened to her in the wood, but with every word she spoke, gold pieces fell from her mouth, until very soon the whole room was covered with them.

"Now look at her arrogance," cried the step-sister, "to throw about gold in that way!" But she was secretly envious of it, and wanted to go into the forest also to seek strawberries.

The mother said, "No, my dear little daughter, it is too cold, thou mightest die of cold."

However, as her daughter let her have no peace, the mother at last yielded, made her a magnificent dress of fur, which she was obliged to put on, and gave her bread-and-butter and cake with her.

The girl went into the forest and straight up to the little house. The three little elves peeped out again, but she did not greet them, and without looking round at them and without speaking to them, she went awkwardly into the room, seated herself by the stove, and began to eat her bread-and-butter and cake.

"Give us some of it," cried the little men.

But she replied, "There is not enough for myself, so how can I give it away to other people?"

When she had done eating, they said, "There is a broom for thee, sweep all clean for us outside by the back-door."

"Humph! Sweep for yourselves," she answered, "I am not your servant."

When she saw that they were not going to give her anything, she went out by the door. Then the little men said to each other, "What shall we give her as she is so naughty, and has a wicked envious heart, that will never let her do a good turn to anyone?"

The first said, "I grant that she may grow uglier every day."

The second said, "I grant that at every word she says, a toad shall spring out of her mouth."

The third said, "I grant that she may die a miserable death."

The maiden looked for strawberries outside, but as she found none, she went angrily home. And when she opened her mouth, and was about to tell her mother what had happened to her in the wood, with every word she said, a toad sprang out of her mouth, so that everyone was seized with horror of her.

Then the step-mother was still more enraged, and thought of nothing but how to do every possible injury to the man's daughter, whose beauty, however, grew daily greater. At length she took a cauldron, set it on the fire, and boiled yarn in it.

When it was boiled, she flung it on the poor girl's shoulder, and gave her an axe in order that she might go on the frozen river, cut a hole in the ice, and rinse the yarn. She was obedient, went thither and cut a hole in the ice; and while she was in the midst of her cutting, a splendid carriage came driving up, in which sat the King.

The carriage stopped, and the King asked, "My child, who art thou, and what art thou doing here?"

"I am a poor girl, and I am rinsing yarn."

Then the King felt compassion, and when he saw that she was so very beautiful, he said to her, "Wilt thou go away with me?"

"Ah, yes, with all my heart," she answered, for she was glad to get away from the mother and sister.

So she got into the carriage and drove away with the King, and when they arrived at his palace, the wedding was celebrated with great pomp, as the little men had granted to the maiden.

Hansel and Grethel

EAR a great forest dwelt a poor wood-cutter with his wife and his two children. The boy was called Hansel and the girl Grethel. He had little to bite and to break, and once when great scarcity fell on the land, he could no longer procure daily bread. Now when he thought over this by night in his bed, and tossed about in his anxiety, he groaned and said to his wife, "What is to become of us? How are we to feed our poor children, when we no longer have anything even for ourselves?"

"I'll tell you what, husband," answered the woman. "Early tomorrow morning we will take the children out into the forest to where it is the thickest, there we will light a fire for them, and give each of them one piece of bread more, and then we will go to our work and leave them alone. They will not find the way home again, and we shall be rid of them."

"No, wife," said the man, "I will not do that; how can I bear to leave my children alone in the forest?—the wild animals would soon come and tear them to pieces."

"O, thou fool!" said she. "Then we must all four die of hunger, thou mayest as well plane the planks for our coffins," and she left him no peace until he consented.

"But I feel very sorry for the poor children, all the same," said the man.

The two children had also not been able to sleep for hunger, and had heard what their step-mother had said to their father. Grethel wept bitter tears, and said to Hansel, "Now all is over with us."

"Be quiet, Grethel," said Hansel, "do not distress thyself, I will soon find a way to help us."

And when the old folks had fallen asleep, he got up, put on his little coat, opened the door below, and crept outside. The moon shone brightly, and the white pebbles which lay in front of the house glittered like real silver pennies. Hansel stooped and put as many of them in the little pocket of his coat as he could possibly get in.

Then he went back and said to Grethel, "Be comforted, dear little sister, and sleep in peace, God will not forsake us," and he lay down again in his bed.

When day dawned, but before the sun had risen, the woman came and awoke the two children, saying, "Get up, you sluggards! we are going into the forest to fetch wood." She gave each a little piece of bread, and said, "There is something for your dinner, but do not eat it up before then, for you will get nothing else."

Grethel took the bread under her apron, as Hansel had the stones in his pocket. Then they all set out together on the way to the forest. When they had walked a short time, Hansel stood still and peeped back at the house, and did so again and again.

His father said, "Hansel, what art thou looking at there and staying behind for? Mind what thou art about, and do not forget how to use thy legs."

"Ah, father," said Hansel, "I am looking at my little white cat, which is sitting up on the roof, and wants to say good-bye to me."

The wife said, "Fool, that is not thy little cat, that is the morning sun which is shining on the chimneys."

Hansel, however, had not been looking back at the cat, but had been constantly throwing one of the white pebble-stones out of his pocket on the road.

When they had reached the middle of the forest, the father said, "Now, children, pile up some wood, and I will light a fire that you may not be cold."

Hansel and Grethel gathered brushwood together, as high as a little hill. The brushwood was lighted, and when the flames were burning very high, the woman said, "Now, children, lay yourselves down by the fire and rest, we will go into the forest and cut some wood. When we have done, we will come back and fetch you away."

Hansel and Grethel sat by the fire, and when noon came, each ate a little piece of bread, and as they heard the strokes of the wood-axe they believed that their father was near. It was not, however, the axe, it was a branch which he had fastened to a withered tree which the wind was blowing backwards and forwards.

And as they had been sitting such a long time, their eyes shut with fatigue, and they fell fast asleep. When at last they awoke, it was already dark night.

Grethel began to cry and said, "How are we to get out of the forest now?"

But Hansel comforted her and said, "Just wait a little, until the moon has risen, and then we will soon find the way."

And when the full moon had risen, Hansel took his little sister by the hand, and followed the pebbles which shone like newly-coined silver pieces, and showed them the way.

They walked the whole night long, and by break of day came once more to their father's house. They knocked at the door, and when the woman opened it and saw that it was Hansel and Grethel, she said,

"You naughty children, why have you slept so long in the forest?—we thought you were never coming back at all!"

The father, however, rejoiced, for it had cut him to the heart to leave them behind alone.

Not long afterwards, there was once more great scarcity in all parts, and the children heard their mother saying at night to their father, "Everything is eaten again, we have one half loaf left, and after that there is an end. The children must go, we will take them farther into the wood, so that they will not find their way out again; there is no other means of saving ourselves!"

The man's heart was heavy, and he thought "it would be better for thee to share the last mouthful with thy children."

The woman, however, would listen to nothing that he had to say, but scolded and reproached him. He who says A must say B, likewise, and as he had yielded the first time, he had to do so a second time also.

The children were, however, still awake and had heard the conversation. When the old folks were asleep, Hansel again got up, and wanted to go out and pick up pebbles, but the woman had locked the door, and Hansel could not get out. Nevertheless he comforted his little sister, and said, "Do not cry, Grethel, go to sleep quietly, the good God will help us."

Early in the morning came the woman, and took the children out of their beds. Their bit of bread was given to them, but it was still smaller than the time before. On the way into the forest Hansel crumbled his in his pocket, and often stood still and threw a morsel on the ground.

"Hansel, why dost thou stop and look round?" said the father, "go on."

"I am looking back at my little pigeon which is sitting on the roof, and wants to say good-bye to me," answered Hansel.

"Simpleton!" said the woman, "that is not thy little pigeon, that is the morning sun that is shining on the chimney."

Hansel, however, little by little, threw all the crumbs on the path.

The woman led the children still deeper into the forest, where they had never in their lives been before. Then a great fire was again made, and the mother said, "Just sit there, you children, and when you are tired, you may sleep a little; we are going into the forest to cut wood, and in the evening when we are done, we will come and fetch you away."

When it was noon, Grethel shared her piece of bread with Hansel, who had scattered his by the way. Then they fell asleep and evening came and went, but no one came to the poor children. They did not awake until it was dark night, and Hansel comforted his little sister and said, "Just wait, Grethel, until the moon rises, and then we shall see the crumbs of bread which I have strewn about, they will show us our way home again."

When the moon came, they set out, but they found no crumbs, for the many thousands of birds which fly about in the woods and fields had picked them all up.

Hansel said to Grethel, "We shall soon find the way," but they did not find it. They walked the whole night and all the next day too from morning till evening, but they did not get out of the forest, and were very hungry, for they had nothing to eat but two or three berries, which grew on the ground. And as they were so weary that their legs would carry them no longer, they lay down beneath a tree and fell asleep.

It was now three mornings since they had left their father's house. They began to walk again, but they always got deeper into the forest, and if help did not come soon, they must die of hunger and weariness. When it was mid-day, they saw a beautiful snow-white bird sitting on a bough, which sang so delightfully that they stood still and listened to it. And when it had finished its song, it spread its wings and flew away before them, and they followed it until they reached a little house, on the roof of which it alighted; and when they came quite up to the little house, they saw that it was built of bread and covered with cakes, but that the windows were of clear sugar.

"We will set to work on that," said Hansel, "and have a good meal. I will eat a bit of the roof, and thou, Grethel, canst eat some of the window, it will taste sweet."

Hansel reached up above, and broke off a little of the roof to try how it tasted, and Grethel leant against the window and nibbled at the panes. Then a soft voice cried from the room,

> "Nibble, nibble, gnaw,
> Who is nibbling at my little house?"

The children answered,

> "The wind, the wind,
> The heaven-born wind,"

and went on eating without disturbing themselves. Hansel, who thought the roof tasted very nice, tore down a great piece of it, and Grethel pushed out the whole of one round window-pane, sat down, and enjoyed herself with it. Suddenly the door opened, and a very, very old woman, who supported herself on crutches, came creeping out.

Hansel and Grethel were so terribly frightened that they let fall what they had in their hands. The old woman, however, nodded her head, and said, "Oh, you dear children, who has brought you here? Do come in, and stay with me. No harm shall happen to you."

She took them both by the hand, and led them into her little house. Then good food was set before them, milk and pancakes, with sugar, apples, and nuts. Afterwards two pretty little beds were covered with clean white linen, and Hansel and Grethel lay down in them, and thought they were in heaven.

The old woman had only pretended to be so kind; she was in reality a wicked witch, who lay in wait for children, and had only built the little house of bread in order to entice them there. When a child fell into her power, she killed it, cooked and ate it, and that was a feast day with

her. Witches have red eyes, and cannot see far, but they have a keen scent like the beasts, and are aware when human beings draw near.

When Hansel and Grethel came into her neighbourhood, she laughed maliciously, and said mockingly, "I have them, they shall not escape me again!"

Early in the morning before the children were awake, she was already up, and when she saw both of them sleeping and looking so pretty, with their plump red cheeks, she muttered to herself, "That will be a dainty mouthful!" Then she seized Hansel with her shrivelled hand, carried him into a little stable, and shut him in with a grated door. He might scream as he liked, that was of no use. Then she went to Grethel, shook her till she awoke, and cried, "Get up, lazy thing, fetch some water, and cook something good for thy brother, he is in the stable outside, and is to be made fat. When he is fat, I will eat him."

Grethel began to weep bitterly, but it was all in vain, she was forced to do what the wicked witch ordered her.

And now the best food was cooked for poor Hansel, but Grethel got nothing but crab-shells. Every morning the woman crept to the little stable, and cried, "Hansel, stretch out thy finger that I may feel if thou wilt soon be fat."

Hansel, however, stretched out a little bone to her, and the old woman, who had dim eyes, could not see it, and thought it was Hansel's finger, and was astonished that there was no way of fattening him. When four weeks had gone by, and Hansel still continued thin, she was seized with impatience and would not wait any longer.

"Hola, Grethel," she cried to the girl, "be active, and bring some water. Let Hansel be fat or lean, tomorrow I will kill him, and cook him."

Ah, how the poor little sister did lament when she had to fetch the water, and how her tears did flow down over her cheeks! "Dear God, do help us!" she cried. "If the wild beasts in the forest had but devoured us, we should at any rate have died together."

"Just keep thy noise to thyself," said the old woman, "all that won't help thee at all."

Early in the morning, Grethel had to go out and hang up the cauldron with the water, and light the fire.

"We will bake first," said the old woman, "I have already heated the oven, and kneaded the dough." She pushed poor Grethel out to the oven, from which flames of fire were already darting. "Creep in," said the witch, "and see if it is properly heated, so that we can shut the bread in."

And when once Grethel was inside, she intended to shut the oven and let her bake in it, and then she would eat her, too. But Grethel saw what she had in her mind, and said, "I do not know how I am to do it; how do you get in?"

"Silly goose," said the old woman. "The door is big enough; just look, I can get in myself!" and she crept up and thrust her head into the oven.

Then Grethel gave her a push that drove her far into it, and shut the iron door, and fastened the bolt. Oh! then she began to howl quite horribly, but Grethel ran away, and the godless witch was miserably burnt to death.

Grethel, however, ran as quick as lightning to Hansel, opened his little stable, and cried, "Hansel, we are saved! The old witch is dead!"

Then Hansel sprang out like a bird from its cage when the door is opened for it. How they did rejoice and embrace each other, and dance about and kiss each other! And as they had no longer any need to fear her, they went into the witch's house, and in every corner there stood chests full of pearls and jewels.

"These are far better than pebbles!" said Hansel, and thrust into his pockets whatever could be got in, and Grethel said, "I, too, will take something home with me," and filled her pinafore full.

"But now we will go away," said Hansel, "that we may get out of the witch's forest."

When they had walked for two hours, they came to a great piece of water.

"We cannot get over," said Hansel, "I see no foot-plank, and no bridge."

"And no boat crosses either," answered Grethel, "but a white duck is swimming there; if I ask her, she will help us over."

Then she cried,

"Little duck, little duck, dost thou see,
Hansel and Grethel are waiting for thee?
There's never a plank, or bridge in sight,
Take us across on thy back so white."

The duck came to them, and Hansel seated himself on its back, and told his sister to sit by him.

"No," replied Grethel, "that will be too heavy for the little duck; she shall take us across, one after the other."

The good little duck did so, and when they were once safely across and had walked for a short time, the forest seemed to be more and more familiar to them, and at length they saw from afar their father's house. Then they began to run, rushed into the parlour, and threw themselves into their father's arms. The man had not known one happy hour since he had left the children in the forest; the woman, however, was dead.

Grethel emptied her pinafore until pearls and precious stones ran about the room, and Hansel threw one handful after another out of his pocket to add to them. Then all anxiety was at an end, and they lived together in perfect happiness.

The Straw, the Coal, and the Bean

HERE lived in a certain village a poor old woman, who had gathered together a dish of beans and wanted to cook them. So she made a fire on her hearth, and that it might burn the quicker, she lighted it with a handful of straw. When she was emptying the beans into the pan, one dropped without her observing it, and lay on the ground beside a straw, and soon afterwards a burning coal from the fire leapt down to the two.

Then the straw began and said, "Dear friends, from whence do you come here?"

The coal replied, "I fortunately sprang out of the fire, and if I had not escaped by main force, my death would have been certain,—I should have been burnt to ashes."

The bean said, "I too have escaped with a whole skin, but if the old woman had got me into the pan, I should have been made into broth without any mercy, like my comrades."

"And would a better fate have fallen to my lot?" said the straw. "The old woman has destroyed all my brethren in fire and smoke; she seized sixty of them at once, and took their lives. I luckily slipped through her fingers."

"But what are we to do now?" said the coal.

"I think," answered the bean, "that as we have so fortunately escaped death, we should keep together like good companions, and lest a new mischance should overtake us here, we should go away together, and repair to a foreign country."

The proposition pleased the two others, and they set out on their way in company. Soon, however, they came to a little brook, and as there was no bridge or foot-plank, they did not know how they were to get over it.

The straw hit on a good idea, and said, "I will lay myself straight across, and then you can walk over on me as on a bridge."

The straw therefore stretched itself from one bank to the other, and the coal, who was of an impetuous disposition, tripped quite boldly on to the newly-built bridge. But when she had reached the middle, and heard the water rushing beneath her, she was, after all, afraid, and stood still, and ventured no farther. The straw, however, began to burn, broke in two pieces, and fell into the stream. The coal slipped after her, hissed when she got into the water, and breathed her last.

The bean, who had prudently stayed behind on the shore, could not but laugh at the event, was unable to stop, and laughed so heartily that she burst. It would have been all over with her, likewise, if, by good fortune, a tailor who was travelling in search of work had not sat down to rest by the brook. As he had a compassionate heart he pulled out his needle and thread, and sewed her together. The bean thanked him most prettily, but as the tailor used black thread, all beans since then have a black seam.

The Fisherman and His Wife

HERE was once on a time a Fisherman who lived with his wife in a miserable hovel close by the sea, and every day he went out fishing. And once as he was sitting with his rod, looking at the clear water, his line suddenly went down, far down below, and when he drew it up again, he brought out a large Flounder. Then the Flounder said to him, "Hark, you Fisherman, I pray you, let me live, I am no Flounder really, but an enchanted prince. What good will it do you to kill me? I should not be good to eat, put me in the water again, and let me go."

"Come," said the Fisherman, "there is no need for so many words about it—a fish that can talk I should certainly let go, anyhow," with that he put him back again into the clear water, and the Flounder went to the bottom, leaving a long streak of blood behind him. Then the Fisherman got up and went home to his wife in the hovel.

"Husband," said the woman, "have you caught nothing today?"

"No," said the man, "I did catch a Flounder, who said he was an enchanted prince, so I let him go again."

"Did you not wish for anything first?" said the woman.

"No," said the man; "what should I wish for?"

"Ah," said the woman, "it is surely hard to have to live always in this dirty hovel; you might have wished for a small cottage for us. Go back and call him. Tell him we want to have a small cottage, he will certainly give us that."

"Ah," said the man, "why should I go there again?"

"Why," said the woman, "you did catch him, and you let him go again; he is sure to do it. Go at once."

The man still did not quite like to go, but did not like to oppose his wife, and went to the sea. When he got there, the sea was all green and yellow, and no longer so smooth; so he stood still and said,

"Flounder, flounder in the sea,
Come, I pray thee, here to me;

For my wife, good Ilsabil,
Wills not as I'd have her will."

Then the Flounder came swimming to him and said, "Well, what does she want, then?"

"Ah," said the man, "I did catch you, and my wife says I really ought to have wished for something. She does not like to live in a wretched hovel any longer; she would like to have a cottage."

"Go, then," said the Flounder, "she has it already."

When the man went home, his wife was no longer in the hovel, but instead of it there stood a small cottage, and she was sitting on a bench before the door. Then she took him by the hand and said to him, "Just come inside, look, now isn't this a great deal better?"

So they went in, and there was a small porch, and a pretty little parlour and bedroom, and a kitchen and pantry, with the best of furniture, and fitted up with the most beautiful things made of tin and brass, whatsoever was wanted. And behind the cottage there was a small yard, with hens and ducks, and a little garden with flowers and fruit.

"Look," said the wife, "is not that nice!"

"Yes," said the husband, "and so we must always think it,—now we will live quite contented."

"We will think about that," said the wife. With that they ate something and went to bed.

Everything went well for a week or a fortnight, and then the woman said, "Hark you, husband, this cottage is far too small for us, and the garden and yard are little; the Flounder might just as well have given us a larger house. I should like to live in a great stone castle; go to the Flounder, and tell him to give us a castle."

"Ah, wife," said the man, "the cottage is quite good enough; why should we live in a castle?"

"What!" said the woman; "just go there, the Flounder can always do that."

"No, wife," said the man, "the Flounder has just given us the cottage, I do not like to go back so soon, it might make him angry."

"Go," said the woman, "he can do it quite easily, and will be glad to do it; just you go to him."

The man's heart grew heavy, and he would not go. He said to himself, "It is not right," and yet he went. And when he came to the sea, the water was quite purple and dark-blue, and grey and thick, and no longer so green and yellow, but it was still quiet.

And he stood there and said,

"Flounder, flounder in the sea,
Come, I pray thee, here to me;
For my wife, good Ilsabil,
Wills not as I'd have her will."

"Well, what does she want, then?" said the Flounder.

84

"Alas," said the man, half scared, "she wants to live in a great stone castle."

"Go to it, then, she is standing before the door," said the Flounder.

Then the man went away, intending to go home, but when he got there, he found a great stone palace, and his wife was just standing on the steps going in, and she took him by the hand and said, "Come in."

So he went in with her, and in the castle was a great hall paved with marble, and many servants, who flung wide the doors; and the walls were all bright with beautiful hangings, and in the rooms were chairs and tables of pure gold, and crystal chandeliers hung from the ceiling, and all the rooms and bed-rooms had carpets, and food and wine of the very best were standing on all the tables so that they nearly broke down beneath it. Behind the house, too, there was a great court-yard, with stables for horses and cows, and the very best of carriages; there was a magnificent large garden, too, with the most beautiful flowers and fruit-trees, and a park quite half a mile long, in which were stags, deer, and hares, and everything that could be desired.

"Come," said the woman, "isn't that beautiful?"

"Yes, indeed," said the man, "now let it be; and we will live in this beautiful castle and be content."

"We will consider about that," said the woman, "and sleep upon it;" thereupon they went to bed.

Next morning the wife awoke first, and it was just daybreak, and from her bed she saw the beautiful country lying before her. Her husband was still stretching himself, so she poked him in the side with her elbow, and said, "Get up, husband, and just peep out of the window. Look you, couldn't we be the King over all that land? Go to the Flounder, we will be the King."

"Ah, wife," said the man, "why should we be King? I do not want to be King."

"Well," said the wife, "if you won't be King, I will; go to the Flounder, for I will be King."

"Ah, wife," said the man, "why do you want to be King? I do not like to say that to him."

"Why not?" said the woman; "go to him this instant; I must be King!"

So the man went, and was quite unhappy because his wife wished to be King. "It is not right; it is not right," thought he. He did not wish to go, but yet he went.

And when he came to the sea, it was quite dark-grey, and the water heaved up from below, and smelt putrid. Then he went and stood by it, and said,

"Flounder, flounder in the sea,
Come, I pray thee, here to me;
For my wife, good Ilsabil,
Wills not as I'd have her will"

"Well, what does she want, then?" said the Flounder.

"Alas," said the man, "she wants to be King."

"Go to her; she is King already."

So the man went, and when he came to the palace, the castle had become much larger, and had a great tower and magnificent ornaments, and the sentinel was standing before the door, and there were numbers of soldiers with kettle-drums and trumpets. And when he went inside the house, everything was of real marble and gold, with velvet covers and great golden tassels. Then the doors of the hall were opened, and there was the court in all its splendour, and his wife was sitting on a high throne of gold and diamonds, with a great crown of gold on her head, and a sceptre of pure gold and jewels in her hand, and on both sides of her stood her maids-in-waiting in a row, each of them always one head shorter than the last.

Then he went and stood before her, and said, "Ah, wife, and now you are King."

"Yes," said the woman, "now I am King."

So he stood and looked at her, and when he had looked at her thus for some time, he said, "And now that you are King, let all else be, now we will wish for nothing more."

"Nay, husband," said the woman, quite anxiously, "I find time pass very heavily, I can bear it no longer; go to the Flounder—I am King, but I must be Emperor, too."

"Alas, wife, why do you wish to be Emperor?"

"Husband," said she, "go to the Flounder. I will be Emperor."

"Alas, wife," said the man, "he cannot make you Emperor; I may not say that to the fish. There is only one Emperor in the land. An Emperor the Flounder cannot make you! I assure you he cannot."

"What!" said the woman, "I am the King, and you are nothing but my husband; will you go this moment? go at once! If he can make a king he can make an emperor. I will be Emperor; go instantly."

So he was forced to go. As the man went, however, he was troubled in mind, and thought to himself, "It will not end well; it will not end well! Emperor is too shameless! The Flounder will at last be tired out."

With that he reached the sea, and the sea was quite black and thick, and began to boil up from below, so that it threw up bubbles, and such a sharp wind blew over it that it curdled, and the man was afraid. Then he went and stood by it, and said,

> "Flounder, flounder in the sea,
> Come, I pray thee, here to me;
> For my wife, good Ilsabil,
> Wills not as I'd have her will."

"Well, what does she want, then?" said the Flounder.

"Alas, Flounder," said he, "my wife wants to be Emperor."

"Go to her," said the Flounder; "she is Emperor already."

So the man went, and when he got there, the whole palace was made of polished marble with alabaster figures and golden ornaments, and soldiers were marching before the door blowing trumpets, and beating cymbals and drums; and in the house, barons, and counts, and dukes were going about as servants. Then they opened the doors to him, which were of pure gold. And when he entered, there sat his wife on a throne, which was made of one piece of gold, and was quite two miles high; and she wore a great golden crown that was three yards high, and set with diamonds and carbuncles, and in one hand she had the sceptre, and in the other the imperial orb; and on both sides of her stood the yeomen of the guard in two rows, each being smaller than the one before him, from the biggest giant, who was two miles high, to the very smallest dwarf, just as big as my little finger. And before it stood a number of princes and dukes.

Then the man went and stood among them, and said, "Wife, are you Emperor now?"

"Yes," said she, "now I am Emperor."

Then he stood and looked at her well, and when he had looked at her thus for some time, he said, "Ah, wife, be content, now that you are Emperor."

"Husband," said she, "why are you standing there? Now, I am Emperor, but I will be Pope too; go to the Flounder."

"Alas, wife," said the man, "what will you not wish for? You cannot be Pope; there is but one in Christendom; he cannot make you Pope."

"Husband," said she, "I will be Pope; go immediately, I must be Pope this very day."

"No, wife," said the man, "I do not like to say that to him; that would not do, it is too much; the Flounder can't make you Pope."

"Husband," said she, "what nonsense! If he can make an emperor he can make a pope. Go to him directly. I am Emperor, and you are nothing but my husband; will you go at once?"

Then he was afraid and went; but he was quite faint, and shivered and shook, and his knees and legs trembled. And a high wind blew over the land, and the clouds flew, and towards evening all grew dark, and the leaves fell from the trees, and the water rose and roared as if it were boiling, and splashed upon the shore; and in the distance he saw ships which were firing guns in their sore need, pitching and tossing on the waves. And yet in the midst of the sky there was still a small bit of blue, though on every side it was as red as in a heavy storm.

So, full of despair, he went and stood in much fear and said,

"Flounder, flounder in the sea,
Come, I pray thee, here to me;
For my wife, good Ilsabil,
Wills not as I'd have her will."

"Well, what does she want, then?" said the Flounder.

"Alas," said the man, "she wants to be Pope."

"Go to her then," said the Flounder; "she is Pope already."

So he went, and when he got there, he saw what seemed to be a large church surrounded by palaces. He pushed his way through the crowd. Inside, however, everything was lighted up with thousands and thousands of candles, and his wife was clad in gold, and she was sitting on a much higher throne, and had three great golden crowns on, and round about her there was much ecclesiastical splendour; and on both sides of her was a row of candles the largest of which was as tall as the very tallest tower, down to the very smallest kitchen candle, and all the emperors and kings were on their knees before her, kissing her shoe.

"Wife," said the man, and looked attentively at her, "are you now Pope?"

"Yes," said she, "I am Pope."

So he stood and looked at her, and it was just as if he was looking at the bright sun. When he had stood looking at her thus for a short time, he said, "Ah, wife, if you are Pope, do let well alone!"

But she looked as stiff as a post, and did not move or show any signs of life. Then said he, "Wife, now that you are Pope, be satisfied, you cannot become anything greater now."

"I will consider about that," said the woman. Thereupon they both went to bed, but she was not satisfied, and greediness let her have no sleep, for she was continually thinking what there was left for her to be.

The man slept well and soundly, for he had run about a great deal during the day; but the woman could not fall asleep at all, and flung herself from one side to the other the whole night through, thinking always what more was left for her to be, but unable to call to mind anything else. At length the sun began to rise, and when the woman saw the red of dawn, she sat up in bed and looked at it. And when, through the window, she saw the sun thus rising, she said, "Cannot I, too, order the sun and moon to rise?"

"Husband," said she, poking him in the ribs with her elbows, "wake up! go to the Flounder, for I wish to be even as God is."

The man was still half asleep, but he was so horrified that he fell out of bed. He thought he must have heard amiss, and rubbed his eyes, and said, "Alas, wife, what are you saying?"

"Husband," said she, "if I can't order the sun and moon to rise, and have to look on and see the sun and moon rising, I can't bear it. I shall not know what it is to have another happy hour, unless I can make them rise myself." Then she looked at him so terribly that a shudder ran over him, and said, "Go at once; I wish to be like unto God."

"Alas, wife," said the man, falling on his knees before her, "the Flounder cannot do that; he can make an emperor and a pope; I beseech you, go on as you are, and be Pope."

Then she fell into a rage, and her hair flew wildly about her head, and she cried, "I will not endure this, I'll not bear it any longer; wilt thou go?"

Then he put on his trousers and ran away like a madman. But outside a great storm was raging, and blowing so hard that he could scarcely keep his feet; houses and trees toppled over, the mountains trembled, rocks rolled into the sea, the sky was pitch black, and it thundered and lightened, and the sea came in with black waves as high as church-towers and mountains, and all with crests of white foam at the top.

Then he cried, but could not hear his own words,

> "Flounder, flounder in the sea,
> Come, I pray thee, here to me;
> For my wife, good Ilsabil,
> Wills not as I'd have her will."

"Well, what does she want, then?" said the Flounder.

"Alas," said he, "she wants to be like unto God."

"Go to her, and you will find her back again in the dirty hovel."

And there they are living still at this very time.

The Valiant Little Tailor

NE summer's morning a little tailor was sitting on his table by the window; he was in good spirits, and sewed with all his might. Then came a peasant woman down the street crying, "Good jams, cheap! Good jams, cheap!"

This rang pleasantly in the tailor's ears; he stretched his delicate head out of the window, and called, "Come up here, dear woman; here you will get rid of your goods."

The woman came up the three steps to the tailor with her heavy basket, and he made her unpack the whole of the pots for him. He inspected all of them, lifted them up, put his nose to them, and at length said, "The jam seems to me to be good, so weigh me out four ounces, dear woman, and if it is a quarter of a pound that is of no consequence."

The woman who had hoped to find a good sale, gave him what he desired, but went away quite angry and grumbling.

"Now, God bless the jam to my use," cried the little tailor, "and give me health and strength;" so he brought the bread out of the cupboard, cut himself a piece right across the loaf and spread the jam over it.

"This won't taste bitter," said he, "but I will just finish the jacket before I take a bite." He laid the bread near him, sewed on, and in his joy, made bigger and bigger stitches.

In the meantime the smell of the sweet jam ascended so to the wall, where the flies were sitting in great numbers, that they were attracted and descended on it in hosts.

"Hola! who invited you?" said the little tailor, and drove the unbidden guests away. The flies, however, who understood no German, would not be turned away, but came back again in ever-increasing companies.

The little tailor at last lost all patience, and got a bit of cloth from the hole under his work-table, and saying, "Wait, and I will give it to you," struck it mercilessly on them. When he drew it away and counted, there lay before him no fewer than seven, dead and with legs stretched out.

"Art thou a fellow of that sort?" said he, and could not help admiring his own bravery. "The whole town shall know of this!" And the little tailor hastened to cut himself a girdle, stitched it, and embroidered on it in large letters, "Seven at one stroke!"

"What, the town!" he continued. "The whole world shall hear of it!" and his heart wagged with joy like a lamb's tail. The tailor put on the girdle, and resolved to go forth into the world, because he thought his workshop was too small for his valour.

Before he went away, he sought about in the house to see if there was anything which he could take with him; however, he found nothing but an old cheese, and that he put in his pocket. In front of the door he observed a bird which had caught itself in the thicket. It had to go into his pocket with the cheese. Now he took to the road boldly, and as he was light and nimble, he felt no fatigue.

The road led him up a mountain, and when he had reached the highest point of it, there sat a powerful giant looking about him quite comfortably. The little tailor went bravely up, spoke to him, and said, "Good day, comrade, so thou art sitting there overlooking the widespread world! I am just on my way thither, and want to try my luck. Hast thou any inclination to go with me?"

The giant looked contemptuously at the tailor, and said, "Thou ragamuffin! Thou miserable creature!"

"Oh, indeed?" answered the little tailor, and unbuttoned his coat, and showed the giant the girdle, "There mayst thou read what kind of a man I am!"

The giant read, "Seven at one stroke," and thought that they had been men whom the tailor had killed, and began to feel a little respect for the tiny fellow. Nevertheless, he wished to try him first, and took a stone in his hand and squeezed it together so that water dropped out of it. "Do that likewise," said the giant, "if thou hast strength?"

"Is that all?" said the tailor, "that is child's play with us!" and put his hand into his pocket, brought out the soft cheese, and pressed it until the liquid ran out of it. "Faith," said he, "that was a little better, wasn't it?"

The giant did not know what to say, and could not believe it of the little man. Then the giant picked up a stone and threw it so high that the eye could scarcely follow it. "Now, little mite of a man, do that likewise."

"Well thrown," said the tailor, "but after all the stone came down to earth again; I will throw you one which shall never come back at all." And he put his hand into his pocket, took out the bird, and threw it into the air. The bird, delighted with its liberty, rose, flew away and did not come back.

"How does that shot please you, comrade?" asked the tailor.

"Thou canst certainly throw," said the giant, "but now we will see if thou art able to carry anything properly." He took the little tailor to a mighty oak tree which lay there felled on the ground, and said, "If thou art strong enough, help me to carry the tree out of the forest."

"Readily," answered the little man; "take thou the trunk on thy shoulders, and I will raise up the branches and twigs; after all, they are the heaviest."

The giant took the trunk on his shoulder, but the tailor seated himself on a branch, and the giant who could not look round, had to carry away the whole tree, and the little tailor into the bargain; he behind, was quite merry and happy, and whistled the song "Three tailors rode forth from the gate," as if carrying the tree were child's play.

The giant, after he had dragged the heavy burden part of the way, could go no further, and cried, "Hark you, I shall have to let the tree fall!"

The tailor sprang nimbly down, seized the tree with both arms as if he had been carrying it, and said to the giant, "Thou art such a great fellow, and yet canst not even carry the tree!"

They went on together, and as they passed a cherry-tree, the giant laid hold of the top of the tree where the ripest fruit was hanging, bent it down, gave it into the tailor's hand, and bade him eat. But the little tailor was much too weak to hold the tree, and when the giant let it go, it sprang back again, and the tailor was hurried into the air with it. When he had fallen down again without injury, the giant said, "What is this? Hast thou not strength enough to hold the weak twig?"

"There is no lack of strength," answered the little tailor. "Dost thou think that could be anything to a man who has struck down seven at one blow? I leapt over the tree because the huntsmen are shooting down there in the thicket. Jump as I did, if thou canst do it." The giant made the attempt, but could not get over the tree, and remained hanging in the branches, so that in this also the tailor kept the upper hand.

The giant said, "If thou art such a valiant fellow, come with me into our cavern and spend the night with us."

The little tailor was willing, and followed him. When they went into the cave, other giants were sitting there by the fire, and each of them had a roasted sheep in his hand and was eating it. The little tailor looked round and thought, "It is much more spacious here than in my workshop."

The giant showed him a bed, and said he was to lie down in it and sleep. The bed, however, was too big for the little tailor; he did not lie down in it, but crept into a corner. When it was midnight, and the giant thought that the little tailor was lying in a sound sleep, he got up, took a great iron bar, cut through the bed with one blow, and thought he had given the grasshopper his finishing stroke.

With the earliest dawn the giants went into the forest, and had quite forgotten the little tailor, when all at once he walked up to them quite merrily and boldly. The giants were terrified; they were afraid that he would strike them all dead, and ran away in a great hurry.

The little tailor went onwards, always following his own pointed nose. After he had walked for a long time, he came to the court-yard of a royal palace, and as he felt weary, he lay down on the grass and fell asleep. Whilst he lay there, the people came and inspected him on all sides, and read on his girdle, "Seven at one stroke."

"Ah!" said they, "What does the great warrior here in the midst of peace? He must be a mighty lord." They went and announced him to the King, and gave it as their opinion that if war should break out, this would be a weighty and useful man who ought on no account to be allowed to depart.

The counsel pleased the King, and he sent one of his courtiers to the little tailor to offer him military service when he awoke. The ambassador remained standing by the sleeper, waited until he stretched his limbs and opened his eyes, and then conveyed to him this proposal.

"For this very reason have I come here," the tailor replied. "I am ready to enter the King's service." He was therefore honourably received, and a separate dwelling was assigned him.

The soldiers, however, were set against the little tailor, and wished him a thousand miles away. "What is to be the end of this?" they said amongst themselves. "If we quarrel with him, and he strikes about him, seven of us will fall at every blow; not one of us can stand against him."

They came therefore to a decision, betook themselves in a body to the King, and begged for their dismissal. "We are not prepared," said they, "to stay with a man who kills seven at one stroke."

The King was sorry that for the sake of one he should lose all his faithful servants, wished that he had never set eyes on the tailor, and would willingly have been rid of him again. But he did not venture to give him his dismissal, for he dreaded lest he should strike him and all his people dead, and place himself on the royal throne.

He thought about it for a long time, and at last found good counsel. He sent to the little tailor and caused him to be informed that as he was such a great warrior, he had one request to make to him. In a forest of his country lived two giants, who caused great mischief with their robbing, murdering, ravaging, and burning, and no one could approach them without putting himself in danger of death. If the tailor conquered and killed these two giants, he would give him his only daughter to wife, and half of his kingdom as a dowry, likewise one hundred horsemen should go with him to assist him.

"That would indeed be a fine thing for a man like me!" thought the little tailor. "One is not offered a beautiful princess and half a kingdom every day of one's life!"

"Oh, yes," he replied, "I will soon subdue the giants, and do not require the help of the hundred horsemen to do it; he who can hit seven with one blow has no need to be afraid of two."

The little tailor went forth, and the hundred horsemen followed him. When he came to the outskirts of the forest, he said to his followers, "Just stay waiting here, I alone will soon finish off the giants."

Then he bounded into the forest and looked about right and left. After a while he perceived both giants. They lay sleeping under a tree, and snored so that the branches waved up and down. The little tailor, not idle, gathered two pocketsful of stones, and with these climbed up the tree. When he was half-way up, he slipped down by a branch, until he sat just above the sleepers, and then let one stone after another fall on the breast of one of the giants.

For a long time the giant felt nothing, but at last he awoke, pushed his comrade, and said, "Why art thou knocking me?"

"Thou must be dreaming," said the other, "I am not knocking thee."

They laid themselves down to sleep again, and then the tailor threw a stone down on the second.

"What is the meaning of this?" cried the other. "Why art thou pelting me?"

"I am not pelting thee," answered the first, growling.

They disputed about it for a time, but as they were weary they let the matter rest, and their eyes closed once more. The little tailor began his game again, picked out the biggest stone, and threw it with all his might on the breast of the first giant.

"That is too bad!" cried he, and sprang up like a madman, and pushed his companion against the tree until it shook. The other paid him back in the same coin, and they got into such a rage that they tore up trees and belaboured each other so long, that at last they both fell down dead on the ground at the same time.

Then the little tailor leapt down. "It is a lucky thing," said he, "that they did not tear up the tree on which I was sitting, or I should have had to spring on to another like a squirrel; but we tailors are nimble."

He drew out his sword and gave each of them a couple of thrusts in the breast, and then went out to the horsemen and said, "The work is done; I have given both of them their finishing stroke, but it was hard work! They tore up trees in their sore need, and defended themselves with them, but all that is to no purpose when a man like myself comes, who can kill seven at one blow."

"But are you not wounded?" asked the horsemen.

"You need not concern yourself about that," answered the tailor. "They have not bent one hair of mine."

The horsemen would not believe him, and rode into the forest; there they found the giants swimming in their blood, and all round about, lay the torn-up trees.

The little tailor demanded of the King the promised reward; he, however, repented of his promise, and again bethought himself how he could get rid of the hero.

"Before thou receivest my daughter, and the half of my kingdom," said he to him, "thou must perform one more heroic deed. In the forest roams a unicorn which does great harm, and thou must catch it first."

"I fear one unicorn still less than two giants. Seven at one blow, is my kind of affair."

He took a rope and an axe with him, went forth into the forest, and again bade those who were sent with him to wait outside. He had not to seek long. The unicorn soon came towards him, and rushed directly on the tailor, as if it would spit him on its horn without more ceremony.

95

"Softly, softly; it can't be done as quickly as that," said he, and stood still and waited until the animal was quite close, and then sprang nimbly behind the tree. The unicorn ran against the tree with all its strength, and struck its horn so fast in the trunk that it had not strength enough to draw it out again, and thus it was caught.

"Now, I have got the bird," said the tailor, and came out from behind the tree and put the rope round its neck, and then with his axe he hewed the horn out of the tree, and when all was ready, he led the beast away and took it to the King.

The King still would not give him the promised reward, and made a third demand. Before the wedding the tailor was to catch him a wild boar that made great havoc in the forest, and the huntsmen should give him their help.

"Willingly," said the tailor, "that is child's play!"

He did not take the huntsmen with him into the forest, and they were well pleased that he did not, for the wild boar had several times received them in such a manner that they had no inclination to lie in wait for him.

When the boar perceived the tailor, it ran on him with foaming mouth and whetted tusks, and was about to throw him to the ground, but the active hero sprang into a chapel which was near, and up to the window at once, and in one bound out again. The boar ran in after him, but the tailor ran round outside and shut the door behind it, and then the raging beast, which was much too heavy and awkward to leap out of the window, was caught.

The little tailor called the huntsmen thither that they might see the prisoner with their own eyes. The hero, however, went to the King, who was now, whether he liked it or not, obliged to keep his promise, and gave him his daughter and the half of his kingdom. Had he known that it was no warlike hero, but a little tailor who was standing before him, it would have gone to his heart still more than it did. The wedding was held with great magnificence and small joy, and out of a tailor a king was made.

After some time the young Queen heard her husband say in his dreams at night, "Boy, make me the doublet, and patch the pantaloons, or else I will rap the yard-measure over thine ears." Then she discovered in what state of life the young lord had been born, and next morning complained of her wrongs to her father, and begged him to help her to get rid of her husband, who was nothing else but a tailor.

The King comforted her and said, "Leave thy bed-room door open this night, and my servants shall stand outside, and when he has fallen asleep shall go in, bind him, and take him on board a ship which shall carry him into the wide world."

The woman was satisfied with this; but the King's armour-bearer, who had heard all, was friendly with the young lord, and informed him of the whole plot.

"I'll put a screw into that business," said the little tailor.

At night he went to bed with his wife at the usual time, and when she thought that he had fallen asleep, she got up, opened the door, and then lay down again. The little tailor, who was only pretending to be asleep, began to cry out in a clear voice, "Boy, make me the doublet and patch me the pantaloons, or I will rap the yard-measure over thine ears. I smote seven at one blow. I killed two giants, I brought away one unicorn and caught a wild boar, and am I to fear those who are standing outside the room."

When these men heard the tailor speaking thus, they were overcome by a great dread, and ran as if the wild huntsman were behind them, and none of them would venture anything further against him. So the little tailor was a king and remained one, to the end of his life.

Cinderella

HE wife of a rich man fell sick, and as she felt that her end was drawing near, she called her only daughter to her bedside and said, "Dear child, be good and pious, and then the good God will always protect thee, and I will look down on thee from heaven and be near thee." Thereupon she closed her eyes and departed.

Every day the maiden went out to her mother's grave and wept, and she remained pious and good. When winter came, the snow spread a white sheet over the grave, and when the spring sun had drawn it off again, the man had taken another wife.

The woman had brought two daughters into the house with her, who were beautiful and fair of face, but vile and black of heart. Now began a bad time for the poor step-child.

"Is the stupid goose to sit in the parlour with us?" said they. "He who wants to eat bread must earn it; out with the kitchen-wench." They took her pretty clothes away from her, put an old grey bedgown on her, and gave her wooden shoes. "Just look at the proud princess, how decked out she is!" they cried, and laughed, and led her into the kitchen.

There she had to do hard work from morning till night, get up before daybreak, carry water, light fires, cook and wash. Besides this, the sisters did her every imaginable injury—they mocked her and emptied her peas and lentils into the ashes, so that she was forced to sit and pick them out again.

In the evening when she had worked till she was weary, she had no bed to go to, but had to sleep by the fireside in the ashes. And as on that account she always looked dusty and dirty, they called her Cinderella.

It happened that the father was once going to the fair, and he asked his two step-daughters what he should bring back for them.

"Beautiful dresses," said one.

"Pearls and jewels," said the second.

"And thou, Cinderella," said he, "what wilt thou have?"

"Father, break off for me the first branch which knocks against your hat on your way home."

So he bought beautiful dresses, pearls and jewels for his two step-daughters, and on his way home, as he was riding through a green thicket, a hazel twig brushed against him and knocked off his hat. Then he broke off the branch and took it with him.

When he reached home, he gave his step-daughters the things which they had wished for, and to Cinderella he gave the branch from the hazel-bush. Cinderella thanked him, went to her mother's grave and planted the branch on it, and wept so much that the tears fell down on it and watered it. It grew, however, and became a handsome tree.

Thrice a day Cinderella went and sat beneath it, and wept and prayed, and a little white bird always came on the tree, and if Cinderella expressed a wish, the bird threw down to her what she had wished for.

It happened, however, that the King appointed a festival which was to last three days, and to which all the beautiful young girls in the country were invited, in order that his son might choose himself a bride. When the two step-sisters heard that they too were to appear among the number, they were delighted, called Cinderella and said, "Comb our hair for us, brush our shoes and fasten our buckles, for we are going to the festival at the King's palace."

Cinderella obeyed, but wept, because she too would have liked to go with them to the dance, and begged her step-mother to allow her to do so.

"Thou go, Cinderella!" said she. "Thou art dusty and dirty, and wouldst go to the festival? Thou hast no clothes and shoes, and yet wouldst dance!"

As, however, Cinderella went on asking, the step-mother at last said, "I have emptied a dish of lentils into the ashes for thee, if thou hast picked them out again in two hours, thou shalt go with us."

The maiden went through the back-door into the garden, and called, "You tame pigeons, you turtle-doves, and all you birds beneath the sky, come and help me to pick

"The good into the pot,
The bad into the crop."

Then two white pigeons came in by the kitchen-window, and afterwards the turtle-doves, and at last all the birds beneath the sky, came whirring and crowding in, and alighted amongst the ashes. And the pigeons nodded with their heads and began pick, pick, pick, pick, and the rest began also pick, pick, pick, pick, and gathered all the good grains into the dish. Hardly had one hour passed before they had finished, and all flew out again.

Then the girl took the dish to her step-mother, and was glad, and believed that now she would be allowed to go with them to the festival. But the step-mother said, "No, Cinderella, thou hast no clothes and thou canst not dance; thou wouldst only be laughed at."

And as Cinderella wept at this, the step-mother said, "If thou canst pick two dishes of lentils out of the ashes for me in one hour, thou shalt go with us." And she thought to herself, "That she most certainly cannot do."

When the step-mother had emptied the two dishes of lentils amongst the ashes, the maiden went through the back-door into the garden and cried, "You tame pigeons, you turtle-doves, and all you birds under heaven, come and help me to pick

> "The good into the pot,
> The bad into the crop."

Then two white pigeons came in by the kitchen-window, and afterwards the turtle-doves, and at length all the birds beneath the sky, came whirring and crowding in, and alighted amongst the ashes. And the doves nodded with their heads and began pick, pick, pick, pick, and the others began also pick, pick, pick, pick, and gathered all the good seeds into the dishes, and before half an hour was over they had already finished, and all flew out again.

Then the maiden carried the dishes to the step-mother and was delighted, and believed that she might now go with them to the festival. But the step-mother said, "All this will not help thee; thou goest not with us, for thou hast no clothes and canst not dance; we should be ashamed of thee!" On this she turned her back on Cinderella, and hurried away with her two proud daughters.

As no one was now at home, Cinderella went to her mother's grave beneath the hazel-tree, and cried,

> "Shiver and quiver, little tree,
> Silver and gold throw down over me."

Then the bird threw a gold and silver dress down to her, and slippers embroidered with silk and silver. She put on the dress with all speed, and went to the festival.

Her step-sisters and the step-mother however did not know her, and thought she must be a foreign princess, for she looked so beautiful in the golden dress. They never once thought of Cinderella, and believed that she was sitting at home in the dirt, picking lentils out of the ashes.

The prince went to meet her, took her by the hand and danced with her. He would dance with no other maiden, and never left loose of her hand, and if anyone else came to invite her, he said, "This is my partner."

She danced till it was evening, and then she wanted to go home. But the King's son said, "I will go with thee and bear thee company," for he wished to see to whom the beautiful maiden belonged.

She escaped from him, however, and sprang into the pigeon-house. The King's son waited until her father came, and then he told him that the stranger maiden had leapt into the pigeon-house.

The old man thought, "Can it be Cinderella?" and they had to bring him an axe and a pickaxe that he might hew the pigeon-house to pieces,

but no one was inside it. And when they got home, Cinderella lay in her dirty clothes among the ashes, and a dim little oil-lamp was burning on the mantle-piece, for Cinderella had jumped quickly down from the back of the pigeon-house and had run to the little hazel-tree, and there she had taken off her beautiful clothes and laid them on the grave, and the bird had taken them away again, and then she had placed herself in the kitchen amongst the ashes in her grey gown.

Next day when the festival began afresh, and her parents and the step-sisters had gone once more, Cinderella went to the hazel-tree and said,

> "Shiver and quiver, my little tree,
> Silver and gold throw down over me."

Then the bird threw down a much more beautiful dress than on the preceding day. And when Cinderella appeared at the festival in this dress, everyone was astonished at her beauty.

The King's son had waited until she came, and instantly took her by the hand and danced with no one but her. When others came and invited her, he said, "She is my partner."

When evening came, she wished to leave, and the King's son followed her and wanted to see into which house she went. But she sprang away from him, and into the garden behind the house. Therein stood a beautiful tall tree on which hung the most magnificent pears. She clambered so nimbly between the branches like a squirrel that the King's son did not know where she was gone.

He waited until her father came, and said to him, "The stranger-maiden has escaped from me, and I believe she has climbed up the pear-tree." The father thought, "Can it be Cinderella?" and had an axe brought and cut the tree down, but no one was on it.

And when they got into the kitchen, Cinderella lay there amongst the ashes, as usual, for she had jumped down on the other side of the tree, had taken the beautiful dress to the bird on the little hazel-tree, and put on her grey gown.

On the third day, when the parents and sisters had gone away, Cinderella went once more to her mother's grave and said to the little tree,

> "Shiver and quiver, my little tree,
> Silver and gold throw down over me."

And now the bird threw down to her a dress which was more splendid and magnificent than any she had yet had, and the slippers were golden. And when she went to the festival in the dress, no one knew how to speak for astonishment. The King's son danced with her only, and if anyone invited her to dance, he said, "She is my partner."

When evening came, Cinderella wished to leave, and the King's son was anxious to go with her, but she escaped from him so quickly that he could not follow her. The King's son had, however, used a stratagem, and had caused the whole staircase to be smeared with pitch, and there, when she ran down, had the maiden's left slipper remained sticking. The King's son picked it up, and it was small and dainty, and all golden.

Next morning, he went with it to the father, and said to him, "No one shall be my wife but she whose foot this golden slipper fits."

Then were the two sisters glad, for they had pretty feet. The eldest went with the shoe into her room and wanted to try it on, and her mother stood by. But she could not get her big toe into it, and the shoe was too small for her.

Then her mother gave her a knife and said, "Cut the toe off; when thou art Queen, thou wilt have no more need to go on foot."

The maiden cut the toe off, forced the foot into the shoe, swallowed the pain, and went out to the King's son. Then he took her on his horse as his bride and rode away with her.

They were, however, obliged to pass the grave, and there, on the hazel-tree, sat the two pigeons and cried,

> "Turn and peep, turn and peep,
> There's blood within the shoe,
> The shoe it is too small for her,
> The true bride waits for you."

Then he looked at her foot and saw how the blood was streaming from it. He turned his horse round and took the false bride home again, and said she was not the true one, and that the other sister was to put the shoe on.

Then this one went into her chamber and got her toes safely into the shoe, but her heel was too large. So her mother gave her a knife and said, "Cut a bit off thy heel; when thou art Queen, thou wilt have no more need to go on foot."

The maiden cut a bit off her heel, forced her foot into the shoe, swallowed the pain, and went out to the King's son. He took her on his horse as his bride, and rode away with her, but when they passed by the hazel-tree, two little pigeons sat on it and cried,

> "Turn and peep, turn and peep,
> There's blood within the shoe,
> The shoe it is too small for her,
> The true bride waits for you."

He looked down at her foot and saw how the blood was running out of her shoe, and how it had stained her white stocking. Then he turned his horse and took the false bride home again.

"This also is not the right one," said he, "have you no other daughter?"

"No," said the man. "There is still a little stunted kitchen-wench which my late wife left behind her, but she cannot possibly be the bride."

The King's son said he was to send her up to him; but the mother answered, "Oh no, she is much too dirty, she cannot show herself!"

He absolutely insisted on it, and Cinderella had to be called. She first washed her hands and face clean, and then went and bowed down before the King's son, who gave her the golden shoe. Then she seated herself on a stool, drew her foot out of the heavy wooden shoe, and put it into the slipper, which fitted like a glove. And when she rose up and the King's son looked at her face, he recognized the beautiful maiden who had danced with him and cried, "That is the true bride!"

The step-mother and the two sisters were terrified and became pale with rage. The King's son, however, took Cinderella on his horse and rode away with her. And soon their wedding was celebrated.

Mother Holle

WIDOW had two daughters, one of whom was pretty and industrious, whilst the other was ugly and idle. But she was much fonder of the ugly and idle one, because she was her own daughter; and the other, who was a step-daughter, was obliged to do all the work, and be the Cinderella of the house. Every day the poor girl had to sit by a well, in the highway, and spin and spin till her fingers bled.

Now it happened that one day the shuttle was marked with her blood, so she dipped it in the well, to wash the mark off; but it dropped out of her hand and fell to the bottom. She began to weep, and ran to her step-mother and told her of the mishap. But she scolded her sharply, and was so merciless as to say, "Since you have let the shuttle fall in, you must fetch it out again."

So the girl went back to the well, and did not know what to do; and in the sorrow of her heart she jumped into the well to get the shuttle. She lost her senses; and when she awoke and came to herself again, she was in a lovely meadow where the sun was shining and many thousands of flowers were growing.

Along this meadow she went, and at last came to a baker's oven full of bread, and the bread cried out, "Oh, take me out! take me out! or I shall burn; I have been baked a long time!" So she went up to it, and took out all the loaves one after another with the bread-shovel.

After that she went on till she came to a tree covered with apples, which called out to her, "Oh, shake me! shake me! we apples are all ripe!" So she shook the tree till the apples fell like rain, and went on shaking till they were all down, and when she had gathered them into a heap, she went on her way.

At last she came to a little house, out of which an old woman peeped; but she had such large teeth that the girl was frightened, and was about to run away.

But the old woman called out to her, "What are you afraid of, dear child? Stay with me; if you will do all the work in the house properly, you shall be the better for it. Only you must take care to make my bed well, and shake it thoroughly till the feathers fly—for then there is snow on the earth. I am Mother Holle."

As the old woman spoke so kindly to her, the girl took courage and agreed to enter her service. She attended to everything to the satisfaction of her mistress, and always shook her bed so vigorously that the feathers flew about like snow-flakes. So she had a pleasant life with her; never an angry word; and boiled or roast meat every day.

She stayed some time with Mother Holle, and then she became sad. At first she did not know what was the matter with her, but found at length that it was home-sickness: although she was many thousand times better off here than at home, still she had a longing to be there.

At last she said to the old woman, "I have a longing for home; and however well off I am down here, I cannot stay any longer; I must go up again to my own people."

Mother Holle said, "I am pleased that you long for your home again, and as you have served me so truly, I myself will take you up again."

Thereupon she took her by the hand, and led her to a large door. The door was opened, and just as the maiden was standing beneath the doorway, a heavy shower of golden rain fell, and all the gold remained sticking to her, so that she was completely covered over with it.

"You shall have that because you have been so industrious," said Mother Holle; and at the same time she gave her back the shuttle which she had let fall into the well. Thereupon the door closed, and the maiden found herself up above upon the earth, not far from her mother's house.

And as she went into the yard the cock was standing by the well-side, and cried,

> "Cock-a-doodle-doo!
> Your golden girl's come back to you!"

So she went in to her mother, and as she arrived thus covered with gold, she was well received, both by her and her sister.

The girl told all that had happened to her; and as soon as the mother heard how she had come by so much wealth, she was very anxious to obtain the same good luck for the ugly and lazy daughter. She had to seat herself by the well and spin; and in order that her shuttle might be stained with blood, she stuck her hand into a thorn bush and pricked her finger. Then she threw her shuttle into the well, and jumped in after it.

She came, like the other, to the beautiful meadow and walked along the very same path. When she got to the oven, the bread again cried, "Oh, take me out! take me out! or I shall burn; I have been baked a long time!"

But the lazy thing answered, "As if I had any wish to make myself dirty?" and on she went.

Soon she came to the apple-tree, which cried, "Oh, shake me! shake me! we apples are all ripe!"

But she answered, "I like that! one of you might fall on my head," and so went on.

When she came to Mother Holle's house, she was not afraid, for she had already heard of her big teeth, and she hired herself to her immediately.

The first day she forced herself to work diligently, and obeyed Mother Holle when she told her to do anything, for she was thinking of all the gold that she would give her. But on the second day she began to be lazy, and on the third day still more so, and then she would not get up in the morning at all. Neither did she make Mother Holle's bed as she ought, and did not shake it so as to make the feathers fly up.

Mother Holle was soon tired of this, and gave her notice to leave. The lazy girl was willing enough to go, and thought that now the golden rain would come. Mother Holle led her too to the great door; but while she was standing beneath it, instead of the gold a big kettleful of pitch was emptied over her.

"That is the reward for your service," said Mother Holle, and shut the door.

So the lazy girl went home; but she was quite covered with pitch, and the cock by the well-side, as soon as he saw her, cried out,

"Cock-a-doodle-doo!
Your pitchy girl's come back to you!"

But the pitch stuck fast to her, and could not be got off as long as she lived.

Little Red-Cap

HERE was once upon a time a dear little girl who was loved by everyone who looked at her, but most of all by her grandmother, and there was nothing that she would not have given to the child. Once she gave her a little cap of red velvet, which suited her so well that she would never wear anything else; so she was always called 'Little Red-Cap.' One day her mother said to her, "Come, Little Red-Cap, here is a piece of cake and a bottle of wine; take them to your grandmother, she is ill and weak, and they will do her good. Set out before it gets hot, and when you are going, walk nicely and quietly and do not run off the path, or you may fall and break the bottle, and then your grandmother will get nothing; and when you go into her room, don't forget to say, 'Good morning,' and don't peep into every corner before you do it."

"I will take great care," said Little Red-Cap to her mother, and gave her hand on it.

The grandmother lived out in the wood, half a league from the village, and just as Little Red-Cap entered the wood, a wolf met her. Red-Cap did not know what a wicked creature he was, and was not at all afraid of him.

"Good day, Little Red-Cap," said he.

"Thank you kindly, wolf."

"Whither away so early, Little Red-Cap?"

"To my grandmother's."

"What have you got in your apron?"

"Cake and wine; yesterday was baking-day, so poor sick grandmother is to have something good, to make her stronger."

"Where does your grandmother live, Little Red-Cap?"

"A good quarter of a league farther on in the wood; her house stands under the three large oak-trees, the nut-trees are just below; you surely must know it," replied Little Red-Cap.

The wolf thought to himself, "What a tender young creature! What a nice plump mouthful—she will be better to eat than the old woman. I must act craftily, so as to catch both."

So he walked for a short time by the side of Little Red-Cap, and then he said, "See, Little Red-Cap, how pretty the flowers are about here— why do you not look round? I believe, too, that you do not hear how sweetly the little birds are singing; you walk gravely along as if you were going to school, while everything else out here in the wood is merry."

Little Red-Cap raised her eyes, and when she saw the sunbeams dancing here and there through the trees, and pretty flowers growing everywhere, she thought, "Suppose I take grandmother a fresh nose-gay; that would please her too. It is so early in the day that I shall still get there in good time;" and so she ran from the path into the wood to look for flowers. And whenever she had picked one, she fancied that she saw a still prettier one farther on, and ran after it, and so got deeper and deeper into the wood.

Meanwhile the wolf ran straight to the grandmother's house and knocked at the door.

"Who is there?"

"Little Red-Cap," replied the wolf. "She is bringing cake and wine; open the door."

"Lift the latch," called out the grandmother. "I am too weak, and cannot get up."

The wolf lifted the latch, the door flew open, and without saying a word he went straight to the grandmother's bed, and devoured her. Then he put on her clothes, dressed himself in her cap, laid himself in bed and drew the curtains.

Little Red-Cap, however, had been running about picking flowers, and when she had gathered so many that she could carry no more, she remembered her grandmother, and set out on the way to her.

She was surprised to find the cottage-door standing open, and when she went into the room, she had such a strange feeling that she said to herself, "Oh dear! how uneasy I feel today, and at other times I like being with grandmother so much."

She called out, "Good morning," but received no answer; so she went to the bed and drew back the curtains. There lay her grandmother with her cap pulled far over her face, and looking very strange.

"Oh! grandmother," she said, "what big ears you have!"

"The better to hear you with, my child," was the reply.

"But, grandmother, what big eyes you have!" she said.

"The better to see you with, my dear."

"But, grandmother, what large hands you have!"

"The better to hug you with."

"Oh! but, grandmother, what a terrible big mouth you have!"

"The better to eat you with!"

And scarcely had the wolf said this, than with one bound he was out of bed and swallowed up Red-Cap.

When the wolf had appeased his appetite, he lay down again in the bed, fell asleep and began to snore very loud. The huntsman was just passing the house, and thought to himself, "How the old woman is snoring! I must just see if she wants anything."

So he went into the room, and when he came to the bed, he saw that the wolf was lying in it. "Do I find thee here, thou old sinner!" said he. "I have long sought thee!"

He killed the wolf and cut open his stomach. Out skipped the little Red-Cap, crying, "Ah, how frightened I have been! How dark it was inside the wolf;" and after that the aged grandmother came out alive also, but scarcely able to breathe.

Then all three were delighted. The huntsman drew off the wolf's skin and went home with it; the grandmother ate the cake and drank the wine which Red-Cap had brought, and revived, but Red-Cap thought to herself, "As long as I live, I will never by myself leave the path, to run into the wood, when my mother has forbidden me to do so!"

The Bremen Town-Musicians

THERE was once a certain man who had a donkey, which had carried the corn-sacks to the mill indefatigably for many a long year; but his strength was going, and he was growing more and more unfit for work. Then his master began to consider how he might best save his keep; but the donkey, seeing that no good wind was blowing, ran away and set out on the road to Bremen. "There," he thought, "I can surely be town-musician."

When he had walked some distance, he found a hound lying on the road, gasping like one who had run till he was tired.

"What are you gasping so for, you big fellow?" asked the donkey.

"Ah," replied the hound, "as I am old, and daily grow weaker, and no longer can hunt, my master wanted to kill me, so I took to flight; but now how am I to earn my bread?"

"I tell you what," said the donkey. "I am going to Bremen, and shall be town-musician there; go with me and engage yourself also as a musician. I will play the lute, and you shall beat the kettledrum."

The hound agreed, and on they went.

Before long they came to a cat, sitting on the path, with a face like three rainy days!

"Now then, old shaver, what has gone askew with you?" asked the donkey.

"Who can be merry when his neck is in danger?" answered the cat. "Because I am now getting old, and my teeth are worn to stumps, and I prefer to sit by the fire and spin, rather than hunt about after mice, my mistress wanted to drown me, so I ran away. But now good advice is scarce. Where am I to go?"

"Go with us to Bremen. You understand night-music, so you can be a town-musician."

The cat thought well of it, and went with them.

After this the three fugitives came to a farm-yard, where the cock was sitting upon the gate, crowing with all his might.

113

"Your crow goes through and through one," said the donkey. "What is the matter?"

"I have been foretelling fine weather, because it is the day on which Our Lady washes the Christ-child's little shirts, and wants to dry them," said the cock; "but guests are coming for Sunday, so the housewife has no pity, and has told the cook that she intends to eat me in the soup tomorrow, and this evening I am to have my head cut off. Now I am crowing at full pitch while I can."

"Ah, but red-comb," said the donkey, "you had better come away with us. We are going to Bremen; you can find something better than death everywhere: you have a good voice, and if we make music together it must have some quality!"

The cock agreed to this plan, and all four went on together. They could not, however, reach the city of Bremen in one day, and in the evening they came to a forest where they meant to pass the night. The donkey and the hound laid themselves down under a large tree, the cat and the cock settled themselves in the branches; but the cock flew right to the top, where he was most safe.

Before he went to sleep he looked round on all the four sides, and thought he saw in the distance a little spark burning; so he called out to his companions that there must be a house not far off, for he saw a light. The donkey said, "If so, we had better get up and go on, for the shelter here is bad." The hound thought that a few bones with some meat on would do him good too!

So they made their way to the place where the light was, and soon saw it shine brighter and grow larger, until they came to a well-lighted robber's house. The donkey, as the biggest, went to the window and looked in.

"What do you see, my grey-horse?" asked the cock.

"What do I see?" answered the donkey; "a table covered with good things to eat and drink, and robbers sitting at it enjoying themselves."

"That would be the sort of thing for us," said the cock.

"Yes, yes; ah, how I wish we were there!" said the donkey.

Then the animals took counsel together how they should manage to drive away the robbers, and at last they thought of a plan. The donkey was to place himself with his fore-feet upon the window-ledge, the hound was to jump on the donkey's back, the cat was to climb upon the dog, and lastly the cock was to fly up and perch upon the head of the cat.

When this was done, at a given signal, they began to perform their music together: the donkey brayed, the hound barked, the cat mewed, and the cock crowed; then they burst through the window into the room, so that the glass clattered!

At this horrible din, the robbers sprang up, thinking no otherwise than that a ghost had come in, and fled in a great fright out into the forest. The four companions now sat down at the table, well content with what was left, and ate as if they were going to fast for a month.

As soon as the four minstrels had done, they put out the light, and each sought for himself a sleeping-place according to his nature and to what suited him. The donkey laid himself down upon some straw in the yard, the hound behind the door, the cat upon the hearth near the warm ashes, and the cock perched himself upon a beam of the roof; and being tired from their long walk, they soon went to sleep.

When it was past midnight, and the robbers saw from afar that the light was no longer burning in their house, and all appeared quiet, the captain said, "We ought not to have let ourselves be frightened out of our wits;" and ordered one of them to go and examine the house.

The messenger finding all still, went into the kitchen to light a candle, and, taking the glistening fiery eyes of the cat for live coals, he held a lucifer-match to them to light it. But the cat did not understand the joke, and flew in his face, spitting and scratching. He was dreadfully frightened, and ran to the back-door, but the dog, who lay there, sprang up and bit his leg; and as he ran across the yard by the straw-heap, the donkey gave him a smart kick with its hind foot. The cock, too, who had been awakened by the noise, and had become lively, cried down from the beam, "Cock-a-doodle-doo!"

Then the robber ran back as fast as he could to his captain, and said, "Ah, there is a horrible witch sitting in the house, who spat on me and scratched my face with her long claws; and by the door stands a man with a knife, who stabbed me in the leg; and in the yard there lies a black monster, who beat me with a wooden club; and above, upon the roof, sits the judge, who called out, 'Bring the rogue here to me!' so I got away as well as I could."

After this the robbers did not trust themselves in the house again; but it suited the four musicians of Bremen so well that they did not care to leave it any more. And the mouth of him who last told this story is still warm.

The Devil with the Three Golden Hairs

HERE was once a poor woman who gave birth to a little son; and as he came into the world with a caul on, it was predicted that in his fourteenth year he would have the King's daughter for his wife. It happened that soon afterwards the King came into the village, and no one knew that he was the King, and when he asked the people what news there was, they answered, "A child has just been born with a caul on; whatever anyone so born undertakes turns out well. It is prophesied, too, that in his fourteenth year he will have the King's daughter for his wife."

The King, who had a bad heart, and was angry about the prophecy, went to the parents, and, seeming quite friendly, said, "You poor people, let me have your child, and I will take care of it."

At first they refused, but when the stranger offered them a large amount of gold for it, and they thought, "It is a luck-child, and everything must turn out well for it," they at last consented, and gave him the child.

The King put it in a box and rode away with it until he came to a deep piece of water; then he threw the box into it and thought, "I have freed my daughter from her unlooked-for suitor."

The box, however, did not sink, but floated like a boat, and not a drop of water made its way into it. And it floated to within two miles of the King's chief city, where there was a mill, and it came to a stand-still at the mill-dam.

A miller's boy, who by good luck was standing there, noticed it and pulled it out with a hook, thinking that he had found a great treasure, but when he opened it, there lay a pretty boy inside, quite fresh and lively. He took him to the miller and his wife, and as they had no children they were glad, and said, "God has given him to us." They took great care of the foundling, and he grew up in all goodness.

It happened that once in a storm the King went into the mill, and he asked the mill-folk if the tall youth was their son.

"No," answered they, "he's a foundling. Fourteen years ago he floated down to the mill-dam in a box, and the mill-boy pulled him out of the water."

117

Then the King knew that it was none other than the luck-child which he had thrown into the water, and he said, "My good people, could not the youth take a letter to the Queen; I will give him two gold pieces as a reward?"

"Just as the King commands," answered they, and they told the boy to hold himself in readiness.

Then the King wrote a letter to the Queen, wherein he said, "As soon as the boy arrives with this letter, let him be killed and buried, and all must be done before I come home."

The boy set out with this letter; but he lost his way, and in the evening came to a large forest. In the darkness he saw a small light; he went towards it and reached a cottage. When he went in, an old woman was sitting by the fire quite alone. She started when she saw the boy, and said, "Whence do you come, and whither are you going?"

"I come from the mill," he answered, "and wish to go to the Queen, to whom I am taking a letter; but as I have lost my way in the forest I should like to stay here over night."

"You poor boy," said the woman, "you have come into a den of thieves, and when they come home, they will kill you."

"Let them come," said the boy, "I am not afraid; but I am so tired that I cannot go any farther," and he stretched himself upon a bench and fell asleep.

Soon afterwards the robbers came, and angrily asked what strange boy was lying there? "Ah," said the old woman, "it is an innocent child who has lost himself in the forest, and out of pity I have let him come in; he has to take a letter to the Queen."

The robbers opened the letter and read it, and in it was written that the boy as soon as he arrived should be put to death. Then the hard-hearted robbers felt pity, and their leader tore up the letter and wrote another, saying, that as soon as the boy came, he should be married at once to the King's daughter. Then they let him lie quietly on the bench until the next morning, and when he awoke, they gave him the letter, and showed him the right way.

And the Queen, when she had received the letter and read it, did as was written in it, and had a splendid wedding-feast prepared, and the King's daughter was married to the luck-child; and as the youth was handsome and agreeable, she lived with him in joy and contentment.

After some time the King returned to his palace and saw that the prophecy was fulfilled, and the luck-child married to his daughter. "How has that come to pass?" said he. "I gave quite another order in my letter."

So the Queen gave him the letter, and said that he might see for himself what was written in it. The King read the letter and saw quite well that it had been exchanged for the other. He asked the youth what had become of the letter entrusted to him, and why he had brought another instead of it.

"I know nothing about it," answered he; "it must have been changed in the night, when I slept in the forest."

The King said in a passion, "You shall not have everything quite so much your own way; whosoever marries my daughter must fetch me from hell three golden hairs from the head of the devil; bring me what I want, and you shall keep my daughter."

In this way the King hoped to be rid of him for ever. But the luck-child answered, "I will fetch the golden hairs, I am not afraid of the Devil;" thereupon he took leave of them and began his journey.

The road led him to a large town, where the watchman by the gates asked him what his trade was, and what he knew.

"I know everything," answered the luck-child.

"Then you can do us a favour," said the watchman, "if you will tell us why our market-fountain, which once flowed with wine has become dry, and no longer gives even water?"

"That you shall know," answered he; "only wait until I come back."

Then he went farther and came to another town, and there also the gatekeeper asked him what was his trade, and what he knew.

"I know everything," answered he.

"Then you can do us a favour and tell us why a tree in our town which once bore golden apples now does not even put forth leaves?"

"You shall know that," answered he; "only wait until I come back."

Then he went on and came to a wide river over which he must go. The ferryman asked him what his trade was, and what he knew.

"I know everything," answered he.

"Then you can do me a favour," said the ferryman, "and tell me why I must always be rowing backwards and forwards, and am never set free?"

"You shall know that," answered he; "only wait until I come back."

When he had crossed the water, he found the entrance to Hell. It was black and sooty within, and the Devil was not at home, but his grandmother was sitting in a large arm-chair.

"What do you want?" said she to him, but she did not look so very wicked.

"I should like to have three golden hairs from the devil's head," answered he, "else I cannot keep my wife."

"That is a good deal to ask for," said she; "if the devil comes home and finds you, it will cost you your life; but as I pity you, I will see if I cannot help you."

She changed him into an ant and said, "Creep into the folds of my dress, you will be safe there."

"Yes," answered he, "so far, so good; but there are three things be-sides that I want to know: why a fountain which once flowed with wine has become dry, and no longer gives even water; why a tree which once bore golden apples does not even put forth leaves; and why a ferry-man must always be going backwards and forwards, and is never set free?"

"Those are difficult questions," answered she, "but only be silent and quiet and pay attention to what the devil says when I pull out the three golden hairs."

As the evening came on, the devil returned home. No sooner had he entered than he noticed that the air was not pure. "I smell man's flesh," said he; "all is not right here." Then he pried into every corner, and searched, but could not find anything.

His grandmother scolded him. "It has just been swept," said she, "and everything put in order, and now you are upsetting it again; you have always got man's flesh in your nose. Sit down and eat your supper."

When he had eaten and drunk, he was tired, and laid his head in his grandmother's lap, and before long he was fast asleep, snoring and breathing heavily. Then the old woman took hold of a golden hair, pulled it out, and laid it down near her.

"Oh!" cried the devil, "what are you doing?"

"I have had a bad dream," answered the grandmother, "so I seized hold of your hair."

"What did you dream then?" said the devil.

"I dreamed that a fountain in a market-place from which wine once flowed was dried up, and not even water would flow out of it; what is the cause of it?"

"Oh, ho! if they did but know it," answered the devil; "there is a toad sitting under a stone in the well; if they killed it, the wine would flow again."

He went to sleep again and snored until the windows shook. Then she pulled the second hair out.

"Ha! what are you doing?" cried the devil angrily.

"Do not take it ill," said she. "I did it in a dream."

"What have you dreamt this time?" asked he.

"I dreamt that in a certain kingdom there stood an apple-tree which had once borne golden apples, but now would not even bear leaves. What, think you, was the reason?"

"Oh! if they did but know," answered the devil. "A mouse is gnawing at the root; if they killed this they would have golden apples again, but if it gnaws much longer the tree will wither altogether. But leave me alone with your dreams: if you disturb me in my sleep again you will get a box on the ear."

The grandmother spoke gently to him until he fell asleep again and snored. Then she took hold of the third golden hair and pulled it out. The devil jumped up, roared out, and would have treated her ill, but she quieted him once more and said, "Who can help bad dreams?"

"What was the dream, then?" asked he, and was quite curious.

"I dreamt of a ferry-man who complained that he must always ferry from one side to the other, and was never released. What is the cause of it?"

"Ah! the fool," answered the devil; "when anyone comes and wants to go across, he must put the oar in his hand, and the other man will have to ferry and he will be free."

As the grandmother had plucked out the three golden hairs, and the three questions were answered, she let the old serpent alone, and he slept until daybreak.

When the devil had gone out again, the old woman took the ant out of the folds of her dress, and gave the luck-child his human shape again.

"There are the three golden hairs for you," said she. "What the Devil said to your three questions, I suppose you heard?"

"Yes," answered he, "I heard, and will take care to remember."

"You have what you want," said she, "and now you can go your way."

He thanked the old woman for helping him in his need, and left hell well content that everything had turned out so fortunately.

When he came to the ferry-man, he was expected to give the promised answer. "Ferry me across first," said the luck-child, "and then I will tell you how you can be set free," and when he had reached the opposite shore, he gave him the devil's advice: "Next time anyone comes, who wants to be ferried over, just put the oar in his hand."

He went on and came to the town wherein stood the unfruitful tree, and there too the watchman wanted an answer. So he told him what he had heard from the devil: "Kill the mouse which is gnawing at its root, and it will again bear golden apples." Then the watchman thanked him, and gave him as a reward two asses laden with gold, which followed him.

At last he came to the town whose well was dry. He told the watchman what the devil had said: "A toad is in the well beneath a stone; you must find it and kill it, and the well will again give wine in plenty." The watchman thanked him, and also gave him two asses laden with gold.

At last the luck-child got home to his wife, who was heartily glad to see him again, and to hear how well he had prospered in everything. To the King he took what he had asked for, the devil's three golden hairs, and when the King saw the four asses laden with gold, he was quite content, and said, "Now all the conditions are fulfilled, and you can keep my daughter. But tell me, dear son-in-law, where did all that gold come from? this is tremendous wealth!"

"I was rowed across a river," answered he, "and got it there; it lies on the shore instead of sand."

"Can I too fetch some of it?" said the King; and he was quite eager about it.

"As much as you like," answered he. "There is a ferry-man on the river; let him ferry you over, and you can fill your sacks on the other side."

The greedy King set out in all haste, and when he came to the river, he beckoned to the ferry-man to put him across. The ferry-man came and bade him get in, and when they got to the other shore, he put the oar in his hand and sprang out.

But from this time forth the King had to ferry, as a punishment for his sins. Perhaps he is ferrying still? If he is, it is because no one has taken the oar from him.

The Three Languages

N AGED count once lived in Switzerland. He had an only son, but he was stupid, and could learn nothing. Then said the father, "Hark thee, my son, I can get nothing into thy head, let me try as I will. Thou must go from hence, I will give thee into the care of a celebrated master, who shall see what he can do with thee."

The youth was sent into a strange town, and remained a whole year with the master. At the end of this time, he came home again, and his father asked, "Now, my son, what hast thou learnt?"

"Father, I have learnt what the dogs say when they bark."

"Lord have mercy on us!" cried the father; "is that all thou hast learnt? I will send thee into another town, to another master."

The youth was taken thither, and stayed a year with this master likewise. When he came back, the father again asked, "My son, what hast thou learnt?"

He answered, "Father, I have learnt what the birds say."

Then the father fell into a rage and said, "Oh, thou lost man, thou hast spent the precious time and learnt nothing; art thou not ashamed to appear before mine eyes? I will send thee to a third master, but if thou learnest nothing this time also, I will no longer be thy father."

The youth remained a whole year with the third master also, and when he came home again, and his father inquired, "My son, what hast thou learnt?" he answered, "Dear father, I have this year learnt what the frogs croak."

Then the father fell into the most furious anger, sprang up, called his people thither, and said, "This man is no longer my son, I drive him forth, and command you to take him out into the forest, and kill him."

They took him forth, but when they should have killed him, they could not do it for pity, and let him go.

The youth wandered on, and after some time came to a fortress where he begged for a night's lodging.

"Yes," said the lord of the castle, "if thou wilt pass the night down there in the old tower, go thither; but I warn thee, it is at the peril of thy life, for it is full of wild dogs, which bark and howl without stopping, and at certain hours a man has to be given to them, whom they at once devour."

The whole district was in sorrow and dismay because of them, and yet no one could do anything to stop this. The youth, however, was without fear, and said, "Just let me go down to the barking dogs, and give me something that I can throw to them; they will do nothing to harm me."

As he himself would have it so, they gave him some food for the wild animals, and led him down to the tower. When he went inside, the dogs did not bark at him, but wagged their tails quite amicably around him, ate what he set before them, and did not hurt one hair of his head.

Next morning, to the astonishment of everyone, he came out again safe and unharmed, and said to the lord of the castle, "The dogs have revealed to me, in their own language, why they dwell there, and bring evil on the land. They are bewitched, and are obliged to watch over a great treasure which is below in the tower, and they can have no rest until it is taken away, and I have likewise learnt, from their discourse, how that is to be done."

Then all who heard this rejoiced, and the lord of the castle said he would adopt him as a son if he accomplished it successfully. He went down again, and as he knew what he had to do, he did it thoroughly, and brought a chest full of gold out with him. The howling of the wild dogs was henceforth heard no more; they had disappeared, and the country was freed from the trouble.

After some time he took it into his head that he would travel to Rome. On the way he passed by a marsh, in which a number of frogs were sitting croaking. He listened to them, and when he became aware of what they were saying, he grew very thoughtful and sad.

At last he arrived in Rome, where the Pope had just died, and there was great difficulty as to whom they should appoint as his successor. They at length agreed that the person should be chosen as pope who should be distinguished by some divine and miraculous token.

And just as that was decided on, the young count entered into the church, and suddenly two snow-white doves flew on his shoulders and remained sitting there. The ecclesiastics recognized therein the token from above, and asked him on the spot if he would be pope.

He was undecided, and knew not if he were worthy of this, but the doves counselled him to do it, and at length he said yes. Then was he anointed and consecrated, and thus was fulfilled what he had heard from the frogs on his way, which had so affected him, that he was to be his Holiness the Pope. Then he had to sing a mass, and did not know one word of it, but the two doves sat continually on his shoulders, and said it all in his ear.

The Wishing-Table, the Gold-Ass, and the Cudgel in the Sack

 HERE was once upon a time a tailor who had three sons, and only one goat. But as the goat supported the whole of them with her milk, she was obliged to have good food, and to be taken every day to pasture. The sons, therefore, did this, in turn. Once the eldest took her to the churchyard, where the finest herbs were to be found, and let her eat and run about there. At night when it was time to go home, he asked, "Goat, hast thou had enough?"

The goat answered,

"I have eaten so much,
Not a leaf more I'll touch, meh! meh!"

"Come home, then," said the youth, and took hold of the cord round her neck, led her into the stable and tied her up securely.

"Well," said the old tailor, "has the goat had as much food as she ought?"

"Oh," answered the son, "she has eaten so much, not a leaf more she'll touch."

But the father wished to satisfy himself, and went down to the stable, stroked the dear animal and asked, "Goat, art thou satisfied?"

The goat answered,

"Wherewithal should I be satisfied?
Among the graves I leapt about,
And found no food, so went without, meh! meh!"

"What do I hear?" cried the tailor, and ran upstairs and said to the youth, "Hollo, thou liar: thou saidest the goat had had enough, and

125

hast let her hunger!" and in his anger he took the yard-measure from the wall, and drove him out with blows.

Next day it was the turn of the second son, who looked out for a place in the fence of the garden, where nothing but good herbs grew, and the goat cleared them all off. At night when he wanted to go home, he asked, "Goat, art thou satisfied?"

The goat answered,

> "I have eaten so much,
> Not a leaf more I'll touch, meh! meh!"

"Come home, then," said the youth, and led her home, and tied her up in the stable.

"Well," said the old tailor, "has the goat had as much food as she ought?"

"Oh," answered the son, "she has eaten so much, not a leaf more she'll touch."

The tailor would not rely on this, but went down to the stable and said, "Goat, hast thou had enough?"

The goat answered,

> "Wherewithal should I be satisfied?
> Among the graves I leapt about,
> And found no food, so went without, meh! meh!"

"The godless wretch!" cried the tailor, "to let such a good animal hunger," and he ran up and drove the youth out of doors with the yard-measure.

Now came the turn of the third son, who wanted to do the thing well, and sought out some bushes with the finest leaves, and let the goat devour them. In the evening when he wanted to go home, he asked, "Goat, hast thou had enough?"

The goat answered,

> "I have eaten so much,
> Not a leaf more I'll touch, meh! meh!"

"Come home, then," said the youth, and led her into the stable, and tied her up.

"Well," said the old tailor, "has the goat had a proper amount of food?"

"She has eaten so much, not a leaf more she'll touch."

The tailor did not trust to that, but went down and asked, "Goat, hast thou had enough?"

The wicked beast answered,

> "Wherewithal should I be satisfied?
> Among the graves I leapt about,
> And found no leaves, so went without, meh! meh!"

"Oh, the brood of liars!" cried the tailor, "each as wicked and forgetful of his duty as the other! Ye shall no longer make a fool of me," and, quite beside himself with anger, he ran upstairs and belaboured the poor young fellow so vigorously with the yard-measure that he sprang out of the house.

The old tailor was now alone with his goat. Next morning he went down into the stable, caressed the goat and said, "Come, my dear little animal, I will take thee to feed myself."

He took her by the rope and conducted her to green hedges, and amongst milfoil, and whatever else goats like to eat. "There thou mayest for once eat to thy heart's content," said he to her, and let her browse till evening. Then he asked, "Goat, art thou satisfied?"

She replied,

> "I have eaten so much,
> Not a leaf more I'll touch, meh! meh!"

"Come home, then," said the tailor, and led her into the stable, and tied her fast.

When he was going away, he turned round again and said, "Well, art thou satisfied for once?"

But the goat did not behave better to him, and cried,

"Wherewithal should I be satisfied?
Among the graves I leapt about,
And found no leaves, so went without, meh! meh!"

When the tailor heard that, he was shocked, and saw clearly that he had driven away his three sons without cause. "Wait, thou ungrateful creature," cried he, "it is not enough to drive thee forth, I will mark thee so that thou wilt no more dare to show thyself amongst honest tailors."

In great haste he ran upstairs, fetched his razor, lathered the goat's head, and shaved her as clean as the palm of his hand. And as the yard-measure would have been too good for her, he brought the horsewhip, and gave her such cuts with it that she ran away in violent haste.

When the tailor was thus left quite alone in his house, he fell into great grief, and would gladly have had his sons back again, but no one knew whither they were gone.

The eldest had apprenticed himself to a joiner, and learnt industriously and indefatigably, and when the time came for him to go travelling, his master presented him with a little table which had no particular appearance, and was made of common wood, but it had one good property: if anyone set it out, and said, "Little table, spread thyself," the good little table was at once covered with a clean little cloth, and a plate was there, and a knife and fork beside it, and dishes with boiled meats and roasted meats, as many as there was room for, and a great glass of red wine shone so that it made the heart glad.

The young journeyman thought, "With this thou hast enough for thy whole life," and went joyously about the world and never troubled himself at all whether an inn was good or bad, or if anything was to be found in it or not.

When it suited him, he did not enter an inn at all, but either in the plain, in a wood, a meadow, or wherever he fancied, he took his little table off his back, set it down before him, and said, "Cover thyself," and then everything appeared that his heart desired.

At length he took it into his head to go back to his father, whose anger would now be appeased, and who would now willingly receive him with his wishing-table. It came to pass that on his way home, he came one evening to an inn which was filled with guests. They bade him welcome, and invited him to sit and eat with them, for otherwise he would have difficulty in getting anything.

"No," answered the joiner, "I will not take the few bites out of your mouths; rather than that, you shall be my guests."

They laughed, and thought he was jesting with them; he, however, placed his wooden table in the middle of the room, and said, "Little table, cover thyself." Instantly it was covered with food, so good that the host could never have procured it, and the smell of it ascended pleasantly to the nostrils of the guests.

"Fall to, dear friends," said the joiner; and the guests when they saw that he meant it, did not need to be asked twice, but drew near, pulled out their knives and attacked it valiantly. And what surprised them the most was that when a dish became empty, a full one instantly took its place of its own accord.

The innkeeper stood in one corner and watched the affair; he did not at all know what to say, but thought, "Thou couldst easily find a use for such a cook as that in thy kitchen."

The joiner and his comrades made merry until late into the night; at length they lay down to sleep, and the young apprentice also went to bed, and set his magic table against the wall. The host's thoughts, however, let him have no rest; it occurred to him that there was a little old table in his lumber-room, which looked just like the apprentice's, and he brought it out quite softly, and exchanged it for the wishing-table.

Next morning, the joiner paid for his bed, took up his table, never thinking that he had got a false one, and went his way. At mid-day he reached his father, who received him with great joy.

"Well, my dear son, what hast thou learnt?" said he to him.

"Father, I have become a joiner."

"A good trade," replied the old man; "but what hast thou brought back with thee from thy apprenticeship?"

"Father, the best thing which I have brought back with me is this little table."

The tailor inspected it on all sides and said, "Thou didst not make a masterpiece when thou mad'st that; it is a bad old table."

"But it is a table which furnishes itself," replied the son. "When I set it out, and tell it to cover itself, the most beautiful dishes stand on it, and a wine also, which gladdens the heart. Just invite all our relations and friends, they shall refresh and enjoy themselves for once, for the table will give them all they require."

When the company was assembled, he put his table in the middle of the room and said, "Little table, cover thyself," but the little table did not bestir itself, and remained just as bare as any other table which did not understand language. Then the poor apprentice became aware that his table had been changed, and was ashamed at having to stand there like a liar.

The relations, however, mocked him, and were forced to go home without having eaten or drunk. The father brought out his patches again, and went on tailoring, but the son went to a master in the craft.

The second son had gone to a miller and had apprenticed himself to him. When his years were over, the master said, "As thou hast conducted thyself so well, I give thee an ass of a peculiar kind, which neither draws a cart nor carries a sack."

"To what use is he put, then?" asked the young apprentice.

"He lets gold drop from his mouth," answered the miller. "If thou settest him on a cloth and sayest 'Bricklebrit,' the good animal will drop gold pieces for thee."

"That is a fine thing," said the apprentice, and thanked the master, and went out into the world. When he had need of gold, he had only to say "Bricklebrit" to his ass, and it rained gold pieces, and he had nothing to do but pick them off the ground. Wheresoever he went, the best of everything was good enough for him, and the dearer the better, for he had always a full purse.

When he had looked about the world for some time, he thought, "Thou must seek out thy father; if thou goest to him with the gold-ass he will forget his anger, and receive thee well."

It came to pass that he came to the same public-house in which his brother's table had been exchanged. He led his ass by the bridle, and the host was about to take the animal from him and tie him up, but the young apprentice said, "Don't trouble yourself, I will take my grey horse into the stable, and tie him up myself too, for I must know where he stands."

This struck the host as odd, and he thought that a man who was forced to look after his ass himself, could not have much to spend; but when the stranger put his hand in his pocket and brought out two gold pieces, and said he was to provide something good for him, the host opened his eyes wide, and ran and sought out the best he could muster.

After dinner the guest asked what he owed. The host did not see why he should not double the reckoning, and said the apprentice must give two more gold pieces. He felt in his pocket, but his gold was just at an end.

"Wait an instant, sir host," said he, "I will go and fetch some money;" but he took the table-cloth with him.

The host could not imagine what this could mean, and being curious, stole after him, and as the guest bolted the stable-door, he peeped through a hole left by a knot in the wood. The stranger spread out the cloth under the animal and cried, "Bricklebrit," and immediately the beast began to let gold pieces fall, so that it fairly rained down money on the ground.

"Eh, my word," said the host, "ducats are quickly coined there! A purse like that is not amiss."

The guest paid his score, and went to bed, but in the night the host stole down into the stable, led away the master of the mint, and tied up another ass in his place. Early next morning the apprentice travelled away with his ass, and thought that he had his gold-ass. At mid-day he reached his father, who rejoiced to see him again, and gladly took him in.

"What hast thou made of thyself, my son?" asked the old man.

"A miller, dear father," he answered.

"What hast thou brought back with thee from thy travels?"

"Nothing else but an ass."

"There are asses enough here," said the father. "I would rather have had a good goat."

"Yes," replied the son, "but it is no common ass, but a gold-ass, when I say 'Bricklebrit,' the good beast opens its mouth and drops a whole sheetful of gold pieces. Just summon all our relations hither, and I will make them rich folks."

"That suits me well," said the tailor, "for then I shall have no need to torment myself any longer with the needle," and ran out himself and called the relations together.

As soon as they were assembled, the miller bade them make way, spread out his cloth, and brought the ass into the room. "Now watch," said he, and cried, "Bricklebrit," but no gold pieces fell, and it was clear that the animal knew nothing of the art, for every ass does not attain such perfection.

Then the poor miller pulled a long face, saw that he was betrayed, and begged pardon of the relatives, who went home as poor as they came. There was no help for it, the old man had to betake him to his needle once more, and the youth hired himself to a miller.

The third brother had apprenticed himself to a turner, and as that is skilled labour, he was the longest in learning. His brothers, however, told him in a letter how badly things had gone with them, and how the inn-keeper had cheated them of their beautiful wishing-gifts on the last evening before they reached home.

When the turner had served his time, and had to set out on his travels, as he had conducted himself so well, his master presented him with a sack and said, "There is a cudgel in it."

"I can put on the sack," said he, "and it may be of good service to me, but why should the cudgel be in it? It only makes it heavy."

"I will tell thee why," replied the master; "if anyone has done anything to injure thee, do but say, 'Out of the sack, Cudgel!' and the cudgel will leap forth among the people, and play such a dance on their backs that they will not be able to stir or move for a week, and it will not leave off until thou sayest, "Into the sack, Cudgel!"

The apprentice thanked him, put the sack on his back, and when anyone came too near him, and wished to attack him, he said, "Out of the sack, Cudgel!" and instantly the cudgel sprang out, and dusted the coat or jacket of one after the other on their backs, and never stopped until it had stripped it off them, and it was done so quickly, that before anyone was aware, it was already his own turn.

In the evening the young turner reached the inn where his brothers had been cheated. He laid his sack on the table before him, and began to talk of all the wonderful things which he had seen in the world.

"Yes," said he, "people may easily find a table which will cover itself, a gold-ass, and things of that kind—extremely good things which I by no means despise—but these are nothing in comparison with the treasure which I have won for myself, and am carrying about with me in my sack there."

The inn-keeper pricked up his ears, "What in the world can that be?" thought he; "the sack must be filled with nothing but jewels; I ought to get them cheap too, for all good things go in threes."

When it was time for sleep, the guest stretched himself on the bench, and laid his sack beneath him for a pillow. When the inn-keeper thought his guest was lying in a sound sleep, he went to him and pushed and pulled quite gently and carefully at the sack to see if he could possibly draw it away and lay another in its place.

The turner had, however, been waiting for this for a long time, and now just as the inn-keeper was about to give a hearty tug, he cried, "Out of the sack, Cudgel!" Instantly the little cudgel came forth, and fell on the inn-keeper, and gave him a sound thrashing.

The host cried for mercy; but the louder he cried, so much the more heavily the cudgel beat the time on his back, until at length he fell to the ground exhausted. Then the turner said, "If thou dost not give back the table which covers itself, and the gold-ass, the dance shall begin afresh."

"Oh, no," cried the host, quite humbly, "I will gladly produce everything, only make the accursed kobold creep back into the sack."

Then said the apprentice, "I will let mercy take the place of justice, but beware of getting into mischief again!"

So he cried, "Into the sack, Cudgel!" and let him have rest.

Next morning the turner went home to his father with the wishing-table, and the gold-ass. The tailor rejoiced when he saw him once more, and asked him likewise what he had learned in foreign parts.

"Dear father," said he, "I have become a turner."

"A skilled trade," said the father. "What hast thou brought back with thee from thy travels?"

"A precious thing, dear father," replied the son, "a cudgel in the sack."

"What!" cried the father, "a cudgel! That's worth thy trouble, indeed! From every tree thou canst cut thyself one."

"But not one like this, dear father. If I say, 'Out of the sack, Cudgel!' the cudgel springs out and leads anyone who means ill with me a weary dance, and never stops until he lies on the ground and prays for fair weather. Look you, with this cudgel have I got back the wishing-table and the gold-ass which the thievish inn-keeper took away from my brothers. Now let them both be sent for, and invite all our kinsmen. I will give them to eat and to drink, and will fill their pockets with gold into the bargain."

The old tailor would not quite believe, but nevertheless got the relatives together. Then the turner spread a cloth in the room and led in the gold-ass, and said to his brother, "Now, dear brother, speak to him."

The miller said, "Bricklebrit," and instantly the gold pieces fell down on the cloth like a thunder-shower, and the ass did not stop until every one of them had so much that he could carry no more. (I can see in thy face that thou also wouldst like to be there.)

Then the turner brought the little table, and said, "Now, dear brother, speak to it." And scarcely had the carpenter said, "Table, cover thyself," than it was spread and amply covered with the most exquisite dishes. Then such a meal took place as the good tailor had never yet known in his house, and the whole party of kinsmen stayed together till far in the night, and were all merry and glad. The tailor locked away

needle and thread, yard-measure and goose, in a press, and lived with his three sons in joy and splendour.

What, however, has become of the goat who was to blame for the tailor driving out his three sons? That I will tell thee. She was ashamed that she had a bald head, and ran to a fox's hole and crept into it. When the fox came home, he was met by two great eyes shining out of the darkness, and was terrified and ran away. A bear met him, and as the fox looked quite disturbed, he said, "What is the matter with thee, brother Fox, why dost thou look like that?"

"Ah," answered Redskin, "a fierce beast is in my cave and stared at me with its fiery eyes."

"We will soon drive him out," said the bear, and went with him to the cave and looked in, but when he saw the fiery eyes, fear seized on him likewise; he would have nothing to do with the furious beast, and took to his heels.

The bee met him, and as she saw that he was ill at ease, she said, "Bear, thou art really pulling a very pitiful face; what has become of all thy gaiety?"

"It is all very well for thee to talk," replied the bear, "a furious beast with staring eyes is in Redskin's house, and we can't drive him out."

The bee said, "Bear, I pity thee, I am a poor weak creature whom thou wouldst not turn aside to look at, but still, I believe, I can help thee."

She flew into the fox's cave, lighted on the goat's smoothly-shorn head, and stung her so violently, that she sprang up, crying "Meh, meh," and ran forth into the world as if mad, and to this hour no one knows where she has gone.

Godfather Death

POOR man had twelve children and was forced to work night and day to give them even bread. When therefore the thirteenth came into the world, he knew not what to do in his trouble, but ran out into the great highway, and resolved to ask the first person whom he met to be godfather. The first to meet him was the good God who already knew what filled his heart, and said to him, "Poor man, I pity thee. I will hold thy child at its christening, and will take charge of it and make it happy on earth."

The man said, "Who art thou?"

"I am God."

"Then I do not desire to have thee for a godfather," said the man; "thou givest to the rich, and leavest the poor to hunger."

Thus spake the man, for he did not know how wisely God apportions riches and poverty. He turned therefore away from the Lord, and went farther.

Then the Devil came to him and said, "What seekest thou? If thou wilt take me as a godfather for thy child, I will give him gold in plenty and all the joys of the world as well."

The man asked, "Who art thou?"

"I am the Devil."

"Then I do not desire to have thee for godfather," said the man; "thou deceivest men and leadest them astray."

He went onwards, and then came Death striding up to him with withered legs, and said, "Take me as godfather."

The man asked, "Who art thou?"

"I am Death, and I make all equal."

Then said the man, "Thou art the right one, thou takest the rich as well as the poor, without distinction; thou shalt be godfather."

Death answered, "I will make thy child rich and famous, for he who has me for a friend can lack nothing."

The man said, "Next Sunday is the christening; be there at the right time."

Death appeared as he had promised, and stood godfather quite in the usual way.

When the boy had grown up, his godfather one day appeared and bade him go with him. He led him forth into a forest, and showed him a herb which grew there, and said, "Now shalt thou receive thy god-father's present. I make thee a celebrated physician. When thou art called to a patient, I will always appear to thee. If I stand by the head of the sick man, thou mayst say with confidence that thou wilt make him well again, and if thou givest him of this herb he will recover; but if I stand by the patient's feet, he is mine, and thou must say that all remedies are in vain, and that no physician in the world could save him. But beware of using the herb against my will, or it might fare ill with thee."

It was not long before the youth was the most famous physician in the whole world. "He had only to look at the patient and he knew his condition at once, and if he would recover, or must needs die." So they said of him, and from far and wide people came to him, sent for him when they had anyone ill, and gave him so much money that he soon became a rich man.

Now it so befell that the King became ill, and the physician was summoned, and was to say if recovery were possible. But when he came to the bed, Death was standing by the feet of the sick man, and the herb did not grow which could save him.

"If I could but cheat Death for once," thought the physician, "he is sure to take it ill if I do, but, as I am his godson, he will shut one eye; I will risk it."

He therefore took up the sick man, and laid him the other way, so that now Death was standing by his head. Then he gave the King some of the herb, and he recovered and grew healthy again.

But Death came to the physician, looking very black and angry, threatened him with his finger, and said, "Thou hast overreached me; this time I will pardon it, as thou art my godson; but if thou venturest it again, it will cost thee thy neck, for I will take thee thyself away with me."

Soon afterwards the King's daughter fell into a severe illness. She was his only child, and he wept day and night, so that he began to lose the sight of his eyes, and he caused it to be made known that whosoever rescued her from death should be her husband and inherit the crown.

When the physician came to the sick girl's bed, he saw Death by her feet. He ought to have remembered the warning given by his godfather, but he was so infatuated by the great beauty of the King's daughter, and the happiness of becoming her husband, that he flung all thought to the winds. He did not see that Death was casting angry glances on him, that he was raising his hand in the air, and threatening him with his withered fist. He raised up the sick girl, and placed her head where her feet had lain. Then he gave her some of the herb, and instantly her cheeks flushed red, and life stirred afresh in her.

When Death saw that for a second time, he was defrauded of his own property, he walked up to the physician with long strides, and said, "All is over with thee, and now the lot falls on thee," and seized him so firmly with his ice-cold hand, that he could not resist, and led him into a cave below the earth.

There he saw how thousands and thousands of candles were burning in countless rows, some large, others half-sized, others small. Every instant some were extinguished, and others again burnt up, so that the flames seemed to leap hither and thither in perpetual change.

"See," said Death, "these are the lights of men's lives. The large ones belong to children, the half-sized ones to married people in their prime, the little ones belong to old people; but children and young folks likewise have often only a tiny candle."

"Show me the light of my life," said the physician, and he thought that it would be still very tall.

Death pointed to a little end which was just threatening to go out, and said, "Behold, it is there."

"Ah, dear godfather," said the horrified physician, "light a new one for me, do it for love of me, that I may enjoy my life, be King, and the husband of the King's beautiful daughter."

"I cannot," answered Death, "one must go out before a new one is lighted."

"Then place the old one on a new one, that will go on burning at once when the old one has come to an end," pleaded the physician.

Death behaved as if he were going to fulfil his wish, and took hold of a tall new candle; but as he desired to revenge himself, he purposely made a mistake in fixing it, and the little piece fell down and was extinguished. Immediately the physician fell on the ground, and now he himself was in the hands of Death.

Clever Elsie

HERE was once a man who had a daughter who was called Clever Elsie. And when she had grown up, her father said, "We will get her married." "Yes," said the mother, "if only any-one would come who would have her."

At length a man came from a distance and wooed her, who was called Hans; but he stipulated that Clever Elsie should be really wise.

"Oh," said the father, "she's sharp enough;" and the mother said, "Oh, she can see the wind coming up the street, and hear the flies coughing."

"Well," said Hans, "if she is not really wise, I won't have her."

When they were sitting at dinner and had eaten, the mother said, "Elsie, go into the cellar and fetch some beer."

Then Clever Elsie took the pitcher from the wall, went into the cel-lar, and tapped the lid briskly as she went, so that the time might not appear long. When she was below, she fetched herself a chair, and set it before the barrel so that she had no need to stoop, and did not hurt her back or do herself any unexpected injury. Then she placed the can before her, and turned the tap, and while the beer was running she would not let her eyes be idle, but looked up at the wall, and after much peering here and there, saw a pick-axe exactly above her, which the masons had accidentally left there.

Then Clever Elsie began to weep, and said, "If I get Hans, and we have a child, and he grows big, and we send him into the cellar here to draw beer, then the pick-axe will fall on his head and kill him." Then she sat and wept and screamed with all the strength of her body, over the misfortune which lay before her.

Those upstairs waited for the drink, but Clever Elsie still did not come. Then the woman said to the servant, "Just go down into the cel-lar and see where Elsie is."

The maid went and found her sitting in front of the barrel, scream-ing loudly. "Elsie, why weepest thou?" asked the maid.

138

"Ah," she answered, "have I not reason to weep? If I get Hans, and we have a child, and he grows big, and has to draw beer here, the pick-axe will perhaps fall on his head, and kill him."

Then said the maid, "What a clever Elsie we have!" and sat down beside her and began loudly to weep over the misfortune.

After a while, as the maid did not come back, and those upstairs were thirsty for the beer, the man said to the boy, "Just go down into the cellar and see where Elsie and the girl are."

The boy went down, and there sat Clever Elsie and the girl both weeping together. Then he asked, "Why are ye weeping?"

"Ah," said Elsie, "have I not reason to weep? If I get Hans, and we have a child, and he grows big, and has to draw beer here, the pick-axe will fall on his head and kill him."

Then said the boy, "What a clever Elsie we have!" and sat down by her, and likewise began to howl loudly.

Upstairs they waited for the boy, but as he still did not return, the man said to the woman, "Just go down into the cellar and see where Elsie is!"

The woman went down, and found all three in the midst of their lamentations, and inquired what was the cause; then Elsie told her also that her future child was to be killed by the pick-axe, when it grew big and had to draw beer, and the pick-axe fell down.

Then said the mother likewise, "What a clever Elsie we have!" and sat down and wept with them.

The man upstairs waited a short time, but as his wife did not come back and his thirst grew ever greater, he said, "I must go into the cellar myself and see where Elsie is."

But when he got into the cellar, and they were all sitting together crying, and he heard the reason, and that Elsie's child was the cause, and that Elsie might perhaps bring one into the world some day, and that it might be killed by the pick-axe, if it should happen to be sitting beneath it, drawing beer just at the very time when it fell down, he cried, "Oh, what a clever Elsie!" and sat down, and likewise wept with them.

The bridegroom stayed upstairs alone for a long time; then as no one would come back he thought, "They must be waiting for me below; I too must go there and see what they are about."

When he got down, five of them were sitting screaming and lamenting quite piteously, each out-doing the other.

"What misfortune has happened then?" asked he.

"Ah, dear Hans," said Elsie, "if we marry each other and have a child, and he is big, and we perhaps send him here to draw something to drink, then the pick-axe which has been left up there might dash his brains out if it were to fall down, so have we not reason to weep?"

"Come," said Hans, "more understanding than that is not needed for my household, as thou art such a clever Elsie, I will have thee," and he seized her hand, took her upstairs with him, and married her.

After Hans had had her some time, he said, "Wife, I am going out to work and earn some money for us; go into the field and cut the corn that we may have some bread."

"Yes, dear Hans, I will do that."

After Hans had gone away, she cooked herself some good broth and took it into the field with her. When she came to the field, she said to herself, "What shall I do; shall I shear first, or shall I eat first? Oh, I will eat first."

Then she emptied her basin of broth, and when she was fully satisfied, she once more said, "What shall I do? Shall I shear first, or shall I sleep first? I will sleep first." Then she lay down among the corn and fell asleep.

Hans had been at home for a long time, but Elsie did not come; then said he, "What a clever Elsie I have; she is so industrious that she does not even come home to eat."

As, however, she still stayed away, and it was evening, Hans went out to see what she had cut, but nothing was cut, and she was lying among the corn asleep. Then Hans hastened home and brought a fowler's net with little bells and hung it round about her, and she still went on sleeping. Then he ran home, shut the house-door, and sat down in his chair and worked.

At length, when it was quite dark, Clever Elsie awoke and when she got up, there was a jingling all round about her, and the bells rang at each step which she took. Then she was alarmed, and became uncertain whether she really was Clever Elsie or not, and said, "Is it I, or is it not I?"

But she knew not what answer to make to this, and stood for a time in doubt; at length she thought, "I will go home and ask if it be I, or if it be not I, they will be sure to know."

140

She ran to the door of her own house, but it was shut; then she knocked at the window and cried, "Hans, is Elsie within?"

"Yes," answered Hans, "she is within."

Hereupon she was terrified, and said, "Ah, heavens! Then it is not I," and went to another door; but when the people heard the jingling of the bells, they would not open it, and she could get in nowhere. Then she ran out of the village, and no one has seen her since.

The Wedding of Mrs. Fox

FIRST STORY

 HERE was once on a time an old fox with nine tails, who believed that his wife was not faithful to him, and wished to try her. He stretched himself out under the bench, did not move a limb, and behaved as if he were stone dead. Mrs. Fox went up to her room, shut herself in, and her maid, Miss Cat, sat by the fire, and did the cooking. When it became known that the old fox was dead, wooers presented themselves. The maid heard someone standing at the house-door, knocking. She went and opened it, and it was a young fox, who said,

> "What may you be about, Miss Cat?
> Do you sleep or do you wake?"

She answered,

> "I am not sleeping, I am waking,
> Wouldst thou know what I am making?
> I am boiling warm beer with butter so nice,
> Will the gentleman enter and drink some likewise?"

"No, thank you, miss," said the fox. "What is Mrs. Fox doing?" The maid replied,

> "She sits all alone,
> And makes her moan,
> Weeping her little eyes quite red,
> Because old Mr. Fox is dead."

"Do just tell her, miss, that a young fox is here, who would like to woo her."
"Certainly, young sir."

> The cat goes up the stairs trip, trap,
> The door she knocks at tap, tap, tap,
> "Mistress Fox, are you inside?"

142

"Oh yes, my little cat," she cried.
"A wooer he stands at the door out there."
"Tell me what he is like, my dear?"

"But has he nine as beautiful tails as the late Mr. Fox?"
"Oh, no," answered the cat, "he has only one."
"Then I will not have him."

Miss Cat went downstairs and sent the wooer away.

Soon afterwards there was another knock, and another fox was at the door who wished to woo Mrs. Fox. He had two tails, but he did not fare better than the first. After this still more came, each with one tail more than the other, but they were all turned away, until at last one came who had nine tails, like old Mr. Fox.

When the widow heard that, she said joyfully to the cat,

"Now open the gates and doors all wide,
And carry old Mr. Fox outside."

But just as the wedding was going to be solemnized, old Mr. Fox stirred under the bench, and cudgelled all the rabble, and drove them and Mrs. Fox out of the house.

SECOND STORY

When old Mr. Fox was dead, the wolf came as a wooer, and knocked at the door, and the cat who was servant to Mrs. Fox, opened it for him. The wolf greeted her, and said,

"Good day, Mrs. Cat of Kehrewit,
How comes it that alone you sit?
What are you making good?"

The cat replied,

"In milk I'm breaking bread so sweet,
Will the gentleman please come in and eat?"

"No, thank you, Mrs. Cat," answered the wolf. "Is Mrs. Fox not at home?"

The cat said,

"She sits upstairs in her room,
Bewailing her sorrowful doom,
Bewailing her trouble so sore,
For old Mr. Fox is no more."

The wolf answered,

"If she's in want of a husband now,
Then will it please her to step below?"
The cat runs quickly up the stair,
And lets her tail fly here and there,
Until she comes to the parlour door.
With her five gold rings at the door she knocks,

143

"Are you within, good Mistress Fox?
If you're in want of a husband now,
Then will it please you to step below?"

Mrs. Fox asked, "Has the gentleman red stockings on, and has he a pointed mouth?"

"No," answered the cat.

"Then he won't do for me."

When the wolf was gone, came a dog, a stag, a hare, a bear, a lion, and all the beasts of the forest, one after the other. But one of the good points which old Mr. Fox had possessed, was always lacking, and the cat had continually to send the wooers away. At length came a young fox.

Then Mrs. Fox said, "Has the gentleman red stockings on, and has he a little pointed mouth?"

"Yes," said the cat, "he has."

"Then let him come upstairs," said Mrs. Fox, and ordered the servant to prepare the wedding-feast.

"Sweep me the room as clean as you can,
Up with the window, fling out my old man!
For many a fine fat mouse he brought,
Yet of his wife he never thought,
But ate up everyone he caught."

Then the wedding was solemnized with young Mr. Fox, and there was much rejoicing and dancing; and if they have not left off, they are dancing still.

The Elves

FIRST STORY

HERE was once a shoemaker who, by no fault of his own, had become so poor that at last he had nothing left but leather for one pair of shoes. So in the evening, he cut out the shoes which he wished to begin to make the next morning, and as he had a good conscience, he lay down quietly in his bed, commended himself to God, and fell asleep.

In the morning, after he had said his prayers, and was just going to sit down to work, the two shoes stood quite finished on his table. He was astounded, and did not know what to say to it. He took the shoes in his hands to observe them closer, and they were so neatly made that there was not one bad stitch in them, just as if they were intended as a masterpiece.

Soon after, a buyer came in, and as the shoes pleased him so well, he paid more for them than was customary, and, with the money, the shoemaker was able to purchase leather for two pairs of shoes. He cut them out at night, and next morning was about to set to work with fresh courage; but he had no need to do so, for, when he got up, they were already made, and buyers also were not wanting, who gave him money enough to buy leather for four pairs of shoes.

The following morning, too, he found the four pairs made; and so it went on constantly, what he cut out in the evening was finished by the morning, so that he soon had his honest independence again, and at last became a wealthy man.

Now it befell that one evening not long before Christmas, when the man had been cutting out, he said to his wife, before going to bed, "What think you if we were to stay up tonight to see who it is that lends us this helping hand?"

The woman liked the idea, and lighted a candle, and then they hid themselves in a corner of the room, behind some clothes which were hanging up there, and watched.

When it was midnight, two pretty little naked men came, sat down by the shoemaker's table, took all the work which was cut out before them and began to stitch, and sew, and hammer so skilfully and so quickly with their little fingers that the shoemaker could not turn away his eyes for astonishment. They did not stop until all was done, and stood finished on the table, and then they ran quickly away.

Next morning the woman said, "The little men have made us rich, and we really must show that we are grateful for it. They run about so, and have nothing on, and must be cold. I'll tell thee what I'll do: I will make them little shirts, and coats, and vests, and trousers, and knit both of them a pair of stockings, and do thou, too, make them two little pairs of shoes."

The man said, "I shall be very glad to do it;" and one night, when everything was ready, they laid their presents all together on the table instead of the cut-out work, and then concealed themselves to see how the little men would behave.

At midnight they came bounding in, and wanted to get to work at once, but as they did not find any leather cut out, but only the pretty little articles of clothing, they were at first astonished, and then they showed intense delight. They dressed themselves with the greatest rapidity, putting the pretty clothes on, and singing,

> "Now we are boys so fine to see,
> Why should we longer cobblers be?"

Then they danced and skipped and leapt over chairs and benches. At last they danced out of doors. From that time forth they came no more, but as long as the shoemaker lived all went well with him, and all his undertakings prospered.

SECOND STORY

HERE was once a poor servant-girl, who was industrious and cleanly, and swept the house every day, and emptied her sweepings on the great heap in front of the door. One morning when she was just going back to her work, she found a letter on this heap, and as she could not read, she put her broom in the corner, and took the letter to her master and mistress, and behold it was an invitation from the elves, who asked the girl to hold a child for them at its christening.

The girl did not know what to do, but at length, after much persuasion, and as they told her that it was not right to refuse an invitation of this kind, she consented. Then three elves came and conducted her to a hollow mountain, where the little folks lived.

Everything there was small, but more elegant and beautiful than can be described. The baby's mother lay in a bed of black ebony ornamented with pearls, the coverlids were embroidered with gold, the cradle was of ivory, the bath of gold.

The girl stood as godmother, and then wanted to go home again, but the little elves urgently entreated her to stay three days with them. So she stayed, and passed the time in pleasure and gaiety, and the little folks did all they could to make her happy.

At last she set out on her way home. Then first they filled her pockets quite full of money, and after that they led her out of the mountain again. When she got home, she wanted to begin her work, and took the broom, which was still standing in the corner, in her hand and began to sweep.

Then some strangers came out of the house, who asked her who she was, and what business she had there? And she had not, as she thought, been three days with the little men in the mountains, but seven years, and in the meantime her former masters had died.

THIRD STORY

T HE elves once took a child away from its mother, and left in its place a changeling with a large head and staring eyes, which would do nothing but eat and drink. In her trouble she went to her neighbour, and asked her advice. The neighbour said that she was to carry the changeling into the kitchen, set it down on the hearth, light a fire, and boil some water in two egg-shells, which would make the changeling laugh, and if he laughed, all would be over with him. The woman did everything that her neighbour bade her.

When she put the egg-shells with water on the fire, the imp said, "I am as old now as the Wester forest, but never yet have I seen anyone boil anything in an egg-shell!"

And he began to laugh at it. Whilst he was laughing, suddenly came a host of little elves, who brought the right child, set it down on the hearth, and took the changeling away with them.

The Robber Bridegroom

HERE was once on a time a miller who had a beautiful daughter, and as she was grown up, he wished that she was provided for, and well married. He thought, "If any good suitor comes and asks for her, I will give her to him." Not long afterwards, a suitor came, who appeared to be very rich, and as the miller had no fault to find with him, he promised his daughter to him. The maiden, however, did not like him quite so much as a girl should like the man to whom she is engaged, and had no confidence in him. Whenever she saw, or thought of him, she felt a secret horror.

Once he said to her, "Thou art my betrothed, and yet thou hast never once paid me a visit."

The maiden replied, "I know not where thy house is."

Then said the bridegroom, "My house is out there in the dark forest."

She tried to excuse herself, and said she could not find the way there.

The bridegroom said, "Next Sunday thou must come out there to me; I have already invited the guests, and I will strew ashes in order that thou mayst find thy way through the forest."

When Sunday came, and the maiden had to set out on her way, she became very uneasy, she herself knew not exactly why, and to mark her way she filled both her pockets full of peas and lentils. Ashes were strewn at the entrance of the forest, and these she followed, but at every step she threw a couple of peas on the ground.

She walked almost the whole day until she reached the middle of the forest, where it was the darkest, and there stood a solitary house, which she did not like, for it looked so dark and dismal. She went inside it, but no one was within, and the most absolute stillness reigned.

Suddenly a voice cried,

"Turn back, turn back, young maiden dear,
'Tis a murderer's house you enter here."

The maiden looked up, and saw that the voice came from a bird, which was hanging in a cage on the wall. Again it cried,

> "Turn back, turn back, young maiden dear,
> 'Tis a murderer's house you enter here."

Then the young maiden went on farther from one room to another, and walked through the whole house, but it was entirely empty and not one human being was to be found. At last she came to the cellar, and there sat an extremely aged woman, whose head shook constantly.

"Can you not tell me," said the maiden, "if my betrothed lives here?"

"Alas, poor child," replied the old woman, "whither hast thou come? Thou art in a murderer's den. Thou thinkest thou art a bride soon to be married, but thou wilt keep thy wedding with death. Look, I have been forced to put a great kettle on there, with water in it, and when they have thee in their power, they will cut thee to pieces without

149

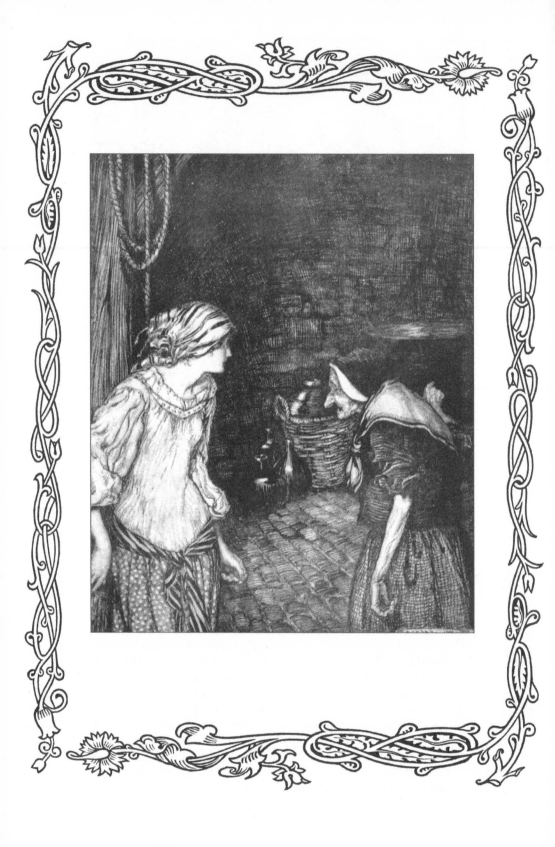

mercy, will cook thee, and eat thee, for they are eaters of human flesh. If I do not have compassion on thee, and save thee, thou art lost."

Thereupon the old woman led her behind a great hogshead where she could not be seen. "Be as still as a mouse," said she, "do not make a sound, or move, or all will be over with thee. At night, when the robbers are asleep, we will escape; I have long waited for an opportunity."

Hardly was this done, than the godless crew came home. They dragged with them another young girl. They were drunk, and paid no heed to her screams and lamentations. They gave her wine to drink, three glasses full, one glass of white wine, one glass of red, and a glass of yellow, and with this her heart burst in twain and she fell down dead.

The poor bride behind the cask trembled and shook, for she saw right well what fate the robbers had destined for her. One of them noticed a gold ring on the little finger of the murdered girl, and as it would not come off at once, he took an axe and cut the finger off, but it sprang up in the air, away over the cask and fell straight into the bride's bosom. The robber took a candle and wanted to look for it, but could not find it.

Then another of them said, "Hast thou looked behind the great hogshead?"

But the old woman cried, "Come and get something to eat, and leave off looking till the morning, the finger won't run away from you."

Then the robbers said, "The old woman is right," and gave up their search, and sat down to eat, and the old woman poured a sleeping-draught in their wine, so that they soon lay down in the cellar, and slept and snored.

When the bride heard that, she came out from behind the hogshead, and had to step over the sleepers, for they lay in rows on the ground, and great was her terror lest she should waken one of them. But God helped her, and she got safely over.

The old woman went up with her, opened the doors, and they hurried out of the murderers' den with all the speed in their power. The wind had blown away the strewn ashes, but the peas and lentils had sprouted and grown up, and showed them the way in the moonlight. They walked the whole night, until in the morning they arrived at the mill, and then the maiden told her father everything exactly as it had happened.

When the day came when the wedding was to be celebrated, the bridegroom appeared, and the Miller had invited all his relations and friends. As they sat at table, each was bidden to relate something. The bride sat still, and said nothing.

Then said the bridegroom to the bride, "Come, my darling, dost thou know nothing? Relate something to us like the rest."

She replied, "Then I will relate a dream. I was walking alone through a wood, and at last I came to a house, in which no living soul was, but on the wall there was a bird in a cage which cried,

'Turn back, turn back, young maiden dear,
'Tis a murderer's house you enter here.'

And this it cried once more. My darling, I only dreamt this. Then I went through all the rooms, and they were all empty, and there was something so horrible about them! At last I went down into the cellar, and there sat a very very old woman, whose head shook; I asked her, 'Does my bridegroom live in this house?' She answered, 'Alas, poor child, thou hast got into a murderer's den, thy bridegroom does live here, but he will hew thee in pieces, and kill thee, and then he will cook thee, and eat thee.' My darling, I only dreamt this. But the old woman hid me behind a great hogshead, and, scarcely was I hidden, when the robbers came home, dragging a maiden with them, to whom they gave three kinds of wine to drink, white, red, and yellow, with which her heart broke in twain, and she died. My darling, I only dreamt this. And one of the robbers saw that there was a ring on her little finger, and as it was hard to draw off, he took an axe and cut it off, but the finger sprang up in the air, and sprang behind the great hogshead, and fell in my bosom. And there is the finger with the ring!"

And with these words she drew it forth, and showed it to those present.

The robber, who had during this story become as pale as ashes, leapt up and wanted to escape, but the guests held him fast, and delivered him over to justice. Then he and his whole troop were executed for their infamous deeds.

Frau Trude

 HERE was once a little girl who was obstinate and inquisitive, and when her parents told her to do anything, she did not obey them, so how could she fare well? One day she said to her parents, "I have heard so much of Frau Trude, I will go to her some day. People say that everything about her does look so strange, and that there are such odd things in her house, that I have become quite curious!"

Her parents absolutely forbade her, and said, "Frau Trude is a bad woman, who does wicked things, and if thou goest to her, thou art no longer our child."

But the maiden did not let herself be turned aside by her parent's prohibition, and still went to Frau Trude.

And when she got to her, Frau Trude said, "Why art thou so pale?"

"Ah," she replied, and her whole body trembled, "I have been so terrified at what I have seen."

"What hast thou seen?"

"I saw a black man on your steps."

"That was a collier."

"Then I saw a green man."

"That was a huntsman."

"After that I saw a blood-red man."

"That was a butcher."

"Ah, Frau Trude, I was terrified; I looked through the window and saw not you, but, as I verily believe, the devil himself with a head of fire."

"Oho!" said she, "then thou hast seen the witch in her proper costume. I have been waiting for thee, and wanting thee a long time already; thou shalt give me some light."

Then she changed the girl into a block of wood, and threw it into the fire. And when it was in full blaze, she sat down close to it, and warmed herself by it, and said, "That shines bright for once in a way!"

Herr Korbes

COCK and a hen once wanted to take a journey together. So the cock built a beautiful carriage, which had four red wheels, and harnessed four mice to it. The hen seated herself in it with the cock, and they drove away together. Not long afterwards they met a cat who said, "Where are you going?" The cock replied, "We are going to the house of Herr Korbes." "Take me with you," said the cat. The cock answered, "Most willingly, get up behind, lest you fall off in front. Take great care not to dirty my little red wheels. And you little wheels, roll on, and you little mice pipe out, as we go forth on our way to the house of Herr Korbes."

After this came a millstone, then an egg, then a duck, then a pin, and at last a needle, who all seated themselves in the carriage, and drove with them. When, however, they reached the house of Herr Korbes, Herr Korbes was not there. The mice drew the carriage into the barn, the hen flew with the cock upon a perch. The cat sat down by the hearth, the duck on the well-pole. The egg rolled itself into a towel, the pin stuck itself into the chair-cushion, the needle jumped on to the bed in the middle of the pillow, and the millstone laid itself over the door.

Then Herr Korbes came home, went to the hearth, and was about to light the fire, when the cat threw a quantity of ashes in his face. He ran into the kitchen in a great hurry to wash it off, and the duck splashed some water in his face. He wanted to dry it with the towel, but the egg rolled up against him, broke, and glued up his eyes. He wanted to rest, and sat down in the chair, and then the pin pricked him. He fell in a passion, and threw himself on his bed, but as soon as he laid his head on the pillow, the needle pricked him, so that he screamed aloud, and was just going to run out into the wide world in his rage, but when he came to the house-door, the millstone leapt down and struck him dead.

Herr Korbes must have been a very wicked man!

Fundevogel (Bird-foundling)

HERE was once a forester who went into the forest to hunt, and as he entered it, he heard a sound of screaming as if a little child were there. He followed the sound, and at last came to a high tree, and at the top of this a little child was sitting, for the mother had fallen asleep under the tree with the child, and a bird of prey had seen it in her arms, had flown down, snatched it away, and set it on the high tree.

The forester climbed up, brought the child down, and thought to himself, "Thou wilt take him home with thee, and bring him up with thy Lina." He took it home, therefore, and the two children grew up together. The one, however, which he had found on a tree was called Fundevogel, because a bird had carried it away. Fundevogel and Lina loved each other so dearly that when they did not see each other they were sad.

The forester, however, had an old cook, who one evening took two pails and began to fetch water, and did not go once only, but many times, out to the spring.

Lina saw this and said, "Hark you, old Sanna, why are you fetching so much water?"

"If thou wilt never repeat it to anyone, I will tell thee why." So Lina said, no, she would never repeat it to anyone, and then the cook said, "Early tomorrow morning, when the forester is out hunting, I will heat the water, and when it is boiling in the kettle, I will throw in Fundevogel, and will boil him in it."

Betimes next morning the forester got up and went out hunting, and when he was gone, the children were still in bed. Then Lina said to Fundevogel, "If thou wilt never leave me, I too will never leave thee."

Fundevogel said, "Neither now, nor ever will I leave thee."

Then said Lina, "Then I will tell thee. Last night, old Sanna carried so many buckets of water into the house that I asked her why she was doing that, and she said that if I would promise not to tell anyone she would tell me, and I said I would be sure not to tell anyone, and she said that early tomorrow morning when father was out hunting, she would set on the kettle full of water, throw thee into it and boil thee; but we will get up quickly, dress ourselves, and go away together."

The two children therefore got up, dressed themselves quickly, and went away. When the water in the kettle was boiling, the cook went into the bedroom to fetch Fundevogel and throw him into it. But when she came in, and went to the beds, both the children were gone. Then she was terribly alarmed, and she said to herself, "What shall I say now when the forester comes home and sees that the children are gone? They must be followed instantly to get them back again."

Then the cook sent three servants after them, who were to run and overtake the children. The children, however, were sitting outside the forest, and when they saw from afar the three servants running, Lina said to Fundevogel, "Never leave me, and I will never leave thee."

Fundevogel said, "Neither now, nor ever."

Then said Lina, "Do thou become a rose-tree, and I the rose upon it."

When the three servants came to the forest, nothing was there but a rose-tree and one rose on it, but the children were nowhere. Then said they, "There is nothing to be done here," and they went home and told the cook that they had seen nothing in the forest but a little rose-bush with one rose on it.

Then the old cook scolded and said, "You simpletons, you should have cut the rose-bush in two, and have broken off the rose and brought it home with you; go, and do it at once."

They had therefore to go out and look for the second time. The children, however, saw them coming from a distance.

Then Lina said, "Fundevogel, never leave me, and I will never leave thee."

Fundevogel said, "Neither now, nor ever."

Said Lina, "Then do thou become a church, and I'll be the chandelier in it."

So when the three servants came, nothing was there but a church, with a chandelier in it. They said therefore to each other, "What can we do here, let us go home."

When they got home, the cook asked if they had not found them; so they said no, they had found nothing but a church, and that there was a chandelier in it. And the cook scolded them and said, "You fools! why did you not pull the church to pieces, and bring the chandelier home with you?"

And now the old cook herself got on her legs, and went with the three servants in pursuit of the children. The children, however, saw from afar that the three servants were coming, and the cook waddling after them.

Then said Lina, "Fundevogel, never leave me, and I will never leave thee."

Then said Fundevogel, "Neither now, nor ever."

Said Lina, "Be a fishpond, and I will be the duck upon it."

The cook, however, came up to them, and when she saw the pond, she lay down by it, and was about to drink it up. But the duck swam quickly to her, seized her head in its beak and drew her into the water, and there the old witch had to drown. Then the children went home together, and were heartily delighted, and if they are not dead, they are living still.

Old Sultan

HERE was once a farmer who had a faithful dog called Sultan, who had grown old, and lost all his teeth, so that he could no longer hold anything fast. One day the farmer was standing with his wife before the house-door, and said, "Tomorrow I intend to shoot Old Sultan, he is no longer of any use."

His wife, who felt pity for the faithful beast, answered, "He has served us so long, and been so faithful, that we might well give him his keep."

"Eh! what?" said the man. "You are not very sharp. He has not a tooth left in his mouth, and not a thief is afraid of him; now he may be off. If he has served us, he has had good feeding for it."

The poor dog, who was lying stretched out in the sun not far off, had heard everything, and was sorry that the morrow was to be his last day. He had a good friend, the wolf, and he crept out in the evening into the forest to him, and complained of the fate that awaited him.

"Hark ye, gossip," said the wolf, "be of good cheer, I will help you out of your trouble. I have thought of something. Tomorrow, early in the morning, your master is going with his wife to make hay, and they will take their little child with them, for no one will be left behind in the house. They are wont, during work-time, to lay the child under the hedge in the shade; you lay yourself there too, just as if you wished to guard it. Then I will come out of the wood, and carry off the child. You must rush swiftly after me, as if you would seize it again from me. I will let it fall, and you will take it back to its parents, who will think that you have saved it, and will be far too grateful to do you any harm; on the contrary, you will be in high favour, and they will never let you want for anything again."

The plan pleased the dog, and it was carried out just as it was arranged. The father screamed when he saw the Wolf running across the field with his child, but when Old Sultan brought it back, then he was full of joy, and stroked him and said, "Not a hair of yours shall be hurt, you shall eat my bread free as long as you live."

And to his wife he said, "Go home at once and make Old Sultan some bread-sop that he will not have to bite, and bring the pillow out of my bed, I will give him that to lie upon."

Henceforward Old Sultan was as well off as he could wish to be.

Soon afterwards the wolf visited him, and was pleased that everything had succeeded so well. "But, gossip," said he, "you will just wink an eye if when I have a chance I carry off one of your master's fat sheep."

"Do not reckon upon that," answered the dog. "I will remain true to my master; I cannot agree to that."

The wolf, who thought that this could not be spoken in earnest, came creeping about in the night and was going to take away the sheep. But the farmer, to whom the faithful Sultan had told the wolf's plan, caught him and dressed his hide soundly with the flail. The wolf had to pack off, but he cried out to the dog, "Wait a bit, you scoundrel, you shall pay for this."

The next morning the wolf sent the boar to challenge the dog to come out into the forest so that they might settle the affair. Old Sultan could find no one to stand by him but a cat with only three legs, and as they went out together the poor cat limped along, and at the same time stretched out her tail into the air with pain.

The wolf and his friend were already on the spot appointed, but when they saw their enemy coming, they thought that he was bringing a sabre with him, for they mistook the outstretched tail of the cat for one. And when the poor beast hopped on its three legs, they could only think every time that it was picking up a stone to throw at them. So they were both afraid; the wild boar crept into the under-wood, and the wolf jumped up a tree.

The dog and the cat, when they came up, wondered that there was no one to be seen. The wild boar, however, had not been able to hide himself altogether; and one of his ears was still to be seen. Whilst the cat was looking carefully about, the boar moved his ear; the cat, who thought it was a mouse moving there, jumped upon it and bit it hard.

The boar made a fearful noise and ran away, crying out, "The guilty one is up in the tree." The dog and cat looked up and saw the wolf, who was ashamed of having shown himself so timid, and made friends with the dog.

The Six Swans

NCE upon a time a certain King was hunting in a great forest, and he chased a wild beast so eagerly that none of his attendants could follow him. When evening drew near, he stopped and looked around him, and then he saw that he had lost his way. He sought a way out, but could find none. Then he perceived an aged woman with a head which nodded perpetually, who came towards him, but she was a witch.

"Good woman," said he to her, "Can you not show me the way through the forest?"

"Oh, yes, Lord King," she answered, "that I certainly can, but on one condition, and if you do not fulfil that, you will never get out of the forest, and will die of hunger in it."

"What kind of condition is it?" asked the King.

"I have a daughter," said the old woman, "who is as beautiful as anyone in the world, and well deserves to be your consort, and if you will make her your Queen, I will show you the way out of the forest."

In the anguish of his heart the King consented, and the old woman led him to her little hut, where her daughter was sitting by the fire. She received the King as if she had been expecting him, and he saw that she was very beautiful, but still she did not please him, and he could not look at her without secret horror. After he had taken the maiden up on his horse, the old woman showed him the way, and the King reached his royal palace again, where the wedding was celebrated.

The King had already been married once, and had by his first wife, seven children, six boys and a girl, whom he loved better than anything else in the world. As he now feared that the step-mother might not treat them well, and even do them some injury, he took them to a lonely castle which stood in the midst of a forest. It lay so concealed, and the way was so difficult to find that he himself would not have found it, if a wise woman had not given him a ball of yarn with wonderful properties. When he threw it down before him, it unrolled itself and showed him his path.

159

The King, however, went so frequently away to his dear children that the Queen observed his absence; she was curious and wanted to know what he did when he was quite alone in the forest. She gave a great deal of money to his servants, and they betrayed the secret to her, and told her likewise of the ball which alone could point out the way.

And now she knew no rest until she had learnt where the King kept the ball of yarn, and then she made little shirts of white silk, and as she had learnt the art of witchcraft from her mother, she sewed a charm inside them. And once when the King had ridden forth to hunt, she took the little shirts and went into the forest, and the ball showed her the way.

The children, who saw from a distance that someone was approaching, thought that their dear father was coming to them, and full of joy, ran to meet him. Then she threw one of the little shirts over each of them, and no sooner had the shirts touched their bodies than they were changed into swans, and flew away over the forest. The Queen went home quite delighted, and thought she had got rid of her step-children, but the girl had not run out with her brothers, and the Queen knew nothing about her.

Next day the King went to visit his children, but he found no one but the little girl.

"Where are thy brothers?" asked the King.

"Alas, dear father," she answered, "they have gone away and left me alone!" and she told him that she had seen from her little window how her brothers had flown away over the forest in the shape of swans, and she showed him the feathers, which they had let fall in the court-yard, and which she had picked up.

The King mourned, but he did not think that the Queen had done this wicked deed, and as he feared that the girl would also be stolen away from him, he wanted to take her away with him. But she was afraid of her step-mother, and entreated the King to let her stay just this one night more in the forest castle.

The poor girl thought, "I can no longer stay here. I will go and seek my brothers." And when night came, she ran away, and went straight into the forest.

She walked the whole night long, and next day also without stopping, until she could go no farther for weariness. Then she saw a forest-hut, and went into it, and found a room with six little beds, but she did not venture to get into one of them, but crept under one, and lay down on the hard ground, intending to pass the night there.

Just before sunset, however, she heard a rustling, and saw six swans come flying in at the window. They alighted on the ground and blew at each other, and blew all the feathers off, and their swan's skins stripped off like a shirt. Then the maiden looked at them and recognized her brothers, was glad and crept forth from beneath the bed. The brothers were not less delighted to see their little sister, but their joy was of short duration.

"Here canst thou not abide," they said to her. "This is a shelter for robbers, if they come home and find thee, they will kill thee."

"But can you not protect me?" asked the little sister.

"No," they replied, "only for one quarter of an hour each evening can we lay aside our swan's skins and have during that time our human form; after that, we are once more turned into swans."

The little sister wept and said, "Can you not be set free?"

"Alas, no," they answered, "the conditions are too hard! For six years thou mayst neither speak nor laugh, and in that time thou must sew together six little shirts of starwort for us. And if one single word falls from thy lips, all thy work will be lost."

And when the brothers had said this, the quarter of an hour was over, and they flew out of the window again as swans.

The maiden, however, firmly resolved to deliver her brothers, even if it should cost her her life. She left the hut, went into the midst of the forest, seated herself on a tree, and there passed the night. Next morning she went out and gathered starwort and began to sew. She could not speak to anyone, and she had no inclination to laugh; she sat there and looked at nothing but her work.

When she had already spent a long time there, it came to pass that the King of the country was hunting in the forest, and his huntsmen came to the tree on which the maiden was sitting.

They called to her and said, "Who art thou?" But she made no answer. "Come down to us," said they. "We will not do thee any harm." She only shook her head.

As they pressed her further with questions, she threw her golden necklace down to them, and thought to content them thus. They, however, did not cease, and then she threw her girdle down to them, and as this also was to no purpose, her garters, and by degrees everything that she had on that she could do without until she had nothing left but her shift.

The huntsmen, however, did not let themselves be turned aside by that, but climbed the tree and fetched the maiden down and led her before the King. The King asked, "Who art thou? What art thou doing on the tree?" But she did not answer. He put the question in every language that he knew, but she remained as mute as a fish.

As she was so beautiful, the King's heart was touched, and he was smitten with a great love for her. He put his mantle on her, took her before him on his horse, and carried her to his castle. Then he caused her to be dressed in rich garments, and she shone in her beauty like bright daylight, but no word could be drawn from her. He placed her by his side at table, and her modest bearing and courtesy pleased him so much that he said, "She is the one whom I wish to marry, and no other woman in the world." And after some days he united himself to her.

The King, however, had a wicked mother who was dissatisfied with this marriage and spoke ill of the young Queen. "Who knows," said she, "from whence the creature who can't speak, comes? She is not worthy of a king!"

After a year had passed, when the Queen brought her first child into the world, the old woman took it away from her, and smeared her mouth with blood as she slept. Then she went to the King and accused the Queen of being a man-eater.

The King would not believe it, and would not suffer anyone to do her any injury. She, however, sat continually sewing at the shirts, and cared for nothing else.

The next time, when she again bore a beautiful boy, the false step-mother used the same treachery, but the King could not bring himself to give credit to her words. He said, "She is too pious and good to do anything of that kind; if she were not dumb, and could defend herself, her innocence would come to light."

But when the old woman stole away the newly-born child for the third time, and accused the Queen, who did not utter one word of defence, the King could do no otherwise than deliver her over to justice, and she was sentenced to suffer death by fire.

When the day came for the sentence to be executed, it was the last day of the six years during which she was not to speak or laugh, and she had delivered her dear brothers from the power of the enchantment. The six shirts were ready, only the left sleeve of the sixth was wanting.

When, therefore, she was led to the stake, she laid the shirts on her arm, and when she stood on high and the fire was just going to be lighted, she looked around and six swans came flying through the air towards her. Then she saw that her deliverance was near, and her heart leapt with joy.

The swans swept towards her and sank down so that she could throw the shirts over them, and as they were touched by them, their swan's skins fell off, and her brothers stood in their own bodily form before her, and were vigorous and handsome. The youngest only lacked his left arm, and had in the place of it a swan's wing on his shoulder.

They embraced and kissed each other, and the Queen went to the King, who was greatly moved, and she began to speak and said, "Dearest husband, now I may speak and declare to thee that I am innocent, and falsely accused." And she told him of the treachery of the old woman who had taken away her three children and hidden them.

Then to the great joy of the King they were brought thither, and as a punishment, the wicked step-mother was bound to the stake, and burnt to ashes. But the King and the Queen with their six brothers lived many years in happiness and peace.

Briar-Rose

N TIMES past there were a King and Queen who said every day, "Ah, if only we had a child!" but they never had one. But it happened that once when the Queen was bathing, a frog crept out of the water on to the land, and said to her, "Your wish shall be fulfilled; before a year has gone by you shall have a daughter."

What the frog had said came true, and the Queen had a little girl who was so pretty that the King could not contain himself for joy, and ordered a great feast. He invited not only his kindred, friends and acquaintance, but also the Wise Women, in order that they might be kind and well-disposed towards the child. There were thirteen of them in his kingdom, but, as he had only twelve golden plates for them to eat out of, one of them had to be left at home.

The feast was held with all manner of splendour, and when it came to an end, the Wise Women bestowed their magic gifts upon the baby: one gave virtue, another beauty, a third riches, and so on with everything in the world that one can wish for.

When eleven of them had made their promises, suddenly the thirteenth came in. She wished to avenge herself for not having been invited, and without greeting, or even looking at anyone, she cried with a loud voice, "The King's daughter shall in her fifteenth year prick herself with a spindle, and fall down dead." And, without saying a word more, she turned round and left the room.

They were all shocked; but the twelfth, whose good wish still remained unspoken, came forward, and as she could not undo the evil sentence, but only soften it, she said, "It shall not be death, but a deep sleep of a hundred years, into which the princess shall fall."

The King, who would fain keep his dear child from the misfortune, gave orders that every spindle in the whole kingdom should be burnt. Meanwhile the gifts of the Wise Women were plenteously fulfilled on the young girl, for she was so beautiful, modest, good-natured, and wise, that everyone who saw her was bound to love her.

It happened that on the very day when she was fifteen years old, the King and Queen were not at home, and the maiden was left in the palace quite alone. So she went round into all sorts of places, looked into rooms and bed-chambers just as she liked, and at last came to an old tower. She climbed up the narrow winding-staircase, and reached a little door. A rusty key was in the lock, and when she turned it the door sprang open, and there in a little room sat an old woman with a spindle, busily spinning her flax.

"Good day, old dame," said the King's daughter; "what are you doing there?"

"I am spinning," said the old woman, and nodded her head.

"What sort of thing is that, that rattles round so merrily?" said the girl, and she took the spindle and wanted to spin too. But scarcely had she touched the spindle when the magic decree was fulfilled, and she pricked her finger with it.

And, in the very moment when she felt the prick, she fell down upon the bed that stood there, and lay in a deep sleep. And this sleep extended over the whole palace; the King and Queen who had just come home, and had entered the great hall, began to go to sleep, and the whole of the court with them. The horses, too, went to sleep in the stable, the dogs in the yard, the pigeons upon the roof, the flies on the wall; even the fire that was flaming on the hearth became quiet and slept, the roast meat left off frizzling, and the cook, who was just going to pull the hair of the scullery boy, because he had forgotten something, let him go, and went to sleep. And the wind fell, and on the trees before the castle not a leaf moved again.

But round about the castle there began to grow a hedge of thorns, which every year became higher, and at last grew close up round the castle and all over it, so that there was nothing of it to be seen, not even the flag upon the roof. But the story of the beautiful sleeping "Briar-

rose," for so the princess was named, went about the country, so that from time to time kings' sons came and tried to get through the thorny hedge into the castle. But they found it impossible, for the thorns held fast together, as if they had hands, and the youths were caught in them, could not get loose again, and died a miserable death.

After long, long years a King's son came again to that country, and heard an old man talking about the thorn-hedge, and that a castle was said to stand behind it in which a wonderfully beautiful princess, named Briar-rose, had been asleep for a hundred years; and that the King and Queen and the whole court were asleep likewise. He had heard, too, from his grandfather, that many kings' sons had already come, and had tried to get through the thorny hedge, but they had remained sticking fast in it, and had died a pitiful death.

Then the youth said, "I am not afraid, I will go and see the beautiful Briar-rose." The good old man might dissuade him as he would, he did not listen to his words.

But by this time the hundred years had just passed, and the day had come when Briar-rose was to awake again. When the King's son came near to the thorn-hedge, it was nothing but large and beautiful flowers, which parted from each other of their own accord, and let him pass unhurt, then they closed again behind him like a hedge. In the castle-yard he saw the horses and the spotted hounds lying asleep; on the roof sat the pigeons with their heads under their wings. And when he entered the house, the flies were asleep upon the wall, the cook in the kitchen was still holding out his hand to seize the boy, and the maid was sitting by the black hen which she was going to pluck.

He went on farther, and in the great hall he saw the whole of the court lying asleep, and up by the throne lay the King and Queen. Then he went on still farther, and all was so quiet that a breath could be heard, and at last he came to the tower, and opened the door into the little room where Briar-rose was sleeping. There she lay, so beautiful that he could not turn his eyes away; and he stooped down and gave her a kiss. But as soon as he kissed her, Briar-rose opened her eyes and awoke, and looked at him quite sweetly.

Then they went down together, and the King awoke, and the Queen, and the whole court, and looked at each other in great astonishment. And the horses in the court-yard stood up and shook themselves; the hounds jumped up and wagged their tails; the pigeons upon the roof pulled out their heads from under their wings, looked round, and flew into the open country; the flies on the wall crept again; the fire in the kitchen burned up and flickered and cooked the meat; the joint began to turn and frizzle again, and the cook gave the boy such a box on the ear that he screamed, and the maid plucked the fowl ready for the spit.

And then the marriage of the King's son with Briar-rose was celebrated with all splendour, and they lived contented to the end of their days.

King Thrushbeard

A KING had a daughter who was beautiful beyond all measure, but so proud and haughty withal that no suitor was good enough for her. She sent away one after the other, and ridiculed them as well.

Once the King made a great feast and invited thereto, from far and near, all the young men likely to marry. They were all marshalled in a row according to their rank and standing; first came the kings, then the grand-dukes, then the princes, the earls, the barons, and the gentry.

Then the King's daughter was led through the ranks, but to everyone she had some objection to make; one was too fat, "The wine-cask," she said. Another was too tall, "Long and thin has little in." The third was too short, "Short and thick is never quick." The fourth was too pale, "As pale as death." The fifth too red, "A fighting-cock." The sixth was not straight enough, "A green log dried behind the stove."

So she had something to say against everyone, but she made herself especially merry over a good king who stood quite high up in the row, and whose chin had grown a little crooked. "Well," she cried and laughed, "he has a chin like a thrush's beak!" and from that time he got the name of King Thrushbeard.

But the old King, when he saw that his daughter did nothing but mock the people, and despised all the suitors who were gathered there, was very angry, and swore that she should have for her husband the very first beggar that came to his doors.

A few days afterwards a fiddler came and sang beneath the windows, trying to earn a small alms. When the King heard him, he said, "Let him come up."

So the fiddler came in, in his dirty, ragged clothes, and sang before the King and his daughter, and when he had ended, he asked for a trifling gift. The King said, "Your song has pleased me so well that I will give you my daughter there, to wife."

The King's daughter shuddered, but the King said, "I have taken an oath to give you to the very first beggar-man, and I will keep it."

All she could say was in vain; the priest was brought, and she had to let herself be wedded to the fiddler on the spot. When that was done, the King said, "Now it is not proper for you, a beggar-woman, to stay any longer in my palace, you may just go away with your husband."

The beggar-man led her out by the hand, and she was obliged to walk away on foot with him. When they came to a large forest, she asked, "To whom does that beautiful forest belong?"

"It belongs to King Thrushbeard; if you had taken him, it would have been yours."

"Ah, unhappy girl that I am, if I had but taken King Thrushbeard!"

Afterwards they came to a meadow, and she asked again, "To whom does this beautiful green meadow belong?"

"It belongs to King Thrushbeard; if you had taken him, it would have been yours."

"Ah, unhappy girl that I am, if I had but taken King Thrushbeard!"

Then they came to a large town, and she asked again, "To whom does this fine large town belong?"

"It belongs to King Thrushbeard; if you had taken him, it would have been yours."

"Ah, unhappy girl that I am, if I had but taken King Thrushbeard!"

"It does not please me," said the fiddler, "to hear you always wishing for another husband; am I not good enough for you?"

At last they came to a very little hut, and she said, "Oh, goodness! what a small house; to whom does this miserable, mean hovel belong?"

The fiddler answered, "That is my house and yours, where we shall live together."

She had to stoop in order to go in at the low door.

"Where are the servants?" said the King's daughter.

"What servants?" answered the beggar-man; "you must yourself do what you wish to have done. Just make a fire at once, and set on water to cook my supper, I am quite tired."

But the King's daughter knew nothing about lighting fires or cooking, and the beggar-man had to lend a hand himself to get anything fairly done. When they had finished their scanty meal, they went to bed; but he forced her to get up quite early in the morning in order to look after the house.

For a few days they lived in this way as well as might be, and finished all their provisions. Then the man said, "Wife, we cannot go on any longer eating and drinking here and earning nothing. You must weave baskets."

He went out, cut some willows, and brought them home. Then she began to weave, but the tough willows wounded her delicate hands.

"I see that this will not do," said the man; "you had better spin, perhaps you can do that better."

She sat down and tried to spin, but the hard thread soon cut her soft fingers so that the blood ran down.

"See," said the man, "you are fit for no sort of work; I have made a bad bargain with you. Now I will try to make a business with pots and earthenware; you must sit in the market-place and sell the ware."

"Alas," thought she, "if any of the people from my father's kingdom come to the market and see me sitting there, selling, how they will mock me?" But it was of no use, she had to yield unless she chose to die of hunger.

For the first time she succeeded well, for the people were glad to buy the woman's wares because she was good-looking, and they paid her what she asked; many even gave her the money and left the pots with her as well. So they lived on what she had earned as long as it lasted, then the husband bought a lot of new crockery. With this she sat down at the corner of the market-place, and set it out round about her ready for sale. But suddenly there came a drunken hussar galloping along, and he rode right amongst the pots so that they were all broken into a thousand bits.

She began to weep, and did not know what to do for fear. "Alas! what will happen to me?" cried she; "what will my husband say to this?"

She ran home and told him of the misfortune. "Who would seat herself at a corner of the market-place with crockery?" said the man; "leave off crying, I see very well that you cannot do any ordinary work, so I have been to our King's palace and have asked whether they cannot find a place for a kitchen-maid, and they have promised me to take you; in that way you will get your food for nothing."

The King's daughter was now a kitchen-maid, and had to be at the cook's beck and call, and do the dirtiest work. In both her pockets she fastened a little jar, in which she took home her share of the leavings, and upon this they lived.

It happened that the wedding of the King's eldest son was to be celebrated, so the poor woman went up and placed herself by the door of the hall to look on. When all the candles were lit, and people, each more beautiful than the other, entered, and all was full of pomp and splendour, she thought of her lot with a sad heart, and cursed the pride and haughtiness which had humbled her and brought her to so great poverty.

The smell of the delicious dishes which were being taken in and out reached her, and now and then the servants threw her a few morsels of them: these she put in her jars to take home.

All at once the King's son entered, clothed in velvet and silk, with gold chains about his neck. And when he saw the beautiful woman standing by the door, he seized her by the hand, and would have danced with her; but she refused and shrank with fear, for she saw that it was King Thrushbeard, her suitor whom she had driven away with scorn. Her struggles were of no avail, he drew her into the hall; but the string by which her pockets were hung broke, the pots fell down, the soup ran out, and the scraps were scattered all about.

And when the people saw it, there arose general laughter and derision, and she was so ashamed that she would rather have been a thousand fathoms below the ground. She sprang to the door and would have run away, but on the stairs a man caught her and brought her back; and when she looked at him, it was King Thrushbeard again. He said to her kindly, "Do not be afraid, I and the fiddler who has been living with you in that wretched hovel are one. For love of you I disguised myself so; and I also was the hussar who rode through your crockery. This was all done to humble your proud spirit, and to punish you for the insolence with which you mocked me."

Then she wept bitterly and said, "I have done great wrong, and am not worthy to be your wife."

But he said, "Be comforted, the evil days are past; now we will celebrate our wedding."

Then the maids-in-waiting came and put on her the most splendid clothing, and her father and his whole court came and wished her happiness in her marriage with King Thrushbeard, and the joy now began in earnest. I wish you and I had been there too.

Little Snow White

T WAS in the middle of winter, when the flakes of snow were falling like feathers from the sky, a queen sat at a window sewing; the frame of the window was made of black ebony. And whilst she was sewing and looking out of the window at the snow, she pricked her finger with the needle, and three drops of blood fell upon the snow.

The red looked pretty on the white snow, and she thought to herself, "I wish that I had a child as white as snow, as red as blood, and as black as the wood of the window frame".

Soon after that, she had a little daughter, who was as white as snow and as red as blood, and her hair was as black as ebony; and she was therefore called Snow White. But when the child was born, the Queen died.

After a year had passed, the King decided to marry another woman. She was beautiful, but proud and haughty, and she could not bear that anyone else should be more beautiful than she was.

She had a wonderful mirror: when she stood in front of it, looked at herself in it, and said:

> "Mirror, mirror, on the wall,
> Who in this land is the fairest of all?"

the mirror answered:

> "You, O Queen, are the fairest of all!"

Then she was satisfied, for she knew that the mirror spoke the truth.

But Snow White was growing up and she was growing more and more beautiful. When she was seven years old, she was as beautiful as the day and more beautiful than the Queen herself. And when the Queen asked her mirror:

> "Mirror, mirror, on the wall,
> Who in this land is the fairest of all?"

it answered:

175

"You are fairer than all who are here, Lady Queen.
But more beautiful still is Snow White, as I've seen ."

Then the Queen was shocked, and turned yellow and green with envy. From that moment on, whenever she looked at Snow White, her heart heaved in her chest, because she hated the girl so much.

Envy and pride grew higher and higher in her heart like a weed, so that she had no peace, day or night.

She called a huntsman and said, "Take the child away into the forest and kill her; I cannot bear to see her any longer".

The huntsman obeyed and took her away; but when he had drawn his knife and was about to pierce Snow White's innocent heart, she began to weep and said, "Ah, dear huntsman, spare my life! I will run away into the wild forest and never come home again."

And she was so beautiful that the huntsman took pity on her and said, "Run away, then, you poor child".

"The wild beasts will soon devour you," he thought, however it seemed as if a stone had been rolled from his heart, as he was no longer expected to kill her.

But now the poor child was all alone in the great forest and so terrified that she looked at every leaf of every tree and did not know what to do. Then she began to run, and she ran over sharp stones and through thorns, and the wild beasts ran past her but did her no harm.

She ran as long as her feet would go until it was almost evening; then she saw a little cottage and went into it to have a rest. Everything in the cottage was small, but neater and cleaner than you can imagine. There was a table with a white tablecloth and seven little plates, and on each plate was a little spoon; in addition, there were seven little knives and forks, and seven little mugs. Against the wall stood seven little beds side by side, covered with snow-white blankets.

Snow White was so hungry and thirsty that she ate some vegetables and bread from each plate and drank a drop of wine out of each mug, for she did not wish to take everything from just one person.

Then, because she was so tired, she laid herself down on one of the little beds, but none of them suited her: one was too long, another too short, but at last she found that the seventh one was right, and so she stayed in it, said her prayers and went to sleep.

When it was quite dark, the owners of the cottage came back home: they were seven dwarfs, who dug and delved in the mountains for ore. They lit their seven candles, and once it was light inside the cottage, they saw that someone had been there, for nothing was in the same place as they had left it.

The first said, "Who has been sitting on my chair?"

The second: "Who has been eating off my plate?"

The third: "Who has been taking some of my bread?"

The fourth: "Who has been eating my vegetables?"

The fifth: "Who has been using my fork?"

The sixth: "Who has been cutting with my knife?"

The seventh: "Who has been drinking out of my mug?"

Then the first looked round and saw that there was a little hollow on his bed, and he said, "Who has been getting into my bed?" The others came up and each called out, "Somebody has been lying in my bed too."

But the seventh, when he looked at his bed, saw Snow White lying asleep there. And he called the others, who came running up, and they shouted with astonishment, and brought their seven little candles and let the light fall on Snow White.

"Oh, heavens! Oh, heavens!" they cried, "what a lovely child!" and they were so glad to see her that they did not wake her up, but let her sleep on in the bed. And the seventh dwarf shared the beds of his companions, spending one hour with each, and so got through the night.

When it was morning, Snow White awoke and was frightened when she saw the seven dwarfs. But they were friendly and asked her what her name was.

"My name is Snow White," she answered.

"How have you come to our house?" said the dwarfs.

Then she told them that her step-mother had wished to have her killed, but that the huntsman had spared her life and that she had run for the whole day, until at last she had found their house.

The dwarfs said, "If you take care of our house, cook, make the beds, wash, sew, and knit, and keep everything neat and clean, you can stay with us and you shall have everything you need".

"Yes," said Snow White, "I will do that with all of my heart," and she stayed with them.

She kept the house in order for them. In the mornings they went to the mountains and looked for copper and gold; in the evenings they came back, and their supper had to be ready.

The girl was alone for the whole day, so the good dwarfs warned her and said, "Beware of your step-mother: she will soon know that you are here; be sure that you don't let anyone come in."

But the Queen, believing that Snow White was dead, could only think that she was again the first and most beautiful of all, so she went to her mirror and said:

"Mirror, mirror, on the wall,
Who in this land is the fairest of all?"

And the mirror answered:

"Oh, Queen, you are the fairest of all I see,
But over the hills, where the seven dwarfs dwell,
Snow White is still alive and well,
And no one is as fair as she."

Then she was astonished, because she knew that the mirror never lied, and she knew that the huntsman had betrayed her and that Snow White was still alive.

And so she thought and thought again about how she could kill her, for so long as she was not the fairest in the whole land, her envy did not let her rest. And when she had at last thought of something to do, she painted her face and dressed herself like an old door-to-door saleswoman, and no one would have recognised her. In this disguise, she went over the seven mountains to the seven dwarfs and knocked at the door and cried, "Pretty things to sell, very cheap, very cheap".

Snow White looked out of the window and called out, "Hello, my good woman, what have you got to sell?"

"Good things, pretty things," she answered; "corset-laces of all colours," and she pulled out one which was woven of brightly coloured silk.

"I think I can let this worthy old woman in," thought Snow White, and she unbolted the door and bought the pretty laces.

"Child," said the old woman, "how terrible you look; come here, I will lace you properly for once".

Snow White suspected nothing, but stood before her and let herself be laced into her corset with the new laces. But the old woman laced so quickly and laced so tightly that Snow White could not breathe and fell down as if she was dead.

"Now I am the most beautiful," said the Queen to herself, and ran away.

Not long afterwards, in the evening, the seven dwarfs came home, but imagine how shocked they were when they saw their dear Snow White lying on the ground, neither stirring nor moving and looking like she was dead. They lifted her up, and, seeing that her corset was laced too tightly, they cut the laces; then she began to breathe a little and after a while came to life again.

When the dwarfs heard what had happened, they said, "The old woman was none other than the wicked Queen; take care and don't let anyone come in when we are not with you."

But the wicked woman, when she had reached home, stood in front of the mirror and asked:

> "Mirror, mirror, on the wall,
> Who in this land is the fairest of all?"

And it answered as before:

> "Oh, Queen, you are the fairest of all I see,
> But over the hills, where the seven dwarfs dwell,
> Snow White is still alive and well,
> And no one is as fair as she."

179

When she heard that, all of her blood rushed to her heart with fear, for she saw plainly that Snow White had come back to life. "But now," she said, "I will think of something that will put an end to you," and with the help of witchcraft, which she understood, she made a poisonous comb. Then she disguised herself and took the shape of another old woman. So she went over the seven mountains to the seven dwarfs, knocked at the door and cried, "Good things to sell, cheap, cheap!"

Snow White looked out and said, "Go away; I cannot let anyone come in."

"I suppose that you can look," said the old woman and pulled the poisonous comb out and held it up.

The girl liked it so much that she let herself be tricked and opened the door.

When they had made a deal, the old woman said, "Now I will comb your hair properly for once".

Poor Snow White suspected nothing and let the old woman do as she wished, but she had only just put the comb in her hair than the poison took effect and the girl fell down senseless.

"You paragon of beauty," said the wicked woman, "you are done for now," and she went away.

But fortunately it was almost evening and time for the seven dwarfs to come home. When they saw Snow White lying on the ground as if she was dead, they at once suspected the step-mother, and they looked and found the poisoned comb sticking in her head. Moments after they had taken it out, Snow White came round and told them what had happened. Then they warned her once more to be on her guard and to not open the door to anyone.

Once the Queen had got home, she stood in front of the mirror and said:

> "Mirror, mirror, on the wall,
> Who in this land is the fairest of all?"

Then it answered as before:

> "Oh, Queen, you are the fairest of all I see.
> But over the hills, where the seven dwarfs dwell,
> Snow White is still alive and well,
> And no one is as fair as she."

When she heard the mirror say this, she trembled and shook with rage. "Snow White shall die," she cried, "even if it costs me my life!"

With that, she went into a quite secret, lonely room, where no one ever went, and there she made a very poisonous apple. Outside it looked pretty, white with a red bloom to it, so that everyone who saw it longed for it; but whoever ate a piece of it must surely die.

When the apple was ready, she painted her face and dressed herself up as a farming woman, and so she went over the seven mountains to the seven dwarfs. She knocked at the door.

Snow White put her head out of the window and said, "I cannot let anyone in; the seven dwarfs have forbidden me to".

"It is all the same to me," answered the woman, "I shall soon get rid of my apples. There, I will give you one."

"No," said Snow White, "I do not dare to take anything".

"Are you afraid of poison?" said the old woman. "Look, I will cut the apple in two pieces; you eat the red side, and I will eat the white."

The apple was so cleverly made that only the red cheek was poisoned. Snow White longed for the fine apple; and when she saw that the woman was eating part of it, she could not resist any longer, stretched out her hand and took the poisonous half. But she had hardly taken a bite out of it than she fell down dead.

Then the Queen looked at her with a dreadful look and laughed out loud and said, "White as snow, red as blood, black as ebony wood! This time the dwarfs cannot wake you up again."

At home she asked the mirror:

> "Mirror, mirror, on the wall,
> Who in this land is the fairest of all?"

It answered at last:

> "Oh, Queen, in this land you are the fairest of all."

Then her envious heart could rest, as much as an envious heart like hers can rest.

The dwarfs, when they came home in the evening, found Snow White lying on the ground; she was not breathing, and was dead.

They lifted her up, looked to see whether they could find anything poisonous, unlaced her, combed her hair, washed her with water and wine, but nothing was any use: the poor child was dead and remained dead.

They laid her on a bier, and all seven of them sat round it and wept for her, for three long days.

Then it was time to bury her, but she still looked as if she was living, and still had her pretty red cheeks. They said, "We cannot bury her in the dark ground," and they had a transparent coffin of glass made, so that she could be seen from all sides, and they laid her in it and wrote her name upon it in golden letters, and wrote that she was a king's daughter. Then they put the coffin out on the mountain, and one of them always stayed by it and watched it.

The birds came, too, and wept for Snow White; first an owl, then a raven, and last a dove. And Snow White lay for a long, long time in the coffin, and she did not change, but looked like she was asleep; for she was as white as snow, as red as blood, and her hair was as black as ebony.

It happened, however, that a king's son came into the forest and went to the dwarfs' house to spend the night. He saw the coffin on the mountain and the beautiful Snow White within it, and read what was written on it in golden letters. Then he said to the dwarfs, "Let me have the coffin, I will give you whatever you want for it".

But the dwarfs answered, "We will not part with it for all the gold in the world".

Then he said, "Let me have it as a gift, for I cannot live without seeing Snow White. I will honour and prize her as my dearest possession."

Because he had spoken in this way, the good dwarfs took pity upon him and gave him the coffin.

And now the King's son had it carried away by his servants on their shoulders. It so happened that they stumbled over a tree stump, and with the bump, the poisonous piece of apple, which Snow White had bitten off, came out of her throat. Before long, she opened her eyes, lifted up the lid of the coffin, sat up, and was alive again.

"Oh, goodness me, where am I?" she cried.

The King's son, full of joy, said, "You are with me," and told her what had happened. He said, "I love you more than everything in the world; come with me to my father's palace, and you shall be my wife".

183

And Snow White was happy to do that and she accompanied him, and their wedding was held with great show and splendour. But Snow White's wicked step-mother was also invited to the feast. She dressed herself in beautiful clothes, stood before the mirror and said:

"Mirror, mirror, on the wall,
Who in this land is the fairest of all?"

The mirror answered:

"Oh, Queen, out of all here the fairest is you, but know
The young Queen is fairer than you, though."

Then the wicked woman uttered a curse and was so wretched, so utterly wretched, that she did not know what to do. At first she did not want to go to the wedding at all, but she could not get any peace and had go to see the young Queen.

When she went in, she recognised Snow White and became so overwhelmed with rage and jealousy that she fell down dead.

Rumpelstiltskin

HERE was once a miller who was poor, but who had a beautiful daughter. Now it happened that he had to go and speak to the King, and in order to make himself appear important he said to him, "I have a daughter who can spin straw into gold."

The King said to the miller, "That is an art which pleases me well; if your daughter is as clever as you say, bring her tomorrow to my palace, and I will try what she can do."

And when the girl was brought to him, he took her into a room which was quite full of straw, gave her a spinning-wheel and a reel, and said, "Now set to work, and if by tomorrow morning early you have not spun this straw into gold during the night, you must die." Thereupon he himself locked up the room, and left her in it alone.

So there sat the poor miller's daughter, and for her life could not tell what to do; she had no idea how straw could be spun into gold, and she grew more and more miserable, until at last she began to weep.

But all at once the door opened, and in came a little man, and said, "Good evening, Mistress Miller; why are you crying so?"

"Alas!" answered the girl, "I have to spin straw into gold, and I do not know how to do it."

"What will you give me," said the manikin, "if I do it for you?"

"My necklace," said the girl.

The little man took the necklace, seated himself in front of the wheel, and "whirr, whirr, whirr," three turns, and the reel was full; then he put another on, and whirr, whirr, whirr, three times round, and the second was full too. And so it went on until the morning, when all the straw was spun, and all the reels were full of gold.

By daybreak the King was already there, and when he saw the gold, he was astonished and delighted, but his heart became only more greedy. He had the miller's daughter taken into another room full of straw, which was much larger, and commanded her to spin that also in one night if she valued her life.

185

The girl knew not how to help herself, and was crying, when the door again opened, and the little man appeared, and said, "What will you give me if I spin the straw into gold for you?"

"The ring on my finger," answered the girl.

The little man took the ring, again began to turn the wheel, and by morning had spun all the straw into glittering gold.

The King rejoiced beyond measure at the sight, but still he had not gold enough; and he had the miller's daughter taken into a still larger room full of straw, and said, "You must spin this, too, in the course of this night; but if you succeed, you shall be my wife."

"Even if she be a miller's daughter," thought he, "I could not find a richer wife in the whole world."

When the girl was alone, the manikin came again for the third time, and said, "What will you give me if I spin the straw for you this time also?"

"I have nothing left that I could give," answered the girl.

"Then promise me, if you should become Queen, your first child."

"Who knows whether that will ever happen?" thought the miller's daughter; and, not knowing how else to help herself in this strait, she promised the manikin what he wanted, and for that he once more span the straw into gold.

And when the King came in the morning, and found all as he had wished, he took her in marriage, and the pretty miller's daughter became a Queen.

A year after, she had a beautiful child, and she never gave a thought to the manikin. But suddenly he came into her room, and said, "Now give me what you promised."

The Queen was horror-struck, and offered the manikin all the riches of the kingdom if he would leave her the child. But the manikin said, "No, something that is living is dearer to me than all the treasures in the world."

Then the Queen began to weep and cry, so that the manikin pitied her. "I will give you three days' time," said he; "if by that time you find out my name, then shall you keep your child."

So the Queen thought the whole night of all the names that she had ever heard, and she sent a messenger over the country to inquire, far and wide, for any other names that there might be. When the manikin came the next day, she began with Caspar, Melchior, Balthazar, and said all the names she knew, one after another; but to everyone the little man said, "That is not my name."

On the second day she had inquiries made in the neighbourhood as to the names of the people there, and she repeated to the manikin the most uncommon and curious. "Perhaps your name is Shortribs, or Sheepshanks, or Laceleg?" but he always answered, "That is not my name."

On the third day the messenger came back again, and said, "I have not been able to find a single new name, but as I came to a high mountain at the end of the forest, where the fox and the hare bid each other good night, there I saw a little house, and before the house a fire was burning, and round about the fire quite a ridiculous little man was jumping: he hopped upon one leg, and shouted—

'Today I bake, tomorrow brew,
The next I'll have the young Queen's child.
Ha! glad am I that no one knew
That Rumpelstiltskin I am styled.'

You may think how glad the Queen was when she heard the name! And when soon afterwards the little man came in, and asked, "Now, Mistress Queen, what is my name?" at first she said, "Is your name Conrad?"

"No."

"Is your name Harry?"

"No."

"Perhaps your name is Rumpelstiltskin?"

"The devil has told you that! the devil has told you that!" cried the little man, and in his anger he plunged his right foot so deep into the earth that his whole leg went in; and then in rage he pulled at his left leg so hard with both hands that he tore himself in two.

The Golden Bird

N THE olden time there was a king, who had behind his palace a beautiful pleasure-garden in which there was a tree that bore golden apples. When the apples were getting ripe, they were counted, but on the very next morning one was missing. This was told to the King, and he ordered that a watch should be kept every night beneath the tree.

The King had three sons, the eldest of whom he sent, as soon as night came on, into the garden; but when midnight came, he could not keep himself from sleeping, and next morning again an apple was gone.

The following night the second son had to keep watch, it fared no better with him; as soon as twelve o'clock had struck he fell asleep, and in the morning an apple was gone.

Now it came to the turn of the third son to watch; and he was quite ready, but the King had not much trust in him, and thought that he would be of less use even than his brothers; but at last he let him go. The youth lay down beneath the tree, but kept awake, and did not let sleep master him.

When it struck twelve, something rustled through the air, and in the moonlight he saw a bird coming whose feathers were all shining with gold. The bird alighted on the tree, and had just plucked off an apple, when the youth shot an arrow at him. The bird flew off, but the arrow had struck his plumage, and one of his golden feathers fell down.

The youth picked it up, and the next morning took it to the King and told him what he had seen in the night. The King called his council together, and everyone declared that a feather like this was worth more than the whole kingdom.

"If the feather is so precious," declared the King, "one alone will not do for me; I must and will have the whole bird!"

The eldest son set out; he trusted to his cleverness, and thought that he would easily find the Golden Bird. When he had gone some distance, he saw a Fox sitting at the edge of a wood, so he cocked his gun and took aim at him.

The Fox cried, "Do not shoot me! and in return I will give you some good counsel. You are on the way to the Golden Bird; and this evening you will come to a village in which stand two inns opposite to one another. One of them is lighted up brightly, and all goes on merrily within, but do not go into it; go rather into the other, even though it seems a bad one."

"How can such a silly beast give wise advice?" thought the King's son, and he pulled the trigger. But he missed the Fox, who stretched out his tail and ran quickly into the wood.

So he pursued his way, and by evening came to the village where the two inns were; in one they were singing and dancing; the other had a poor, miserable look. "I should be a fool, indeed," he thought, "if I were to go into the shabby tavern, and pass by the good one." So he went into the cheerful one, lived there in riot and revel, and forgot the bird and his father, and all good counsels.

When some time had passed, and the eldest son for month after month did not come back home, the second set out, wishing to find the Golden Bird. The Fox met him as he had met the eldest, and gave him the good advice of which he took no heed. He came to the two inns, and his brother was standing at the window of the one from which came the music, and called out to him. He could not resist, but went inside and lived only for pleasure.

Again some time passed, and then the King's youngest son wanted to set off and try his luck, but his father would not allow it. "It is of no use," said he, "he will find the Golden Bird still less than his brothers, and if a mishap were to befall him he knows not how to help himself; he is a little wanting at the best." But at last, as he had no peace, he let him go.

Again the Fox was sitting outside the wood, and begged for his life, and offered his good advice. The youth was good-natured, and said, "Be easy, little Fox, I will do you no harm."

"You shall not repent it," answered the Fox; "and that you may get on more quickly, get up behind on my tail."

And scarcely had he seated himself when the Fox began to run, and away he went over stock and stone till his hair whistled in the wind. When they came to the village, the youth got off; he followed the good advice, and without looking round turned into the little inn, where he spent the night quietly.

The next morning, as soon as he got into the open country, there sat the Fox already, and said, "I will tell you further what you have to do. Go on quite straight, and at last you will come to a castle, in front of which a whole regiment of soldiers is lying, but do not trouble yourself about them, for they will all be asleep and snoring. Go through the midst of them straight into the castle, and go through all the rooms, till at last you will come to a chamber where a Golden Bird is hanging in a wooden cage. Close by, there stands an empty gold cage for show, but

beware of taking the bird out of the common cage and putting it into the fine one, or it may go badly with you."

With these words the Fox again stretched out his tail, and the King's son seated himself upon it, and away he went over stock and stone till his hair whistled in the wind.

When he came to the castle, he found everything as the Fox had said. The King's son went into the chamber where the Golden Bird was shut up in a wooden cage, whilst a golden one stood hard by; and the three golden apples lay about the room. "But," thought he, "it would be absurd if I were to leave the beautiful bird in the common and ugly cage," so he opened the door, laid hold of it, and put it into the golden cage. But at the same moment the bird uttered a shrill cry. The soldiers awoke, rushed in, and took him off to prison.

The next morning he was taken before a court of justice, and as he confessed everything, was sentenced to death. The King, however, said that he would grant him his life on one condition—namely, if he brought him the Golden Horse which ran faster than the wind; and in that case he should receive, over and above, as a reward, the Golden Bird.

The King's son set off, but he sighed and was sorrowful, for how was he to find the Golden Horse? But all at once he saw his old friend the Fox sitting on the road.

"Look you," said the Fox, "this has happened because you did not give heed to me. However, be of good courage. I will give you my help, and tell you how to get to the Golden Horse. You must go straight on, and you will come to a castle, where in the stable stands the horse. The grooms will be lying in front of the stable; but they will be asleep and snoring, and you can quietly lead out the Golden Horse. But of one thing you must take heed; put on him the common saddle of wood and leather, and not the golden one, which hangs close by, else it will go ill with you."

Then the Fox stretched out his tail, the King's son seated himself upon it, and away he went over stock and stone until his hair whistled in the wind.

Everything happened just as the Fox had said; the prince came to the stable in which the Golden Horse was standing, but just as he was going to put the common saddle upon him, he thought, "It will be a shame to such a beautiful beast, if I do not give him the good saddle which belongs to him by right." But scarcely had the golden saddle touched the horse than he began to neigh loudly. The grooms awoke, seized the youth, and threw him into prison.

The next morning he was sentenced by the court to death; but the King promised to grant him his life, and the Golden Horse as well, if he could bring back the beautiful princess from the Golden Castle.

With a heavy heart the youth set out; yet luckily for him he soon found the trusty Fox. "I ought only to leave you to your ill-luck," said the Fox, "but I pity you, and will help you once more out of your trouble. This road takes you straight to the Golden Castle, you will reach it by eventide; and at night, when everything is quiet, the beautiful princess goes to the bathing-house to bathe. When she enters it, run up to her and give her a kiss, then she will follow you, and you can take her away with you; only do not allow her to take leave of her parents first, or it will go ill with you."

Then the Fox stretched out his tail, the King's son seated himself upon it, and away the Fox went, over stock and stone, till his hair whistled in the wind.

When he reached the Golden Castle, it was just as the Fox had said. He waited until midnight, when everything lay in deep sleep, and the beautiful princess was going to the bathing-house. Then he sprang out and gave her a kiss. She said that she would like to go with him, but she asked him pitifully, and with tears, to allow her first to take leave of her parents. At first he withstood her prayer, but when she wept more and more, and fell at his feet, he at last gave in. But no sooner had the maiden reached the bedside of her father than he and all the rest in the castle awoke, and the youth was laid hold of and put into prison.

The next morning the King said to him, "Your life is forfeited, and you can only find mercy if you take away the hill which stands in front of my windows, and prevents my seeing beyond it; and you must finish it all within eight days. If you do that you shall have my daughter as your reward."

The King's son began, and dug and shovelled without leaving off, but when after seven days he saw how little he had done, and how all his work was as good as nothing, he fell into great sorrow and gave up all hope. But on the evening of the seventh day the Fox appeared and said, "You do not deserve that I should take any trouble about you; but just go away and lie down to sleep, and I will do the work for you."

The next morning when he awoke and looked out of the window, the hill had gone. The youth ran, full of joy, to the King, and told him that the task was fulfilled, and whether he liked it or not, the King had to hold to his word and give him his daughter.

So the two set forth together, and it was not long before the trusty Fox came up with them. "You have certainly got what is best," said he, "but the Golden Horse also belongs to the maiden of the Golden Castle."

"How shall I get it?" asked the youth.

"That I will tell you," answered the Fox. "First take the beautiful maiden to the King who sent you to the Golden Castle. There will be unheard-of rejoicing; they will gladly give you the Golden Horse, and will bring it out to you. Mount it as soon as possible, and offer your hand to all in farewell; last of all to the beautiful maiden. And as soon as you have taken her hand swing her up on to the horse, and gallop away, and no one will be able to bring you back, for the horse runs faster than the wind."

All was carried out successfully, and the King's son carried off the beautiful princess on the Golden Horse.

The Fox did not remain behind, and he said to the youth, "Now I will help you to get the Golden Bird. When you come near to the castle where the Golden Bird is to be found, let the maiden get down, and I will take her into my care. Then ride with the Golden Horse into the castle-yard; there will be great rejoicing at the sight, and they will bring out the Golden Bird for you. As soon as you have the cage in your hand gallop back to us, and take the maiden away again. ”

When the plan had succeeded, and the King's son was about to ride home with his treasures, the Fox said, “Now you shall reward me for my help.”

“What do you require for it?” asked the youth.

“When you get into the wood yonder, shoot me dead, and chop off my head and feet.”

“That would be fine gratitude,” said the King's son. “I cannot possibly do that for you.”

The Fox said, “If you will not do it I must leave you, but before I go away I will give you a piece of good advice. Be careful about two things. Buy no gallows'-flesh, and do not sit at the edge of any well.” And then he ran into the wood.

The youth thought, "That is a wonderful beast, he has strange whims; who is going to buy gallows'-flesh? and the desire to sit at the edge of a well it has never yet seized me."

He rode on with the beautiful maiden, and his road took him again through the village in which his two brothers had remained. There was a great stir and noise, and, when he asked what was going on, he was told that two men were going to be hanged. As he came nearer to the place, he saw that they were his brothers, who had been playing all kinds of wicked pranks, and had squandered all their wealth. He inquired whether they could not be set free.

"If you will pay for them," answered the people; "but why should you waste your money on wicked men, and buy them free."

He did not think twice about it, but paid for them, and when they were set free, they all went on their way together.

They came to the wood where the Fox had first met them, and, as it was cool and pleasant within it, whilst the sun shone hotly, the two brothers said, "Let us rest a little by the well, and eat and drink."

He agreed, and whilst they were talking he forgot himself, and sat down upon the edge of the well without thinking of any evil. But the two brothers threw him backwards into the well, took the maiden, the Horse, and the Bird, and went home to their father.

"Here we bring you not only the Golden Bird," said they; "we have won the Golden Horse also, and the maiden from the Golden Castle."

Then was there great joy; but the Horse would not eat, the Bird would not sing, and the maiden sat and wept.

But the youngest brother was not dead. By good fortune the well was dry, and he fell upon soft moss without being hurt, but he could not get out again. Even in this strait the faithful Fox did not leave him: it came and leapt down to him, and upbraided him for having forgotten its advice.

"But yet I cannot give it up so," he said; "I will help you up again into daylight." He bade him grasp his tail and keep tight hold of it; and then he pulled him up.

"You are not out of all danger yet," said the Fox. "Your brothers were not sure of your death, and have surrounded the wood with watchers, who are to kill you if you let yourself be seen."

But a poor man was sitting upon the road, with whom the youth changed clothes, and in this way he got to the King's palace. No one knew him, but the Bird began to sing, the Horse began to eat, and the beautiful maiden left off weeping.

The King, astonished, asked, "What does this mean?"

Then the maiden said, "I do not know, but I have been so sorrowful and now I am so happy! I feel as if my true bridegroom had come." She told him all that had happened, although the other brothers had threatened her with death if she were to betray anything.

The King commanded that all people who were in his castle should be brought before him; and amongst them came the youth in his ragged clothes; but the maiden knew him at once and fell upon his neck.

The wicked brothers were seized and put to death, but he was married to the beautiful maiden and declared heir to the King.

But how did it fare with the poor Fox? Long afterwards the King's son was once again walking in the wood, when the Fox met him and said, "You have everything now that you can wish for, but there is never an end to my misery, and yet it is in your power to free me," and again he asked him with tears to shoot him dead and to chop off his head and feet. So he did it, and scarcely was it done when the Fox was changed into a man, and was no other than the brother of the beautiful princess, who at last was freed from the magic charm which had been laid upon him. And now nothing more was wanting to their happiness as long as they lived.

Frederick and Catherine

HERE was once on a time a man who was called Frederick and a woman called Catherine, who had married each other and lived together as young married folks. One day Frederick said, "I will now go and plough, Catherine; when I come back, there must be some roast meat on the table for hunger, and a fresh draught for thirst."

"Just go, Frederick," answered Kate, "just go, I will have all ready for you."

Therefore when dinner-time drew near, she got a sausage out of the chimney, put it in the frying-pan, put some butter to it, and set it on the fire. The sausage began to fry and to hiss, Catherine stood beside it and held the handle of the pan, and had her own thoughts as she was doing it.

Then it occurred to her, "While the sausage is getting done thou couldst go into the cellar and draw beer." So she set the frying-pan safely on the fire, took a can, and went down into the cellar to draw beer.

The beer ran into the can and Kate watched it, and then she thought, "Oh, dear! The dog upstairs is not fastened up, it might get the sausage out of the pan. Well thought of." And in a trice she was up the cellar-steps again, but the Spitz had the sausage in its mouth already, and trailed it away on the ground.

But Catherine, who was not idle, set out after it, and chased it a long way into the field. The dog, however, was swifter than Catherine and did not let the sausage journey easily, but skipped over the furrows with it.

"What's gone is gone!" said Kate, and turned round, and as she had run till she was weary, she walked quietly and comfortably, and cooled herself. During this time the beer was still running out of the cask, for Kate had not turned the tap. And when the can was full and there was no other place for it, it ran into the cellar and did not stop until the whole cask was empty.

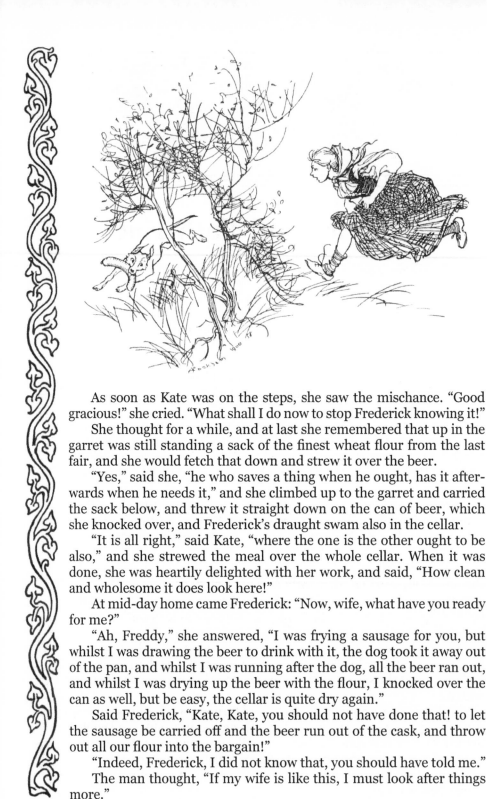

As soon as Kate was on the steps, she saw the mischance. "Good gracious!" she cried. "What shall I do now to stop Frederick knowing it!"

She thought for a while, and at last she remembered that up in the garret was still standing a sack of the finest wheat flour from the last fair, and she would fetch that down and strew it over the beer.

"Yes," said she, "he who saves a thing when he ought, has it afterwards when he needs it," and she climbed up to the garret and carried the sack below, and threw it straight down on the can of beer, which she knocked over, and Frederick's draught swam also in the cellar.

"It is all right," said Kate, "where the one is the other ought to be also," and she strewed the meal over the whole cellar. When it was done, she was heartily delighted with her work, and said, "How clean and wholesome it does look here!"

At mid-day home came Frederick: "Now, wife, what have you ready for me?"

"Ah, Freddy," she answered, "I was frying a sausage for you, but whilst I was drawing the beer to drink with it, the dog took it away out of the pan, and whilst I was running after the dog, all the beer ran out, and whilst I was drying up the beer with the flour, I knocked over the can as well, but be easy, the cellar is quite dry again."

Said Frederick, "Kate, Kate, you should not have done that! to let the sausage be carried off and the beer run out of the cask, and throw out all our flour into the bargain!"

"Indeed, Frederick, I did not know that, you should have told me."

The man thought, "If my wife is like this, I must look after things more."

Now he had got together a good number of thalers which he changed into gold, and said to Catherine, "Look, these are counters for playing games; I will put them in a pot and bury them in the stable under the cow's manger, but mind you keep away from them, or it will be the worse for you."

Said she, "Oh, no, Frederick, I certainly will not go."

And when Frederick was gone, some pedlars came into the village who had cheap earthen-bowls and pots, and asked the young woman if there was nothing she wanted to bargain with them for?

"Oh, dear people," said Catherine, "I have no money and can buy nothing, but if you have any use for yellow counters, I will buy of you."

"Yellow counters, why not? But just let us see them."

"Then go into the stable and dig under the cow's manger, and you will find the yellow counters. I am not allowed to go there."

The rogues went thither, dug and found pure gold. Then they laid hold of it, ran away, and left their pots and bowls behind in the house. Catherine thought she must use her new things, and as she had no lack in the kitchen already without these, she knocked the bottom out of every pot, and set them all as ornaments on the paling which went round about the house.

When Frederick came and saw the new decorations, he said, "Catherine, what have you been about?"

"I have bought them, Frederick, for the counters which were under the cow's manger. I did not go there myself, the pedlars had to dig them out for themselves."

"Ah, wife," said Frederick, "what have you done? Those were not counters, but pure gold, and all our wealth; you should not have done that."

"Indeed, Frederick," said she, "I did not know that, you should have forewarned me."

Catherine stood for a while and bethought herself; then she said, "Listen, Frederick, we will soon get the gold back again, we will run after the thieves."

"Come, then," said Frederick, "we will try it; but take with you some butter and cheese that we may have something to eat on the way."

"Yes, Frederick, I will take them."

They set out, and as Frederick was the better walker, Catherine followed him. "It is to my advantage," thought she, "when we turn back, I shall be a little way in advance."

Then she came to a hill where there were deep ruts on both sides of the road. "There one can see," said Catherine, "how they have torn and skinned and galled the poor earth, it will never be whole again as long as it lives," and in her heart's compassion she took her butter and smeared the ruts right and left, that the earth might not be so hurt by the wheels, and as she was thus bending down in her charity, one of the cheeses rolled out of her pocket down the hill.

Said Catherine, "I have made my way once up here, I will not go down again; another may run and fetch it back."

So she took another cheese and rolled it down. But the cheeses did not come back, so she let a third run down, thinking, "Perhaps they are waiting for company, and do not like to walk alone."

As all three stayed away she said, "I do not know what that can mean, but it may perhaps be that the third has not found the way, and has gone wrong, I will just send the fourth to call it."

But the fourth did no better than the third. Then Catherine was angry, and threw down the fifth and sixth as well, and these were her last.

She remained standing for some time watching for their coming, but when they still did not come, she said, "Oh, you are good folks to send in search of death, you stay a fine long time away! Do you think I will wait any longer for you? I shall go my way, you may run after me; you have younger legs than I."

Catherine went on and found Frederick, who was standing waiting for her because he wanted something to eat. "Now just let us have what you have brought with you," said he.

She gave him the dry bread.

"Where have you the butter and the cheeses?" asked the man.

"Ah, Freddy," said Catherine, "I smeared the cart-ruts with the butter and the cheeses will come soon; one ran away from me, so I sent the others after to call it."

Said Frederick, "You should not have done that, Catherine, to smear the butter on the road, and let the cheeses run down the hill!"

"Really, Frederick, you should have told me."

Then they ate the dry bread together, and Frederick said, "Catherine, did you make the house safe when you came away?"

"No, Frederick, you should have told me to do it before."

"Then go home again, and make the house safe before we go any farther, and bring with you something else to eat. I will wait here for you."

Catherine went back and thought, "Frederick wants something more to eat; he does not like butter and cheese, so I will take with me a handkerchief full of dried pears and a pitcher of vinegar for him to drink."

Then she bolted the upper half of the door fast, but unhinged the lower door, and took it on her back, believing that when she had placed the door in security the house must be well taken care of. Catherine took her time on the way, and thought, "Frederick will rest himself so much the longer."

When she had once more got up to him, she said, "Here is the house-door for you, Frederick, and now you can take care of the house yourself."

"Oh, heavens," said he, "what a wise wife I have! She takes the under-door off the hinges that everything may run in, and bolts the upper one. It is now too late to go back home again, but since you have brought the door here, you shall just carry it farther."

"I will carry the door, Frederick, but the dried pears and the vinegar-jug will be too heavy for me; I will hang them on the door, it may carry them."

And now they went into the forest, and sought the rogues, but did not find them. At length as it grew dark, they climbed into a tree and resolved to spend the night there. Scarcely, however, had they sat down at the top of it than the rascals came thither who carry away with them what does not want to go, and find things before they are lost. They sat down under the very tree in which Frederick and Catherine were sitting, lighted a fire, and were about to share their booty.

Frederick got down on the other side and collected some stones together. Then he climbed up again with them, and wished to throw them at the thieves and kill them. The stones, however, did not hit them, and the knaves cried, "It will soon be morning, the wind is shaking down the fir-apples."

Catherine still had the door on her back, and as it pressed so heavily on her, she thought it was the fault of the dried pears, and said, "Frederick, I must throw the pears down."

"No, Catherine, not now," he replied, "they might betray us."

"Oh, but, Frederick, I must! They weigh me down far too much."

"Do it, then, and be hanged!"

Then the dried pears rolled down between the branches, and the rascals below said, "The leaves are falling."

A short time afterwards, as the door was still heavy, Catherine said, "Ah, Frederick, I must pour out the vinegar."

"No, Catherine, you must not, it might betray us."

"Ah, but, Frederick, I must, it weighs me down far too much."

"Then do it and be hanged!"

So she emptied out the vinegar, and it besprinkled the robbers. They said amongst themselves, "The dew is already falling."

At length Catherine thought, "Can it really be the door which weighs me down so?" and said, "Frederick, I must throw the door down."

"No, not now, Catherine, it might discover us."

"Oh, but, Frederick, I must. It weighs me down far too much."

"Oh, no, Catherine, do hold it fast."

"Ah, Frederick, I am letting it fall!"

"Let it go, then, in the devil's name."

Then it fell down with a violent clatter, and the rascals below cried, "The devil is coming down the tree!" and they ran away and left everything behind them.

Early next morning, when the two came down, they found all their gold again, and carried it home. When they were once more at home, Frederick said, "And now, Catherine, you, too, must be industrious and work."

"Yes, Frederick, I will soon do that, I will go into the field and cut corn."

When Catherine got into the field, she said to herself, "Shall I eat before I cut, or shall I sleep before I cut? Oh, I will eat first." Then Catherine ate and eating made her sleepy, and she began to cut, and half in a dream cut all her clothes to pieces, her apron, her gown, and her shift.

When Catherine awoke again after a long sleep, she was standing there half-naked, and said to herself, "Is it I, or is it not I? Alas, it is not I."

In the meantime night came, and Catherine ran into the village, knocked at her husband's window, and cried, "Frederick!"

"What is the matter?"

"I should very much like to know if Catherine is in?"

"Yes, yes," replied Frederick, "she must be in and asleep."

Said she, "'Tis well, then I am certainly at home already," and ran away.

Outside Catherine found some vagabonds who were going to steal. Then she went to them and said, "I will help you to steal."

The rascals thought that she knew the situation of the place, and were willing. Catherine went in front of the houses, and cried, "Good folks, have you anything? We want to steal."

The thieves thought to themselves, "That's a fine way of doing things," and wished themselves once more rid of Catherine. Then they said to her, "Outside the village the pastor has some turnips in the field. Go there and pull up some turnips for us."

Catherine went to the ground, and began to pull them up, but was so idle that she did not gather them together. Then a man came by, saw her, and stood still and thought that it was the devil who was thus rooting amongst the turnips. He ran away into the village to the pastor, and said, "Mr. Pastor, the devil is in your turnip-ground, rooting up turnips."

"Ah, heavens," answered the pastor, "I have a lame foot, I cannot go out and drive him away!"

Said the man, "Then I will carry you on my back," and he carried him out on his back.

And when they came to the ground, Catherine arose and stood up her full height.

"Ah, the devil!" cried the pastor, and both hurried away, and in his great fright the pastor could run better with his lame foot than the man who had carried him on his back could do with his sound one.

The Queen Bee

WO kings' sons once went out in search of adventures, and fell into a wild, disorderly way of living, so that they never came home again. The youngest, who was called Simpleton, set out to seek his brothers, but when at length he found them, they mocked him for thinking that he with his simplicity could get through the world, when they two could not make their way, and yet were so much cleverer.

They all three travelled away together, and came to an ant-hill. The two elder wanted to destroy it, to see the little ants creeping about in their terror, and carrying their eggs away, but Simpleton said, "Leave the creatures in peace; I will not allow you to disturb them."

Then they went onwards and came to a lake, on which a great number of ducks were swimming. The two brothers wanted to catch a couple and roast them, but Simpleton would not permit it, and said, "Leave the creatures in peace, I will not suffer you to kill them."

At length they came to a bee's nest, in which there was so much honey that it ran out of the trunk of the tree where it was. The two wanted to make a fire beneath the tree, and suffocate the bees in order to take away the honey, but Simpleton again stopped them and said, "Leave the creatures in peace, I will not allow you to burn them."

At length the three brothers arrived at a castle where stone horses were standing in the stables, and no human being was to be seen, and they went through all the halls until, quite at the end, they came to a door in which were three locks. In the middle of the door, however, there was a little pane, through which they could see into the room.

There they saw a little grey man, who was sitting at a table. They called him, once, twice, but he did not hear; at last they called him for the third time, when he got up, opened the locks, and came out. He said nothing, however, but conducted them to a handsomely-spread table, and when they had eaten and drunk, he took each of them to a bedroom.

Next morning the little grey man came to the eldest, beckoned to him, and conducted him to a stone table, on which were inscribed three

tasks, by the performance of which the castle could be delivered. The first was that in the forest, beneath the moss, lay the princess's pearls, a thousand in number, which must be picked up, and if by sunset one single pearl was wanting, he who had looked for them would be turned into stone.

The eldest went thither, and sought the whole day, but when it came to an end, he had only found one hundred, and what was written on the table came to pass, and he was changed into stone.

Next day, the second brother undertook the adventure; it did not, however, fare much better with him than with the eldest; he did not find more than two hundred pearls, and was changed to stone.

At last the turn came to Simpleton also, who sought in the moss. It was, however, so hard to find the pearls, and he got on so slowly, that he seated himself on a stone, and wept. And while he was thus sitting, the King of the ants whose life he had once saved, came with five thousand ants, and before long the little creatures had got all the pearls together, and laid them in a heap.

The second task, however, was to fetch out of the lake the key of the King's daughter's bed-chamber. When Simpleton came to the lake, the ducks which he had saved, swam up to him, dived down, and brought the key out of the water.

But the third task was the most difficult: from amongst the three sleeping daughters of the King was the youngest and dearest to be sought out. They, however, resembled each other exactly, and were only to be distinguished by their having eaten different sweetmeats before they fell asleep: the eldest a bit of sugar, the second a little syrup, and the youngest a spoonful of honey.

Then the Queen of the bees, which Simpleton had protected from the fire, came and tasted the lips of all three, and at last she remained sitting on the mouth which had eaten honey, and thus the King's son recognized the right princess. Then the enchantment was at an end; everything was released from sleep, and those who had been turned to stone received once more their natural forms.

Simpleton married the youngest and sweetest princess, and after her father's death became King, and his two brothers received the two other sisters.

The Three Feathers

HERE was once on a time a King who had three sons, of whom two were clever and wise, but the third did not speak much, and was simple, and was called the Simpleton. When the King had become old and weak, and was thinking of his end, he did not know which of his sons should inherit the kingdom after him. Then he said to them, "Go forth, and he who brings me the most beautiful carpet shall be King after my death." And that there should be no dispute amongst them, he took them outside his castle, blew three feathers in the air, and said, "You shall go as they fly."

One feather flew to the east, the other to the west, but the third flew straight up and did not fly far, but soon fell to the ground. And now one brother went to the right, and the other to the left, and they mocked Simpleton, who was forced to stay where the third feather had fallen.

He sat down and was sad, then all at once he saw that there was a trap-door close by the feather. He raised it up, found some steps, and went down them, and then he came to another door, knocked at it, and heard somebody inside calling,

"Little green maiden small,
Hopping hither and thither;
Hop to the door,
And quickly see who is there."

The door opened, and he saw a great, fat toad sitting, and round about her a crowd of little toads. The fat toad asked what he wanted?

He answered, "I should like to have the prettiest and finest carpet in the world."

Then she called a young one and said,

"Little green maiden small,
Hopping hither and thither,
Hop quickly and bring me
The great box here."

The young toad brought the box, and the fat toad opened it, and gave Simpleton a carpet out of it, so beautiful and so fine, that on the earth above, none could have been woven like it. Then he thanked her, and ascended again.

The two others had, however, looked on their youngest brother as so stupid that they believed he would find and bring nothing at all. "Why should we give ourselves a great deal of trouble to search?" said they, and got some coarse handkerchiefs from the first shepherds' wives whom they met, and carried them home to the King.

At the same time Simpleton also came back, and brought his beautiful carpet, and when the King saw it, he was astonished, and said, "If justice be done, the kingdom belongs to the youngest."

But the two others let their father have no peace, and said that it was impossible that Simpleton, who in everything lacked understanding, should be King, and entreated him to make a new agreement with them.

Then the father said, "He who brings me the most beautiful ring shall inherit the kingdom," and led the three brothers out, and blew into the air three feathers, which they were to follow. Those of the two eldest again went east and west, and Simpleton's feather flew straight up, and fell down near the door into the earth.

Then he went down again to the fat toad, and told her that he wanted the most beautiful ring. She at once ordered her great box to be brought, and gave him a ring out of it, which sparkled with jewels, and was so beautiful that no goldsmith on earth would have been able to make it.

The two eldest laughed at Simpleton for going to seek a golden ring. They gave themselves no trouble, but knocked the nails out of an old carriage-ring, and took it to the King; but when Simpleton produced his golden ring, his father again said, "The kingdom belongs to him."

The two eldest did not cease from tormenting the King until he made a third condition, and declared that the one who brought the most beautiful woman home, should have the kingdom. He again blew the three feathers into the air, and they flew as before.

Then Simpleton without more ado went down to the fat toad, and said, "I am to take home the most beautiful woman!"

"Oh," answered the toad, "the most beautiful woman! She is not at hand at the moment, but still thou shalt have her." She gave him a yellow turnip which had been hollowed out, to which six mice were harnessed.

Then Simpleton said quite mournfully, "What am I to do with that?"

The toad answered, "Just put one of my little toads into it."

Then he seized one at random out of the circle, and put her into the yellow coach, but hardly was she seated inside it than she turned into a wonderfully beautiful maiden, and the turnip into a coach, and the six mice into horses. So he kissed her, and drove off quickly with the horses, and took her to the King.

His brothers came afterwards; they had given themselves no trouble at all to seek beautiful girls, but had brought with them the first peasant women they chanced to meet.

When the King saw them, he said, "After my death the kingdom belongs to my youngest son."

But the two eldest deafened the King's ears afresh with their clamour, "We cannot consent to Simpleton's being King," and demanded that the one whose wife could leap through a ring which hung in the centre of the hall should have the preference. They thought, "The peasant women can do that easily; they are strong enough, but the delicate maiden will jump herself to death."

The aged King agreed likewise to this. Then the two peasant women jumped, and jumped through the ring, but were so stout that they fell, and their coarse arms and legs broke in two. And then the pretty maiden whom Simpleton had brought with him, sprang, and sprang through as lightly as a deer, and all opposition had to cease.

So he received the crown, and has ruled wisely for a length of time.

The Golden Goose

HERE was a man who had three sons, the youngest of whom was called Dummling[1], and was despised, mocked, and put down on every occasion. It happened that the eldest wanted to go into the forest to hew wood, and before he went, his mother gave him a beautiful sweet cake and a bottle of wine in order that he might not suffer from hunger or thirst.

When he entered the forest, there met him a little grey-haired old man who bade him good-day, and said, "Do give me a piece of cake out of your pocket, and let me have a draught of your wine; I am so hungry and thirsty."

But the prudent youth answered, "If I give you my cake and wine, I shall have none for myself; be off with you," and he left the little man standing and went on. But when he began to hew down a tree, it was not long before he made a false stroke, and the axe cut him in the arm, so that he had to go home and have it bound up. And this was the little grey man's doing.

After this the second son went into the forest, and his mother gave him, like the eldest, a cake and a bottle of wine. The little old grey man met him likewise, and asked him for a piece of cake and a drink of

---

[1] Simpleton.

wine. But the second son, too, said with much reason, "What I give you will be taken away from myself; be off!" and he left the little man standing and went on. His punishment, however, was not delayed; when he had made a few strokes at the tree, he struck himself in the leg, so that he had to be carried home.

Then Dummling said, "Father, do let me go and cut wood."

The father answered, "Your brothers have hurt themselves with it, leave it alone, you do not understand anything about it." But Dummling begged so long that at last he said, "Just go then, you will get wiser by hurting yourself."

His mother gave him a cake made with water and baked in the cinders, and with it a bottle of sour beer. When he came to the forest, the little old grey man met him likewise, and greeting him, said, "Give me a piece of your cake and a drink out of your bottle; I am so hungry and thirsty."

Dummling answered, "I have only cinder-cake and sour beer; if that pleases you, we will sit down and eat."

So they sat down, and when Dummling pulled out his cinder-cake, it was a fine sweet cake, and the sour beer had become good wine. So they ate and drank, and after that the little man said, "Since you have a good heart, and are willing to divide what you have, I will give you good luck. There stands an old tree, cut it down, and you will find something at the roots." Then the little man took leave of him.

Dummling went and cut down the tree, and when it fell, there was a goose sitting in the roots with feathers of pure gold. He lifted her up, and taking her with him, went to an inn where he thought he would stay the night.

Now the host had three daughters, who saw the goose and were curious to know what such a wonderful bird might be, and would have liked to have one of its golden feathers.

The eldest thought, "I shall soon find an opportunity of pulling out a feather," and as soon as Dummling had gone out, she seized the goose by the wing, but her finger and hand remained sticking fast to it.

The second came soon afterwards, thinking only of how she might get a feather for herself, but she had scarcely touched her sister than she was held fast.

At last the third also came with the like intent, and the others screamed out, "Keep away; for goodness' sake keep away!" But she did not understand why she was to keep away. "The others are there," she thought, "I may as well be there too," and ran to them; but as soon as she had touched her sister, she remained sticking fast to her. So they had to spend the night with the goose.

The next morning Dummling took the goose under his arm and set out, without troubling himself about the three girls who were hanging on to it. They were obliged to run after him continually, now left, now right, just as he was inclined to go.

In the middle of the fields the parson met them, and when he saw the procession, he said, "For shame, you good-for-nothing girls, why are you running across the fields after this young man? is that seemly?" At the same time he seized the youngest by the hand in order to pull her away, but as soon as he touched her, he likewise stuck fast, and was himself obliged to run behind.

Before long the sexton came by and saw his master, the parson, running on foot behind three girls. He was astonished at this and called out, "Hi! your reverence, whither away so quickly? do not forget that we have a christening today!" and running after him he took him by the sleeve, but was also held fast to it.

Whilst the five were trotting thus one behind the other, two labourers came with their hoes from the fields; the parson called out to them and begged that they would set him and the sexton free. But they had scarcely touched the sexton when they were held fast, and now there were seven of them running behind Dummling and the goose.

Soon afterwards he came to a city, where a king ruled who had a daughter who was so serious that no one could make her laugh. So he had put forth a decree that whosoever should be able to make her laugh should marry her.

When Dummling heard this, he went with his goose and all her train before the King's daughter, and as soon as she saw the seven people running on and on, one behind the other, she began to laugh quite loudly, and as if she would never leave off. Thereupon Dummling asked to have her for his wife, and the wedding was celebrated.

After the King's death, Dummling inherited the kingdom, and lived a long time contentedly with his wife.

Allerleirauh

HERE was once on a time a King who had a wife with golden hair, and she was so beautiful that her equal was not to be found on earth. It came to pass that she lay ill, and as she felt that she must soon die, she called the King and said, "If thou wishest to marry again after my death, take no one who is not quite as beautiful as I am, and who has not just such golden hair as I have: this thou must promise me." And after the King had promised her this she closed her eyes and died.

For a long time the King could not be comforted, and had no thought of taking another wife. At length his councillors said, "There is no help for it, the King must marry again, that we may have a Queen." And now messengers were sent about far and wide, to seek a bride who equalled the late Queen in beauty. In the whole world, however, none was to be found, and even if one had been found, still there would have been no one who had such golden hair. So the messengers came home as they went.

Now the King had a daughter, who was just as beautiful as her dead mother, and had the same golden hair. When she was grown up, the King looked at her one day, and saw that in every respect she was like his late wife, and suddenly felt a violent love for her. Then he spake to his councillors, "I will marry my daughter, for she is the counterpart of my late wife, otherwise I can find no bride who resembles her."

When the councillors heard that, they were shocked, and said, "God has forbidden a father to marry his daughter, no good can come from such a crime, and the kingdom will be involved in the ruin."

The daughter was still more shocked when she became aware of her father's resolution, but hoped to turn him from his design. Then she said to him, "Before I fulfil your wish, I must have three dresses, one as golden as the sun, one as silvery as the moon, and one as bright as the stars; besides this, I wish for a mantle of a thousand different kinds of fur and hair joined together, and one of every kind of animal in your kingdom must give a piece of his skin for it."

But she thought, "To get that will be quite impossible, and thus I shall divert my father from his wicked intentions."

The King, however, did not give it up, and the cleverest maidens in his kingdom had to weave the three dresses, one as golden as the sun, one as silvery as the moon, and one as bright as the stars, and his huntsmen had to catch one of every kind of animal in the whole of his

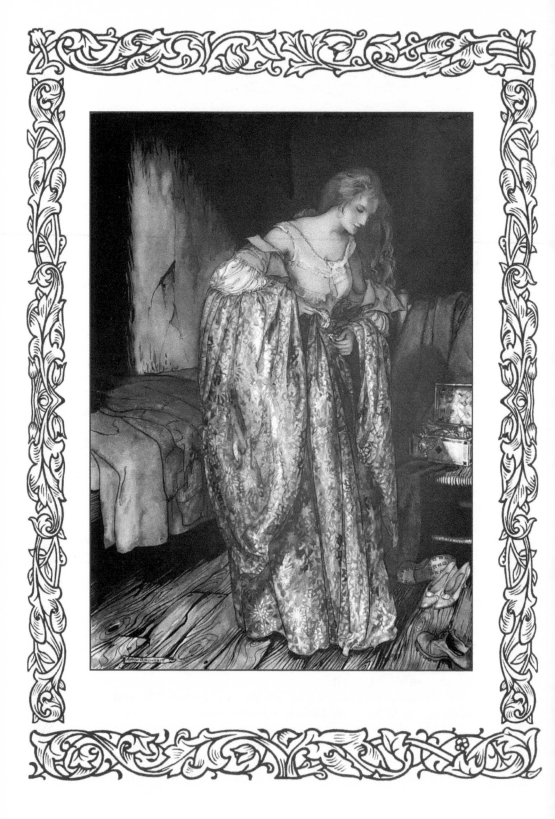

kingdom, and take from it a piece of its skin, and out of these was made a mantle of a thousand different kinds of fur.

At length, when all was ready, the King caused the mantle to be brought, spread it out before her, and said, "The wedding shall be to-morrow."

When, therefore, the King's daughter saw that there was no longer any hope of turning her father's heart, she resolved to run away from him. In the night whilst everyone was asleep, she got up, and took three different things from her treasures, a golden ring, a golden spinning-wheel, and a golden reel. The three dresses of the sun, moon, and stars she put into a nutshell, put on her mantle of all kinds of fur, and blackened her face and hands with soot. Then she commended herself to God, and went away, and walked the whole night until she reached a great forest. And as she was tired, she got into a hollow tree, and fell asleep.

The sun rose, and she slept on, and she was still sleeping when it was full day. Then it so happened that the King to whom this forest belonged, was hunting in it. When his dogs came to the tree, they snuffed, and ran barking round about it. The King said to the huntsmen, "Just see what kind of wild beast has hidden itself in there."

The huntsmen obeyed his order, and when they came back, they said, "A wondrous beast is lying in the hollow tree; we have never before seen one like it. Its skin is fur of a thousand different kinds, but it is lying asleep."

Said the King, "See if you can catch it alive, and then fasten it on the carriage, and we will take it with us."

When the huntsmen laid hold of the maiden, she awoke full of terror, and cried to them, "I am a poor child, deserted by father and mother; have pity on me, and take me with you."

Then said they, "Allerleirauh, thou wilt be useful in the kitchen, come with us, and thou canst sweep up the ashes."

So they put her in the carriage, and took her home to the royal palace. There they pointed out to her a closet under the stairs, where no daylight entered, and said, "Hairy animal, there canst thou live and sleep."

Then she was sent into the kitchen, and there she carried wood and water, swept the hearth, plucked the fowls, picked the vegetables, raked the ashes, and did all the dirty work.

Allerleirauh lived there for a long time in great wretchedness. Alas, fair princess, what is to become of thee now! It happened, however, that one day a feast was held in the palace, and she said to the cook, "May I go up-stairs for a while, and look on? I will place myself outside the door."

The cook answered, "Yes, go, but you must be back here in half-an-hour to sweep the hearth."

Then she took her oil-lamp, went into her den, put off her fur-dress, and washed the soot off her face and hands, so that her full beauty once more came to light. And she opened the nut, and took out her dress which shone like the sun, and when she had done that, she went up to the festival, and everyone made way for her, for no one knew her, and thought no otherwise than that she was a king's daughter.

The King came to meet her, gave his hand to her, and danced with her, and thought in his heart, "My eyes have never yet seen anyone so beautiful!"

When the dance was over, she curtsied; and when the King looked round again, she had vanished, and none knew whither. The guards who stood outside the palace were called and questioned, but no one had seen her.

She had, however, run into her little den, had quickly taken off her dress, made her face and hands black again, put on the fur-mantle, and again was Allerleirauh.

And now when she went into the kitchen, and was about to get to her work and sweep up the ashes, the cook said, "Leave that alone till morning, and make me the soup for the King; I, too, will go upstairs awhile, and take a look; but let no hairs fall in, or in future thou shalt have nothing to eat."

So the cook went away, and Allerleirauh made the soup for the King, and made bread soup and the best she could, and when it was ready, she fetched her golden ring from her little den, and put it in the bowl in which the soup was served. When the dancing was over, the King had his soup brought and ate it, and he liked it so much that it seemed to him he had never tasted better. But when he came to the bottom of the bowl, he saw a golden ring lying, and could not conceive how it could have got there. Then he ordered the cook to appear before him.

The cook was terrified when he heard the order, and said to Allerleirauh, "Thou hast certainly let a hair fall into the soup, and if thou hast, thou shalt be beaten for it."

When he came before the King, the latter asked who had made the soup? The cook replied, "I made it."

But the King said, "That is not true, for it was much better than usual, and cooked differently."

He answered, "I must acknowledge that I did not make it, it was made by the rough animal."

The King said, "Go and bid it come up here."

When Allerleirauh came, the King said, "Who art thou?"

"I am a poor girl who no longer has any father or mother."

He asked further, "Of what use art thou in my palace?"

She answered, "I am good for nothing but to have boots thrown at my head."

He continued, "Where didst thou get the ring which was in the soup?"

She answered, "I know nothing about the ring." So the King could learn nothing, and had to send her away again.

After a while, there was another festival, and then, as before, Allerleirauh begged the cook for leave to go and look on. He answered, "Yes, but come back again in half-an-hour, and make the King the bread soup which he so much likes."

Then she ran into her den, washed herself quickly, and took out of the nut the dress which was as silvery as the moon, and put it on. Then she went up and was like a princess, and the King stepped forward to meet her, and rejoiced to see her once more, and as the dance was just beginning they danced it together.

But when it was at end, she again disappeared so quickly that the King could not observe where she went. She, however, sprang into her den, and once more made herself a hairy animal, and went into the kitchen to prepare the bread soup. When the cook had gone up-stairs, she fetched the little golden spinning-wheel, and put it in the bowl so that the soup covered it.

Then it was taken to the King, who ate it, and liked it as much as before, and had the cook brought, who this time likewise was forced to confess that Allerleirauh had prepared the soup. Allerleirauh again came before the King, but she answered that she was good for nothing else but to have boots thrown at her head, and that she knew nothing at all about the little golden spinning-wheel.

When, for the third time, the King held a festival, all happened just as it had done before. The cook said, "Faith, rough-skin, thou art a witch, and always puttest something in the soup which makes it so good that the King likes it better than that which I cook," but as she begged so hard, he let her go up at the appointed time.

And now she put on the dress which shone like the stars, and thus entered the hall. Again the King danced with the beautiful maiden, and thought that she never yet had been so beautiful. And whilst she was dancing, he contrived, without her noticing it, to slip a golden ring on her finger, and he had given orders that the dance should last a very long time.

When it was ended, he wanted to hold her fast by her hands, but she tore herself loose, and sprang away so quickly through the crowd that she vanished from his sight. She ran as fast as she could into her den beneath the stairs, but as she had been too long, and had stayed more than half-an-hour she could not take off her pretty dress, but only threw over it her fur-mantle, and in her haste she did not make herself quite black, but one finger remained white. Then Allerleirauh ran into the kitchen, and cooked the bread soup for the King, and as the cook was away, put her golden reel into it.

When the King found the reel at the bottom of it, he caused Allerleirauh to be summoned, and then he espied the white finger, and saw the ring which he had put on it during the dance. Then he grasped her by the hand, and held her fast, and when she wanted to release herself and run away, her fur-mantle opened a little, and the star-dress shone forth.

The King clutched the mantle and tore it off. Then her golden hair shone forth, and she stood there in full splendour, and could no longer hide herself. And when she had washed the soot and ashes from her face, she was more beautiful than anyone who had ever been seen on earth.

The King said, "Thou art my dear bride, and we will never more part from each other."

Thereupon the marriage was solemnized, and they lived happily until their death.

The Hare's Bride

HERE was once a woman and her daughter who lived in a pretty garden with cabbages; and a little hare came into it, and during the winter time ate all the cabbages. Then says the mother to the daughter, "Go into the garden, and chase the hare away." The girl says to the little hare, "Sh-sh, hare, you are still eating up all our cabbages." Says the hare, "Come, maiden, and seat yourself on my little hare's tail, and come with me into my little hare's hut." The girl will not do it.

Next day the hare comes again and eats the cabbages, then says the mother to the daughter, "Go into the garden, and drive the hare away." The girl says to the hare, "Sh-sh, little hare, you are still eating all the cabbages." The little hare says, "Maiden, seat thyself on my little hare's tail, and come with me into my little hare's hut." The maiden refuses.

The third day the hare comes again, and eats the cabbages. On this the mother says to the daughter, "Go into the garden, and hunt the hare away." Says the maiden, "Sh-sh, little hare, you are still eating all our cabbages." Says the little hare, "Come, maiden, seat thyself on my little hare's tail, and come with me into my little hare's hut." The girl seats herself on the little hare's tail, and then the hare takes her far away to his little hut, and says, "Now cook green cabbage and millet-seed, and I will invite the wedding-guests."

Then all the wedding-guests assembled. (Who were the wedding-guests?) That I can tell you as another told it to me. They were all hares, and the crow was there as parson to marry the bride and bridegroom, and the fox as clerk, and the altar was under the rainbow.

The girl, however, was sad, for she was all alone. The little hare comes and says, "Open the doors, open the doors, the wedding-guests are merry." The bride says nothing, but weeps.

The little hare goes away. The little hare comes back and says, "Take off the lid, take off the lid, the wedding-guests are hungry." The bride again says nothing, and weeps.

The little hare goes away. The little hare comes back and says, "Take off the lid, take off the lid, the wedding-guests are waiting." Then the bride says nothing, and the hare goes away, but she dresses a straw-doll in her clothes, and gives her a spoon to stir with, and sets her by the pan with the millet-seed, and goes back to her mother.

The little hare comes once more and says, "Take off the lid, take off the lid," and gets up, and strikes the doll on the head so that her cap falls off. Then the little hare sees that it is not his bride, and goes away and is sorrowful.

The Twelve Huntsmen

HERE was once a King's son who was betrothed to a maiden whom he loved very much. And when he was sitting beside her and very happy, news came that his father lay sick unto death, and desired to see him once again before his end. Then he said to his beloved, "I must now go and leave thee, I give thee a ring as a remembrance of me. When I am King, I will return and fetch thee."

So he rode away, and when he reached his father, the latter was dangerously ill, and near his death. He said to him, "Dear son, I wished to see thee once again before my end, promise me to marry as I wish," and he named a certain King's daughter who was to be his wife.

The son was in such trouble that he did not think what he was doing, and said, "Yes, dear father, your will shall be done," and thereupon the King shut his eyes, and died.

When therefore the son had been proclaimed King, and the time of mourning was over, he was forced to keep the promise which he had given his father, and caused the King's daughter to be asked in marriage, and she was promised to him. His first betrothed heard of this, and fretted so much about his faithlessness that she nearly died.

Then her father said to her, "Dearest child, why art thou so sad? Thou shalt have whatsoever thou wilt."

She thought for a moment and said, "Dear father, I wish for eleven girls exactly like myself in face, figure, and size."

The father said, "If it be possible, thy desire shall be fulfilled," and he caused a search to be made in his whole kingdom, until eleven young maidens were found who exactly resembled his daughter in face, figure, and size.

When they came to the King's daughter, she had twelve suits of huntsmen's clothes made, all alike, and the eleven maidens had to put on the huntsmen's clothes, and she herself put on the twelfth suit. Thereupon she took leave of her father, and rode away with them, and rode to the court of her former betrothed, whom she loved so dearly. Then she inquired if he required any huntsmen, and if he would take the whole of them into his service.

The King looked at her and did not know her, but as they were such handsome fellows, he said, "Yes," and that he would willingly take them, and now they were the King's twelve huntsmen.

The King, however, had a lion which was a wondrous animal, for he knew all concealed and secret things. It came to pass that one evening he said to the King, "Thou thinkest thou hast twelve huntsmen?"

"Yes," said the King, "they are twelve huntsmen."

The lion continued, "Thou art mistaken, they are twelve girls."

The King said, "That cannot be true! How wilt thou prove that to me?"

"Oh, just let some peas be strewn in thy ante-chamber," answered the lion, "and then thou wilt soon see it. Men have a firm step, and when they walk over peas, none of them stir, but girls trip and skip, and drag their feet, and the peas roll about."

The King was well pleased with the counsel, and caused the peas to be strewn.

There was, however, a servant of the King's who favoured the huntsmen, and when he heard that they were going to be put to this test, he went to them and repeated everything, and said, "The lion wants to make the King believe that you are girls."

Then the King's daughter thanked him, and said to her maidens, "Put on some strength, and step firmly on the peas."

So next morning when the King had the twelve huntsmen called before him, and they came into the ante-chamber where the peas were lying, they stepped so firmly on them, and had such a strong, sure walk, that not one of the peas either rolled or stirred.

Then they went away again, and the King said to the lion, "Thou hast lied to me, they walk just like men."

The lion said, "They have got to know that they were going to be put to the test, and have assumed some strength. Just let twelve spinning-wheels be brought into the ante-chamber some day, and they will go to them and be pleased with them, and that is what no man would do."

The King liked the advice, and had the spinning-wheels placed in the ante-chamber.

But the servant, who was well disposed to the huntsmen, went to them, and disclosed the project. Then when they were alone, the King's daughter said to her eleven girls, "Put some constraint on yourselves, and do not look round at the spinning-wheels."

And next morning when the King had his twelve huntsmen summoned, they went through the ante-chamber, and never once looked at the spinning wheels.

Then the King again said to the lion, "Thou hast deceived me, they are men, for they have not looked at the spinning-wheels."

The lion replied, "They have learnt that they were going to be put to the test, and have restrained themselves."

The King, however, would no longer believe the lion.

The twelve huntsmen always followed the King to the chase, and his liking for them continually increased. Now it came to pass that once when they were out hunting, news came that the King's betrothed was approaching. When the true bride heard that, it hurt her so much that her heart was almost broken, and she fell fainting to the ground.

223

The King thought something had happened to his dear huntsman, ran up to him, wanted to help him, and drew his glove off. Then he saw the ring which he had given to his first bride, and when he looked in her face, he recognized her. Then his heart was so touched that he kissed her, and when she opened her eyes, he said, "Thou art mine, and I am thine, and no one in the world can alter that."

He sent a messenger to the other bride, and entreated her to return to her own kingdom, for he had a wife already, and a man who had just found an old dish did not require a new one. Thereupon the wedding was celebrated, and the lion was again taken into favour, because, after all, he had told the truth.

Jorinda and Joringel

HERE was once an old castle in the midst of a large and thick forest, and in it an old woman who was a witch dwelt all alone. In the day-time she changed herself into a cat or a screech-owl, but in the evening she took her proper shape again as a human being. She could lure wild beasts and birds to her, and then she killed and boiled and roasted them. If anyone came within one hundred paces of the castle he was obliged to stand still, and could not stir from the place until she bade him be free. But whenever an innocent maiden came within this circle, she changed her into a bird, and shut her up in a wicker-work cage, and carried the cage into a room in the castle. She had about seven thousand cages of rare birds in the castle.

Now, there was once a maiden who was called Jorinda, who was fairer than all other girls. She and a handsome youth named Joringel had promised to marry each other. They were still in the days of betrothal, and their greatest happiness was being together.

One day in order that they might be able to talk together in quiet they went for a walk in the forest. "Take care," said Joringel, "that you do not go too near the castle."

It was a beautiful evening; the sun shone brightly between the trunks of the trees into the dark green of the forest, and the turtle-doves sang mournfully upon the young boughs of the birch-trees.

Jorinda wept now and then; she sat down in the sunshine and was sorrowful. Joringel was sorrowful too; they were as sad as if they were about to die. Then they looked around them, and were quite at a loss, for they did not know by which way they should go home. The sun was still half above the mountain and half set.

Joringel looked through the bushes, and saw the old walls of the castle close at hand. He was horror-stricken and filled with deadly fear.

Jorinda was singing—

> "My little bird, with the necklace red,
> Sings sorrow, sorrow, sorrow,
> He sings that the dove must soon be dead,
> Sings sorrow, sor—— jug, jug, jug."

Joringel looked for Jorinda. She was changed into a nightingale, and sang "jug, jug, jug."

A screech-owl with glowing eyes flew three times round about her, and three times cried "to-whoo, to-whoo, to-whoo!"

Joringel could not move: he stood there like a stone, and could neither weep nor speak, nor move hand or foot.

The sun had now set. The owl flew into the thicket, and directly afterwards there came out of it a crooked old woman, yellow and lean, with large red eyes and a hooked nose, the point of which reached to her chin. She muttered to herself, caught the nightingale, and took it away in her hand.

Joringel could neither speak nor move from the spot; the nightingale was gone. At last the woman came back, and said in a hollow voice, "Greet thee, Zachiel. If the moon shines on the cage, Zachiel, let him loose at once."

Then Joringel was freed. He fell on his knees before the woman and begged that she would give him back his Jorinda, but she said that he should never have her again, and went away. He called, he wept, he lamented, but all in vain, "Ah, what is to become of me?"

Joringel went away, and at last came to a strange village; there he kept sheep for a long time. He often walked round and round the castle, but not too near to it. At last he dreamt one night that he found a blood-red flower, in the middle of which was a beautiful large pearl; that he picked the flower and went with it to the castle, and that everything he touched with the flower was freed from enchantment; he also dreamt that by means of it he recovered his Jorinda.

In the morning, when he awoke, he began to seek over hill and dale if he could find such a flower. He sought until the ninth day, and then, early in the morning, he found the blood-red flower. In the middle of it there was a large dew-drop, as big as the finest pearl.

Day and night he journeyed with this flower to the castle. When he was within a hundred paces of it, he was not held fast, but walked on to the door. Joringel was full of joy; he touched the door with the flower, and it sprang open. He walked in through the courtyard, and listened for the sound of the birds. At last he heard it. He went on and found the room from whence it came, and there the witch was feeding the birds in the seven thousand cages.

When she saw Joringel, she was angry, very angry, and scolded and spat poison and gall at him, but she could not come within two paces of him. He did not take any notice of her, but went and looked at the cages with the birds; but there were many hundred nightingales, how was he to find his Jorinda again?

Just then he saw the old woman quietly take away a cage with a bird in it, and go towards the door.

Swiftly he sprang towards her, touched the cage with the flower, and also the old woman. She could now no longer bewitch anyone; and Jorinda was standing there, clasping him round the neck, and she was as beautiful as ever!

The Three Sons of Fortune

 FATHER once called his three sons before him, and he gave to the first a cock, to the second a scythe, and to the third a cat. "I am already aged," said he, "my death is nigh, and I have wished to take thought for you before my end; money I have not, and what I now give you seems of little worth, but all depends on your making a sensible use of it. Only seek out a country where such things are still unknown, and your fortune is made."

After the father's death the eldest went away with his cock, but wherever he came the cock was already known; in the towns he saw him from a long distance, sitting upon the steeples and turning round with the wind, and in the villages he heard more than one crowing; no one would show any wonder at the creature, so that it did not look as if he would make his fortune by it.

At last, however, it happened that he came to an island where the people knew nothing about cocks, and did not even understand how to divide their time. They certainly knew when it was morning or evening, but at night, if they did not sleep through it, not one of them knew how to find out the time.

"Look!" said he, "what a proud creature! it has a ruby-red crown upon its head, and wears spurs like a knight; it calls you three times during the night, at fixed hours, and when it calls for the last time, the sun soon rises. But if it crows by broad daylight, then take notice, for there will certainly be a change of weather."

The people were well pleased; for a whole night they did not sleep, and listened with great delight as the cock at two, four, and six o'clock, loudly and clearly proclaimed the time. They asked if the creature were for sale, and how much he wanted for it?

"About as much gold as an ass can carry," answered he.

"A ridiculously small price for such a precious creature!" they cried unanimously, and willingly gave him what he had asked.

When he came home with his wealth, his brothers were astonished, and the second said, "Well, I will go forth and see whether I cannot get rid of my scythe as profitably." But it did not look as if he would, for labourers met him everywhere, and they had scythes upon their shoulders as well as he.

At last, however, he chanced upon an island where the people knew nothing of scythes. When the corn was ripe there, they took cannon out

229

to the fields and shot it down. Now this was rather an uncertain affair; many shot right over it, others hit the ears instead of the stems, and shot them away, whereby much was lost, and besides all this, it made a terrible noise.

So the man set to work and mowed it down so quietly and quickly that the people opened their mouths with astonishment. They agreed to give him what he wanted for the scythe, and he received a horse laden with as much gold as it could carry.

And now the third brother wanted to take his cat to the right man. He fared just like the others; so long as he stayed on the mainland there was nothing to be done. Every place had cats, and there were a great many of them.

At last he sailed over to an island, and it luckily happened that no cats had ever yet been seen there, and that the mice had got the upper hand so much that they danced upon the tables and benches whether the master were at home or not. The people complained bitterly of the plague; the King himself in his palace did not know how to secure himself against them; mice squeaked in every corner, and gnawed whatever they could lay hold of with their teeth.

But now the cat began her chase, and soon cleared a couple of rooms, and the people begged the King to buy the wonderful beast for the country. The King willingly gave what was asked, which was a mule laden with gold, and the third brother came home with the greatest treasure of all.

The cat made herself merry with the mice in the royal palace, and killed so many that they could not be counted.

At last she grew warm with the work and thirsty, so she stood still, lifted up her head and cried, "Mew! mew!" When they heard this strange cry, the King and all his people were frightened, and in their terror ran all at once out of the palace. Then the King took counsel what was best to be done; at last it was determined to send a herald to the cat, and demand that she should leave the palace, or if not, she was to expect that force would be used against her.

The councillors said, "Rather will we let ourselves be plagued with the mice, for to that misfortune we are accustomed, than give up our lives to such a monster as this."

A noble youth, therefore, was sent to ask the cat "whether she would peaceably quit the castle?"

But the cat, whose thirst had become still greater, merely answered, "Mew! mew!"

The youth understood her to say, "Most certainly not! most certainly not!" and took this answer to the King.

"Then," said the councillors, "she shall yield to force."

Cannon were brought out, and the palace was soon in flames. When the fire reached the room where the cat was sitting, she sprang safely out of the window; but the besiegers did not leave off until the whole palace was shot down to the ground.

How Six Men Got on in the World

HERE was once a man who understood all kinds of arts; he served in war, and behaved well and bravely, but when the war was over, he received his dismissal, and three farthings for his expenses on the way. "Stop," said he, "I shall not be content with this. If I can only meet with the right people, the King will yet have to give me all the treasure of the country."

Then full of anger he went into the forest, and saw a man standing therein who had plucked up six trees as if they were blades of corn. He said to him, "Wilt thou be my servant and go with me?"

"Yes," he answered, "but, first, I will take this little bundle of sticks home to my mother," and he took one of the trees, and wrapped it round the five others, lifted the bundle on his back, and carried it away.

Then he returned and went with his master, who said, "We two ought to be able to get through the world very well," and when they had walked on for a short while, they found a huntsman who was kneeling, had shouldered his gun, and was about to fire. The master said to him, "Huntsman, what art thou going to shoot?"

He answered, "Two miles from here a fly is sitting on the branch of an oak-tree, and I want to shoot its left eye out."

"Oh, come with me," said the man, "if we three are together, we certainly ought to be able to get on in the world!"

The huntsman was ready, and went with him, and they came to seven windmills whose sails were turning round with great speed, and yet no wind was blowing either on the right or the left, and no leaf was stirring.

Then said the man, "I know not what is driving the windmills, not a breath of air is stirring," and he went onwards with his servants, and when they had walked two miles, they saw a man sitting on a tree who was shutting one nostril, and blowing out of the other. "Good gracious! what are you doing up there?"

He answered, "Two miles from here are seven windmills; look, I am blowing them till they turn round."

"Oh, come with me," said the man. "If we four are together, we shall carry the whole world before us!"

Then the blower came down and went with him, and after a while they saw a man who was standing on one leg and had taken off the other, and laid it beside him. Then the master said, "You have arranged things very comfortably to have a rest."

"I am a runner," he replied, "and to stop myself running far too fast, I have taken off one of my legs, for if I run with both, I go quicker than any bird can fly."

"Oh, go with me. If we five are together, we shall carry the whole world before us."

So he went with them, and it was not long before they met a man who wore a cap, but had put it quite on one ear. Then the master said to him, "Gracefully, gracefully, don't stick your cap on one ear, you look just like a tom-fool!"

"I must not wear it otherwise," said he, "for if I set my hat straight, a terrible frost comes on, and all the birds in the air are frozen, and drop dead on the ground."

"Oh, come with me," said the master. "If we six are together, we can carry the whole world before us."

Now the six came to a town where the King had proclaimed that whosoever ran a race with his daughter and won the victory, should be her husband, but whosoever lost it, must lose his head.

Then the man presented himself and said, "I will, however, let my servant run for me."

The King replied, "Then his life also must be staked, so that his head and thine are both set on the victory."

When that was settled and made secure, the man buckled the other leg on the runner, and said to him, "Now be nimble, and help us to win."

It was fixed that the one who was the first to bring some water from a far distant well, was to be the victor. The runner received a pitcher, and the King's daughter one too, and they began to run at the same time, but in an instant, when the King's daughter had got a very little way, the people who were looking on could see no more of the runner, and it was just as if the wind had whistled by.

In a short time he reached the well, filled his pitcher with water, and turned back. Half-way home, however, he was overcome with fatigue, and set his pitcher down, lay down himself, and fell asleep. He had, however, made a pillow of a horse's skull which was lying on the ground, in order that he might lie uncomfortably, and soon wake up again.

In the meantime the King's daughter, who could also run very well—quite as well as any ordinary mortal can—had reached the well, and was hurrying back with her pitcher full of water, and when she saw the runner lying there asleep, she was glad and said, "My enemy is delivered over into my hands," emptied his pitcher, and ran on.

And now all would have been lost if by good luck the huntsman had not been standing at the top of the castle, and had not seen everything with his sharp eyes. Then said he, "The King's daughter shall still not prevail against us;" and he loaded his gun, and shot so cleverly, that he shot the horse's skull away from under the runner's head without hurting him.

Then the runner awoke, leapt up, and saw that his pitcher was empty, and that the King's daughter was already far in advance. He did not lose heart, however, but ran back to the well with his pitcher, again drew some water, and was still at home again, ten minutes before the King's daughter.

"Behold!" said he, "I have not bestirred myself till now, it did not deserve to be called running before."

But it pained the King, and still more his daughter, that she should be carried off by a common disbanded soldier like that; so they took counsel with each other how to get rid of him and his companions. Then said the King to her, "I have thought of a way; don't be afraid, they shall not come back again."

And he said to them, "You shall now make merry together, and eat and drink," and he conducted them to a room which had a floor of iron, and the doors also were of iron, and the windows were guarded with iron bars. There was a table in the room covered with delicious food, and the King said to them, "Go in, and enjoy yourselves."

And when they were inside, he ordered the doors to be shut and bolted. Then he sent for the cook, and commanded him to make a fire under the room until the iron became red-hot. This the cook did, and the six who were sitting at table began to feel quite warm, and they thought the heat was caused by the food; but as it became still greater, and they wanted to get out, and found that the doors and windows were bolted, they became aware that the King must have an evil intention, and wanted to suffocate them.

"He shall not succeed, however," said the one with the cap. "I will cause a frost to come, before which the fire shall be ashamed, and creep away."

Then he put his cap on straight, and immediately there came such a frost that all heat disappeared, and the food on the dishes began to freeze.

When an hour or two had passed by, and the King believed that they had perished in the heat, he had the doors opened to behold them himself. But when the doors were opened, all six were standing there, alive and well, and said that they should very much like to get out to warm themselves, for the very food was fast frozen to the dishes with the cold.

Then, full of anger, the King went down to the cook, scolded him, and asked why he had not done what he had been ordered to do. But the cook replied, "There is heat enough there, just look yourself." Then the King saw that a fierce fire was burning under the iron room, and perceived that there was no getting the better of the six in this way.

Again the King considered how to get rid of his unpleasant guests, and caused their chief to be brought and said, "If thou wilt take gold and renounce my daughter, thou shalt have as much as thou wilt."

"Oh, yes, Lord King," he answered, "give me as much as my servant can carry, and I will not ask for your daughter."

On this the King was satisfied, and the other continued, "In fourteen days, I will come and fetch it."

Thereupon he summoned together all the tailors in the whole kingdom, and they were to sit for fourteen days and sew a sack. And when it was ready, the strong one who could tear up trees had to take it on his back, and go with it to the King.

Then said the King, "Who can that strong fellow be who is carrying a bundle of linen on his back that is as big as a house?" and he was alarmed and said, "What a lot of gold he can carry away!"

Then he commanded a ton of gold to be brought; it took sixteen of his strongest men to carry it, but the strong one snatched it up in one hand, put it in his sack, and said, "Why don't you bring more at the same time?—that hardly covers the bottom!"

Then, little by little, the King caused all his treasure to be brought thither, and the strong one pushed it into the sack, and still the sack was not half full with it. "Bring more," cried he, "these few crumbs don't fill it."

Then seven thousand carts with gold had to be gathered together in the whole kingdom, and the strong one thrust them and the oxen harnessed to them into his sack.

"I will examine it no longer," said he, "but will just take what comes, so long as the sack is but full." When all that was inside, there was still room for a great deal more; then he said, "I will just make an end of the thing; people do sometimes tie up a sack even when it is not full." So he took it on his back, and went away with his comrades.

When the King now saw how one single man was carrying away the entire wealth of the country, he became enraged, and bade his horsemen mount and pursue the six, and ordered them to take the sack away from the strong one. Two regiments speedily overtook the six,

235

and called out, "You are prisoners, put down the sack with the gold, or you will all be cut to pieces!"

"What say you?" cried the blower, "that we are prisoners! Rather than that should happen, all of you shall dance about in the air."

And he closed one nostril, and with the other blew on the two regiments. Then they were driven away from each other, and carried into the blue sky over all the mountains—one here, the other there. One sergeant cried for mercy; he had nine wounds, and was a brave fellow who did not deserve ill treatment.

The blower stopped a little so that he came down without injury, and then the blower said to him, "Now go home to thy King, and tell him he had better send some more horsemen, and I will blow them all into the air."

When the King was informed of this, he said, "Let the rascals go. They have the best of it."

Then the six conveyed the riches home, divided it amongst them, and lived in content until their death.

Clever Grethel

HERE was once a cook named Grethel, who wore shoes with red rosettes, and when she walked out with them on, she turned herself this way and that, and thought, "You certainly are a pretty girl!" And when she came home, she drank, in her gladness of heart, a draught of wine, and as wine excites a desire to eat, she tasted the best of whatever she was cooking until she was satisfied, and said, "The cook must know what the food is like."

It came to pass that the master one day said to her, "Grethel, there is a guest coming this evening; prepare me two fowls very daintily."

"I will see to it, master," answered Grethel. She killed two fowls, scalded them, plucked them, put them on the spit, and towards evening set them before the fire, that they might roast. The fowls began to turn brown, and were nearly ready, but the guest had not yet arrived.

Then Grethel called out to her master, "If the guest does not come, I must take the fowls away from the fire, but it will be a sin and a shame if they are not eaten directly, when they are juiciest."

The master said, "I will run myself, and fetch the guest."

When the master had turned his back, Grethel laid the spit with the fowls on one side, and thought, "Standing so long by the fire here makes one hot and thirsty; who knows when they will come? Meanwhile, I will run into the cellar, and take a drink."

She ran down, set a jug, said, "God bless it to thy use, Grethel," and took a good drink, and took yet another hearty draught.

Then she went and put the fowls down again to the fire, basted them, and drove the spit merrily round. But as the roast meat smelt so good, Grethel thought, "Something might be wrong, it ought to be tasted!"

She touched it with her finger, and said, "Ah! how good fowls are! It certainly is a sin and a shame that they are not eaten directly!"

She ran to the window, to see if the master was not coming with his guest, but she saw no one, and went back to the fowls and thought, "One of the wings is burning! I had better take it off and eat it."

So she cut it off, ate it, and enjoyed it, and when she had done, she thought, "the other must go down too, or else master will observe that something is missing."

When the two wings were eaten, she went and looked for her master, and did not see him. It suddenly occurred to her, "Who knows? They are perhaps not coming at all, and have turned in somewhere."

Then she said, "Hallo, Grethel, enjoy yourself, one fowl has been cut into, take another drink, and eat it up entirely; when it is eaten, you will have some peace, why should God's good gifts be spoilt?"

So she ran into the cellar again, took an enormous drink and ate up the one chicken in great glee.

When one of the chickens was swallowed down, and still her master did not come, Grethel looked at the other and said, "Where one is, the other should be likewise, the two go together; what's right for the one is right for the other; I think if I were to take another draught it would do me no harm."

So she took another hearty drink, and let the second chicken rejoin the first.

When she was just in the best of the eating, her master came and cried, "Haste thee, Grethel, the guest is coming directly after me!"

"Yes, sir, I will soon serve up," answered Grethel.

Meantime the master looked to see that the table was properly laid, and took the great knife, wherewith he was going to carve the chickens, and sharpened it on the steps.

Presently the guest came, and knocked politely and courteously at the house-door. Grethel ran, and looked to see who was there, and when she saw the guest, she put her finger to her lips and said, "Hush! hush! get away as quickly as you can, if my master catches you it will be the worse for you; he certainly did ask you to supper, but his intention is to cut off your two ears. Just listen how he is sharpening the knife for it!"

The guest heard the sharpening, and hurried down the steps again as fast as he could.

Grethel was not idle; she ran screaming to her master, and cried, "You have invited a fine guest!"

"Eh, why, Grethel? What do you mean by that?"

"Yes," said she, "he has taken the chickens which I was just going to serve up, off the dish, and has run away with them!"

"That's a nice trick!" said her master, and lamented the fine chickens. "If he had but left me one, so that something remained for me to eat."

He called to him to stop, but the guest pretended not to hear. Then he ran after him with the knife still in his hand, crying, "Just one, just one," meaning that the guest should leave him just one chicken, and not take both.

The guest, however, thought no otherwise than that he was to give up one of his ears, and ran as if fire were burning under him, in order to take them both home with him.

Hans in Luck

ANS had served his master for seven years, so he said to him, "Master, my time is up; now I should be glad to go back home to my mother; give me my wages." The master answered, "You have served me faithfully and honestly; as the service was so shall the reward be;" and he gave Hans a piece of gold as big as his head. Hans pulled his handkerchief out of his pocket, wrapped up the lump in it, put it on his shoulder, and set out on the way home.

As he went on, always putting one foot before the other, he saw a horseman trotting quickly and merrily by on a lively horse. "Ah!" said Hans quite loud, "what a fine thing it is to ride! There you sit as on a chair; you stumble over no stones, you save your shoes, and get on, you don't know how."

The rider, who had heard him, stopped and called out, "Hollo! Hans, why do you go on foot, then?"

"I must," answered he, "for I have this lump to carry home; it is true that it is gold, but I cannot hold my head straight for it, and it hurts my shoulder."

"I will tell you what," said the rider, "we will exchange: I will give you my horse, and you can give me your lump."

"With all my heart," said Hans, "but I can tell you, you will have to crawl along with it."

The rider got down, took the gold, and helped Hans up; then gave him the bridle tight in his hands and said, "If you want to go at a really good pace, you must click your tongue and call out, "Jup! Jup!"

Hans was heartily delighted as he sat upon the horse and rode away so bold and free. After a little while he thought that it ought to go faster, and he began to click with his tongue and call out, "Jup! Jup!" The horse put himself into a sharp trot, and before Hans knew where he was, he was thrown off and lying in a ditch which separated the field from the highway. The horse would have gone off too if it had not been stopped by a countryman, who was coming along the road and driving a cow before him.

Hans got his limbs together and stood up on his legs again, but he was vexed, and said to the countryman, "It is a poor joke, this riding, especially when one gets hold of a mare like this, that kicks and throws one off, so that one has a chance of breaking one's neck. Never again will I mount it. Now I like your cow, for one can walk quietly behind her, and have, over and above, one's milk, butter and cheese every day without fail. What would I not give to have such a cow."

"Well," said the countryman, "if it would give you so much pleasure, I do not mind giving the cow for the horse." Hans agreed with the greatest delight; the countryman jumped upon the horse, and rode quickly away.

Hans drove his cow quietly before him, and thought over his lucky bargain. "If only I have a morsel of bread—and that can hardly fail me—I can eat butter and cheese with it as often as I like; if I am thirsty, I can milk my cow and drink the milk. Good heart, what more can I want?"

When he came to an inn, he made a halt, and in his great content ate up what he had with him—his dinner and supper—and all he had, and with his last few farthings had half a glass of beer. Then he drove his cow onwards along the road to his mother's village.

As it drew nearer mid-day, the heat was more oppressive, and Hans found himself upon a moor which it took about an hour to cross. He felt it very hot and his tongue clave to the roof of his mouth with thirst.

"I can find a cure for this," thought Hans; "I will milk the cow now and refresh myself with the milk." He tied her to a withered tree, and as he had no pail he put his leather cap underneath; but try as he would, not a drop of milk came. And as he set himself to work in a clumsy way, the impatient beast at last gave him such a blow on his head with its hind foot, that he fell on the ground, and for a long time could not think where he was.

By good fortune a butcher just then came along the road with a wheel-barrow, in which lay a young pig. "What sort of a trick is this?" cried he, and helped the good Hans up.

Hans told him what had happened. The butcher gave him his flask and said, "Take a drink and refresh yourself. The cow will certainly give no milk, it is an old beast; at the best it is only fit for the plough, or for the butcher."

"Well, well," said Hans, as he stroked his hair down on his head, "who would have thought it? Certainly it is a fine thing when one can kill a beast like that at home; what meat one has! But I do not care much for beef, it is not juicy enough for me. A young pig like that now is the thing to have, it tastes quite different; and then there are the sausages!"

"Hark ye, Hans," said the butcher, "out of love for you I will exchange, and will let you have the pig for the cow."

"Heaven repay you for your kindness!" said Hans as he gave up the cow, whilst the pig was unbound from the barrow, and the cord by which it was tied was put in his hand.

Hans went on, and thought to himself how everything was going just as he wished; if he did meet with any vexation it was immediate-

241

ly set right. Presently there joined him a lad who was carrying a fine white goose under his arm. They said good morning to each other, and Hans began to tell of his good luck, and how he had always made such good bargains.

The boy told him that he was taking the goose to a christening-feast. "Just lift her," added he, and laid hold of her by the wings; "how heavy she is—she has been fattened up for the last eight weeks. Whoever has a bit of her when she is roasted will have to wipe the fat from both sides of his mouth."

"Yes," said Hans, as he weighed her in one hand, "she is a good weight, but my pig is no bad one."

Meanwhile the lad looked suspiciously from one side to the other, and shook his head. "Look here," he said at length, "it may not be all right with your pig. In the village through which I passed, the Mayor himself had just had one stolen out of its sty. I fear—I fear that you have got hold of it there. They have sent out some people and it would be a bad business if they caught you with the pig; at the very least, you would be shut up in the dark hole."

The good Hans was terrified. "Goodness!" he said, "help me out of this fix; you know more about this place than I do, take my pig and leave me your goose."

"I shall risk something at that game," answered the lad, "but I will not be the cause of your getting into trouble." So he took the cord in his hand, and drove away the pig quickly along a by-path.

The good Hans, free from care, went homewards with the goose under his arm. "When I think over it properly," said he to himself, "I have even gained by the exchange: first there is the good roast-meat, then the quantity of fat which will drip from it, and which will give me dripping for my bread for a quarter of a year, and lastly the beautiful white feathers; I will have my pillow stuffed with them, and then indeed I shall go to sleep without rocking. How glad my mother will be!"

As he was going through the last village, there stood a scissors-grinder with his barrow; as his wheel whirred he sang—

> "I sharpen scissors and quickly grind,
> My coat blows out in the wind behind."

Hans stood still and looked at him; at last he spoke to him and said, "All's well with you, as you are so merry with your grinding."

"Yes," answered the scissors-grinder, "the trade has a golden foundation. A real grinder is a man who as often as he puts his hand into his pocket finds gold in it. But where did you buy that fine goose?"

"I did not buy it, but exchanged my pig for it."

"And the pig?"

"That I got for a cow."

"And the cow?"

"I took that instead of a horse."

"And the horse?"

"For that I gave a lump of gold as big as my head."

"And the gold?"

"Well, that was my wages for seven years' service."

"You have known how to look after yourself each time," said the grinder. "If you can only get on so far as to hear the money jingle in your pocket whenever you stand up, you will have made your fortune."

"How shall I manage that?" said Hans. "You must be a grinder, as I am; nothing particular is wanted for it but a grindstone, the rest finds itself. I have one here; it is certainly a little worn, but you need not give me anything for it but your goose; will you do it?"

"How can you ask?" answered Hans. "I shall be the luckiest fellow on earth; if I have money whenever I put my hand in my pocket, what need I trouble about any longer?" and he handed him the goose and received the grindstone in exchange.

"Now," said the grinder, as he took up an ordinary heavy stone that lay by him, "here is a strong stone for you into the bargain; you can hammer well upon it, and straighten your old nails. Take it with you and keep it carefully."

Hans loaded himself with the stones, and went on with a contented heart; his eyes shone with joy. "I must have been born with a caul," he cried; "everything I want happens to me just as if I were a Sunday-child."

Meanwhile, as he had been on his legs since daybreak, he began to feel tired. Hunger also tormented him, for in his joy at the bargain by which he got the cow he had eaten up all his store of food at once. At last he could only go on with great trouble, and was forced to stop every minute; the stones, too, weighed him down dreadfully. Then he could not help thinking how nice it would be if he had not to carry them just then.

He crept like a snail to a well in a field, and there he thought that he would rest and refresh himself with a cool draught of water, but in order that he might not injure the stones in sitting down, he laid them carefully by his side on the edge of the well. Then he sat down on it, and was about to stoop and drink, when he made a slip, pushed against the stones, and both of them fell into the water.

When Hans saw them with his own eyes sinking to the bottom, he jumped for joy, and then knelt down, and with tears in his eyes thanked God for having shown him this favour also, and delivered him in so good a way, and without his having any need to reproach himself, from those heavy stones which had been the only things that troubled him.

"There is no man under the sun so fortunate as I," he cried out. With a light heart and free from every burden he now ran on until he was with his mother at home.

The Fox and the Geese

HE fox once came to a meadow in which was a flock of fine fat geese, on which he smiled and said, "I come at the nick of time, you are sitting together quite beautifully, so that I can eat you up one after the other." The geese cackled with terror, sprang up, and began to wail and beg piteously for their lives. But the fox would listen to nothing, and said, "There is no mercy to be had! You must die."

At length one of them took heart and said, "If we poor geese are to yield up our vigorous young lives, show us the only possible favour and allow us one more prayer, that we may not die in our sins, and then we will place ourselves in a row, so that you can always pick yourself out the fattest."

"Yes," said the fox, "that is reasonable, and a pious request. Pray away, I will wait till you are done."

Then the first began a good long prayer, for ever saying, "Ga! Ga!" and as she would make no end, the second did not wait until her turn came, but began also, "Ga! Ga!" The third and fourth followed her, and soon they were all cackling together.

When they have done praying, the story shall be continued further, but at present they are still praying without stopping.

The Singing, Soaring Lark

HERE was once on a time a man who was about to set out on a long journey, and on parting he asked his three daughters what he should bring back with him for them. Whereupon the eldest wished for pearls, the second wished for diamonds, but the third said, "Dear father, I should like a singing, soaring lark." The father said, "Yes, if I can get it, you shall have it," kissed all three, and set out.

Now when the time had come for him to be on his way home again, he had brought pearls and diamonds for the two eldest, but he had sought everywhere in vain for a singing, soaring lark for the youngest, and he was very unhappy about it, for she was his favourite child. Then his road lay through a forest, and in the midst of it was a splendid castle, and near the castle stood a tree, but quite on the top of the tree, he saw a singing, soaring lark.

"Aha, you come just at the right moment!" he said, quite delighted, and called to his servant to climb up and catch the little creature.

But as he approached the tree, a lion leapt from beneath it, shook himself, and roared till the leaves on the tree trembled. "He who tries to steal my singing, soaring lark," he cried, "will I devour."

Then the man said, "I did not know that the bird belonged to thee. I will make amends for the wrong I have done and ransom myself with a large sum of money, only spare my life."

The lion said, "Nothing can save thee, unless thou wilt promise to give me for mine own what first meets thee on thy return home; and if thou wilt do that, I will grant thee thy life, and thou shalt have the bird for thy daughter, into the bargain."

But the man hesitated and said, "That might be my youngest daughter, she loves me best, and always runs to meet me on my return home."

The servant, however, was terrified and said, "Why should your daughter be the very one to meet you, it might as easily be a cat, or dog?"

Then the man allowed himself to be over-persuaded, took the singing, soaring lark, and promised to give the lion whatsoever should first meet him on his return home.

When he reached home and entered his house, the first who met him was no other than his youngest and dearest daughter, who came

running up, kissed and embraced him, and when she saw that he had brought with him a singing, soaring lark, she was beside herself with joy.

The father, however, could not rejoice, but began to weep, and said, "My dearest child, I have bought the little bird dear. In return for it, I have been obliged to promise thee to a savage lion, and when he has thee, he will tear thee in pieces and devour thee," and he told her all, just as it had happened, and begged her not to go there, come what might.

But she consoled him and said, "Dearest father, indeed your promise must be fulfilled. I will go thither and soften the lion, so that I may return to thee safely."

Next morning she had the road pointed out to her, took leave, and went fearlessly out into the forest. The lion, however, was an enchanted prince and was by day a lion, and all his people were lions with him, but in the night they resumed their natural human shapes. On her arrival she was kindly received and led into the castle.

When night came, the lion turned into a handsome man, and their wedding was celebrated with great magnificence. They lived happily together, remained awake at night, and slept in the daytime.

One day he came and said, "Tomorrow there is a feast in thy father's house, because thy eldest sister is to be married, and if thou art inclined to go there, my lions shall conduct thee."

She said, "Yes, I should very much like to see my father again," and went thither, accompanied by the lions.

There was great joy when she arrived, for they had all believed that she had been torn in pieces by the lion, and had long ceased to live. But she told them what a handsome husband she had, and how well off she was, remained with them while the wedding-feast lasted, and then went back again to the forest.

When the second daughter was about to be married, and she was again invited to the wedding, she said to the lion, "This time I will not be alone, thou must come with me."

The lion, however, said that it was too dangerous for him, for if when there a ray from a burning candle fell on him, he would be changed into a dove, and for seven years long would have to fly about with the doves.

She said, "Ah, but do come with me, I will take great care of thee, and guard thee from all light."

So they went away together, and took with them their little child as well. She had a chamber built there, so strong and thick that no ray could pierce through it; in this he was to shut himself up when the candles were lit for the wedding-feast. But the door was made of green wood which warped and left a little crack which no one noticed.

The wedding was celebrated with magnificence, but when the procession with all its candles and torches came back from church, and passed by this apartment, a ray about the breadth of a hair fell on the King's son, and when this ray touched him, he was transformed in an instant, and when she came in and looked for him, she did not see him, but a white dove was sitting there.

The dove said to her, "For seven years must I fly about the world, but at every seventh step that thou takest I will let fall a drop of red blood and a white feather, and these will show thee the way, and if thou followest the trace thou canst release me." Thereupon the dove flew out at the door, and she followed him, and at every seventh step a red drop of blood and a little white feather fell down and showed her the way.

So she went continually further and further in the wide world, never looking about her or resting, and the seven years were almost past; then she rejoiced and thought that they would soon be delivered, and yet they were so far from it! Once when they were thus moving onwards, no little feather and no drop of red blood fell, and when she raised her eyes, the dove had disappeared. And as she thought to herself, "In this no man can help thee," she climbed up to the sun, and said to him, "Thou shinest into every crevice, and over every peak, hast not thou seen a white dove flying?"

"No," said the sun, "I have seen none, but I present thee with a casket, open it when thou art in sorest need."

Then she thanked the sun, and went on until evening came and the moon appeared; she then asked her, "Thou shinest the whole night through, and on every field and forest, hast thou not seen a white dove flying?"

"No," said the moon, "I have seen no dove, but here I give thee an egg, break it when thou art in great need."

She thanked the moon, and went on until the night wind came up and blew on her, then she said to it, "Thou blowest over every tree and under every leaf, hast thou not seen a white dove flying?"

"No," said the night wind, "I have seen none, but I will ask the three other winds, perhaps they have seen it."

The east wind and the west wind came, and had seen nothing, but the south wind said, "I have seen the white dove, it has flown to the Red Sea, where it has become a lion again, for the seven years are over, and the lion is there fighting with a dragon; the dragon, however, is an enchanted princess."

The night wind then said to her, "I will advise thee; go to the Red Sea, on the right bank are some tall reeds, count them, break off the eleventh, and strike the dragon with it, then the lion will be able to subdue it, and both then will regain their human form. After that, look round and thou wilt see the griffin which is by the Red Sea; swing thyself, with thy beloved, on to his back, and the bird will carry you over the sea to your own home. Here is a nut for thee, when thou art above the centre of the sea, let the nut fall, it will immediately shoot up, and a tall nut-tree will grow out of the water on which the griffin may rest; for if he cannot rest, he will not be strong enough to carry you across, and if thou forgettest to throw down the nut, he will let you fall into the sea."

Then she went thither, and found everything as the night wind had said. She counted the reeds by the sea, and cut off the eleventh, struck the dragon therewith, whereupon the lion overcame it, and immediately both of them regained their human shapes. But when the princess, who had before been the dragon, was delivered from enchantment, she took the youth by the arm, seated herself on the griffin, and carried him off with her.

There stood the poor maiden who had wandered so far and was again forsaken. She sat down and cried, but at last she took courage and said, "Still I will go as far as the wind blows and as long as the cock crows, until I find him."

And she went forth by long, long roads, until at last she came to the castle where both of them were living together; there she heard that soon a feast was to be held, in which they would celebrate their wedding, but she said, "God still helps me," and opened the casket that the sun had given her. A dress lay therein as brilliant as the sun itself. So she took it out and put it on, and went up into the castle, and everyone, even the bride herself, looked at her with astonishment.

The dress pleased the bride so well that she thought it might do for her wedding-dress, and asked if it was for sale?

"Not for money or land," answered she, "but for flesh and blood." The bride asked her what she meant by that, and she said, "Let me sleep a night in the chamber where the bridegroom sleeps." The bride would not, yet wanted very much to have the dress; at last she consented, but the page was to give the prince a sleeping-draught.

When it was night, therefore, and the youth was already asleep, she was led into the chamber; she seated herself on the bed and said, "I have followed after thee for seven years. I have been to the sun and the moon, and the four winds, and have enquired for thee, and have helped thee against the dragon; wilt thou, then, quite forget me?"

But the prince slept so soundly that it only seemed to him as if the wind were whistling outside in the fir-trees.

When therefore day broke, she was led out again, and had to give up the golden dress. And as that even had been of no avail, she was sad, went out into a meadow, sat down there, and wept.

While she was sitting there, she thought of the egg which the moon had given her; she opened it, and there came out a clucking hen with twelve chickens all of gold, and they ran about chirping, and crept again under the old hen's wings; nothing more beautiful was ever seen in the world!

Then she arose, and drove them through the meadow before her, until the bride looked out of the window. The little chickens pleased her so much that she immediately came down and asked if they were for sale.

"Not for money or land, but for flesh and blood; let me sleep another night in the chamber where the bridegroom sleeps."

The bride said, "Yes," intending to cheat her as on the former evening. But when the prince went to bed, he asked the page what the murmuring and rustling in the night had been? On this the page told all; that he had been forced to give him a sleeping-draught, because a poor girl had slept secretly in the chamber, and that he was to give him another that night. The prince said, "Pour out the draught by the bed-side."

At night, she was again led in, and when she began to relate how ill all had fared with her, he immediately recognized his beloved wife by her voice, sprang up and cried, "Now I really am released! I have been as it were in a dream, for the strange princess has bewitched me so that I have been compelled to forget thee, but God has delivered me from the spell at the right time."

Then they both left the castle secretly in the night, for they feared the father of the princess, who was a sorcerer, and they seated themselves on the griffin which bore them across the Red Sea, and when they were in the midst of it, she let fall the nut. Immediately a tall nut-tree grew up, whereon the bird rested, and then carried them home, where they found their child, who had grown tall and beautiful, and they lived thenceforth happily until their death.

The Young Giant

NCE on a time there lived a countryman who had a son who was as big as a thumb, and did not become any bigger, and during several years did not grow one hair's breadth. Once when the father was going out to plough, the little one said, "Father, I will go out with you."

"Thou wouldst go out with me?" said the father. "Stay here, thou wilt be of no use out there, besides thou mightest get lost!"

Then Thumbling began to cry, and for the sake of peace his father put him in his pocket, and took him with him. When he was outside in the field, he took him out again, and set him in a freshly-cut furrow. Whilst he was there, a great giant came over the hill.

"Dost thou see that great bogie?" said the father, for he wanted to frighten the little fellow to make him good; "he is coming to fetch thee."

The giant, however, had scarcely taken two steps with his long legs before he was in the furrow. He took up little Thumbling carefully with two fingers, examined him, and without saying one word went away with him.

His father stood by, but could not utter a sound for terror, and he thought nothing else but that his child was lost, and that as long as he lived he should never set eyes on him again.

The giant, however, carried him home, suckled him, and Thumbling grew and became tall and strong after the manner of giants. When two years had passed, the old giant took him into the forest, wanted to try him, and said, "Pull up a stick for thyself."

Then the boy was already so strong that he tore up a young tree out of the earth by the roots. But the giant thought, "We must do better than that," took him back again, and suckled him two years longer. When he tried him, his strength had increased so much that he could tear an old tree out of the ground. That was still not enough for the giant; he again suckled him for two years, and when he then went with him into the forest and said, "Now, just tear up a proper stick for me," the boy tore up the strongest oak-tree from the earth, so that it split, and that was a mere trifle to him.

"Now that will do," said the giant, "thou art perfect," and took him back to the field from whence he had brought him.

His father was there following the plough. The young giant went up to him, and said, "Does my father see what a fine man his son has grown into?"

The farmer was alarmed, and said, "No, thou art not my son; I don't want thee—leave me!"

"Truly I am your son; allow me to do your work, I can plough as well as you, nay better."

"No, no, thou art not my son, and thou canst not plough—go away!"

However, as he was afraid of this great man, he left hold of the plough, stepped back and stood at one side of the piece of land. Then the youth took the plough, and just pressed it with one hand, but his grasp was so strong that the plough went deep into the earth.

The farmer could not bear to see that, and called to him, "If thou art determined to plough, thou must not press so hard on it, that makes bad work."

The youth, however, unharnessed the horses, and drew the plough himself, saying, "Just go home, father, and bid my mother make ready a large dish of food, and in the meantime I will go over the field."

Then the farmer went home, and ordered his wife to prepare the food; but the youth ploughed the field which was two acres large, quite alone, and then he harnessed himself to the harrow, and harrowed the whole of the land, using two harrows at once.

When he had done it, he went into the forest, and pulled up two oak-trees, laid them across his shoulders, and hung on them one harrow behind and one before, and also one horse behind and one before, and carried all as if it had been a bundle of straw, to his parents' house.

When he entered the yard, his mother did not recognize him, and asked, "Who is that horrible tall man?"

The farmer said, "That is our son."

She said, "No, that cannot be our son, we never had such a tall one, ours was a little thing." She called to him, "Go away, we do not want thee!"

The youth was silent, but led his horses to the stable, gave them some oats and hay, and all that they wanted. When he had done this, he went into the parlour, sat down on the bench and said, "Mother, now I should like something to eat, will it soon be ready?"

Then she said, "Yes," and brought in two immense dishes full of food, which would have been enough to satisfy herself and her husband for a week. The youth, however, ate the whole of it himself, and asked if she had nothing more to set before him. "No," she replied, "that is all we have."

"But that was only a taste, I must have more." She did not dare to oppose him, and went and put a huge caldron full of food on the fire, and when it was ready, carried it in. "At length come a few crumbs," said he, and ate all there was, but it was still not sufficient to appease his hunger.

Then said he, "Father, I see well that with you I shall never have food enough; if you will get me an iron staff which is strong, and which I cannot break against my knees, I will go out into the world."

The farmer was glad, put his two horses in his cart, and fetched from the smith a staff so large and thick that the two horses could only just bring it away. The youth laid it across his knees, and snap! he broke it in two in the middle like a beanstalk, and threw it away. The father then harnessed four horses, and brought a bar which was so long and thick, that the four horses could only just drag it. The son snapped this also in twain against his knees, threw it away, and said, "Father, this can be of no use to me, you must harness more horses, and bring a stronger staff." So the father harnessed eight horses, and brought one which was so long and thick, that the eight horses could only just carry it. When the son took it in his hand, he broke off a bit from the top of it also, and said, "Father, I see that you will not be able to procure me any such staff as I want, I will remain no longer with you."

So he went away, and gave out that he was a smith's apprentice. He arrived at a village, wherein lived a smith who was a greedy fellow, who never did a kindness to anyone, but wanted everything for himself. The youth went into the smithy to him, and asked if he needed a journeyman. "Yes," said the smith, and looked at him, and thought, "That is a strong fellow who will strike out well, and earn his bread." So he asked, "How much wages dost thou want?"

"I don't want any at all," he replied, "only every fortnight, when the other journeymen are paid, I will give thee two blows, and thou must bear them."

The miser was heartily satisfied, and thought he would thus save much money.

Next morning, the strange journeyman was to begin to work, but when the master brought the glowing bar, and the youth struck his first blow, the iron flew asunder, and the anvil sank so deep into the earth, that there was no bringing it out again. Then the miser grew angry, and said, "Oh, but I can't make any use of you, you strike far too powerfully; what will you have for the one blow?"

Then said he, "I will only give you quite a small blow, that's all." And he raised his foot, and gave him such a kick that he flew away over four loads of hay. Then he sought out the thickest iron bar in the smithy for himself, took it as a stick in his hand and went onwards.

When he had walked for some time, he came to a small farm, and asked the bailiff if he did not require a head-servant. "Yes," said the bailiff, "I can make use of one; you look a strong fellow who can do something, how much a year do you want as wages?" He again replied that he wanted no wages at all, but that every year he would give him three blows, which he must bear. Then the bailiff was satisfied, for he, too, was a covetous fellow.

Next morning all the servants were to go into the wood, and the others were already up, but the head-servant was still in bed. Then one of them called to him, "Get up, it is time; we are going into the wood, and thou must go with us."

"Ah," said he quite roughly and surlily, "you may just go, then; I shall be back again before any of you."

Then the others went to the bailiff, and told him that the head-man was still lying in bed, and would not go into the wood with them. The bailiff said they were to awake him again, and tell him to harness the horses.

The head-man, however, said as before, "Just go there, I shall be back again before any of you." And then he stayed in bed two hours longer.

At length he arose from the feathers, but first he got himself two bushels of peas from the loft, made himself some broth with them, ate it at his leisure, and when that was done, went and harnessed the horses, and drove into the wood.

Not far from the wood was a ravine through which he had to pass, so he first drove the horses on, and then stopped them, and went behind the cart, took trees and brushwood, and made a great barricade, so that no horse could get through.

When he was entering the wood, the others were just driving out of it with their loaded carts to go home; then said he to them, "Drive on, I will still get home before you do."

He did not drive far into the wood, but at once tore two of the very largest trees of all out of the earth, threw them on his cart, and turned round. When he came to the barricade, the others were still standing there, not able to get through.

"Don't you see," said he, "that if you had stayed with me, you would have got home just as quickly, and would have had another hour's sleep?"

He now wanted to drive on, but his horses could not work their way through, so he unharnessed them, laid them on the top of the cart, took the shafts in his own hands, and pulled it all through, and he did this just as easily as if it had been laden with feathers.

When he was over, he said to the others, "There, you see, I have got over quicker than you," and drove on, and the others had to stay where they were. In the yard, however, he took a tree in his hand, showed it to the bailiff, and said, "Isn't that a fine bundle of wood?"

Then said the bailiff to his wife, "The servant is a good one, if he does sleep long, he is still home before the others."

So he served the bailiff for a year, and when that was over, and the other servants were getting their wages, he said it was time for him to have his too. The bailiff, however, was afraid of the blows which he was to receive, and earnestly entreated him to excuse him from having them; for rather than that, he himself would be head-servant, and the youth should be bailiff.

"No," said he, "I will not be a bailiff, I am head-servant, and will remain so, but I will administer that which we agreed on."

The bailiff was willing to give him whatsoever he demanded, but it was of no use, the head-servant said no to everything. Then the bailiff did not know what to do, and begged for a fortnight's delay, for he wanted to find some way of escape. The head-servant consented to this delay.

The bailiff summoned all his clerks together, and they were to think the matter over, and give him advice. The clerks pondered for a long time, but at last they said that no one was sure of his life with the head-servant, for he could kill a man as easily as a midge, and that the bailiff ought to make him get into the well and clean it, and when he was down below, they would roll up one of the mill-stones which was lying there, and throw it on his head; and then he would never return to daylight.

The advice pleased the bailiff, and the head-servant was quite willing to go down the well. When he was standing down below at the bottom, they rolled down the largest mill-stone and thought they had broken his skull, but he cried, "Chase away those hens from the well, they are scratching in the sand up there, and throwing the grains into my eyes, so that I can't see."

So the bailiff cried, "Sh-sh," and pretended to frighten the hens away.

When the head-servant had finished his work, he climbed up and said, "Just look what a beautiful neck-tie I have on," and behold it was the mill-stone which he was wearing round his neck.

The head-servant now wanted to take his reward, but the bailiff again begged for a fortnight's delay. The clerks met together and advised him to send the head-servant to the haunted mill to grind corn by night, for from thence as yet no man had ever returned in the morning alive.

The proposal pleased the bailiff, he called the head-servant that very evening, and ordered him to take eight bushels of corn to the mill, and grind it that night, for it was wanted. So the head-servant went to the loft, and put two bushels in his right pocket, and two in his left, and took four in a wallet, half on his back, and half on his breast, and thus laden went to the haunted mill.

The miller told him that he could grind there very well by day, but not by night, for the mill was haunted, and that up to the present time whosoever had gone into it at night had been found in the morning lying dead inside. He said, "I will manage it, just you go away to bed." Then he went into the mill, and poured out the corn.

About eleven o'clock he went into the miller's room, and sat down on the bench. When he had sat there a while, a door suddenly opened, and a large table came in, and on the table, wine and roasted meats placed themselves, and much good food besides, but everything came of itself, for no one was there to carry it. After this the chairs pushed themselves up, but no people came, until all at once he beheld fingers, which handled knives and forks, and laid food on the plates, but with this exception he saw nothing.

As he was hungry, and saw the food, he, too, placed himself at the table, ate with those who were eating, and enjoyed it. When he had had enough, and the others also had quite emptied their dishes, he distinctly heard all the candles being suddenly snuffed out, and as it was now pitch dark, he felt something like a box on the ear.

Then he said, "If anything of that kind comes again, I shall strike out in return." And when he had received a second box on the ear, he, too, struck out. And so it continued the whole night. He took nothing without returning it, but repaid everything with interest, and did not lay about him in vain.

At daybreak, however, everything ceased. When the miller had got up, he wanted to look after him, and wondered if he were still alive. Then the youth said, "I have eaten my fill, have received some boxes on the ear, but I have given some in return."

The miller rejoiced, and said that the mill was now released from the spell, and wanted to give him much money as a reward. But he said, "Money, I will not have, I have enough of it."

So he took his meal on his back, went home, and told the bailiff that he had done what he had been told to do, and would now have the reward agreed on. When the bailiff heard that, he was seriously alarmed and quite beside himself; he walked backwards and forwards in the room, and drops of perspiration ran down from his forehead. Then he opened the window to get some fresh air, but before he was aware, the head-servant had given him such a kick that he flew through the window out into the air, and so far away that no one ever saw him again.

257

Then said the head-servant to the bailiff's wife, "If he does not come back, you must take the other blow." She cried, "No, no, I cannot bear it," and opened the other window, because drops of perspiration were running down her forehead.

Then he gave her such a kick that she, too, flew out, and as she was lighter she went much higher than her husband. Her husband cried, "Do come to me," but she replied, "Come thou to me, I cannot come to thee."

And they hovered about there in the air, and could not get to each other, and whether they are still hovering about, or not, I do not know, but the young giant took up his iron bar, and went on his way.

The Raven

HERE was once on a time a Queen who had a little daughter who was still so young that she could not walk. One day the child was naughty, and the mother might say what she liked, but the child would not be quiet. Then she became impatient, and as the ravens were flying about the palace, she opened the window and said, "I wish you were a raven and would fly away, and then I should have some rest."

Scarcely had she spoken the words, before the child was changed into a raven, and flew from her arms out of the window. It flew into a dark forest, and stayed in it a long time, and the parents heard nothing of their child.

Then one day a man was on his way through this forest and heard the raven crying, and followed the voice, and when he came nearer, the bird said, "I am a king's daughter by birth, and am bewitched, but thou canst set me free."

"What am I to do?" asked he.

She said, "Go further into the forest, and thou wilt find a house, wherein sits an aged woman, who will offer thee meat and drink, but thou must accept nothing; for if thou eatest or drinkest anything, thou wilt fall into a sleep, and then thou wilt not be able to deliver me. In the garden behind the house there is a great heap of tan, and on this thou shalt stand and wait for me. For three days I will come every afternoon at two o'clock in a carriage. On the first day four white horses will be harnessed to it, then four chestnut horses, and lastly four black ones; but if thou art not awake, but sleeping, I shall not be set free."

The man promised to do everything that she desired, but the raven said, "Alas! I know already that thou wilt not deliver me; thou wilt accept something from the woman."

Then the man once more promised that he would certainly not touch anything either to eat or to drink. But when he entered the house, the old woman came to him and said, "Poor man, how faint you are; come and refresh yourself; eat and drink."

"No," said the man, "I will not eat or drink."

She, however, let him have no peace, and said, "If you will not eat, take one drink out of the glass; one is nothing."

Then he let himself be persuaded, and drank. Shortly before two o'clock in the afternoon he went into the garden to the tan heap to wait for the raven. As he was standing there, his weariness all at once became so great that he could not struggle against it, and lay down for a short time, but he was determined not to go to sleep. Hardly, however, had he lain down, than his eyes closed of their own accord, and he fell asleep and slept so soundly that nothing in the world could have aroused him.

At two o'clock the raven came driving up with four white horses, but she was already in deep grief and said, "I know he is asleep." And when she came into the garden, he was indeed lying there asleep on the heap of tan. She alighted from the carriage, went to him, shook him, and called him, but he did not awake.

Next day about noon, the old woman came again and brought him food and drink, but he would not take any of it. But she let him have no rest and persuaded him until at length he again took one drink out of the glass.

Towards two o'clock he went into the garden to the tan heap to wait for the raven, but all at once felt such a great weariness that his limbs would no longer support him. He could not stand upright, and was forced to lie down, and fell into a heavy sleep.

When the raven drove up with four brown horses, she was already full of grief, and said, "I know he is asleep." She went to him, but there he lay sleeping, and there was no wakening him.

Next day the old woman asked what was the meaning of this? He was neither eating nor drinking anything; did he want to die? He replied, "I am not allowed to eat or drink, and will not do so."

She, however, set a dish with meat, and a glass with wine before him, and when he smelt it, he could not resist, and swallowed a deep draught. When the time came, he went out into the garden to the heap of tan, and waited for the King's daughter; but he became still more weary than on the day before, and lay down and slept as soundly as if he had been a stone.

At two o'clock the raven came with four black horses, and the coachman and everything else was black. She was already in the deepest grief, and said, "I know that he is asleep and cannot deliver me."

When she came to him, there he was lying fast asleep. She shook him and called him, but she could not waken him. Then she laid a loaf beside him, and after that a piece of meat, and thirdly a bottle of wine, and he might consume as much of all of them as he liked, but they would never grow less. After this she took a gold ring from her finger, and put it on his, and her name was graven on it.

Lastly, she laid a letter beside him wherein was written what she had given him, and that none of the things would ever grow less; and in it was also written, "I see right well that here thou wilt never be able to deliver me, but if thou art still willing to deliver me, come to the golden castle of Stromberg; it lies in thy power, of that I am certain." And when she had given him all these things, she seated herself in her carriage, and drove to the golden castle of Stromberg.

When the man awoke and saw that he had slept, he was sad at heart, and said, "She has certainly driven by, and I have not set her free." Then he perceived the things which were lying beside him, and read the letter wherein was written how everything had happened. So he arose and went away, intending to go to the golden castle of Stromberg, but he did not know where it was.

After he had walked about the world for a long time, he entered into a dark forest, and walked for fourteen days without stopping, and still could not find his way out. Then it was once more evening, and he was so tired that he lay down in a thicket and fell asleep. Next day he went onwards, and in the evening, as he was again about to lie down beneath some bushes, he heard such a howling and crying that he could not go to sleep. And at the time when people light the candles, he saw one glimmering, and arose and went towards it. Then he came to a house which seemed very small, for in front of it a great giant was standing. He thought to himself, "If I go in, and the giant sees me, it will very likely cost me my life."

At length he ventured it and went in. When the giant saw him, he said, "It is well that thou comest, for it is long since I have eaten; I will at once eat thee for my supper."

"I'd rather you would leave that alone," said the man, "I do not like to be eaten; but if thou hast any desire to eat, I have quite enough here to satisfy thee."

"If that be true," said the giant, "thou mayst be easy, I was only going to devour thee because I had nothing else."

Then they went, and sat down to the table, and the man took out the bread, wine, and meat which would never come to an end.

"This pleases me well," said the giant, and ate to his heart's content.

Then the man said to him, "Canst thou tell me where the golden castle of Stromberg is?"

The giant said, "I will look at my map; all the towns, and villages, and houses are to be found on it."

He brought out the map which he had in the room and looked for the castle, but it was not to be found on it. "It's no matter!" said he. "I have some still larger maps in my cupboard upstairs, and we will look in them." But there, too, it was in vain.

The man now wanted to go onwards, but the giant begged him to wait a few days longer until his brother, who had gone out to bring some provisions, came home. When the brother came home, they inquired about the golden castle of Stromberg.

He replied, "When I have eaten and have had enough, I will look in the map."

Then he went with them up to his chamber, and they searched in his map, but could not find it. Then he brought out still older maps, and they never rested until they found the golden castle of Stromberg, but

it was many thou-
sand miles away.

"How am I to
get there?" asked
the man.

The giant said,
"I have two hours'
time, during which
I will carry you
into the neighbour-
hood, but after that
I must be at home
to suckle the child
that we have." So
the giant carried
the man to about
a hundred leagues
from the castle,
and said, "Thou
canst very well
walk the rest of the
way alone." And he
turned back, but

the man went onwards day and night, until at length he came to the
golden castle of Stromberg.

It stood on a glass-mountain, and the bewitched maiden drove
in her carriage round the castle, and then went inside it. He rejoiced
when he saw her and wanted to climb up to her, but when he began to
do so, he always slipped down the glass again.

And when he saw that he could not reach her, he was filled with
trouble, and said to himself, "I will stay down here below, and wait for
her." So he built himself a hut and stayed in it for a whole year, and
every day saw the King's daughter driving about above, but never could
go to her.

Then one day he saw from his hut three robbers who were beating
each other, and cried to them, "God be with ye!" They stopped when
they heard the cry, but as they saw no one, they once more began to
beat each other, and that too most dangerously. So he again cried,
"God be with ye!" Again they stopped, looked round about, but as they
saw no one they went on beating each other. Then he cried for the third
time, "God be with ye," and thought, "I must see what these three are
about," and went thither and asked why they were beating each other
so furiously.

One of them said that he had found a stick, and that when he
struck a door with it, that door would spring open. The next said that
he had found a mantle, and that whenever he put it on, he was invis-
ible, but the third said he had found a horse on which a man could ride
everywhere, even up the glass-mountain. And now they did not know

whether they ought to have these things in common, or whether they ought to divide them.

Then the man said, "I will give you something in exchange for these three things. Money indeed have I not, but I have other things of more value; but first I must try yours to see if you have told the truth."

Then they put him on the horse, threw the mantle round him, and gave him the stick in his hand, and when he had all these things, they were no longer able to see him. So he gave them some vigorous blows and cried, "Now, vagabonds, you have got what you deserve, are you satisfied?"

And he rode up the glass-mountain, but when he came in front of the castle at the top, it was shut. Then he struck the door with his stick, and it sprang open immediately. He went in and ascended the stairs until he came to the hall where the maiden was sitting with a golden cup full of wine before her.

She, however, could not see him because he had the mantle on. And when he came up to her, he drew from his finger the ring which she had given him, and threw it into the cup so that it rang.

Then she cried, "That is my ring, so the man who is to set me free must be here." They searched the whole castle and did not find him, but he had gone out, and had seated himself on the horse and thrown off the mantle.

When they came to the door, she saw him and cried aloud in her delight. Then he alighted and took the King's daughter in his arms, but she kissed him and said, "Now hast thou set me free, and tomorrow we will celebrate our wedding."

The Water of Life

HERE was once a King who had an illness, and no one believed that he would come out of it with his life. He had three sons who were much distressed about it, and went down into the palace-garden and wept. There they met an old man who inquired as to the cause of their grief. They told him that their father was so ill that he would most certainly die, for nothing seemed to cure him.

Then the old man said, "I know of one more remedy, and that is the water of life; if he drinks of it he will become well again; but it is hard to find."

The eldest said, "I will manage to find it," and went to the sick King, and begged to be allowed to go forth in search of the water of life, for that alone could save him.

"No," said the King, "the danger of it is too great. I would rather die." But he begged so long that the King consented.

The prince thought in his heart, "If I bring the water, then I shall be best beloved of my father, and shall inherit the kingdom."

So he set out, and when he had ridden forth a little distance, a dwarf stood there in the road who called to him and said, "Whither away so fast?"

"Silly shrimp," said the prince, very haughtily, "it is nothing to do with you," and rode on. But the little dwarf had grown angry, and had wished an evil wish.

Soon after this the prince entered a ravine, and the further he rode the closer the mountains drew together, and at last the road became so narrow that he could not advance a step further; it was impossible either to turn his horse or to dismount from the saddle, and he was shut in there as if in prison.

The sick King waited long for him, but he came not. Then the second son said, "Father, let me go forth to seek the water," and thought to himself, "If my brother is dead, then the kingdom will fall to me."

At first the King would not allow him to go either, but at last he yielded, so the prince set out on the same road that his brother had taken, and he too met the dwarf, who stopped him to ask, whither he was going in such haste? "Little shrimp," said the prince, "that is nothing to thee," and rode on without giving him another look. But the dwarf bewitched him, and he, like the other, got into a ravine, and could neither go forwards nor backwards. So fare haughty people.

As the second son also remained away, the youngest begged to be allowed to go forth to fetch the water, and at last the King was obliged to let him go. When he met the dwarf and the latter asked him whither he was going in such haste, he stopped, gave him an explanation, and said, "I am seeking the water of life, for my father is sick unto death."

"Dost thou know, then, where that is to be found?"

"No," said the prince.

"As thou hast borne thyself as is seemly, and not haughtily like thy false brothers, I will give thee the information and tell thee how thou mayst obtain the water of life. It springs from a fountain in the court-yard of an enchanted castle, but thou wilt not be able to make thy way to it, if I do not give thee an iron wand and two small loaves of bread. Strike thrice with the wand on the iron door of the castle, and it will spring open: inside lie two lions with gaping jaws, but if thou throwest a loaf to each of them, they will be quieted. Then hasten to fetch some of the water of life before the clock strikes twelve, else the door will shut again, and thou wilt be imprisoned."

The prince thanked him, took the wand and the bread, and set out on his way. When he arrived, everything was as the dwarf had said. The door sprang open at the third stroke of the wand, and when he had appeased the lions with the bread, he entered the castle, and came in a large and splendid hall, wherein sat some enchanted princes whose rings he drew off their fingers. A sword and a loaf of bread were lying there, which he carried away.

After this, he entered a chamber, in which was a beautiful maiden who rejoiced when she saw him, kissed him, and told him that he had delivered her, and should have the whole of her kingdom, and that if he would return in a year their wedding should be celebrated; likewise she told him where the spring of the water of life was, and that he was to hasten and draw some of it before the clock struck twelve.

Then he went onwards, and at last entered a room where there was a beautiful newly-made bed, and as he was very weary, he felt inclined to rest a little. So he lay down and fell asleep. When he awoke, it was striking a quarter to twelve. He sprang up in a fright, ran to the spring, drew some water in a cup which stood near, and hastened away.

But just as he was passing through the iron door, the clock struck twelve, and the door fell to with such violence that it carried away a piece of his heel. He, however, rejoicing at having obtained the water of life, went homewards, and again passed the dwarf.

When the latter saw the sword and the loaf, he said, "With these thou hast won great wealth; with the sword thou canst slay whole armies, and the bread will never come to an end."

But the prince would not go home to his father without his brothers, and said, "Dear dwarf, canst thou not tell me where my two brothers are? They went out before I did in search of the water of life, and have not returned."

"They are imprisoned between two mountains," said the dwarf. "I have condemned them to stay there, because they were so haughty."

Then the prince begged until the dwarf released them; he warned him, however, and said, "Beware of them, for they have bad hearts."

When his brothers came, he rejoiced, and told them how things had gone with him, that he had found the water of life, and had brought a cupful away with him, and had rescued a beautiful princess, who was willing to wait a year for him, and then their wedding was to be celebrated, and he would obtain a great kingdom.

After that they rode on together, and chanced upon a land where war and famine reigned, and the King already thought he must perish, for the scarcity was so great. Then the prince went to him and gave him the loaf, wherewith he fed and satisfied the whole of his kingdom, and then the prince gave him the sword also, wherewith he slew the hosts of his enemies, and could now live in rest and peace.

The prince then took back his loaf and his sword, and the three brothers rode on. But after this they entered two more countries where war and famine reigned, and each time the prince gave his loaf and his sword to the Kings, and had now delivered three kingdoms, and after that they went on board a ship and sailed over the sea.

During the passage, the two eldest conversed apart and said, "The youngest has found the water of life and not we, for that our father will give him the kingdom—the kingdom which belongs to us, and he will rob us of all our fortune."

They then began to seek revenge, and plotted with each other to destroy him. They waited until they found him fast asleep, then they poured the water of life out of the cup, and took it for themselves, but into the cup they poured salt sea-water.

Now therefore, when they arrived home, the youngest took his cup to the sick King in order that he might drink out of it, and be cured. But scarcely had he drunk a very little of the salt sea-water than he became still worse than before. And as he was lamenting over this, the two eldest brothers came, and accused the youngest of having intended to poison him, and said that they had brought him the true water of life, and handed it to him. He had scarcely tasted it, when he felt his sickness departing, and became strong and healthy as in the days of his youth.

After that they both went to the youngest, mocked him, and said, "You certainly found the water of life, but you have had the pain, and we the gain; you should have been sharper, and should have kept your eyes open. We took it from you whilst you were asleep at sea, and when a year is over, one of us will go and fetch the beautiful princess. But beware that you do not disclose aught of this to our father; indeed he does not trust you, and if you say a single word, you shall lose your life into the bargain, but if you keep silent, you shall have it as a gift."

The old King was angry with his youngest son, and thought he had plotted against his life. So he summoned the court together, and had sentence pronounced upon his son, that he should be secretly shot. And once when the prince was riding forth to the chase, suspecting no evil, the King's huntsman had to go with him, and when they were quite alone in the forest, the huntsman looked so sorrowful that the prince said to him, "Dear huntsman, what ails you?"

The huntsman said, "I cannot tell you, and yet I ought."

Then the prince said, "Say openly what it is, I will pardon you."

"Alas!" said the huntsman, "I am to shoot you dead, the King has ordered me to do it."

Then the prince was shocked, and said, "Dear huntsman, let me live; there, I give you my royal garments; give me your common ones in their stead."

The huntsman said, "I will willingly do that, indeed I should not have been able to shoot you."

Then they exchanged clothes, and the huntsman returned home; the prince, however, went further into the forest.

After a time three waggons of gold and precious stones came to the King for his youngest son, which were sent by the three Kings who had slain their enemies with the prince's sword, and maintained their people with his bread, and who wished to show their gratitude for it. The old King then thought, "Can my son have been innocent?" and said to his people, "Would that he were still alive, how it grieves me that I have suffered him to be killed!"

"He still lives," said the huntsman, "I could not find it in my heart to carry out your command," and told the King how it had happened. Then a stone fell from the King's heart, and he had it proclaimed in every country that his son might return and be taken into favour again.

The princess, however, had a road made up to her palace which was quite bright and golden, and told her people that whosoever came riding straight along it to her, would be the right wooer and was to be admitted, and whoever rode by the side of it, was not the right one, and was not to be admitted. As the time was now close at hand, the eldest thought he would hasten to go to the King's daughter, and give himself out as her deliverer, and thus win her for his bride, and the kingdom to boot.

Therefore he rode forth, and when he arrived in front of the palace, and saw the splendid golden road, he thought it would be a sin and a shame if he were to ride over that, and turned aside, and rode on the right side of it. But when he came to the door, the servants told him that he was not the right man, and was to go away again.

Soon after this the second prince set out, and when he came to the golden road, and his horse had put one foot on it, he thought it would be a sin and a shame to tread a piece of it off, and he turned aside and rode on the left side of it, and when he reached the door, the attendants told him he was not the right one, and he was to go away again.

When at last the year had entirely expired, the third son likewise wished to ride out of the forest to his beloved, and with her to forget his sorrows. So he set out and thought of her so incessantly, and wished to be with her so much, that he never noticed the golden road at all. So his horse rode onwards up the middle of it, and when he came to the door, it was opened and the princess received him with joy, and said he was her deliverer, and lord of the kingdom, and their wedding was celebrated with great rejoicing.

When it was over, she told him that his father invited him to come to him, and had forgiven him. So he rode thither, and told him everything; how his brothers had betrayed him, and how he had nevertheless kept silence. The old King wished to punish them, but they had put to sea, and never came back as long as they lived.

The Peasant's Wise Daughter

HERE was once a poor peasant who had no land, but only a small house, and one daughter. Then said the daughter, "We ought to ask our lord the King for a bit of newly-cleared land." When the King heard of their poverty, he presented them with a bit of land, which she and her father dug up, and intended to sow with a little corn and grain of that kind. When they had dug nearly the whole of the field, they found in the earth a mortar made of pure gold. "Listen," said the father to the girl, "as our lord the King has been so gracious and presented us with the field, we ought to give him this mortar in return for it."

The daughter, however, would not consent to this, and said, "Father, if we have the mortar without having the pestle as well, we shall have to get the pestle, so you had much better say nothing about it."

He would, however, not obey her, but took the mortar and carried it to the King, said that he had found it in the cleared land, and asked if he would accept it as a present. The King took the mortar, and asked if he had found nothing besides that? "No," answered the countryman. Then the King said that he must now bring him the pestle. The peasant said they had not found that, but he might just as well have spoken to the wind; he was put in prison, and was to stay there until he produced the pestle.

The servants had daily to carry him bread and water, which is what people get in prison, and they heard how the man cried out continually, "Ah! if I had but listened to my daughter! Alas, alas, if I had but listened to my daughter!"

Then the servants went to the King and told him how the prisoner was always crying, "Ah! if I had but listened to my daughter!" and would neither eat nor drink.

So he commanded the servants to bring the prisoner before him, and then the King asked the peasant why he was always crying, "Ah! if I had but listened to my daughter!" and what it was that his daughter had said.

"She told me that I ought not to take the mortar to you, for I should have to produce the pestle as well."

"If you have a daughter who is as wise as that, let her come here."

She was therefore obliged to appear before the King, who asked her if she really was so wise, and said he would set her a riddle, and

270

if she could guess that, he would marry her. She at once said yes, she would guess it.

Then said the King, "Come to me not clothed, not naked, not riding, not walking, not in the road, and not out of the road, and if thou canst do that I will marry thee."

So she went away, put off everything she had on, and then she was not clothed, and took a great fishing net, and seated herself in it and wrapped it entirely round and round her, so that she was not naked, and she hired an ass, and tied the fisherman's net to its tail, so that it was forced to drag her along, and that was neither riding nor walking. The ass had also to drag her in the ruts, so that she only touched the ground with her great toe, and that was neither being in the road nor out of the road.

And when she arrived in that fashion, the King said she had guessed the riddle and fulfilled all the conditions. Then he ordered her father to be released from the prison, took her to wife, and gave into her care all the royal possessions.

Now when some years had passed, the King was once drawing up his troops on parade, when it happened that some peasants who had been selling wood stopped with their waggons before the palace; some of them had oxen yoked to them, and some horses. There was one peasant who had three horses, one of which was delivered of a young foal, and it ran away and lay down between two oxen which were in front of the waggon.

When the peasants came together, they began to dispute, to beat each other and make a disturbance, and the peasant with the oxen wanted to keep the foal, and said one of the oxen had given birth to it, and the other said his horse had had it, and that it was his.

271

The quarrel came before the King, and he gave the verdict that the foal should stay where it had been found, and so the peasant with the oxen, to whom it did not belong, got it. Then the other went away, and wept and lamented over his foal.

Now he had heard how gracious his lady the Queen was because she herself had sprung from poor peasant folks, so he went to her and begged her to see if she could not help him to get his foal back again. Said she, "Yes, I will tell thee what to do, if thou wilt promise me not to betray me.

Early tomorrow morning, when the King parades the guard, place thyself there in the middle of the road by which he must pass, take a great fishing-net and pretend to be fishing; go on fishing too, and empty out the net as if thou hadst got it full"—and then she told him also what he was to say if he was questioned by the King.

The next day, therefore, the peasant stood there, and fished on dry ground. When the King passed by and saw that, he sent his messenger to ask what the stupid man was about? He answered, "I am fishing." The messenger asked how he could fish when there was no water there? The peasant said, "It is as easy for me to fish on dry land as it is for an ox to have a foal."

The messenger went back and took the answer to the King, who ordered the peasant to be brought to him and told him that this was not his own idea, and he wanted to know whose it was? The peasant must confess that at once. The peasant, however, would not do so, and said always, God forbid he should! the idea was his own. They laid him, however, on a heap of straw, and beat him and tormented him so long that at last he admitted that he had got the idea from the Queen.

When the King reached home again, he said to his wife, "Why hast thou behaved so falsely to me? I will not have thee any longer for a wife; thy time is up, go back to the place from whence thou camest—to thy peasant's hut."

One favour, however, he granted her; she might take with her the one thing that was dearest and best in her eyes; and thus was she dismissed.

She said, "Yes, my dear husband, if you command this, I will do it," and she embraced him and kissed him, and said she would take leave of him. Then she ordered a powerful sleeping draught to be brought, to drink farewell to him; the King took a long draught, but she took only a little.

He soon fell into a deep sleep, and when she perceived that, she called a servant and took a fair white linen cloth and wrapped the King in it, and the servant was forced to carry him into a carriage that stood before the door, and she drove with him to her own little house.

She laid him in her own little bed, and he slept one day and one night without awakening, and when he awoke, he looked round and said, "Good God! where am I?" He called his attendants, but none of them were there.

At length his wife came to his bedside and said, "My dear lord and King, you told me I might bring away with me from the palace that which was dearest and most precious in my eyes—I have nothing more precious and dear than yourself, so I have brought you with me."

Tears rose to the King's eyes and he said, "Dear wife, thou shalt be mine and I will be thine," and he took her back with him to the royal palace and was married again to her, and at the present time they are very likely still living.

Doctor Knowall

HERE was once on a time a poor peasant called Crabb, who drove with two oxen a load of wood to the town, and sold it to a doctor for two thalers. When the money was being counted out to him, it so happened that the doctor was sitting at table, and when the peasant saw how daintily he ate and drank, his heart desired what he saw, and he would willingly have been a doctor too. So he remained standing a while, and at length inquired if he too could not be a doctor.

"Oh, yes," said the doctor, "that is soon managed."

"What must I do?" asked the peasant.

"In the first place, buy thyself an ABC book of the kind which has a cock on the frontispiece; in the second, turn thy cart and thy two oxen into money, and get thyself some clothes, and whatsoever else pertains to medicine; thirdly, have a sign painted for thyself with the words, "I am Doctor Knowall," and have that nailed up above thy house door."

The peasant did everything that he had been told to do.

When he had doctored people awhile, but not long, a rich and great lord had some money stolen. Then he was told about Doctor Knowall who lived in such and such a village, and must know what had become of the money. So the lord had the horses put in his carriage, drove out to the village, and asked Crabb if he were Doctor Knowall? Yes, he was, he said. Then he was to go with him and bring back the stolen money. "Oh, yes, but Grethe, my wife, must go too." The lord was willing, and let both of them have a seat in the carriage, and they all drove away together.

When they came to the nobleman's castle, the table was spread, and Crabb was told to sit down and eat. "Yes, but my wife, Grethe, too," said he, and he seated himself with her at the table.

And when the first servant came with a dish of delicate fare, the peasant nudged his wife, and said, "Grethe, that was the first," meaning that was the servant who brought the first dish. The servant, however, thought he intended by that to say, "That is the first thief," and as he actually was so, he was terrified, and said to his comrade outside, "The doctor knows all: we shall fare ill, he said I was the first."

The second did not want to go in at all, but was forced. So when he went in with his dish, the peasant nudged his wife, and said, "Grethe, that is the second." This servant was just as much alarmed, and he got out.

The third did not fare better, for the peasant again said, "Grethe, that is the third."

The fourth had to carry in a dish that was covered, and the lord told the doctor that he was to show his skill, and guess what was beneath the cover. The doctor looked at the dish, had no idea what to say, and cried, "Ah, poor Crabb." When the lord heard that, he cried, "There! he knows it, he knows who has the money!"

On this the servants looked terribly uneasy, and made a sign to the doctor that they wished him to step outside for a moment. When therefore he went out, all four of them confessed to him that they had stolen the money, and said that they would willingly restore it and give him a heavy sum into the bargain, if he would not denounce them, for if he did they would be hanged.

They led him to the spot where the money was concealed. With this the doctor was satisfied, and returned to the hall, sat down to the table, and said, "My lord, now will I search in my book where the gold is hidden."

The fifth servant, however, crept into the stove to hear if the doctor knew still more. The Doctor, however, sat still and opened his ABC book, turned the pages backwards and forwards, and looked for the cock. As he could not find it immediately he said, "I know you are there, so you had better show yourself."

Then the fellow in the stove thought that the doctor meant him, and full of terror, sprang out, crying, "That man knows everything!"

Then Doctor Knowall showed the count where the money was, but did not say who had stolen it, and received from both sides much money in reward, and became a renowned man.

Wise Folks

NE day a peasant took his good hazel-stick out of the corner and said to his wife, "Trina, I am going across country, and shall not return for three days. If during that time the cattle-dealer should happen to call and want to buy our three cows, you may strike a bargain at once, but not unless you can get two hundred thalers for them; nothing less, do you hear?"

"For heaven's sake just go in peace," answered the woman, "I will manage that."

"You, indeed," said the man. "You once fell on your head when you were a little child, and that affects you even now; but let me tell you this, if you do anything foolish, I will make your back black and blue, and not with paint, I assure you, but with the stick which I have in my hand, and the colouring shall last a whole year, you may rely on that." And having said that, the man went on his way.

Next morning the cattle-dealer came, and the woman had no need to say many words to him. When he had seen the cows and heard the price, he said, "I am quite willing to give that, honestly speaking, they are worth it. I will take the beasts away with me at once."

He unfastened their chains and drove them out of the byre, but just as he was going out of the yard-door, the woman clutched him by the sleeve and said, "You must give me the two hundred thalers now, or I cannot let the cows go."

"True," answered the man, "but I have forgotten to buckle on my money-belt. Have no fear, however, you shall have security for my paying. I will take two cows with me and leave one, and then you will have a good pledge."

The woman saw the force of this, and let the man go away with the cows, and thought to herself, "How pleased Hans will be when he finds how cleverly I have managed it!"

The peasant came home on the third day as he had said he would, and at once inquired if the cows were sold?

"Yes, indeed, dear Hans," answered the woman, "and as you said, for two hundred thalers. They are scarcely worth so much, but the man took them without making any objection."

"Where is the money?" asked the peasant.

"Oh, I have not got the money," replied the woman; "he had happened to forget his money-belt, but he will soon bring it, and he left good security behind him."

"What kind of security?" asked the man.

"One of the three cows, which he shall not have until he has paid for the other two. I have managed very cunningly, for I have kept the smallest, which eats the least."

The man was enraged and lifted up his stick, and was just going to give her the beating he had promised her. Suddenly he let the stick fall and said, "You are the stupidest goose that ever waddled on God's earth, but I am sorry for you. I will go out into the highways and wait for three days to see if I find anyone who is still stupider than you. If I succeed in doing so, you shall go scot-free, but if I do not find him, you shall receive your well-deserved reward without any discount."

He went out into the great highways, sat down on a stone, and waited for what would happen. Then he saw a peasant's waggon coming towards him, and a woman was standing upright in the middle of it, instead of sitting on the bundle of straw which was lying beside her, or walking near the oxen and leading them.

The man thought to himself, "That is certainly one of the kind I am in search of," and jumped up and ran backwards and forwards in front of the waggon like one who is not very wise.

"What do you want, my friend?" said the woman to him; "I don't know you, where do you come from?"

"I have fallen down from Heaven," replied the man, "and don't know how to get back again, couldn't you drive me up?"

"No," said the woman, "I don't know the way, but if you come from Heaven you can surely tell me how my husband, who has been there these three years, is. You must have seen him?"

"Oh, yes, I have seen him, but all men can't get on well. He keeps sheep, and the sheep give him a great deal to do. They run up the mountains and lose their way in the wilderness, and he has to run after them and drive them together again. His clothes are all torn to pieces too, and will soon fall off his body. There is no tailor there, for Saint Peter won't let any of them in, as you know by the story."

"Who would have thought it?" cried the woman, "I tell you what, I will fetch his Sunday coat which is still hanging at home in the cupboard, he can wear that and look respectable. You will be so kind as to take it with you."

"That won't do very well," answered the peasant; "people are not allowed to take clothes into Heaven, they are taken away from one at the gate."

"Then hark you," said the woman, "I sold my fine wheat yesterday and got a good lot of money for it, I will send that to him. If you hide the purse in your pocket, no one will know that you have it."

"If you can't manage it any other way," said the peasant, "I will do you that favour."

"Just sit still where you are," said she, "and I will drive home and fetch the purse, I shall soon be back again. I do not sit down on the bundle of straw, but stand up in the waggon, because it makes it lighter for the cattle."

She drove her oxen away, and the peasant thought, "That woman has a perfect talent for folly, if she really brings the money, my wife may think herself fortunate, for she will get no beating."

It was not long before she came in a great hurry with the money, and with her own hands put it in his pocket. Before she went away, she thanked him again a thousand times for his courtesy.

When the woman got home again, she found her son who had come in from the field. She told him what unlooked-for things had befallen her, and then added, "I am truly delighted at having found an opportunity of sending something to my poor husband. Who would ever have imagined that he could be suffering for want of anything up in Heaven?"

The son was full of astonishment. "Mother," said he, "it is not every day that a man comes from Heaven in this way, I will go out immediately, and see if he is still to be found; he must tell me what it is like up there, and how the work is done."

He saddled the horse and rode off with all speed. He found the peasant who was sitting under a willow-tree, and was just going to count the money in the purse.

"Have you seen the man who has fallen down from Heaven?" cried the youth to him.

"Yes," answered the peasant, "he has set out on his way back there, and has gone up that hill, from whence it will be rather nearer; you could still catch him up, if you were to ride fast."

"Alas," said the youth, "I have been doing tiring work all day, and the ride here has completely worn me out; you know the man, be so kind as to get on my horse, and go and persuade him to come here."

"Aha!" thought the peasant, "here is another who has no wick in his lamp!"

"Why should I not do you this favour?" said he, and mounted the horse and rode off in a quick trot.

The youth remained sitting there till night fell, but the peasant never came back. "The man from Heaven must certainly have been in a great hurry, and would not turn back," thought he, "and the peasant has no doubt given him the horse to take to my father."

He went home and told his mother what had happened, and that he had sent his father the horse so that he might not have to be always running about. "Thou hast done well," answered she, "thy legs are younger than his, and thou canst go on foot."

When the peasant got home, he put the horse in the stable beside the cow which he had as a pledge, and then went to his wife and said, "Trina, as your luck would have it, I have found two who are still sillier fools than you; this time you escape without a beating, I will store it up for another occasion."

Then he lighted his pipe, sat down in his grandfather's chair, and said, "It was a good stroke of business to get a sleek horse and a great purse full of money into the bargain, for two lean cows. If stupidity always brought in as much as that I would be quite willing to hold it in honour."

So thought the peasant, but you no doubt prefer the simple folks.

The Spirit in the Bottle

HERE was once a poor woodcutter who toiled from early morning till late night. When at last he had laid by some money, he said to his boy, "You are my only child, I will spend the money which I have earned with the sweat of my brow on your education; if you learn some honest trade you can support me in my old age, when my limbs have grown stiff and I am obliged to stay at home." Then the boy went to a High School and learned diligently so that his masters praised him, and he remained there a long time.

When he had worked through two classes, but was still not yet perfect in everything, the little pittance which the father had earned was all spent, and the boy was obliged to return home to him. "Ah," said the father, sorrowfully, "I can give you no more, and in these hard times I cannot earn a farthing more than will suffice for our daily bread."

"Dear father," answered the son, "don't trouble yourself about it, if it is God's will, it will turn to my advantage I shall soon accustom myself to it." When the father wanted to go into the forest to earn money by helping to pile and stack wood and also to chop it, the son said, "I will go with you and help you."

"Nay, my son," said the father, "that would be hard for you; you are not accustomed to rough work, and will not be able to bear it, besides I have only one axe and no money left wherewith to buy another."

"Just go to the neighbour," answered the son, "he will lend you his axe until I have earned one for myself."

The father then borrowed an axe of the neighbour, and next morning at break of day they went out into the forest together. The son helped his father and was quite merry and brisk about it.

But when the sun was right over their heads, the father said, "We will rest, and have our dinner, and then we shall work as well again."

The son took his bread in his hands, and said, "Just you rest, father, I am not tired; I will walk up and down a little in the forest, and look for birds' nests."

"Oh, you fool," said the father, "why should you want to run about there? Afterwards you will be tired, and no longer able to raise your arm; stay here, and sit down beside me."

The son, however, went into the forest, ate his bread, was very merry and peered in among the green branches to see if he could discover a bird's nest anywhere. So he went up and down to see if he could find a bird's nest until at last he came to a great dangerous-looking oak, which certainly was already many hundred years old, and which five men could not have spanned.

He stood still and looked at it, and thought, "Many a bird must have built its nest in that." Then all at once it seemed to him that he heard a voice. He listened and became aware that someone was crying in a very smothered voice, "Let me out, let me out!"

He looked around, but could discover nothing; nevertheless, he fancied that the voice came out of the ground. Then he cried, "Where art thou?"

The voice answered, "I am down here amongst the roots of the oak-tree. Let me out! Let me out!"

The scholar began to loosen the earth under the tree, and search among the roots, until at last he found a glass bottle in a little hollow. He lifted it up and held it against the light, and then saw a creature shaped like a frog, springing up and down in it.

"Let me out! Let me out!" it cried anew, and the scholar thinking no evil, drew the cork out of the bottle. Immediately a spirit ascended from it, and began to grow, and grew so fast that in a very few moments he stood before the scholar, a terrible fellow as big as half the tree by which he was standing.

"Knowest thou," he cried in an awful voice, "what thy wages are for having let me out?"

"No," replied the scholar fearlessly, "how should I know that?"

"Then I will tell thee," cried the spirit; "I must strangle thee for it."

"Thou shouldst have told me that sooner," said the scholar, "for I should then have left thee shut up, but my head shall stand fast for all thou canst do; more persons than one must be consulted about that."

"More persons here, more persons there," said the spirit. "Thou shalt have the wages thou hast earned. Dost thou think that I was shut up there for such a long time as a favour. No, it was a punishment for me. I am the mighty Mercurius. Whoso releases me, him must I strangle."

"Softly," answered the scholar, "not so fast. I must first know that thou really wert shut up in that little bottle, and that thou art the right spirit. If, indeed, thou canst get in again, I will believe, and then thou mayst do as thou wilt with me."

The spirit said haughtily, "That is a very trifling feat," drew himself together, and made himself as small and slender as he had been at first, so that he crept through the same opening, and right through the neck of the bottle in again. Scarcely was he within than the scholar thrust the cork he had drawn back into the bottle, and threw it among the roots of the oak into its old place, and the spirit was betrayed.

And now the scholar was about to return to his father, but the spirit cried very piteously, "Ah, do let me out! ah, do let me out!"

"No," answered the scholar, "not a second time! He who has once tried to take my life shall not be set free by me, now that I have caught him again."

"If thou wilt set me free," said the spirit, "I will give thee so much that thou wilt have plenty all the days of thy life."

"No," answered the scholar, "thou wouldst cheat me as thou didst the first time."

"Thou art playing away thy own good luck," said the spirit; "I will do thee no harm, but will reward thee richly."

The scholar thought, "I will venture it, perhaps he will keep his word, and anyhow he shall not get the better of me." Then he took out the cork, and the spirit rose up from the bottle as he had done before, stretched himself out and became as big as a giant.

"Now thou shalt have thy reward," said he, and handed the scholar a little bag just like a plaster, and said, "If thou spreadest one end of this over a wound it will heal, and if thou rubbest steel or iron with the other end it will be changed into silver."

"I must just try that," said the scholar, and went to a tree, tore off the bark with his axe, and rubbed it with one end of the plaster. It immediately closed together and was healed. "Now, it is all right," he said to the spirit, "and we can part." The spirit thanked him for his release, and the scholar thanked the spirit for his present, and went back to his father.

"Where hast thou been racing about?" said the father; "why hast thou forgotten thy work? I said at once that thou wouldst never get on with anything."

"Be easy, father, I will make it up."

"Make it up indeed," said the father angrily, "there's no art in that."

"Take care, father, I will soon hew that tree there, so that it will split."

Then he took his plaster, rubbed the axe with it, and dealt a mighty blow, but as the iron had changed into silver, the edge turned.

"Hollo, father, just look what a bad axe you've given me, it has become quite crooked."

The father was shocked and said, "Ah, what hast thou done? Now I shall have to pay for that, and have not the wherewithal, and that is all the good I have got by thy work."

"Don't get angry," said the son, "I will soon pay for the axe."

"Oh, thou blockhead," cried the father, "wherewith wilt thou pay for it? Thou hast nothing but what I give thee. These are students' tricks that are sticking in thy head, but thou hast no idea of wood-cutting."

After a while the scholar said, "Father, I can really work no more, we had better take a holiday."

"Eh, what!" answered he. "Dost thou think I will sit with my hands lying in my lap like thee? I must go on working, but thou mayst take thyself off home."

"Father, I am here in this wood for the first time, I don't know my way alone. Do go with me."

As his anger had now abated, the father at last let himself be persuaded and went home with him. Then he said to the son, "Go and sell thy damaged axe, and see what thou canst get for it, and I must earn the difference, in order to pay the neighbour."

The son took the axe, and carried it into town to a goldsmith, who tested it, laid it in the scales, and said, "It is worth four hundred thalers, I have not so much as that by me."

The son said, "Give me what you have, I will lend you the rest."

The goldsmith gave him three hundred thalers, and remained a hundred in his debt. The son thereupon went home and said, "Father, I have got the money, go and ask the neighbour what he wants for the axe."

"I know that already," answered the old man, "one thaler, six groschen."

"Then give him two thalers, twelve groschen, that is double and enough; see, I have money in plenty," and he gave the father a hundred thalers, and said, "You shall never know want, live as comfortably as you like."

"Good heavens!" said the father, "how hast thou come by these riches?"

The scholar then told how all had come to pass, and how he, trusting in his luck, had made such a good hit. But with the money that was left, he went back to the High School and went on learning more, and as he could heal all wounds with his plaster, he became the most famous doctor in the whole world.

Sweet Porridge

HERE was a poor but good little girl who lived alone with her mother, and they no longer had anything to eat. So the child went into the forest, and there an aged woman met her who was aware of her sorrow, and presented her with a little pot, which when she said, "Cook, little pot, cook," would cook good, sweet porridge, and when she said, "Stop, little pot," it ceased to cook.

The girl took the pot home to her mother, and now they were freed from their poverty and hunger, and ate sweet porridge as often as they chose. Once on a time when the girl had gone out, her mother said, "Cook, little pot, cook."

And it did cook and she ate till she was satisfied, and then she wanted the pot to stop cooking, but did not know the word. So it went on cooking and the porridge rose over the edge, and still it cooked on until the kitchen and whole house were full, and then the next house, and then the whole street, just as if it wanted to satisfy the hunger of the whole world, and there was the greatest distress, but no one knew how to stop it.

At last when only one single house remained, the child came home and just said, "Stop, little pot," and it stopped and gave up cooking, and whosoever wished to return to the town had to eat his way back.

The Little Folks' Presents

 TAILOR and a goldsmith were travelling together, and one evening when the sun had sunk behind the mountains, they heard the sound of distant music, which became more and more distinct. It sounded strange, but so pleasant that they forgot all their weariness and stepped quickly onwards. The moon had already arisen when they reached a hill on which they saw a crowd of little men and women, who had taken each other's hands, and were whirling round in the dance with the greatest pleasure and delight.

They sang to it most charmingly, and that was the music which the travellers had heard. In the midst of them sat an old man who was rather taller than the rest. He wore a parti-coloured coat, and his iron-grey beard hung down over his breast. The two remained standing full of astonishment, and watched the dance. The old man made a sign that they should enter, and the little folks willingly opened their circle.

The goldsmith, who had a hump, and like all hunchbacks was brave enough, stepped in; the tailor felt a little afraid at first, and held back, but when he saw how merrily all was going, he plucked up his courage, and followed. The circle closed again directly, and the little folks went on singing and dancing with the wildest leaps. The old man, however, took a large knife which hung to his girdle, whetted it, and when it was sufficiently sharpened, he looked round at the strangers.

They were terrified, but they had not much time for reflection, for the old man seized the goldsmith and with the greatest speed, shaved the hair of his head clean off, and then the same thing happened to the tailor. But their fear left them when, after he had finished his work, the old man clapped them both on the shoulder in a friendly manner, as much as to say, they had behaved well to let all that be done to them willingly, and without any struggle. He pointed with his finger to a heap of coals which lay at one side, and signified to the travellers by his gestures that they were to fill their pockets with them. Both of them obeyed, although they did not know of what use the coals would be to them, and then they went on their way to seek a shelter for the night. When they had got into the valley, the clock of the neighbouring monastery struck twelve, and the song ceased. In a moment all had vanished, and the hill lay in solitude in the moonlight.

The two travellers found an inn, and covered themselves up on their straw-beds with their coats, but in their weariness forgot to take the coals out of them before doing so. A heavy weight on their limbs awakened them earlier than usual. They felt in the pockets, and could not believe their eyes when they saw that they were not filled with coals, but with pure gold; happily, too, the hair of their heads and beards was there again as thick as ever.

They had now become rich folks, but the goldsmith, who, in accordance with his greedy disposition, had filled his pockets better, was as rich again as the tailor. A greedy man, even if he has much, still wishes to have more, so the goldsmith proposed to the tailor that they should wait another day, and go out again in the evening in order to bring back still greater treasures from the old man on the hill.

The tailor refused, and said, "I have enough and am content; now I shall be a master, and marry my dear object (for so he called his sweetheart), and I am a happy man." But he stayed another day to please him.

In the evening the goldsmith hung a couple of bags over his shoulders that he might be able to stow away a great deal, and took the road to the hill. He found, as on the night before, the little folks at their singing and dancing, and the old man again shaved him clean, and signed to him to take some coal away with him. He was not slow about sticking as much into his bags as would go, went back quite delighted, and covered himself over with his coat.

"Even if the gold does weigh heavily," said he, "I will gladly bear that," and at last he fell asleep with the sweet anticipation of waking in the morning an enormously rich man.

When he opened his eyes, he got up in haste to examine his pockets, but how amazed he was when he drew nothing out of them but black coals, and that howsoever often he put his hands in them. "The gold I got the night before is still there for me," thought he, and went and brought it out, but how shocked he was when he saw that it likewise had again turned into coal.

He smote his forehead with his dusty black hand, and then he felt that his whole head was bald and smooth, as was also the place where his beard should have been. But his misfortunes were not yet over; he now remarked for the first time that in addition to the hump on his back, a second, just as large, had grown in front on his breast. Then he recognized the punishment of his greediness, and began to weep aloud.

The good tailor, who was wakened by this, comforted the unhappy fellow as well as he could, and said, "Thou hast been my comrade in my travelling time; thou shalt stay with me and share in my wealth." He kept his word, but the poor goldsmith was obliged to carry the two humps as long as he lived, and to cover his bald head with a cap.

The Old Woman in the Wood

POOR servant-girl was once travelling with the family with which she was in service, through a great forest, and when they were in the midst of it, robbers came out of the thicket, and murdered all they found. All perished together except the girl, who had jumped out of the carriage in a fright, and hidden herself behind a tree.

When the robbers had gone away with their booty, she came out and beheld the great disaster. Then she began to weep bitterly, and said, "What can a poor girl like me do now? I do not know how to get out of the forest, no human being lives in it, so I must certainly starve."

She walked about and looked for a road, but could find none. When it was evening, she seated herself under a tree, gave herself into God's keeping, and resolved to sit waiting there and not go away, let what might happen.

When, however, she had sat there for a while, a white dove came flying to her with a little golden key in its mouth. It put the little key in her hand, and said, "Dost thou see that great tree, therein is a little lock, it opens with the tiny key, and there thou wilt find food enough, and suffer no more hunger."

Then she went to the tree and opened it, and found milk in a little dish, and white bread to break into it, so that she could eat her fill. When she was satisfied, she said, "It is now the time when the hens at home go to roost, I am so tired I could go to bed too."

Then the dove flew to her again, and brought another golden key in its bill, and said, "Open that tree there, and thou wilt find a bed."

So she opened it, and found a beautiful white bed, and she prayed God to protect her during the night, and lay down and slept. In the morning the dove came for the third time, and again brought a little key, and said, "Open that tree there, and thou wilt find clothes."

And when she opened it, she found garments beset with gold and with jewels, more splendid than those of any king's daughter. So she lived there for some time, and the dove came every day and provided her with all she needed, and it was a quiet good life.

Once, however, the dove came and said, "Wilt thou do something for my sake?"

"With all my heart," said the girl.

Then said the little dove, "I will guide thee to a small house; enter it, and inside it, an old woman will be sitting by the fire and will say, 'Good day.' But on thy life give her no answer, let her do what she will, but pass by her on the right side; further on, there is a door, which open, and thou wilt enter into a room where a quantity of rings of all kinds are lying, amongst which are some magnificent ones with shining stones; leave them, however, where they are, and seek out a plain one, which must likewise be amongst them, and bring it here to me as quickly as thou canst."

The girl went to the little house, and came to the door. There sat an old woman who stared when she saw her, and said, "Good day, my child." The girl gave her no answer, and opened the door. "Whither away," cried the old woman, and seized her by the gown, and wanted to hold her fast, saying, "That is my house; no one can go in there if I choose not to allow it."

But the girl was silent, got away from her, and went straight into the room. Now there lay on the table an enormous quantity of rings, which gleamed and glittered before her eyes. She turned them over and looked for the plain one, but could not find it.

While she was seeking, she saw the old woman and how she was stealing away, and wanting to get off with a bird-cage which she had in

her hand. So she went after her and took the cage out of her hand, and when she raised it up and looked into it, a bird was inside which had the plain ring in its bill. Then she took the ring, and ran quite joyously home with it, and thought the little white dove would come and get the ring, but it did not. Then she leant against a tree and determined to wait for the dove, and, as she thus stood, it seemed just as if the tree was soft and pliant, and was letting its branches down.

And suddenly the branches twined around her, and were two arms, and when she looked round, the tree was a handsome man, who embraced and kissed her heartily, and said, "Thou hast delivered me from the power of the old woman, who is a wicked witch. She had changed me into a tree, and every day for two hours I was a white dove, and so long as she possessed the ring I could not regain my human form."

Then his servants and his horses, who had likewise been changed into trees, were freed from the enchantment also, and stood beside him. And he led them forth to his kingdom, for he was a King's son, and they married, and lived happily.

One-eye, Two-eyes, and Three-eyes

 HERE was once a woman who had three daughters, the eldest of whom was called One-eye, because she had only one eye in the middle of her forehead, and the second, Two-eyes, because she had two eyes like other folks, and the youngest, Three-eyes, because she had three eyes; and her third eye was also in the centre of her forehead. However, as Two-eyes saw just as other human beings did, her sisters and her mother could not endure her. They said to her, "Thou, with thy two eyes, art no better than the common people; thou dost not belong to us!" They pushed her about, and threw old clothes to her, and gave her nothing to eat but what they left, and did everything that they could to make her unhappy.

It came to pass that Two-eyes had to go out into the fields and tend the goat, but she was still quite hungry, because her sisters had given her so little to eat. So she sat down on a ridge and began to weep, and so bitterly that two streams ran down from her eyes. And once when she looked up in her grief, a woman was standing beside her, who said, "Why art thou weeping, little Two-eyes?"

Two-eyes answered, "Have I not reason to weep, when I have two eyes like other people, and my sisters and mother hate me for it, and push me from one corner to another, throw old clothes at me, and give me nothing to eat but the scraps they leave? Today they have given me so little that I am still quite hungry."

Then the wise woman said, "Wipe away thy tears, Two-eyes, and I will tell thee something to stop thee ever suffering from hunger again; just say to thy goat,

> "Bleat, my little goat, bleat,
> Cover the table with something to eat,"

and then a clean well-spread little table will stand before thee, with the most delicious food upon it of which thou mayst eat as much as thou art inclined for, and when thou hast had enough, and hast no more need of the little table, just say,

> "Bleat, bleat, my little goat, I pray,
> And take the table quite away,"

and then it will vanish again from thy sight." Hereupon the wise woman departed.

But Two-eyes thought, "I must instantly make a trial, and see if what she said is true, for I am far too hungry," and she said,

> "Bleat, my little goat, bleat,
> Cover the table with something to eat,"

and scarcely had she spoken the words than a little table, covered with a white cloth, was standing there, and on it was a plate with a knife and fork, and a silver spoon; and the most delicious food was there also, warm and smoking as if it had just come out of the kitchen.

Then Two-eyes said the shortest prayer she knew, "Lord God, be with us always, Amen," and helped herself to some food, and enjoyed it. And when she was satisfied, she said, as the wise woman had taught her,

> "Bleat, bleat, my little goat, I pray,
> And take the table quite away,"

and immediately the little table and everything on it was gone again. "That is a delightful way of keeping house!" thought Two-eyes, and was quite glad and happy.

In the evening, when she went home with her goat, she found a small earthenware dish with some food, which her sisters had set ready for her, but she did not touch it. Next day she again went out with her goat, and left the few bits of broken bread which had been handed to her, lying untouched.

The first and second time that she did this, her sisters did not remark it at all, but as it happened every time, they did observe it, and said, "There is something wrong about Two-eyes, she always leaves her food untasted, and she used to eat up everything that was given her; she must have discovered other ways of getting food."

In order that they might learn the truth, they resolved to send One-eye with Two-eyes when she went to drive her goat to the pasture, to observe what Two-eyes did when she was there, and whether anyone brought her anything to eat and drink. So when Two-eyes set out the next time, One-eye went to her and said, "I will go with you to the pasture, and see that the goat is well taken care of, and driven where there is food."

But Two-eyes knew what was in One-eye's mind, and drove the goat into high grass and said, "Come, One-eye, we will sit down, and I will sing something to you."

One-eye sat down and was tired with the unaccustomed walk and the heat of the sun, and Two-eyes sang constantly,

> "One eye, wakest thou?
> One eye, sleepest thou?

until One-eye shut her one eye, and fell asleep, and as soon as Two-eyes saw that One-eye was fast asleep, and could discover nothing, she said,

> "Bleat, my little goat, bleat,
> Cover the table with something to eat,"

and seated herself at her table, and ate and drank until she was satisfied, and then she again cried,

> "Bleat, bleat, my little goat, I pray,
> And take the table quite away,"

and in an instant all was gone.

Two-eyes now awakened One-eye, and said, "One-eye, you want to take care of the goat, and go to sleep while you are doing it, and in the meantime the goat might run all over the world. Come, let us go home again."

So they went home, and again Two-eyes let her little dish stand untouched, and One-eye could not tell her mother why she would not eat it, and to excuse herself said, "I fell asleep when I was out."

Next day the mother said to Three-eyes, "This time thou shalt go and observe if Two-eyes eats anything when she is out, and if anyone fetches her food and drink, for she must eat and drink in secret."

So Three-eyes went to Two-eyes, and said, "I will go with you and see if the goat is taken proper care of, and driven where there is food."

But Two-eyes knew what was in Three-eyes' mind, and drove the goat into high grass and said, "We will sit down, and I will sing something to you, Three-eyes." Three-eyes sat down and was tired with the walk and with the heat of the sun, and Two-eyes began the same song as before, and sang,

> "Three eyes, are you waking?"

but then, instead of singing,

> "Three eyes, are you sleeping?"

as she ought to have done, she thoughtlessly sang,

> "Two eyes, are you sleeping?"

and sang all the time,

> "Three eyes, are you waking?
> Two eyes, are you sleeping?"

Then two of the eyes which Three-eyes had, shut and fell asleep, but the third, as it had not been named in the song, did not sleep.

It is true that Three-eyes shut it, but only in her cunning, to pretend it was asleep too, but it blinked, and could see everything very well. And when Two-eyes thought that Three-eyes was fast asleep, she used her little charm,

> "Bleat, my little goat, bleat,
> Cover the table with something to eat,"

and ate and drank as much as her heart desired, and then ordered the table to go away again,

> "Bleat, bleat, my little goat, I pray,
> And take the table quite away,"

and Three-eyes had seen everything.

Then Two-eyes came to her, waked her and said, "Have you been asleep, Three-eyes? You are a good care-taker! Come, we will go home."

And when they got home, Two-eyes again did not eat, and Three-eyes said to the mother, "Now, I know why that high-minded thing there does not eat. When she is out, she says to the goat,

> "Bleat, my little goat, bleat,
> Cover the table with something to eat,"

and then a little table appears before her covered with the best of food, much better than any we have here, and when she has eaten all she wants, she says,

> "Bleat, bleat, my little goat, I pray,
> And take the table quite away,"

and all disappears. I watched everything closely. She put two of my eyes to sleep by using a certain form of words, but luckily the one in my forehead kept awake."

Then the envious mother cried, "Dost thou want to fare better than we do? The desire shall pass away," and she fetched a butcher's knife, and thrust it into the heart of the goat, which fell down dead.

When Two-eyes saw that, she went out full of trouble, seated herself on the ridge of grass at the edge of the field, and wept bitter tears. Suddenly the wise woman once more stood by her side, and said, "Two-eyes, why art thou weeping?"

"Have I not reason to weep?" she answered. "The goat which covered the table for me every day when I spoke your charm, has been killed by my mother, and now I shall again have to bear hunger and want."

The wise woman said, "Two-eyes, I will give thee a piece of good advice; ask thy sisters to give thee the entrails of the slaughtered goat, and bury them in the ground in front of the house, and thy fortune will be made."

Then she vanished, and Two-eyes went home and said to her sisters, "Dear sisters, do give me some part of my goat; I don't wish for what is good, but give me the entrails."

Then they laughed and said, "If that's all you want, you can have it."

So Two-eyes took the entrails and buried them quietly in the evening, in front of the house-door, as the wise woman had counselled her to do.

Next morning, when they all awoke, and went to the house-door, there stood a strangely magnificent tree with leaves of silver, and fruit of gold hanging among them, so that in all the wide world there was nothing more beautiful or precious. They did not know how the tree could have come there during the night, but Two-eyes saw that it had grown up out of the entrails of the goat, for it was standing on the exact spot where she had buried them.

Then the mother said to One-eye, "Climb up, my child, and gather some of the fruit of the tree for us."

One-eye climbed up, but when she was about to get hold of one of the golden apples, the branch escaped from her hands, and that happened each time, so that she could not pluck a single apple, let her do what she might.

Then said the mother, "Three-eyes, do you climb up; you with your three eyes can look about you better than One-eye."

One-eye slipped down, and Three-eyes climbed up. Three-eyes was not more skilful, and might search as she liked, but the golden apples always escaped her.

At length the mother grew impatient, and climbed up herself, but could get hold of the fruit no better than One-eye and Three-eyes, for she always clutched empty air.

Then said Two-eyes, "I will just go up, perhaps I may succeed better."

The sisters cried, "You indeed, with your two eyes, what can you do?"

But Two-eyes climbed up, and the golden apples did not get out of her way, but came into her hand of their own accord, so that she could pluck them one after the other, and brought a whole apronful down with her. The mother took them away from her, and instead of treating poor Two-eyes any better for this, she and One-eye and Three-eyes were only envious, because Two-eyes alone had been able to get the fruit, and they treated her still more cruelly.

It so befell that once when they were all standing together by the tree, a young knight came up. "Quick, Two-eyes," cried the two sisters, "creep under this, and don't disgrace us!" and with all speed they turned an empty barrel which was standing close by the tree over poor Two-eyes, and they pushed the golden apples which she had been gathering, under it too.

When the knight came nearer, he was a handsome lord, who stopped and admired the magnificent gold and silver tree, and said to the two sisters, "To whom does this fine tree belong? Anyone who would bestow one branch of it on me might in return for it ask whatsoever he desired."

Then One-eye and Three-eyes replied that the tree belonged to them, and that they would give him a branch. They both took great trouble, but they were not able to do it, for the branches and fruit both moved away from them every time.

Then said the knight, "It is very strange that the tree should belong to you, and that you should still not be able to break a piece off."

They again asserted that the tree was their property. Whilst they were saying so, Two-eyes rolled out a couple of golden apples from under the barrel to the feet of the knight, for she was vexed with One-eye and Three-eyes, for not speaking the truth.

When the knight saw the apples, he was astonished, and asked where they came from. One-eye and Three-eyes answered that they had another sister, who was not allowed to show herself, for she had only two eyes like any common person. The knight, however, desired to see her, and cried, "Two-eyes, come forth."

Then Two-eyes, quite comforted, came from beneath the barrel, and the knight was surprised at her great beauty, and said, "Thou, Two-eyes, canst certainly break off a branch from the tree for me."

"Yes," replied Two-eyes, "that I certainly shall be able to do, for the tree belongs to me." And she climbed up, and with the greatest ease broke off a branch with beautiful silver leaves and golden fruit, and gave it to the knight.

Then said the knight, "Two-eyes, what shall I give thee for it?"

"Alas!" answered Two-eyes, "I suffer from hunger and thirst, grief and want, from early morning till late night; if you would take me with you, and deliver me from these things, I should be happy."

So the knight lifted Two-eyes on to his horse, and took her home with him to his father's castle, and there he gave her beautiful clothes, and meat and drink to her heart's content, and as he loved her so much he married her, and the wedding was solemnized with great rejoicing.

When Two-eyes was thus carried away by the handsome knight, her two sisters grudged her good fortune in downright earnest. "The wonderful tree, however, still remains with us," thought they, "and even if we can gather no fruit from it, still everyone will stand still and look at it, and come to us and admire it. Who knows what good things may be in store for us?"

But next morning, the tree had vanished, and all their hopes were at an end. And when Two-eyes looked out of the window of her own little room, to her great delight it was standing in front of it, and so it had followed her.

Two-eyes lived a long time in happiness. Once two poor women came to her in her castle, and begged for alms. She looked in their faces, and recognized her sisters, One-eye, and Three-eyes, who had fallen into such poverty that they had to wander about and beg their bread from door to door. Two-eyes, however, made them welcome, and was kind to them, and took care of them, so that they both with all their hearts repented the evil that they had done their sister in their youth.

The Star-Money

HERE was once on a time a little girl whose father and mother were dead, and she was so poor that she no longer had any little room to live in, or bed to sleep in, and at last she had nothing else but the clothes she was wearing and a little bit of bread in her hand which some charitable soul had given her. She was, however, good and pious. And as she was thus forsaken by all the world, she went forth into the open country, trusting in the good God. Then a poor man met her, who said, "Ah, give me something to eat, I am so hungry!"

She reached him the whole of her piece of bread, and said, "May God bless it to thy use," and went onwards.

Then came a child who moaned and said, "My head is so cold, give me something to cover it with."

So she took off her hood and gave it to him; and when she had walked a little farther, she met another child who had no jacket and was frozen with cold. Then she gave it her own; and a little farther on one begged for a frock, and she gave away that also.

At length she got into a forest and it had already become dark, and there came yet another child, and asked for a little shirt, and the good little girl thought to herself, "It is a dark night and no one sees thee, thou canst very well give thy little shirt away," and took it off, and gave away that also. And as she so stood, and had not one single thing left, suddenly some stars from heaven fell down, and they were nothing else but hard smooth pieces of money, and although she had just given her little shirt away, she had a new one which was of the very finest linen.

Then she gathered together the money into this, and was rich all the days of her life.

Iron John

HERE was once on a time a King who had a great forest near his palace, full of all kinds of wild animals. One day he sent out a huntsman to shoot him a roe, but he did not come back. "Perhaps some accident has befallen him," said the King, and the next day he sent out two more huntsmen who were to search for him, but they too stayed away. Then on the third day, he sent for all his huntsmen, and said, "Scour the whole forest through, and do not give up until ye have found all three." But of these also, none came home again, and of the pack of hounds which they had taken with them, none were seen more.

From that time forth, no one would any longer venture into the forest, and it lay there in deep stillness and solitude, and nothing was seen of it, but sometimes an eagle or a hawk flying over it. This lasted for many years, when a strange huntsman announced himself to the King as seeking a situation, and offered to go into the dangerous forest.

The King, however, would not give his consent, and said, "It is not safe in there; I fear it would fare with thee no better than with the others, and thou wouldst never come out again."

The huntsman replied, "Lord, I will venture it at my own risk, of fear I know nothing."

The huntsman therefore betook himself with his dog to the forest. It was not long before the dog fell in with some game on the way, and wanted to pursue it; but hardly had the dog run two steps when it stood before a deep pool, could go no farther, and a naked arm stretched itself out of the water, seized it, and drew it under. When the huntsman saw that, he went back and fetched three men to come with buckets and bale out the water.

When they could see to the bottom, there lay a wild man whose body was brown like rusty iron, and whose hair hung over his face down to his knees. They bound him with cords, and led him away to the castle. There was great astonishment over the wild man; the King, however, had him put in an iron cage in his court-yard, and forbade the door to be opened on pain of death, and the Queen herself was to take the key into her keeping. And from this time forth everyone could again go into the forest with safety.

The King had a son of eight years, who was once playing in the court-yard, and while he was playing, his golden ball fell into the cage. The boy ran thither and said, "Give me my ball out."

"Not till thou hast opened the door for me," answered the man.

"No," said the boy, "I will not do that; the King has forbidden it," and ran away.

The next day he again went and asked for his ball; the wild man said, "Open my door," but the boy would not.

On the third day the King had ridden out hunting, and the boy went once more and said, "I cannot open the door even if I wished, for I have not the key."

Then the wild man said, "It lies under thy mother's pillow, thou canst get it there."

The boy, who wanted to have his ball back, cast all thought to the winds, and brought the key. The door opened with difficulty, and the boy pinched his fingers. When it was open, the wild man stepped out, gave him the golden ball, and hurried away. The boy had become afraid; he called and cried after him, "Oh, wild man, do not go away, or I shall be beaten!" The wild man turned back, took him up, set him on his shoulder, and went with hasty steps into the forest. When the King came home, he observed the empty cage, and asked the Queen how that had happened? She knew nothing about it, and sought the key, but it was gone. She called the boy, but no one answered. The King sent out people to seek for him in the fields, but they did not find him. Then he could easily guess what had happened, and much grief reigned in the royal court.

When the wild man had once more reached the dark forest, he took the boy down from his shoulder, and said to him, "Thou wilt never see thy father and mother again, but I will keep thee with me, for thou hast set me free, and I have compassion on thee. If thou dost all I bid thee, thou shalt fare well. Of treasure and gold have I enough, and more than anyone in the world." He made a bed of moss for the boy on which he slept, and the next morning the man took him to a well, and said, "Behold, the gold well is as bright and clear as crystal, thou shalt sit beside it, and take care that nothing falls into it, or it will be polluted. I will come every evening to see if thou hast obeyed my order."

The boy placed himself by the margin of the well, and often saw a golden fish or a golden snake show itself therein, and took care that nothing fell in. As he was thus sitting, his finger hurt him so violently that he involuntarily put it in the water. He drew it quickly out again, but saw that it was quite gilded, and whatsoever pains he took to wash the gold off again, all was to no purpose.

In the evening Iron John came back, looked at the boy, and said, "What has happened to the well?"

"Nothing, nothing," he answered, and held his finger behind his back, that the man might not see it.

But he said, "Thou hast dipped thy finger into the water, this time it may pass, but take care thou dost not again let anything go in."

By daybreak the boy was already sitting by the well and watching it. His finger hurt him again and he passed it over his head, and then unhappily a hair fell down into the well. He took it quickly out, but it was already quite gilded.

Iron John came, and already knew what had happened. "Thou hast let a hair fall into the well," said he. "I will allow thee to watch by it once more, but if this happens for the third time then the well is polluted, and thou canst no longer remain with me."

On the third day, the boy sat by the well, and did not stir his finger, however much it hurt him. But the time was long to him, and he looked at the reflection of his face on the surface of the water. And as he still bent down more and more while he was doing so, and trying to look straight into the eyes, his long hair fell down from his shoulders into the water. He raised himself up quickly, but the whole of the hair of his head was already golden and shone like the sun. You may imagine how terrified the poor boy was! He took his pocket-handkerchief and tied it round his head, in order that the man might not see it.

When he came, he already knew everything, and said, "Take the handkerchief off." Then the golden hair streamed forth, and let the boy excuse himself as he might, it was of no use.

"Thou hast not stood the trial, and canst stay here no longer. Go forth into the world, there thou wilt learn what poverty is. But as thou hast not a bad heart, and as I mean well by thee, there is one thing I will grant thee; if thou fallest into any difficulty, come to the forest and cry, "Iron John," and then I will come and help thee. My power is great, greater than thou thinkest, and I have gold and silver in abundance."

Then the King's son left the forest, and walked by beaten and unbeaten paths ever onwards until at length he reached a great city. There he looked for work, but could find none, and he had learnt nothing by which he could help himself. At length he went to the palace, and asked if they would take him in. The people about court did not at all know what use they could make of him, but they liked him, and told him to stay.

At length the cook took him into his service, and said he might carry wood and water, and rake the cinders together. Once when it so happened that no one else was at hand, the cook ordered him to carry the food to the royal table, but as he did not like to let his golden hair be seen, he kept his little cap on.

Such a thing as that had never yet come under the King's notice, and he said, "When thou comest to the royal table, thou must take thy hat off."

He answered, "Ah, Lord, I cannot; I have a bad sore place on my head."

Then the King had the cook called before him and scolded him, and asked how he could take such a boy as that into his service; and that he was to turn him off at once. The cook, however, had pity on him, and exchanged him for the gardener's boy.

And now the boy had to plant and water the garden, hoe and dig, and bear the wind and bad weather. Once in summer when he was working alone in the garden, the day was so warm he took his little

cap off that the air
might cool him. As the
sun shone on his hair
it glittered and flashed
so that the rays fell into
the bed-room of the
King's daughter, and up
she sprang to see what
that could be. Then she
saw the boy, and cried
to him, "Boy, bring me
a wreath of flowers."

He put his cap
on with all haste, and
gathered wild field-
flowers and bound
them together. When
he was ascending the
stairs with them, the
gardener met him, and
said, "How canst thou
take the King's daugh-
ter a garland of such
common flowers? Go
quickly, and get anoth-
er, and seek out the prettiest and rarest."

"Oh, no," replied the boy, "the wild ones have more scent, and will
please her better."

When he got into the room, the King's daughter said, "Take thy cap
off, it is not seemly to keep it on in my presence."

He again said, "I may not, I have a sore head."

She, however, caught at his cap and pulled it off, and then his gold-
en hair rolled down on his shoulders, and it was splendid to behold.
He wanted to run out, but she held him by the arm, and gave him a
handful of ducats.

With these he departed, but he cared nothing for the gold pieces.
He took them to the gardener, and said, "I present them to thy children, they can play with them."

The following day the King's daughter again called to him that he
was to bring her a wreath of field-flowers, and when he went in with it,
she instantly snatched at his cap, and wanted to take it away from him,
but he held it fast with both hands.

She again gave him a handful of ducats, but he would not keep
them, and gave them to the gardener for playthings for his children.
On the third day things went just the same; she could not get his cap
away from him, and he would not have her money.

Not long afterwards, the country was overrun by war. The King
gathered together his people, and did not know whether or not he

could offer any opposition to the enemy, who was superior in strength and had a mighty army. Then said the gardener's boy, "I am grown up, and will go to the wars also, only give me a horse."

The others laughed, and said, "Seek one for thyself when we are gone, we will leave one behind us in the stable for thee."

When they had gone forth, he went into the stable, and got the horse out; it was lame of one foot, and limped hobblety jig, hobblety jig; nevertheless he mounted it, and rode away to the dark forest.

When he came to the outskirts, he called "Iron John," three times so loudly that it echoed through the trees. Thereupon the wild man appeared immediately, and said, "What dost thou desire?"

"I want a strong steed, for I am going to the wars."

"That thou shalt have, and still more than thou askest for."

Then the wild man went back into the forest, and it was not long before a stable-boy came out of it, who led a horse that snorted with its nostrils, and could hardly be restrained, and behind them followed a great troop of soldiers entirely equipped in iron, and their swords flashed in the sun. The youth made over his three-legged horse to the stable-boy, mounted the other, and rode at the head of the soldiers.

When he got near the battle-field, a great part of the King's men had already fallen, and little was wanting to make the rest give way. Then the youth galloped thither with his iron soldiers, broke like a hurricane over the enemy, and beat down all who opposed him. They began to fly, but the youth pursued, and never stopped, until there was not a single man left. Instead, however, of returning to the King, he conducted his troop by bye-ways back to the forest, and called forth Iron John.

"What dost thou desire?" asked the wild man.

"Take back thy horse and thy troops, and give me my three-legged horse again."

All that he asked was done, and soon he was riding on his three-legged horse.

When the King returned to his palace, his daughter went to meet him, and wished him joy of his victory. "I am not the one who carried away the victory," said he, "but a stranger knight who came to my assistance with his soldiers." The daughter wanted to hear who the strange knight was, but the King did not know, and said, "He followed the enemy, and I did not see him again."

She inquired of the gardener where his boy was, but he smiled, and said, "He has just come home on his three-legged horse, and the others have been mocking him, and crying, 'Here comes our hobblety jig back again!' They asked, too, 'Under what hedge hast thou been lying sleeping all the time?' He, however, said, 'I did the best of all, and it would have gone badly without me.' And then he was still more ridiculed."

The King said to his daughter, "I will proclaim a great feast that shall last for three days, and thou shalt throw a golden apple. Perhaps the unknown will come to it." When the feast was announced, the youth went out to the forest, and called Iron John.

"What dost thou desire?" asked he.

"That I may catch the King's daughter's golden apple."

"It is as safe as if thou hadst it already," said Iron John. "Thou shalt likewise have a suit of red armour for the occasion, and ride on a spirited chestnut-horse."

When the day came, the youth galloped to the spot, took his place amongst the knights, and was recognized by no one. The King's daughter came forward, and threw a golden apple to the knights, but none of them caught it but he, only as soon as he had it he galloped away.

On the second day Iron John equipped him as a white knight, and gave him a white horse. Again he was the only one who caught the apple, and he did not linger an instant, but galloped off with it.

The King grew angry, and said, "That is not allowed; he must appear before me and tell his name." He gave the order that if the knight who caught the apple, should go away again they should pursue him, and if he would not come back willingly, they were to cut him down and stab him.

On the third day, he received from Iron John a suit of black armour and a black horse, and again he caught the apple. But when he was riding off with it, the King's attendants pursued him, and one of them got so near him that he wounded the youth's leg with the point of his sword. The youth nevertheless escaped from them, but his horse leapt so violently that the helmet fell from the youth's head, and they could see that he had golden hair. They rode back and announced this to the King.

The following day the King's daughter asked the gardener about his boy.

"He is at work in the garden; the queer creature has been at the festival too, and only came home yesterday evening; he has likewise shown my children three golden apples which he has won."

The King had him summoned into his presence, and he came and again had his little cap on his head. But the King's daughter went up to him and took it off, and then his golden hair fell down over his shoulders, and he was so handsome that all were amazed.

"Art thou the knight who came every day to the festival, always in different colours, and who caught the three golden apples?" asked the King.

"Yes," answered he, "and here the apples are," and he took them out of his pocket, and returned them to the King. "If you desire further proof, you may see the wound which your people gave me when they followed me. But I am likewise the knight who helped you to your victory over your enemies."

"If thou canst perform such deeds as that, thou art no gardener's boy; tell me, who is thy father?"

"My father is a mighty King, and gold have I in plenty as great as I require."

"I well see," said the King, "that I owe thanks to thee; can I do anything to please thee?"

"Yes," answered he, "that indeed you can. Give me your daughter to wife."

The maiden laughed, and said, "He does not stand much on ceremony, but I have already seen by his golden hair that he was no gardener's boy," and then she went and kissed him.

His father and mother came to the wedding, and were in great delight, for they had given up all hope of ever seeing their dear son again. And as they were sitting at the marriage-feast, the music suddenly stopped, the doors opened, and a stately King came in with a great retinue. He went up to the youth, embraced him and said, "I am Iron John, and was by enchantment a wild man, but thou hast set me free; all the treasures which I possess, shall be thy property."

The Goose-Girl at the Well

HERE was once upon a time a very old woman, who lived with her flock of geese in a waste place among the mountains, and there had a little house. The waste was surrounded by a large forest, and every morning the old woman took her crutch and hobbled into it. There, however, the dame was quite active, more so than anyone would have thought, considering her age, and collected grass for her geese, picked all the wild fruit she could reach, and carried everything home on her back. Anyone would have thought that the heavy load would have weighed her to the ground, but she always brought it safely home.

If anyone met her, she greeted him quite courteously. "Good day, dear countryman, it is a fine day. Ah! you wonder that I should drag grass about, but everyone must take his burthen on his back."

Nevertheless, people did not like to meet her if they could help it, and took by preference a round-about way, and when a father with his boys passed her, he whispered to them, "Beware of the old woman. She has claws beneath her gloves; she is a witch."

One morning, a handsome young man was going through the forest. The sun shone bright, the birds sang, a cool breeze crept through the leaves, and he was full of joy and gladness. He had as yet met no one, when he suddenly perceived the old witch kneeling on the ground cutting grass with a sickle. She had already thrust a whole load into her cloth, and near it stood two baskets, which were filled with wild apples and pears.

"But, good little mother," said he, "how canst thou carry all that away?"

"I must carry it, dear sir," answered she, "rich folk's children have no need to do such things, but with the peasant folk the saying goes, don't look behind you, you will only see how crooked your back is!"

"Will you help me?" she said, as he remained standing by her. "You have still a straight back and young legs, it would be a trifle to you. Besides, my house is not so very far from here, it stands there on the heath behind the hill. How soon you would bound up thither."

The young man took compassion on the old woman.

"My father is certainly no peasant," replied he, "but a rich count; nevertheless, that you may see that it is not only peasants who can carry things, I will take your bundle."

"If you will try it," said she, "I shall be very glad. You will certainly have to walk for an hour, but what will that signify to you; only you must carry the apples and pears as well?"

It now seemed to the young man just a little serious, when he heard of an hour's walk, but the old woman would not let him off, packed the bundle on his back, and hung the two baskets on his arm.

"See, it is quite light," said she.

"No, it is not light," answered the count, and pulled a rueful face.

"Verily, the bundle weighs as heavily as if it were full of cobble stones, and the apples and pears are as heavy as lead! I can scarcely breathe."

He had a mind to put everything down again, but the old woman would not allow it.

"Just look," said she mockingly, "the young gentleman will not carry what I, an old woman, have so often dragged along. You are ready with fine words, but when it comes to be earnest, you want to take to your heels. Why are you standing loitering there?" she continued. "Step out. No one will take the bundle off again."

As long as he walked on level ground, it was still bearable, but when they came to the hill and had to climb, and the stones rolled down under his feet as if they were alive, it was beyond his strength. The drops of perspiration stood on his forehead, and ran, hot and cold, down his back.

"Dame," said he, "I can go no farther. I want to rest a little."

"Not here," answered the old woman, "when we have arrived at our journey's end, you can rest; but now you must go forward. Who knows what good it may do you?"

"Old woman, thou art becoming shameless!" said the count, and tried to throw off the bundle, but he laboured in vain; it stuck as fast to his back as if it grew there. He turned and twisted, but he could not get rid of it. The old woman laughed at this, and sprang about quite delighted on her crutch.

"Don't get angry, dear sir," said she, "you are growing as red in the face as a turkey-cock! Carry your bundle patiently. I will give you a good present when we get home."

What could he do? He was obliged to submit to his fate, and crawl along patiently behind the old woman. She seemed to grow more and more nimble, and his burden still heavier.

All at once she made a spring, jumped on to the bundle and seated herself on the top of it. And however withered she might be, she was yet heavier than the stoutest country lass. The youth's knees trembled, but when he did not go on, the old woman hit him about the legs with a switch and with stinging-nettles. Groaning continually, he climbed the mountain, and at length reached the old woman's house, when he was just about to drop.

When the geese perceived the old woman, they flapped their wings, stretched out their necks, ran to meet her, cackling all the while. Behind the flock walked, stick in hand, an old wench, strong and big, but ugly as night.

"Good mother," said she to the old woman, "has anything happened to you, you have stayed away so long?"

"By no means, my dear daughter," answered she, "I have met with nothing bad, but, on the contrary, with this kind gentleman, who has carried my burthen for me; only think, he even took me on his back when I was tired. The way, too, has not seemed long to us; we have been merry, and have been cracking jokes with each other all the time."

At last the old woman slid down, took the bundle off the young man's back, and the baskets from his arm, looked at him quite kindly, and said, "Now seat yourself on the bench before the door, and rest. You have fairly earned your wages, and they shall not be wanting."

Then she said to the goose-girl, "Go into the house, my dear daughter, it is not becoming for thee to be alone with a young gentleman; one must not pour oil on to the fire, he might fall in love with thee."

The count knew not whether to laugh or to cry. "Such a sweetheart as that," thought he, "could not touch my heart, even if she were thirty years younger."

In the meantime the old woman stroked and fondled her geese as if they were children, and then went into the house with her daughter. The youth lay down on the bench, under a wild apple-tree.

The air was warm and mild; on all sides stretched a green meadow, which was set with cowslips, wild thyme, and a thousand other flowers; through the midst of it rippled a clear brook on which the sun sparkled, and the white geese went walking backwards and forwards, or paddled in the water.

"It is quite delightful here," said he, "but I am so tired that I cannot keep my eyes open; I will sleep a little. If only a gust of wind does not come and blow my legs off my body, for they are as rotten as tinder."

When he had slept a little while, the old woman came and shook him till he awoke. "Sit up," said she, "thou canst not stay here; I have certainly treated thee hardly, still it has not cost thee thy life. Of money and land thou hast no need, here is something else for thee."

Thereupon she thrust a little book into his hand, which was cut out of a single emerald. "Take great care of it," said she, "it will bring thee good fortune."

The count sprang up, and as he felt that he was quite fresh, and had recovered his vigour, he thanked the old woman for her present, and set off without even once looking back at the beautiful daughter. When he was already some way off, he still heard in the distance the noisy cry of the geese.

For three days the count had to wander in the wilderness before he could find his way out. He then reached a large town, and as no one knew him, he was led into the royal palace, where the King and Queen were sitting on their throne. The count fell on one knee, drew the emerald book out of his pocket, and laid it at the Queen's feet.

She bade him rise and hand her the little book. Hardly, however, had she opened it, and looked therein, than she fell as if dead to the ground. The count was seized by the King's servants, and was being

311

led to prison, when the Queen opened her eyes, and ordered them to release him, and everyone was to go out, as she wished to speak with him in private.

When the Queen was alone, she began to weep bitterly, and said:

"Of what use to me are the splendours and honours with which I am surrounded; every morning I awake in pain and sorrow. I had three daughters, the youngest of whom was so beautiful that the whole world looked on her as a wonder. She was as white as snow, as rosy as apple-blossom, and her hair as radiant as sunbeams. When she cried, not tears fell from her eyes, but pearls and jewels only. When she was fifteen years old, the King summoned all three sisters to come before his throne. You should have seen how all the people gazed when the youngest entered, it was just as if the sun were rising! Then the King spoke, "My daughters, I know not when my last day may arrive; I will today decide what each shall receive at my death. You all love me, but the one of you who loves me best, shall fare the best." Each of them said she loved him best. "Can you not express to me," said the King, "how much you do love me, and thus I shall see what you mean?" The eldest spoke, "I love my father as dearly as the sweetest sugar." The second, "I love my father as dearly as my prettiest dress." But the youngest was silent. Then the father said, "And thou, my dearest child, how much dost thou love me?" "I do not know, and can compare my love with nothing." But her father insisted that she should name something. So she said at last, "The best food does not please me without salt, therefore I love my father like salt." When the King heard that, he fell into a passion, and said, "If thou lovest me like salt, thy love shall also be repaid thee with salt." Then he divided the kingdom between the two elder, but caused a sack of salt to be bound on the back of the youngest, and two servants had to lead her forth into the wild forest. We all begged and prayed for her," said the Queen, "but the King's anger was not to be appeased. How she cried when she had to leave us! The whole road was strewn with the pearls which flowed from her eyes. The King soon afterwards repented of his great severity, and had the whole forest searched for the poor child, but no one could find her. When I think that the wild beasts have devoured her, I know not how to contain myself for sorrow; many a time I console myself with the hope that she is still alive, and may have hidden herself in a cave, or has found shelter with compassionate people. But picture to yourself, when I opened your little emerald book, a pearl lay therein, of exactly the same kind as those which used to fall from my daughter's eyes; and then you can also imagine how the sight of it stirred my heart. You must tell me how you came by that pearl."

The count told her that he had received it from the old woman in the forest, who had appeared very strange to him, and must be a witch, but he had neither seen nor hear anything of the Queen's child.

The King and the Queen resolved to seek out the old woman. They thought that there where the pearl had been, they would obtain news of their daughter.

The old woman was sitting in that lonely place at her spinning-wheel, spinning. It was already dusk, and a log which was burning on the hearth gave a scanty light.

All at once there was a noise outside, the geese were coming home from the pasture, and uttering their hoarse cries. Soon afterwards the daughter also entered. But the old woman scarcely thanked her, and only shook her head a little. The daughter sat down beside her, took her spinning-wheel, and twisted the threads as nimbly as a young girl.

Thus they both sat for two hours, and exchanged never a word. At last something rustled at the window, and two fiery eyes peered in. It was an old night-owl, which cried, "Uhu!" three times.

The old woman looked up just a little, then she said, "Now, my little daughter, it is time for thee to go out and do thy work."

She rose and went out, and where did she go? Over the meadows ever onward into the valley.

At last she came to a well, with three old oak-trees standing beside it; meanwhile the moon had risen large and round over the mountain, and it was so light that one could have found a needle. She removed a skin which covered her face, then bent down to the well, and began to wash herself.

When she had finished, she dipped the skin also in the water, and then laid it on the meadow, so that it should bleach in the moonlight, and dry again. But how the maiden was changed! Such a change as that was never seen before!

When the gray mask fell off, her golden hair broke forth like sunbeams, and spread about like a mantle over her whole form. Her eyes shone out as brightly as the stars in heaven, and her cheeks bloomed a soft red like apple-blossom.

But the fair maiden was sad. She sat down and wept bitterly. One tear after another forced itself out of her eyes, and rolled through her long hair to the ground.

There she sat, and would have remained sitting a long time, if there had not been a rustling and cracking in the boughs of the neighbouring tree. She sprang up like a roe which has been overtaken by the shot of the hunter. Just then the moon was obscured by a dark cloud, and in an instant the maiden had put on the old skin and vanished, like a light blown out by the wind.

She ran back home, trembling like an aspen-leaf. The old woman was standing on the threshold, and the girl was about to relate what had befallen her, but the old woman laughed kindly, and said, "I already know all."

She led her into the room and lighted a new log. She did not, however, sit down to her spinning again, but fetched a broom and began to sweep and scour. "All must be clean and sweet," she said to the girl.

"But, mother," said the maiden, "why do you begin work at so late an hour? What do you expect?"

"Dost thou know then what time it is?" asked the old woman.

314

"Not yet midnight," answered the maiden, "but already past eleven o'clock."

"Dost thou not remember," continued the old woman, "that it is three years today since thou camest to me? Thy time is up, we can no longer remain together."

The girl was terrified, and said, "Alas! dear mother, will you cast me off? Where shall I go? I have no friends, and no home to which I can go. I have always done as you bade me, and you have always been satisfied with me; do not send me away."

The old woman would not tell the maiden what lay before her. "My stay here is over," she said to her, "but when I depart, house and parlour must be clean: therefore do not hinder me in my work. Have no care for thyself, thou shalt find a roof to shelter thee, and the wages which I will give thee shall also content thee."

"But tell me what is about to happen," the maiden continued to entreat.

"I tell thee again, do not hinder me in my work. Do not say a word more, go to thy chamber, take the skin off thy face, and put on the silken gown which thou hadst on when thou camest to me, and then wait in thy chamber until I call thee."

But I must once more tell of the King and Queen, who had journeyed forth with the count in order to seek out the old woman in the wilderness.

The count had strayed away from them in the wood by night, and had to walk onwards alone.

Next day it seemed to him that he was on the right track. He still went forward, until darkness came on, then he climbed a tree, intending to pass the night there, for he feared that he might lose his way.

When the moon illumined the surrounding country, he perceived a figure coming down the mountain. She had no stick in her hand, but yet he could see that it was the goose-girl, whom he had seen before in the house of the old woman.

"Oho," cried he, "there she comes, and if I once get hold of one of the witches, the other shall not escape me!"

But how astonished he was, when she went to the well, took off the skin and washed herself, when her golden hair fell down all about her, and she was more beautiful than anyone whom he had ever seen in the whole world.

He hardly dared to breathe, but stretched his head as far forward through the leaves as he dared, and stared at her. Either he bent over too far, or whatever the cause might be, the bough suddenly cracked, and that very moment the maiden slipped into the skin, sprang away like a roe, and as the moon was suddenly covered, disappeared from his eyes. Hardly had she disappeared, before the count descended from the tree, and hastened after her with nimble steps. He had not been gone long before he saw, in the twilight, two figures coming over the meadow. It was the King and Queen, who had perceived from a distance the light shining in the old woman's little house, and were going to it. The count told them what wonderful things he had seen by the well, and they did not doubt that it had been their lost daughter.

They walked onwards full of joy, and soon came to the little house. The geese were sitting all round it, and had thrust their heads under their wings and were sleeping, and not one of them moved.

The King and Queen looked in at the window, the old woman was sitting there quite quietly spinning, nodding her head and never looking round. The room was perfectly clean, as if the little mist men, who carry no dust on their feet, lived there. Their daughter, however, they did not see. They gazed at all this for a long time, at last they took heart, and knocked softly at the window.

The old woman appeared to have been expecting them; she rose, and called out quite kindly, "Come in,—I know you already."

When they had entered the room, the old woman said, "You might have spared yourself the long walk, if you had not three years ago unjustly driven away your child, who is so good and loveable. No harm has come to her; for three years she has had to tend the geese; with them she has learnt no evil, but has preserved her purity of heart. You, however, have been sufficiently punished by the misery in which you have lived."

Then she went to the chamber and called, "Come out, my little daughter."

Thereupon the door opened, and the princess stepped out in her silken garments, with her golden hair and her shining eyes, and it was as if an angel from heaven had entered. She went up to her father and mother, fell on their necks and kissed them; there was no help for it, they all had to weep for joy.

The young count stood near them, and when she perceived him she became as red in the face as a moss-rose, she herself did not know why.

The King said, "My dear child, I have given away my kingdom, what shall I give thee?"

"She needs nothing," said the old woman. "I give her the tears that she has wept on your account; they are precious pearls, finer than those that are found in the sea, and worth more than your whole kingdom, and I give her my little house as payment for her services."

When the old woman had said that, she disappeared from their sight. The walls rattled a little, and when the King and Queen looked round, the little house had changed into a splendid palace, a royal table had been spread, and the servants were running hither and thither.

The story goes still further, but my grandmother, who related it to me, had partly lost her memory, and had forgotten the rest.

I shall always believe that the beautiful princess married the count, and that they remained together in the palace, and lived there in all happiness so long as God willed it.

Whether the snow-white geese, which were kept near the little hut, were verily young maidens (no one need take offence,) whom the old woman had taken under her protection, and whether they now received their human form again, and stayed as handmaids to the young Queen, I do not exactly know, but I suspect it.

This much is certain, that the old woman was no witch, as people thought, but a wise woman, who meant well. Very likely it was she who, at the princess's birth, gave her the gift of weeping pearls instead of tears. That does not happen nowadays, or else the poor would soon become rich.

Snow-White and Rose-Red

HERE was once a poor widow who lived in a lonely cottage. In front of the cottage was a garden wherein stood two rose-trees, one of which bore white and the other red roses. She had two children who were like the two rose-trees, and one was called Snow-white, and the other Rose-red. They were as good and happy, as busy and cheerful as ever two children in the world were, only Snow-white was more quiet and gentle than Rose-red. Rose-red liked better to run about in the meadows and fields seeking flowers and catching butterflies; but Snow-white sat at home with her mother, and helped her with her house-work, or read to her when there was nothing to do.

The two children were so fond of each other that they always held each other by the hand when they went out together, and when Snow-white said, "We will not leave each other," Rose-red answered, "Never so long as we live," and their mother would add, "What one has she must share with the other."

They often ran about the forest alone and gathered red berries, and no beasts did them any harm, but came close to them trustfully. The little hare would eat a cabbage-leaf out of their hands, the roe grazed by their side, the stag leapt merrily by them, and the birds sat still upon the boughs, and sang whatever they knew.

No mishap overtook them; if they had stayed too late in the forest, and night came on, they laid themselves down near one another upon the moss, and slept until morning came, and their mother knew this and had no distress on their account.

Once when they had spent the night in the wood and the dawn had roused them, they saw a beautiful child in a shining white dress sitting near their bed. He got up and looked quite kindly at them, but said nothing and went away into the forest. And when they looked round, they found that they had been sleeping quite close to a precipice, and would certainly have fallen into it in the darkness if they had gone only a few paces further. And their mother told them that it must have been the angel who watches over good children.

Snow-white and Rose-red kept their mother's little cottage so neat that it was a pleasure to look inside it. In the summer Rose-red took care of the house, and every morning laid a wreath of flowers by her mother's bed before she awoke, in which was a rose from each tree. In the winter Snow-white lit the fire and hung the kettle on the wrekin.

The kettle was of copper and shone like gold, so brightly was it polished.

In the evening, when the snowflakes fell, the mother said, "Go, Snow-white, and bolt the door," and then they sat round the hearth, and the mother took her spectacles and read aloud out of a large book, and the two girls listened as they sat and span. And close by them lay a lamb upon the floor, and behind them upon a perch sat a white dove with its head hidden beneath its wings.

One evening, as they were thus sitting comfortably together, someone knocked at the door as if he wished to be let in. The mother said, "Quick, Rose-red, open the door, it must be a traveller who is seeking shelter." Rose-red went and pushed back the bolt, thinking that it was a poor man, but it was not; it was a bear that stretched his broad, black head within the door.

Rose-red screamed and sprang back, the lamb bleated, the dove fluttered, and Snow-white hid herself behind her mother's bed. But the bear began to speak and said, "Do not be afraid, I will do you no harm! I am half-frozen, and only want to warm myself a little beside you."

"Poor bear," said the mother, "lie down by the fire, only take care that you do not burn your coat." Then she cried, "Snow-white, Rose-red, come out, the bear will do you no harm, he means well."

So they both came out, and by-and-by the lamb and dove came nearer, and were not afraid of him. The bear said, "Here, children, knock the snow out of my coat a little;" so they brought the broom and swept the bear's hide clean; and he stretched himself by the fire and growled contentedly and comfortably.

It was not long before they grew quite at home, and played tricks with their clumsy guest. They tugged his hair with their hands, put their feet upon his back and rolled him about, or they took a hazel-switch and beat him, and when he growled, they laughed. But the bear took it all in good part, only when they were too rough, he called out, "Leave me alive, children,

> "Snowy-white, Rosy-red,
> Will you beat your lover dead?"

When it was bed-time, and the others went to bed, the mother said to the bear, "You can lie there by the hearth, and then you will be safe from the cold and the bad weather." As soon as day dawned the two children let him out, and he trotted across the snow into the forest.

Henceforth the bear came every evening at the same time, laid himself down by the hearth, and let the children amuse themselves with him as much as they liked; and they got so used to him that the doors were never fastened until their black friend had arrived.

When spring had come and all outside was green, the bear said one morning to Snow-white, "Now I must go away, and cannot come back for the whole summer."

"Where are you going, then, dear bear?" asked Snow-white.

"I must go into the forest and guard my treasures from the wicked dwarfs. In the winter, when the earth is frozen hard, they are obliged to stay below and cannot work their way through; but now, when the sun has thawed and warmed the earth, they break through it, and come out to pry and steal; and what once gets into their hands, and in their caves, does not easily see daylight again."

Snow-white was quite sorry for his going away, and as she unbolted the door for him, and the bear was hurrying out, he caught against the bolt and a piece of his hairy coat was torn off, and it seemed to Snow-white as if she had seen gold shining through it, but she was not sure about it. The bear ran away quickly, and was soon out of sight behind the trees.

A short time afterwards the mother sent her children into the forest to get fire-wood. There they found a big tree which lay felled on the ground, and close by the trunk something was jumping backwards and forwards in the grass, but they could not make out what it was. When they came nearer, they saw a dwarf with an old withered face and a snow-white beard a yard long. The end of the beard was caught in a crevice of the tree, and the little fellow was jumping backwards and forwards like a dog tied to a rope, and did not know what to do.

He glared at the girls with his fiery red eyes and cried, "Why do you stand there? Can you not come here and help me?"

"What are you about there, little man?" asked Rose-red.

"You stupid, prying goose!" answered the dwarf; "I was going to split the tree to get a little wood for cooking. The little bit of food that one of us wants gets burnt up directly with thick logs; we do not swallow so much as you coarse, greedy folk. I had just driven the wedge safely in, and everything was going as I wished; but the wretched wood was too smooth and suddenly sprang asunder, and the tree closed so quickly that I could not pull out my beautiful white beard; so now it is tight in and I cannot get away, and the silly, sleek, milk-faced things laugh! Ugh! how odious you are!"

The children tried very hard, but they could not pull the beard out, it was caught too fast.

"I will run and fetch someone," said Rose-red.

"You senseless goose!" snarled the dwarf; "why should you fetch someone? You are already two too many for me; can you not think of something better?"

"Don't be impatient," said Snow-white, "I will help you," and she pulled her scissors out of her pocket, and cut off the end of the beard.

As soon as the dwarf felt himself free he laid hold of a bag which lay amongst the roots of the tree, and which was full of gold, and lifted it up, grumbling to himself, "Uncouth people, to cut off a piece of my fine beard. Bad luck to you!" and then he swung the bag upon his back, and went off without even once looking at the children.

Some time after that Snow-white and Rose-red went to catch a dish of fish. As they came near the brook they saw something like a large grasshopper jumping towards the water, as if it were going to leap in.

They ran to it and found it was the dwarf. "Where are you going?" said Rose-red; "you surely don't want to go into the water?"

"I am not such a fool!" cried the dwarf; "don't you see that the accursed fish wants to pull me in?"

The little man had been sitting there fishing, and unluckily the wind had twisted his beard with the fishing-line; just then a big fish bit, and the feeble creature had not strength to pull it out; the fish kept the upper hand and pulled the dwarf towards him. He held on to all the reeds and rushes, but it was of little good, he was forced to follow the movements of the fish, and was in urgent danger of being dragged into the water.

The girls came just in time; they held him fast and tried to free his beard from the line, but all in vain, beard and line were entangled fast together. Nothing was left but to bring out the scissors and cut the beard, whereby a small part of it was lost.

When the dwarf saw that, he screamed out, "Is that civil, you toad-stool, to disfigure one's face? Was it not enough to clip off the end of my beard? Now you have cut off the best part of it. I cannot let myself be seen by my people. I wish you had been made to run the soles off your shoes!" Then he took out a sack of pearls which lay in the rushes, and without saying a word more he dragged it away and disappeared behind a stone.

It happened that soon afterwards the mother sent the two children to the town to buy needles and thread, and laces and ribbons. The road led them across a heath upon which huge pieces of rock lay strewn here and there. Now they noticed a large bird hovering in the air, flying slowly round and round above them; it sank lower and lower, and at last settled near a rock not far off. Directly afterwards they heard a loud, piteous cry. They ran up and saw with horror that the eagle had seized their old acquaintance the dwarf, and was going to carry him off.

The children, full of pity, at once took tight hold of the little man, and pulled against the eagle so long that at last he let his booty go. As soon as the dwarf had recovered from his first fright he cried with his shrill voice, "Could you not have done it more carefully! You dragged at my brown coat so that it is all torn and full of holes, you helpless clumsy creatures!"

Then he took up a sack full of precious stones, and slipped away again under the rock into his hole. The girls, who by this time were used to his thanklessness, went on their way and did their business in the town.

As they crossed the heath again on their way home they surprised the dwarf, who had emptied out his bag of precious stones in a clean spot, and had not thought that anyone would come there so late. The evening sun shone upon the brilliant stones; they glittered and sparkled with all colours so beautifully that the children stood still and looked at them.

"Why do you stand gaping there?" cried the dwarf, and his ashen-gray face became copper-red with rage. He was going on with his bad

322

words when a loud growling was heard, and a black bear came trotting towards them out of the forest. The dwarf sprang up in a fright, but he could not get to his cave, for the bear was already close.

Then in the dread of his heart he cried, "Dear Mr. Bear, spare me, I will give you all my treasures; look, the beautiful jewels lying there! Grant me my life; what do you want with such a slender little fellow as I? you would not feel me between your teeth. Come, take these two wicked girls, they are tender morsels for you, fat as young quails; for mercy's sake eat them!"

The bear took no heed of his words, but gave the wicked creature a single blow with his paw, and he did not move again.

The girls had run away, but the bear called to them, "Snow-white and Rose-red, do not be afraid; wait, I will come with you." Then they knew his voice and waited, and when he came up to them, suddenly his bearskin fell off, and he stood there, a handsome man, clothed all in gold. "I am a King's son," he said, "and I was bewitched by that wicked dwarf, who had stolen my treasures; I have had to run about the forest as a savage bear until I was freed by his death. Now he has got his well-deserved punishment."

Snow-white was married to him, and Rose-red to his brother, and they divided between them the great treasure which the dwarf had gathered together in his cave. The old mother lived peacefully and happily with her children for many years. She took the two rose-trees with her, and they stood before her window, and every year bore the most beautiful roses, white and red.

Maid Maleen

HERE was once a King who had a son who asked in marriage the daughter of a mighty King; she was called Maid Maleen, and was very beautiful. As her father wished to give her to another, the prince was rejected; but as they both loved each other with all their hearts, they would not give each other up, and Maid Maleen said to her father, "I can and will take no other for my husband."

Then the King flew into a passion, and ordered a dark tower to be built, into which no ray of sunlight or moonlight should enter. When it was finished, he said, "Therein shalt thou be imprisoned for seven years, and then I will come and see if thy perverse spirit is broken."

Meat and drink for the seven years were carried into the tower, and then she and her waiting-woman were led into it and walled up, and thus cut off from the sky and from the earth. There they sat in the darkness, and knew not when day or night began. The King's son often went round and round the tower, and called their names, but no sound from without pierced through the thick walls. What else could they do but lament and complain?

Meanwhile the time passed, and by the diminution of the food and drink they knew that the seven years were coming to an end. They thought the moment of their deliverance was come; but no stroke of the hammer was heard, no stone fell out of the wall, and it seemed to Maid Maleen that her father had forgotten her.

As they only had food for a short time longer, and saw a miserable death awaiting them, Maid Maleen said, "We must try our last chance, and see if we can break through the wall."

She took the bread-knife, and picked and bored at the mortar of a stone, and when she was tired, the waiting-maid took her turn. With great labour they succeeded in getting out one stone, and then a second, and a third, and when three days were over, the first ray of light fell on their darkness, and at last the opening was so large that they could look out.

The sky was blue, and a fresh breeze played on their faces; but how melancholy everything looked all around! Her father's castle lay in ruins, the town and the villages were, so far as could be seen, destroyed by fire, the fields far and wide laid to waste, and no human being was visible.

When the opening in the wall was large enough for them to slip through, the waiting-maid sprang down first, and then Maid Maleen

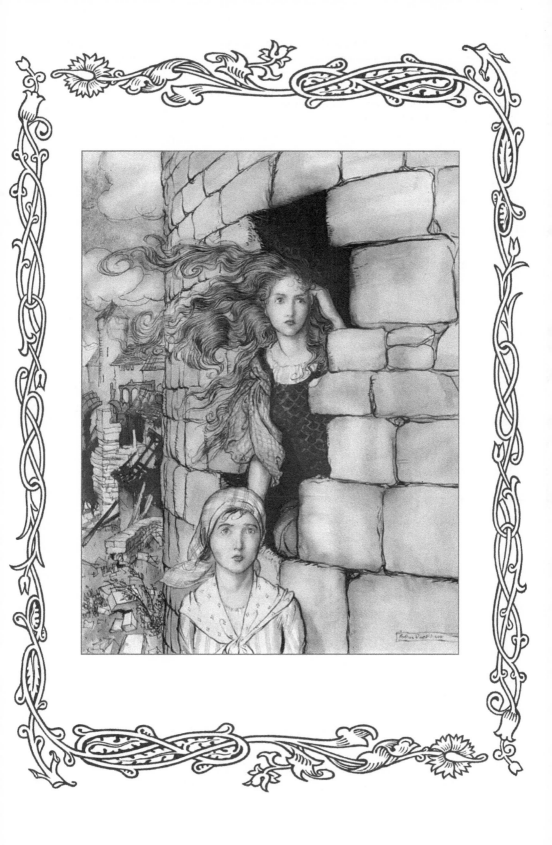

followed. But where were they to go? The enemy had ravaged the whole kingdom, driven away the King, and slain all the inhabitants.

They wandered forth to seek another country, but nowhere did they find a shelter, or a human being to give them a mouthful of bread, and their need was so great that they were forced to appease their hunger with nettles. When, after long journeying, they came into another country, they tried to get work everywhere; but wherever they knocked they were turned away, and no one would have pity on them.

At last they arrived in a large city and went to the royal palace. There also they were ordered to go away, but at last the cook said that they might stay in the kitchen and be scullions.

The son of the King in whose kingdom they were, was, however, the very man who had been betrothed to Maid Maleen. His father had chosen another bride for him, whose face was as ugly as her heart was wicked. The wedding was fixed, and the maiden had already arrived: because of her great ugliness, however, she shut herself in her room, and allowed no one to see her, and Maid Maleen had to take her her meals from the kitchen.

When the day came for the bride and the bridegroom to go to church, she was ashamed of her ugliness, and afraid that if she showed herself in the streets, she would be mocked and laughed at by the people. Then said she to Maid Maleen, "A great piece of luck has befallen thee. I have sprained my foot, and cannot well walk through the streets; thou shalt put on my wedding-clothes and take my place; a greater honour than that thou canst not have!"

Maid Maleen, however, refused it, and said, "I wish for no honour which is not suitable for me." It was in vain, too, that the bride offered her gold. At last she said angrily, "If thou dost not obey me, it shall cost thee thy life. I have but to speak the word, and thy head will lie at thy feet." Then she was forced to obey, and put on the bride's magnificent clothes and all her jewels.

When she entered the royal hall, everyone was amazed at her great beauty, and the King said to his son, "This is the bride whom I have chosen for thee, and whom thou must lead to church."

The bridegroom was astonished, and thought, "She is like my Maid Maleen, and I should believe that it was she herself, but she has long been shut up in the tower, or dead."

He took her by the hand and led her to church. On the way was a nettle-plant, and she said,

> "Oh, nettle-plant,
> Little nettle-plant,
> What dost thou here alone?
> I have known the time
> When I ate thee unboiled,
> When I ate thee unroasted."

"What art thou saying?" asked the King's son.

"Nothing," she replied, "I was only thinking of Maid Maleen."

He was surprised that she knew about her, but kept silence. When they came to the foot-plank into the churchyard, she said,

> "Foot-bridge, do not break,
> I am not the true bride."

"What art thou saying there?" asked the King's son.

"Nothing," she replied, "I was only thinking of Maid Maleen."

"Dost thou know Maid Maleen?"

"No," she answered, "how should I know her; I have only heard of her."

When they came to the church-door, she said once more,

> "Church-door, break not,
> I am not the true bride."

"What art thou saying there?" asked he.

"Ah," she answered, "I was only thinking of Maid Maleen."

Then he took out a precious chain, put it round her neck, and fastened the clasp. Thereupon they entered the church, and the priest joined their hands together before the altar, and married them. He led her home, but she did not speak a single word the whole way.

When they got back to the royal palace, she hurried into the bride's chamber, put off the magnificent clothes and the jewels, dressed herself in her gray gown, and kept nothing but the jewel on her neck, which she had received from the bridegroom.

When the night came, and the bride was to be led into the prince's apartment, she let her veil fall over her face, that he might not observe the deception.

As soon as everyone had gone away, he said to her, "What didst thou say to the nettle-plant which was growing by the wayside?"

"To which nettle-plant?" asked she; "I don't talk to nettle-plants."

"If thou didst not do it, then thou art not the true bride," said he.

So she bethought herself, and said,

> "I must go out unto my maid,
> Who keeps my thoughts for me."

She went out and sought Maid Maleen. "Girl, what hast thou been saying to the nettle?"

"I said nothing but,

> "Oh, nettle-plant,
> Little nettle-plant,
> What dost thou here alone?
> I have known the time
> When I ate thee unboiled,
> When I ate thee unroasted."

The bride ran back into the chamber, and said, "I know now what I said to the nettle," and she repeated the words which she had just heard.

"But what didst thou say to the foot-bridge when we went over it?" asked the King's son.

"To the foot-bridge?" she answered. "I don't talk to foot-bridges."

"Then thou art not the true bride."

She again said,

> "I must go out unto my maid,
> Who keeps my thoughts for me,"

and ran out and found Maid Maleen, "Girl, what didst thou say to the foot-bridge?"

"I said nothing but,

> "Foot-bridge, do not break,
> I am not the true bride."

"That costs thee thy life!" cried the bride, but she hurried into the room, and said, "I know now what I said to the foot-bridge," and she repeated the words.

"But what didst thou say to the church-door?"

"To the church-door?" she replied; "I don't talk to church-doors."

"Then thou art not the true bride."

She went out and found Maid Maleen, and said, "Girl, what didst thou say to the church-door?"

"I said nothing but,

> "Church-door, break not,
> I am not the true bride."

"That will break thy neck for thee!" cried the bride, and flew into a terrible passion, but she hastened back into the room, and said, "I know now what I said to the church-door," and she repeated the words.

"But where hast thou the jewel which I gave thee at the church-door?"

"What jewel?" she answered; "thou didst not give me any jewel."

"I myself put it round thy neck, and I myself fastened it; if thou dost not know that, thou art not the true bride."

He drew the veil from her face, and when he saw her immeasureable ugliness, he sprang back terrified, and said, "How comest thou here? Who art thou?"

"I am thy betrothed bride, but because I feared lest the people should mock me when they saw me out of doors, I commanded the scullery-maid to dress herself in my clothes, and to go to church instead of me."

"Where is the girl?" said he; "I want to see her, go and bring her here."

She went out and told the servants that the scullery-maid was an impostor, and that they must take her out into the court-yard and strike off her head. The servants laid hold of Maid Maleen and wanted to drag her out, but she screamed so loudly for help, that the King's son heard her voice, hurried out of his chamber and ordered them to set the maiden free instantly.

Lights were brought, and then he saw on her neck the gold chain which he had given her at the church-door. "Thou art the true bride," said he, "who went with me to church; come with me now to my room."

When they were both alone, he said, "On the way to the church thou didst name Maid Maleen, who was my betrothed bride; if I could believe it possible, I should think she was standing before me—thou art like her in every respect."

She answered, "I am Maid Maleen, who for thy sake was imprisoned seven years in the darkness, who suffered hunger and thirst, and has lived so long in want and poverty. Today, however, the sun is shining on me once more. I was married to thee in the church, and I am thy lawful wife."

Then they kissed each other, and were happy all the days of their lives. The false bride was rewarded for what she had done by having her head cut off.

The tower in which Maid Maleen had been imprisoned remained standing for a long time, and when the children passed by it, they sang,

> "Kling, klang, gloria.
> Who sits within this tower?
> A King's daughter, she sits within,
> A sight of her I cannot win,
> The wall it will not break,
> The stone cannot be pierced.
> Little Hans, with your coat so gay,
> Follow me, follow me, fast as you may."

The Golden Key

N THE winter time, when deep snow lay on the ground, a poor boy was forced to go out on a sledge to fetch wood. When he had gathered it together, and packed it, he wished, as he was so frozen with cold, not to go home at once, but to light a fire and warm himself a little. So he scraped away the snow, and as he was thus clearing the ground, he found a tiny, gold key. Hereupon he thought that where the key was, the lock must be also, and dug in the ground and found an iron chest. "If the key does but fit it!" thought he; "no doubt there are precious things in that little box." He searched, but no keyhole was there. At last he discovered one, but so small that it was hardly visible. He tried it, and the key fitted it exactly. Then he turned it once round, and now we must wait until he has quite unlocked it and opened the lid, and then we shall learn what wonderful things were lying in that box.